THE GHOSTS OF LONE JACK

Lance Lee Noel

SPI[Mid Continent Public Library
15616 E US HWY 24
Independence, MO 64050]RESS

THIS BOOK IS DEDICATED TO THE MEN AND WOMEN WHO LOST THEIR LIVES DURING ONE OF THE MOST TROUBLED TIMES IN OUR NATION'S HISTORY... THE AMERICAN CIVIL WAR

To learn more about the historic Battle of Lone Jack, or to make a donation to help preserve the Lone Jack battlefield and cemetery, please visit **www.historiclonejack.org**

Library of Congress Control Number: 2007907992

ISBN-13: 978-0-9800369-0-9

Cover art by Paul Mirocha(www.paulmirocha.com), Tucson
Cover/interior design and layout by Campana Design (www.campanadesign.com), Petaluma
Printed by The Covington Group (www.covingtongroup.net), Kansas City
Published by Spinning Moon Press, Phoenix
Printed and bound in The United States of America

ACKNOWLEDGEMENTS

In completing this book, I would be remiss not to thank those who helped and encouraged me along the way. As a result, I must acknowledge the contributions and support offered freely to me by several amazing people. Their insight and generosity made this story possible, and I am sincerely grateful to all of them. First, a special thanks goes to Alinda Miller, President of the Lone Jack Historical Society, whose breadth of knowledge of the bloody conflict was invaluable. Alinda's enthusiasm and dedication to preserving the hallowed site is truly to be admired and commended. Next, I wish to thank Civil War historian and author, Carolyn Bartels. Carolyn has written over 25 books on the American Civil War; and is an expert on the numerous skirmishes in Missouri and the war's lasting impact on the state. I also wish to thank military historians, Matt Matthews and Kip Lindberg. Their wonderful article, "Shot All to Pieces," was invaluable to my understanding of the tactical elements of the battle, and offered great insight into the battle's major participants. (Their comprehensive account, as well as other fascinating information about the battle, can be found at **www.historiclonejack.org**.)

Next, I wish to extend my gratitude to the team of outstanding professionals who dedicated themselves to the many details and features of this book. Rosanne Catalano is a masterful editor, having worked on numerous books of young adult fiction. Paul Mirocha did an amazing job on the artwork for the cover and far exceeded my expectations. Nancy Campana created a wonderful cover and did an excellent job on the interior design. The Covington Group brought it all together in this wonderfully packaged final product. I couldn't have been more impressed with the efforts and talents of all these people.

Most importantly, I want to thank my family and friends whose support has been unwavering.

Thanks to all of you for trusting in me and helping me bring this story to life.

I

A southern wind burst across the field. Carrying the cries of lost souls, the wind howled as it swept towards Jared Millhouse. The right fielder held tight to his baseball cap and winced. The swirling cloud of dust hammered the ten-year-old boy, nearly sweeping him off his feet. Jared pulled the cap over his face and coughed. Rolling through him and beyond, the wind slammed into the trees. The leaves sizzled and hissed. Jared's eyes watered. He rolled his tongue in his dry mouth and spit out the gritty dirt. "*The key...the key,*" echoed through the trees. Jared turned and looked behind him, searching for the source of the strange whisper. The trees settled. Jared shook his head, not sure what he'd heard, and returned his attention to the game.

His Stars had the lead with Timmy Brickshaw marching to the plate. The bulky league MVP rested the aluminum bat against his shoulder and glared at Beans, the Stars' ace hurler. As Beans went into his elaborate windup, Jared bent at the waist and smacked his fist inside his glove like he'd seen the big leaguers do.

"Please don't hit it to me. Please don't hit to me," he mumbled under his breath.

Ping! The sound of the aluminum bat rippled through the air. Jared stood frozen; the ball sailed towards him like a screaming torpedo. *Get down!* his mind hollered, but, as the right fielder for the Lone Jack Stars, Jared had several responsibilities.

In fact, in his brief ten years of life he had taken on all types of responsibilities. Jared hated being the responsible one. He also hated baseball. But when his mother died four years ago from ovarian cancer, he'd started playing for his father. Jared assumed his dad, who loved baseball, would find brief moments of joy by watching his son run the bases. So far, his dad had never made it to one of his games. The heartbroken man was simply too depressed to attend. His grandfather, on the other hand, never missed a game until this one. After his mother's death, Jared and his dad had spent every summer with his grandfather. But his grandfather was suffering from emphysema, and the disease was steadily chipping away at the only pillar of strength Jared had in his life.

But Jared counted himself lucky that his grandfather hadn't felt well enough to come to this particular game. He'd already struck out four times and made an error that cost his team dearly. A tough day for the right fielder considering he generally occupied a seat on the bench. It never mattered to his grandfather that Jared wasn't much of a ball player, but it did matter to Jared. He didn't know why. He hated baseball.

The Stars had an 8-7 lead over the team from Lee's Summit, Paddy O'Quigley's Bar & Grill, when Timmy Brickshaw came to the plate in the top of the last inning. There were two outs with a man on second. One more out and the Stars would advance into the playoffs. With a little over three weeks left before Jared returned to Overland Park, Kansas for school, being the hero of the game that launched his team into championship play would've been the perfect way to end the summer. He just didn't want to have to catch anything.

The echo of the aluminum bat connecting squarely with the ball reverberated in the trees. Jared watched as the ball continued to climb. Normally he could hear the crowd, but with all his focus on the ball it was like he was alone in the field. He took three steps back, then four forward, and then three steps back again. He prayed that the centerfielder, their best player–the best player in the league, for that matter—Suds Davis, would flash by and save the day as he'd done a hundred times before. As the ball inevitably started its decent, Jared realized there was no rescue in sight. Suds had too far to run this time. He was on his own.

Jared danced under the ball as it screamed through the air, getting closer and closer. He reached his mitt high above his head and winced, but there was no sound of a ball smacking leather. Instead he heard the *thud* of the live grenade hitting the ground and bouncing off behind him towards the trees.

He stood motionless with his mouth open, trying to catch his breath. He thought he'd pass out, but there was no time for that. The crowd let out a thunderous, collective moan and then, in unison, screamed, "Get the ball!"

Jared remained frozen for what seemed like an eternity until the feeling returned to his limbs and instinct took over—his second instinct, not his first. His first instinct was to cry. He dug into the dry grass with his cleats (which had seen little action in twelve games, since he'd only connected with the ball twice—a dribbler back to the pitcher and a pop up to the shortstop—and only ten balls had been hit his way when he occupied right field rather than his usual seat on the bench), spun to his left, and darted off after the ball.

On two separate occasions, the citizens of Lone Jack had voted to complete Caleb Winfrey Field, but the small expense of grading, seeding, repairing bleachers and, most importantly for Jared, fixing the outfield fence was too much for the town finances. As it was now, the baseball field next to the elementary school had no metal fence in left and center, and the fence that separated the woods from right field, the shortest section of the outfield by a hundred feet, had collapsed several steamy summers ago. The citizens' vote to fix up Winfrey Field was mostly a symbolic gesture of support for the town youth. It all made sense too, considering the condition of Lone Jack's two main roads. The money was simply needed elsewhere.

That unfortunately was of little consolation to Jared as he scampered towards the woods to retrieve the ball. His heart pounded with every step he made and the ball wasn't slowing down. In fact, it seemed to gain speed with every bounce. The dry, solid ground was like concrete. It hadn't rained in weeks, making for the most miserable Missouri July on record and nearly canceling fireworks shows all over the county for fear of fire.

"Please don't go in the woods! Please don't go in the woods!" he pleaded, hoping to save himself from his awful fate. With one final ricochet off of a stump, the ball hurtled into the shadows of the thick vegetation and drove a dagger into Jared's chest.

Jared knew he was running out of time—Timmy Brickshaw was as big as a high school kid and fast as a deer. The frantic boy dove into the thicket. Like barbed wire, the dense brush poked and pricked him as he crawled. He could barely see or move in the grips of the thorny bushes. Close to losing all hope, he spotted the ball through an opening and reached, but it was too far. Like sharp needles, the prickly thorns poked his skin. He fought with the spiny branches until he finally broke through. He tumbled onto his back and, opening his eyes, spotted the ball sitting next to his head. He grabbed it and scrambled to his feet, clutching it as if his whole life depended on it.

He spotted an easier way out of the brush to his left and raced down the path. As he leaped over a fallen tree, to his dismay, a pale-skinned woman in a long black dress appeared directly in front of him.

Startled, Jared jumped backwards, tumbling over the fallen tree. "Ahh!" he screamed, dropping the ball he'd battled so hard to retrieve.

The lady floated towards him, as if walking on air, and put her sunken, pale face within inches of his. A foul odor drifted from her gaunt body causing Jared to cringe. She smiled with wild, hollow eyes, showing gray, jagged teeth. The woman extended her bony hands towards his face. Jared instinctively pushed away. Her smile suddenly changed into an evil grin. She hissed like a wild cat, piercing his ears.

"Ahhh!" Jared yelled again, shutting his eyes. When he opened them moments later, she was gone. Jared sat motionless, breathing heavily. His costly error had turned into a nightmare so terrible that he was seeing things. Then he remembered. Timmy Brickshaw. The ball.

Scrambling to his feet, Jared scooped up the ball, and raced clumsily out of the woods into right field. Sprinting through the grass, he spotted Suds. "Suds!" he hollered, rushing towards the centerfielder as if he was flagging down a rescue plane. "Suds! I have the ball! Throw it in! Help me, please! Please, Suds! Help me!" Jared tossed the ball to his teammate. He rushed to Suds, grabbed the lanky boy's shoulder and attempted to spin him towards the infield so he could save the day. "Come on, Suds! Please! Throw the ball in! Throw it!"

"Millhouse," Suds responded, "what are you doing? He done scored man. Heck, Brickshaw coulda circled the bases ten times by now. Relax. What was you doin' in there? I done thought ya just went ahead and ran to your grandpa's farm or something. I figured we was never gonna see you again."

"He scored?" Jared asked, not wanting to accept it.

"Heck, yeah. Of course he done scored. Nobody I can remember's ever hit a ball that high. But he does got a mustache and all…even though it ain't like my dad's or nothing. But, we all been waiting on you. We still gotta get one more out, man."

Jared slowly turned his head towards the infield only to find his nightmare had gotten worse. Everyone was waiting for him. His team in the field stood with their hands on their hips, most shaking their heads in annoyance. The parents in the stands sat with their arms crossed, also shaking their heads in disgust. Even the Lee's Summit coach had grown tired and lost his patience as he stood kicking dirt, talking to himself. With head hung low, Jared returned to his position in the middle of right field, though his spirit ran and hid under the bleachers.

***

Willie Wilder, a lean lefty and Lone Jack Stars' ace pitcher, heaved a fearsome fastball. Unfortunately for Willie, however, he had trouble with control and generally hit or walked as many batters as he struck out. Every game he racked up quite an impressive and disturbing number in all categories. As a result, his fellow Stars nicknamed him 'Beans', short for beanball. Beans' family of eight made up a good portion of the African-Americans in the town, since Lone Jack's black population was about five-percent of a total number of seven hundred citizens.

Behind the plate, Russ Parker, a chunky, freckled redhead with a pudgy face, made a hefty target as catcher. He came from a family of six, his parents and three brothers, all resembling redheaded rhinoceroses. And unfortunately for Russ, Parker rhymed too well with 'Porker' to go unnoticed. Luckily for the chubby boy, his feisty personality and thick skin made it a name he seemed to accept. Together the pitcher-catcher duo made 'Pork and Beans', a nickname that even the town newsletter had adopted when reporting their feats on the diamond.

Beans closed out the top half of the inning by striking out the Lee's Summit third baseman, but it did little to cheer up Jared or prevent his teammates from alienating and, in a couple of instances, verbally abusing him. But there was hope. Even if Jared hadn't really thought about it, there was hope. It was only the top of the inning, after all—the Stars still had one more at bat and were only down by one run. And they had Suds Davis. Suds was due to bat third in the inning, and Suds could hit anybody. He'd even launched a rocket off a thirteen year old when he was only seven. Tons of people had seen him do it. Batting cleanup, Suds generally cleaned up.

Jared stood alone by the far end of the bench feeling like he had a contagious disease. No one would go near him. He clutched the fence so tightly his fingers started turning blue. The sweat poured down his red cheeks. His stomach ached for relief as his mind begged for forgiveness and rescue.

The first batter in the bottom of the inning was Jeremiah Shanks. Shanks, as his friends and teammates called him, was a tiny boy with the energy of a hummingbird. Born prematurely, Shanks didn't have much of a chance early in life, but more than made up for it later by buzzing around the streets of Lone Jack, mouthing off to everyone he met. The positive side of the ornery, hyperactive, filthy ten-year-old boy was that his abundance of energy and catlike reflexes made him one fine shortstop. He played the middle-infield position like a maniac, gobbling up one ball after another. In the box, however, Shanks wasn't much of a hitter. Batting second in the lineup, he generally made his way to first via bloop singles and grounders through the holes. Too impatient to take a walk, the little sweat bee swung at everything.

Shanks tapped home plate with his aluminum bat and spit in the dirt. The Lee's Summit pitcher went into his windup and hurled a fastball high and away. The ball was two feet over Shanks' head, but, as everyone could have predicted, the little shortstop swung anyway. He made good contact with the ball, causing Jared to tense in a brief moment of joy, but Shanks caught the ball late, sending a line drive directly to the first baseman. One out.

Lone Jack's lanky first baseman, Daniel Kinser, batted next. Daniel was a tall kid, but fairly slow and deliberate in his movements—almost like a sloth. The Kinsers moved to Lone Jack from Sugar Creek, Missouri, which ultimately gave Daniel his nickname, 'Sweetwater'. And one thing that the quiet, reserved Sweetwater did well, and with enthusiasm, was hit. Next to Suds, his bat was the most important in the lineup, driving in one run after another every season since he'd moved to town.

Sweetwater slowly walked to the batter's box and dug his cleats into the dirt. The Lee's Summit pitcher attempted another fastball up and away, but Sweets was too smart and patient to go chasing. Not wanting to go behind in the count on the dangerous hitter, the pitcher attempted another fastball on the inside corner. Sweets jumped all over it, cranking the ball sharply on a one-hopper to third. The boy at the hot corner reached his glove out and turned his head in fear of being mauled by the mighty blast. But unlike Jared's play in right, the boy miraculously came up with the ball. Since Sweets wasn't much of a runner, the boy threw him out by ten feet at first. Two away.

The third baseman's shock and surprise of actually coming up with the ball was only equaled by Jared's despair as he continued to clutch the fence inside the dugout. But, like everyone in the stands at Winfrey Ballpark, Jared knew that the Stars' last chance was their best one. Suds marched to the plate.

Curren Davis, Jr. was a handsome, athletic kid. He had a relaxed, often lazy demeanor and a genuine, contagious 'aw-shucks' attitude, something he inherited from his dad. His dad, Curren, Sr., worked for a beer distributor in Blue Springs and his large, round belly illustrated that the man had taken a lot of work home with him. Everybody in town called him 'Keg' and through simple country logic, Curren, Jr. was naturally nicknamed 'Suds'.

The centerfielder strolled to the plate with the same enthusiasm and energy he'd use to walk himself off to bed. As he stepped in the batter's box, the Lee's Summit coach called for 'time' from the dugout and marched out to talk to his visibly concerned pitcher. Jared put his head in his hands, pulled his hat over his eyes, and pleaded with the baseball gods for a Suds' round-tripper and ultimate redemption.

Initially, Lone Jack's Coach Jerry Miles assumed the Lee's Summit team would intentionally walk Suds, but putting the tying run on first, even if it were Suds Davis who batted .477, wasn't a viable option. They were going to have to pitch to the slugger.

The Lee's Summit pitcher started with a curveball, hoping Suds would chase after it, but the batter simply watched it curl into the dirt and bounce to the backstop. They would have to do better than that. The next pitch was a fastball inside. Suds pounced on it, crushing the meat pitch to left field. The people in the stands gasped as they watched the ball sail through the air. He had hammered it. Suds sprinted to first and went quickly on his way to second. Jared and the rest of the Lone Jack Stars screamed for joy, sure that the game would be tied and go into extra innings. Jared would be vindicated.

"Run, Suds! Run!" Jared hollered. "Tie the game! Tie the game!"

The left fielder turned and ran back, hoping to get under the ball, but Suds had blasted it way over his head. The left fielder didn't have a prayer. As the ball started humming to the ground, Suds rounded third and would have nearly reached home before the rocket even touched earth…had Timmy Brickshaw not been playing center. Out of nowhere, the large kid appeared and snatched the ball out of the air within inches of the missile hitting solid ground.

"He's out!" the third base umpire yelled with a jerk of his thumb.

Jared's heart sank. He wanted to crawl into a hole. He glanced down the bench to see his fellow Stars tossing helmets and bats to the dirt and several crying. The tears swelled in his eyes as well, not because of the loss, though he was disappointed, but because he had caused it.

"Freakin' Timmy Brickshaw!" Porker yelled as he kicked his shin guards and slammed his catcher's mitt on the bench.

"Dude. Whatta ya expect?" Sweets responded solemnly. "The kid's got a mustache."

"You kiddin' me?" the scornful Shanks hollered. "That ain't no mustache! Old man Lovelace's got a mustache! Brickshaw's is all thin and don't really cover nothin'!"

"It's still a mustache," Sweets countered.

"Blow it out your hole, Sweetwater!" Shanks retaliated. The obnoxious shortstop kicked the dirt and caught Jared staring at him from the end of the dugout. "What you lookin' at, Millhouse? You're the reason we lost! You shoulda caught that ball! Moron!"

"Really," Porker added, "you can't catch. You can't throw. You can't hit and you can't run. You're worthless. We'd be better off having my little brother play right field."

***

Jared waited in the dugout for everyone to leave: the players, the parents, the spectators. He simply couldn't face anyone. As the sun began to set and stillness came over the field he crawled out of the dugout and walked to his bicycle with his shoulders slumped and tears welling in his eyes. When he got to the rack and unlocked his only means of transportation, he realized that his handlebars were gone. It was his final humiliation. Tears trickling down his cheeks, he pulled what remained of his bike from the rack and started pushing it towards his grandfather's farm, four miles away. He had a long walk ahead of him and it was getting dark.

He journeyed past the police station, the public library, and the Crossroads Café. Having traveled over a mile he decided to rest, too exhausted to carry on. Jared stopped near the tiny cemetery off Bynum Road and headed towards the row of trees that lined its entrance. The boy stumbled up the grass, across the gravel parking lot, and set his bike against one of the trees. As he started to sit down against a nearby tree, he heard something stirring in the cemetery behind him. The whippoorwills and crickets sang and screeched, getting louder as the sun dropped over the horizon. But something in the air, besides the birds and bugs, gave him the uncomfortable feeling that he was not alone. Scanning the shadows of the cemetery he quickly remembered the creepy woman he had encountered chasing after that ball, something he'd actually forgotten about with the catastrophic consequences of his blunder in right field. With the vision of the pale woman's gnarly teeth and cold eyes dancing in his head, his heart started to pound, pulsing through his whole body in rhythm with the lightening bugs that shone and faded all around him. He felt as if something, he did not know what, grew closer. Without even realizing what he was doing Jared leaped to his feet and grabbed his bike. As he turned towards the road, a figure appeared in front of him, blocking his escape.

"Ahhh!" Jared screamed.

"Ahhh!" the dark form yelled in response. "What the heck you doing? You done scared the bejesus outta me!"

Jared breathed a huge sigh of relief. He didn't know how much more he could take in one day. "Golly, Sirus. I'm sorry. I thought you were a ghost."

The old man pulled a handkerchief from the back pocket of his overalls and wiped his brow. "Geez. Thanks, kid. Didn't know I was looking so bad. Here I am, a black man, and a pale white kid is tellin' me I look like a ghost. Ain't that somethin'?"

"What are you doing out here?" Jared asked.

"Workin'. I clean up the cemetery for the city once a week."

"I thought you were a farmer. I mean, you worked for my grandpa last summer."

Sirus returned the handkerchief to his pocket and scratched his gray head. "I do a lotta stuff, kid. I'm a handyman. Ever since I retired from Ferrell Gas, I make me a little extra money by doin' odd jobs for folks, like helpin' your grandpa with his cornfields. And it keeps me from gettin' bored. A man's gotta have somethin' to do. How is your grandpa, anyway?"

Jared dropped his head. "Well, he's been sick. Dad thinks he's starting to get dementia 'cause he forgets stuff and does a lot of crazy things. And then he's got emphysema, too."

"Yeah, well, that's what happens sometimes when folks get old. Others got to do the rememberin' for 'em. He always doted on you. And how's your dad?"

Jared paused for a second. His father was a sensitive subject for the ten year old and he wanted to protect him at all costs. "Oh. He's okay. He's here now. He's in between jobs, so he figured he'd come and help Grandpa out for awhile until I have to start school back in Overland Park."

Sirus nodded as if he understood, and he actually understood more than Jared realized. "Well, I'm sure he misses your ma. She was a good lady. I'm sure you miss her too."

Jared cleared his throat. "Yeah," he responded timidly.

"Anyway, what you doin' out here, sittin' next to this here cemetery?"

Jared pushed his bike in front of him as if he needed to show the old man the evidence. "My bike is broke. The handlebars are gone, so I have to walk home."

"Walk home? Heck, boy, that's close to three miles from here and it's getting too dark for a kid to be out alone. That road ain't got no shoulder and it's dangerous." Sirus grabbed the bike, his wrinkled hand like thick, worn leather. "I'll drive ya home. Let me throw this here in the back of my truck and then you help me pick up the rest of this here brush and these tree limbs, and we'll head on outta here."

Wanting to politely decline the invitation, but feeling the needed warmth of someone being kind to him, Jared accepted the offer and began helping the old black man clear the rest of the debris he had piled in the cemetery. Though worn out both physically and mentally, Jared was a man of his word. He cradled a large bundle of sticks and leaves in his arms and tossed them over the side of Sirus' old Ford truck, as the old worker picked up the larger, heavier logs he had dissected with his rusty chainsaw.

"So, how was your baseball game?" Sirus asked.

The boy hesitated. "You already heard about our game?"

"No. I'm askin' you. You got your gray Stars uniform on. Didn't figure you wore it around town 'cause it looked cool."

Jared sighed. He knew he'd have to face the barrage of questions sometime or another, so he'd might as well get used to it. "We lost. We didn't make the playoffs…all 'cause of me."

"'Cause of you?"

Jared nodded in shame. "Yeah. Timmy Brickshaw hit a ball over my head. I tried to catch it. I really did try, but I just couldn't do it. I suck at baseball and cost my team the game. They all hate me."

"Timmy Brickshaw? Ain't he the big kid from Lee's Summit who's already growin' hisself a mustache?" Jared nodded again. "Well, that boy'll be at the higher division next summer, so you won't have to worry about him for at least another season."

"Who cares? I'm not playing next year. My whole team hates me. I prayed no one would hit the ball to me. I prayed a thousand times. I've prayed a thousand times every game I've had to play. But God didn't care. Why couldn't he have hit it to Suds? Suds woulda caught it." Sirus heaved a large limb into the bed of the truck, banging it off the metal. "So you've prayed a thousand times every game? Well, how many balls been hit your way this season?"

"I don't know," Jared responded as he gathered more debris. "I don't get to play every game. The only reason I played this one was 'cause Joey Tanner is flunking summer school, Hoyt Williams was on vacation, and Doyle Madison broke his arm on his skateboard. I guess maybe the ball's been hit to me twelve or so times this year."

Sirus rested his arm on the beat-up Ford and looked down at the boy. "Ya see there? You pray a thousand times a game and only twelve balls was hit to you all year. I'd say that's pretty good. God's looking down on ya, son. Watchin' over ya."

Lowering his eyes to the ground, Jared bit his lip. "Yeah, but He didn't on that one today, and that one was the most important one of all."

Sirus pulled his mower to the back of the truck and hoisted it into the bed, setting the greasy machine on top of the brush pile. "Well, I think we're all done here. It's too hard too see if we got everything, as dark as it is tonight. I'll come back tomorrow to make sure she's all cleaned up." The old timer retrieved his handkerchief and wiped the sweat beads from his forehead. "Hop on in and you can tell me about this hit on the way to your grandpa's. Maybe it wadn't your fault as much as ya think."

Skipping a couple of beats, the rusty Ford rumbled down the bumpy road. With both weathered hands on the wheel and failing eyesight, Sirus wrestled the truck, fighting to keep it between the lines. "So, tell me about this hit that went over your head."

"What's the point?" Jared asked as he slouched in the passenger seat.

"Well, I played me some minor league ball in Wichita when I was younger. Maybe I can help ya out."

Surprised by this revelation, Jared perked up in his seat. "I didn't know that."

"Well, that was a long time ago—so long ago I can barely remember it. But tell me about this shot that went over your head."

"Well…I was in right field, like I said, praying he wouldn't hit it my way. Beans went into his windup and the next thing I know the ball is coming at me."

"Was it on a line or did he hit it high in the air?"

"It was high. Real high. The highest and farthest hit I've ever seen. It went over my head and bounced into the woods."

"Well, see there," Sirus smacked the boy on his thigh, "it wadn't your fault. First off, right field at Winfrey Ballpark is short and it's got them trees and thick brush behind it. If you're playing center or left, where there's no trees, just grass, then you coulda got it before he scored."

Jared reflected on the information. "Well, it is kind of unfair that right field is so short and has the woods behind it with no fence."

"Also, the wind was blowing outta the south today. I noticed that when I was cleanin' up the cemetery. The trees was bending, practically wanting to snap in half. The wind was gusting so bad, it probably carried that ball another fifty feet and woulda made it hard as all get-out to catch. It was swirlin' like mad."

Jared scratched his head, taking in the old man's weather report. "It was awful windy out there. I remember my hat blew off in the top of the fourth."

"Well, there you go. Nobody coulda caught that ball in them conditions." Sirus smiled at his passenger. "Ya see, it wadn't your fault. So what did you do after the ball went over your head?"

"First I just stood there like a moron. I didn't know what to do, but everybody yelled 'run' and that's what I did. But I'm so slow I couldn't catch up to it. It bounced into the woods at the back of right field. I dove in after it, but it was like all the bushes and trees were fighting me." Jared could feel the thorns pricking his tender skin. "It was almost like they came alive. Like they were trying to grab me."

Sirus glanced at the boy. "I'm sure that was just your mind playin' tricks on you. That thick brush and undergrowth is almost impossible for even a person like me to get through. They shoulda cleared it out a long time ago. Don't let it bother you."

Jared was focused on his ill-fated trip into the shadows of the forest. "But that wasn't all I saw in there."

"What do ya mean, kid?"

"You're going to laugh at me or think I'm crazy." Jared swallowed hard, his Adam's apple bouncing from his chin to his chest before settling again. "I saw a lady dressed in black with her hair in a bun. Her teeth were crooked and jagged and her eyes had dark circles around them. It was like she was coming after me...but...not running. It was like she was floating."

Sirus stared at his passenger. "Yeah...what happened next?"

"She appeared out of nowhere in front of me. I screamed and fell over a dead tree. While I couldn't move, she got her face within inches of mine. She had this scary look in her eye. She put her hand up towards my face. Her fingers were pale and crooked and her nails were like a monster's claws." Jared told the story, reliving each detail. When he stopped, Sirus didn't respond, but sat stiffly in the driver's seat. Fearing he'd said too much, Jared changed his demeanor and stared at the old man. "You think I'm crazy, don't you? I know I was just seeing things. I'm not crazy. It was that ball. I got so upset about not catching it that I started seeing things. I'm okay now. I just wish I never would've played this summer. I hate baseball."

"Yeah, kid," Sirus mumbled, his mind preoccupied with visions of his own.

***

Sirus slowly turned the Ford onto the gravel drive leading to the Millhouse farm. The drive stretched two hundred yards from the blacktop to the front of the quaint home, and with each passing winter new potholes appeared making it more and more hazardous. Jared's grandfather was simply too sick to keep up with repairs around the farm. The front of the truck bounced and shook as if it might fall apart at any moment as Sirus pressed forward. The elder Millhouse owned over six-hundred acres and, at one time, had made a small fortune farming throughout the area. But, like many farmers, he fell on hard times. Knowing there was a bleak future in crops, he'd sent his two sons off to college to find a better way to make a living.

Sirus pulled the truck to a stop in front of the house and put it in park. "Okay, now," the gray-bearded man said, "you's home. I'll keep your bike and see if I can't find you some handlebars. I'll fix it good as new for ya. Tell your pa and your grandpa I said hey."

"Thanks for the ride." The large door squeaked as Jared pushed it open with his shoulder. He leaped from the truck, firmly hit the ground with both feet, and started to run for the door of the farmhouse.

When he was several yards away, Sirus suddenly called out to him, "Hey, kid. Wait a minute."

Jared turned back, the lights of the truck shining brightly in his eyes. He could barely make out Sirus, now standing next to the Ford. "Yeah?" Shielding his eyes from the lights, he approached the old man.

Sirus wiped his brow with his handkerchief and sighed. "Look. I can't let you run off into that house thinking you gone crazy and are seein' things." The man hesitated. "You see, you ain't crazy. What you seen out there in them woods…I…I've seen too."

"You have?"

"Yeah. You ain't crazy. Look, what I'm about to tell ya, you can't tell nobody. It's strictly between us." Sirus waited to see the boy's response. Jared slowly nodded that he understood. "That lady ain't a figment of your imagination. She's real. But she idn't real by our understandin' of real. She's a ghost."

"A ghost?" Jared shouted.

"Yeah. A ghost." Sirus glanced at the house to see if anyone had heard the boy's yell and come to the door. "Just relax. Look, there's a lot you don't know about Lone Jack. This place here may be a small country town, but it's got its fair share of history and strange stuff. Plenty of it, in fact. Ya see, when I first moved here thirty-eight years ago everybody talked about the spirits of the Civil War battle that was fought right here in this town bein' restless and the place bein' haunted. Most folks said they felt things and seen orbs…you know what an orb is?"

Jared shook his head no. "Well, an orb is like a small floatin' ball of light. They say it's an apparition…or ghost. They also say that all these floatin' balls of ghosts are lookin' for a portal to get to the other side, like they's all caught in between worlds, if you know what I mean. But then I started seein' actual ghosts, like full-bodied spirits from beyond the grave. I started telling people about what I was seein' and they started sayin' I was crazy, 'cause nobody else was seein' what I was. After that I kept it to myself. But I keep me a journal and write down every time I see one of them spirits. So far, only one other feller had seen one the way I have, 'cept me, until you saw that lady in the black dress today."

Not fully understanding, but his mind filled with questions, Jared stared at the old man. "So…who… who…is she?" he stuttered.

Sirus' head dropped as he prepared his answer to the question. There was no fast explanation. "Well, shucks. Hop back in and I'll tell ya what I think. These bugs are gonna start eatin' us alive and I oughtta shut off my truck 'fore it starts overheatin' or something."

Jared climbed into the truck and waited. Sirus killed the engine. The crickets chirped loudly in the tall overgrown weeds on both sides of the narrow driveway. So dark that neither could make out the other's face, Sirus broke the silence with his deep voice. "Okay, like I done told ya, this here is strictly between me and you. Nobody else needs to know what I'm about to tell ya. Make me a promise."

"I promise," Jared muttered.

"Good. Look, son, there's a lot you don't know about Lone Jack. Ya see, a battle took place back on August 16, 1862, that most folks claim was the bloodiest battle of the Civil War in Missouri. Now, you may not know nothin' about that war right now, but you will. Just keep up with me now, so you know what's goin' on here.

The battle took place in the middle of town. I won't go into all the details about it just yet, but the Union had hunkered down in the middle of town usin' some homes, the blacksmith shop, and even Dr. Caleb Winfrey's home for protection."

"Caleb Winfrey?" Jared recognized the name. "That's the name of our ball field."

"Yeah. Ya see, Lone Jack folks mostly supported the Confederates and, when the war broke out, he left bein' a doctor and joined up with the Rebels, as a captain with his own company of men. In fact, in the battle of Lone Jack, he and some of his men recaptured his own home from the Federal soldiers that had seized it." Sirus paused to reflect on where his story should go next.

"But anyway, another buildin' that the Union used was south of Winfrey's place. It was the Cave Hotel. Now, the Cave Hotel was this huge two-story place built by Bart Cave and his wife, Lucinda. Everybody in town thought the hotel was a little dumb to have, 'cause it was so big. It could fit more guests in a night than the town got in an entire year. But when the battle broke out, the head of the Union army, Major Emory Foster, used the Cave Hotel as a hospital for the injured soldiers—both Confederate prisoners who was hurt and Federal troops. Foster was a brave man and great leader."

"How do you know all of this?" Jared interrupted.

"When you seen the things I seen, you start to learn about things. If you don't, you really will go crazy," Sirus explained. "And it's best you hear it, too. But back to the Cave Hotel—when the fightin broke out, Foster made it into his hospital and even put a yellow flag on it so the Rebels would know it was not to be considered part of the fight. That was kind of an accepted among gentlemen kind of a thing in war. But around nine o'clock that mornin' a Rebel officer, Lieutenant Colonel Sidney Jackman, a great and brave leader in his own right, had three of his men killed by a Union sniper hidin' out in the Cave Hotel. Jackman gave the order to set the huge building on fire. The dry wood went to blazin' in seconds.

"The Federals got all the wounded out as best they could, but one badly wounded Confederate war prisoner was burned alive. As the hotel went up in flames, Mrs. Lucinda Cave ran out with her three small children. She ran to some tall weeds behind a fence for cover, trying to avoid the hail of bullets sailin' through the air. But she was shot in the chest while tendin' to one of her young'ns." Sirus paused and cleared his throat. "She died five weeks later in front of her heartbroken children."

Jared gasped. His mother had basically died in front of him, too. Something he would never forget. "Her kids saw her die?"

"Yeah."

"But she didn't do anything. She was trying to help the hurt soldiers and take care of her kids."

"Look, son," Sirus turned towards the boy. "I ain't tellin' you this to upset ya. The fact is, I think that woman in the black dress that you and I seen is Lucinda Cave, the woman who died in front of her kids. Her ghost is runnin' through town probably ever since. I know it ain't a story for a little boy to be hearin', but you seen her, so you had to know. Had to know who she is and why I think she's hauntin' this place."

Jared squirmed with discomfort. "But why me? I don't want to know her. I don't want to see her ever again. Why did she come after me?"

"I'm not sure, kid. It could've been 'cause you was so upset at not catchin' that ball that your mind went to places unkown. But it ain't uncommon for children to see ghosts in the first place. It's like a child's mind ain't got no concept of reality, so they's open to seein' what is goin' on in the spirit world as easily as our own. Children often talk of ghost sightings. Just nobody believes 'em or pays no mind to it. Don't let it upset or frighten you. Right now, we gotta figure out what's goin' on with these ghosts."

"Then how come you're seeing the ghosts?"

Sirus reflected on the question. "Heck. I guess I'm as foolish and simpleminded as a dang kid. Ain't that another sad thing about me? I ain't no smarter than no kid." The man chuckled. "But actually, old folks tend to see 'em, but it idn't from the same reasons. When they say old folks are losin' their minds, many times it's 'cause they're seein' things that others don't. It's like their minds are headin' for the afterlife and the spirits is callin' out to 'em so they're ready…to make it so they aren't scared when they cross over. That's the way I see it, anyway.

"Old folks ain't as crazy as some might think. The brain is a mighty vast thing that's hard to understand. A part of it shuts down when ya get old, but another part kicks into gear and reaches over to the other side." Sirus stared into the dark hollow night. "But something's goin on. I just know it. These here ghosts of Lone Jack are disturbed. Actin' all funny."

"What do you mean?" Jared asked.

"You seen that lady ghost durin' daylight, in the evenin' and in an area I ain't known her to go before. I've seen me a lot of stuff, like I done told ya, but I really seen, felt, and heard me a lot lately. Somethin's goin' on and I ain't sure what it is."

"What…what have you seen?"

"A lot," Sirus replied. "More than usual. I won't go into any details now 'cause I don't want to scare you and who knows if you'll ever see another one of 'em again."

"I hope not. I don't ever want to see her or any of 'em, ever again. That's for sure." Jared rubbed his sweaty hands together. "How do you know something is going to happen?"

Sirus shifted in his seat and scratched his gray beard. "It's just a hunch. Nothin' for you to be worryin' about. But, since nobody believed me and they all thought I was crazy, I kinda had to clear my head for my own sanity. I done me a lot of research on ghost activity and, like I said, I keep me a journal of everythin' I see. Some things I know for sure.

"These ghosts are usually active at night, which makes me wonder why Mrs. Cave showed herself to ya durin' daytime. They also are more active before thunderstorms, or other times when the air is more charged, which means they most disturbed durin' the spring and summer. They're struggling to me and tryin' to fight their way to the other side, but they don't know how to get there. It's like they're lost or something." Sirus wiped the perspiration from his lip. "Sometimes I see 'em doin' the same thing over and over again, like they's caught in a loop or vicious cycle, trapped between two worlds."

"What kinds of things have you seen?" Jared persisted though he wasn't sure he wanted to hear what the old man might tell him.

"I've seen Confederates and Union soldiers fight back and forth for the same ground or to capture the same cannons the Federals had with 'em. The scenes and things them ghosts do are pretty much the same every time. Men in gray and blue blasting each other with shotguns, and rifles, and pistols. Men fighting with sabers, hacking away at each other. Both sides chargin' on horseback. They do it over and over again." Sirus shook his head. "I think they's fightin' the battle of Lone Jack, still fightin' after all this time. Fightin' that battle over and over again. Still tryin' ta kill each other and win the battle after all these years."

Having heard Sirus' tale of the haunting of Lone Jack, Jared leaped from the truck and hurried to the front door of his grandpa's farmhouse. To his relief and disappointment, nobody was there waiting for him. *It's better off,* he thought. He didn't have the heart to tell his grandfather or his dad about causing his team to lose the game. He also couldn't tell them about his conversation with Sirus—he'd be in trouble for telling tall tales.

His stomach growling, he walked quietly through the kitchen. He hadn't eaten since lunch, but no plate lay on the table for his dinner, and no note to tell him about a meal waiting in the refrigerator was in sight either. Though he was disappointed, Jared fully understood and fought his hunger. His grandfather was too ill to think about his stomach and his dad was simply too depressed and, on this night, too drunk. Jared spotted the empty whisky bottle sitting on the table next to the recliner where his father had passed out. His stomach rolling with hunger pains, Jared tiptoed past his dad, not wanting to disturb him, and made his way to his bedroom. So exhausted he could barely raise his arms, he pulled his gray uniform off, tossed it to the floor, and crawled into bed, thankful that his nightmarish, bewildering day was finally over.

2

Jared crawled from bed late in the morning to the smell of scrambled eggs and bacon permeating the air. Exhausted from the prior day's stressful events, he had slept until nine o'clock, which was rather late for him since generally he was awake and bustling about by seven.

The farmhouse was built in 1955 by his grandpa's own calloused hands after he'd returned home from the Korean War two years prior in '53. Because money was tight and Virgil wasn't much of a carpenter he made the home small and simple. It was most assuredly no architectural wonder as it was a perfect square with each side the same length and height as the others. He painted the home white with a red door and matching red shudders and trim. By 1960 Virgil and his wife, Helen, had two boys, Robert and Daniel, had acquired another five hundred connecting acres to the property, and added a chicken coup, hay barn, and grain bin. Virgil eventually added a cattle barn which was slightly removed from the other structures to the southwest. All the structures were painted red, as most barns and farm buildings were, and matched the red trim and doors of the house.

Though money was tight life was good on the Millhouse farm, until Helen died. Nine years later Sara, Jared's mother, passed on after her battle with ovarian cancer. Since the two deaths, it seemed as if the Millhouse family had fallen into a deep, dark hole and couldn't find their way out. They'd gotten accustomed to hard times; they bounced back, fighting even harder to simply have a good life. But Helen and Sara's deaths were too much to bear.

Rob turned into a shell of a man, not capable of taking care of himself, let alone his son. Virgil, who had depended on Helen like no other, started a gradual decline as well. His mind began to fade. The farm he'd worked so hard to build gradually became more of a burden rather than the labor of love it had been for so many years in the past. The paint cracked and peeled on the house and nearby structures. Weeds and wild grass infested the yard Virgil had kept so tidy. The fields produced less and less.

In the four years since his mother died, Jared's pain had faded little. His dad's pain seemed to grow, aging the forty-eight-year-old man. Rob simply wasn't there. Not mentally, anyway, and physically crumbling right before Jared's eyes. He tried to be strong for his father; he helped out as best he could and never caused problems. He was extremely bright, always the top in his class, and consistently one of the teacher's favorites. But it didn't seem to help.

As Jared scurried into the kitchen, his stomach still girgling with hunger, he noticed his grandpa was having one of his better days, a blessing for the boy, who continued to torture himself about dropping the ball. His arthritic grandpa cracked an egg and dropped it into a frying pan. A towel hung from his belt and he whistled a song Jared couldn't recognize.

"Morning, kiddo," Virgil greeted his grandson as the boy pulled a chair away from the kitchen table and sat down. "How was the game?"

"Uhh...we lost," Jared answered.

"Well, that's okay. Can't win 'em all and you wouldn't have beat them boys from Grandview in the playoffs anyway. They're giants."

"Yeah," Jared mumbled.

"Well, you only got three weeks left 'till school starts, so you better make the most of it." Virgil pulled the towel from his waist and covered his mouth as he began coughing. "Doggone this emphysema. Got my lungs aching and burnin' all the time."

Virgil piled bacon, scrambled eggs, hash browns, and biscuits and gravy onto a plate, heaped so high the food fell over the side, and slid it in front of Jared. Jared didn't know where to start. Hungry as he was, he dove right in. With his cheeks stretched to their limits and his lips smacking, Jared looked up at the gaunt man working in front of the stove. "We lost because I didn't catch the ball and Timmy Brickshaw scored a homerun. It was all my fault," he confessed as he reached for his glass of orange juice. "Everybody hates me now. I'm not gonna play next year."

"Not gonna play?" the old man responded. "if you don't want to play you don't have to. You should play 'cause it's fun. But everybody drops a ball, son. You might want to think about that ball and how you're gonna catch it next time. It doesn't matter how good you are or aren't, and you're probably better than you think. You're too hard on yourself. Just like your father."

Virgil wiped off the kitchen counter and took a seat next to his grandson. "Look, kiddo, in life it's not how many times you fall. It's how many times you get back up. And the fact is, it's just a game. What does it really matter in life? You're a good boy. You're kind to everybody. You're smart. You never complain. You always do your best and you always do what's right. You're gonna do great things in your life, and the one thing I know is that all the tough stuff you go through makes you ready for those great things. You'll do things you never thought possible. And you'll probably look back and be thankful that you made it through the tough times and that they helped mold you. You're a good boy. I'm very proud of you." Virgil struggled to his feet, rubbed his grandson's head, and returned to the stove.

As Jared started in on a second helping of eggs, his father staggered into the kitchen, regretting his choice of alcohol for dinner the night before. "Morning, Dad," Jared said with a bright grin, offering his dad a little cheer.

"Morning," Rob responded with less enthusiasm. He headed straight for the coffee pot and poured himself a cup as Virgil prepared him a plate.

"You want ketchup for your hash browns, Rob?" Virgil asked.

"I'm not that hungry, Dad. I'll just make me a bacon sandwich," Rob answered sharply and took a seat at the table.

"A bacon sandwich? I made enough food to feed an army."

Rob rubbed his forehead. "Well, nobody told you to get up and make breakfast, Dad. You shouldn't be doing it anyway. Besides, I've got another one of my headaches coming on."

Virgil frowned as he grabbed the plate he'd prepared for his son. The old man sat down at the table and started eating. "What time you two taking off to go fishing?"

"I'm not feeling well," Rob replied. "I wish these headaches would go away."

Virgil glanced at his son and then at Jared. "You might want to start by not drinking your dinner. It's not healthy."

Rob dropped his hand on the table, smacking the surface. "Don't start in on me this morning, Dad. I've had constant headaches off and on for months now and you know it. I told you I'd run the brush hog out front and I'll do it when I'm feeling up to it."

"You also promised Jared you'd take him fishing this evening," the old man responded through another coughing fit.

"Dad, where's your oxygen tank? You should be using that as much as possible."

"I use it plenty. I can't cook and push around a darn oxygen tank. You want me to blow up and this house along with me? Besides, it makes me look like an alien or something."

Rob turned to his son. "I don't think I'm going to be able to go fishing, li'l man. My head's hurting worse than usual today."

The disappointment nothing new, Jared attempted a smile. "That's okay. I don't really like fishing that much anyway." He dropped his chin to the table and ran his greasy fingers across the surface. "Can I be excused?"

"Of course," Virgil replied, sending Jared to his feet, scampering towards the door. "Hey, kiddo." Jared stopped and turned to his grandpa. "I'm heading into town to play chess. Why don't you tag along with me? You're leaving in a few weeks and I want to spend as much time with you as I can until then."

"Dad, do you really think you ought to be going into town?" Rob criticized. "You need to relax. You haven't been feeling well. Besides, they'll all be playing chess up there next week and the week after. They got nothing better to do. You won't be missing anything."

"Yeah, I will be missing something, son. I won't be playin' chess or getting out and seeing my friends. I've been cooped up in this house for most of the summer. And Jared has too. He's ten years old, for crying out loud, and sits around playing video games by himself all day. The boy needs to get out and run around like boys do…and I want to be around him as much as possible until you take him back to Overland Park."

Rob dropped his head and huffed. "Don't start with me, Dad. You know I'm fighting my own health issues. I'd love to do more stuff with Jared, but these headaches have just left me immobile. And what's he going to do while you're playing chess? Wait by the phone to call an ambulance when one of you-all keels over?"

Jared left the two men arguing, something they'd done more often lately, and headed out into the bright morning sunshine. It was a comfortable day for August. A slight breeze offered merciful relief from the blistering heat. Jared ran to the north side of the house where his one refuge resided. A mighty oak tree, with limbs the circumference of tires, sat on the property line separating his grandpa's farm from a development of immense two-story homes. Jared hoisted his body into the arms of his dependable friend, climbed a quarter of the way up the towering tree, and nestled into his customary spot with his back resting against the trunk. Perched there, he pretended to be strapped into a large rocket, like the great astronauts of the Mercury Program in the 50s and 60s that his grandpa told him amazing stories about. He was Alan Shepard, Gordo Cooper, Wally Schirra, or John Glenn preparing for his voyage into outerspace and the unknown.

As the brave space traveler started his countdown to the far reaches of the Milky Way, a soft voice called out from the tall dense grass on the property line. "Hey. What are you doing up there?"

Startled—and worried someone had seen him playing in his pretend world—Jared responded loudly, "Nothing. Just up here, sitting in my tree. Who's down there?"

The stranger stomped through the grass as Jared strained to see who it was. A lanky girl about his age appeared just over the fence. Her long, flowing brown hair and big brown eyes instantly took Jared's breath away. "Hi. I'm Molly Overkamp. What's your name?"

Reeling from his unsuspected guest, Jared hesitated. "Uhh…I'm Jared. Jared Millhouse. This is my grandpa's farm."

"Well, we live here." The pretty girl nodded her head to the back of the house directly behind her. "Can we come up?"

Excited to finally meet someone, especially a girl that pretty, Jared shouted, "Sure! Come on up. My grandpa says this tree is probably over a hundred and fifty years old. There's plenty of room and it's easy to climb. Just watch."

As he hopped from one large branch to another, hoping in vain to impress his new acquaintance, another girl with short blond hair, a pointy nose, and glasses worked her way to the fence. The girls stepped through the gaps between the lines of barbed wire and walked to the base of the tree. "Hi. I'm Jan Beasley," the skinny blond said in a nasally voice. "I live a couple houses down from Molly. We're best friends."

Though Jared didn't know it because he went to school in Kansas, the summer had been very good to Molly Overkamp. The short, chubby girl, who had always been cute, grew three inches during the summer break and lost all of her baby fat. She had blossomed into a beautiful, delicate creature and Jared was absolutely smitten with his new friend.

As the three kids maneuvered through the organic jungle gym, Jared continued trying to impress his new friends. He talked of space travel and sports heroes. He told tall tales of his own gallant deeds and world travel, which, to this point, consisted of not crying when he crashed his bicycle and traveling from Kansas to Missouri like it was a trip around the world. Though the girls showed little interest, the three laughed and teased until it seemed like they'd been friends forever.

They sat halfway up the enormous oak with their legs dangling until Virgil crept around the side of the house. "Jared, let's go. I told them fellas I'd be up there at ten and here it is a quarter to eleven."

Jared looked at his new friends and sighed. He stepped to a branch below his feet and started his descent. "I have to go," he moaned. "I told my grandpa I'd go with him into town."

Virgil walked gingerly to the tree he'd known most of his life. He coughed into a handkerchief and stared up into the dense leaves. "Oh. I didn't know you had you some friends out here, kiddo," he said as he spotted the two young girls. "You can stay here if you want, so you-all can play."

Jared leaped from the last branch, hitting the ground with a *thud*. He knew that he should go into town to keep an eye on his grandfather, though he desperately wanted to stay with his new companions. He really had no friends and the thought of leaving the two girls, especially Molly, made for a tough decision. Staring at the frail man in front of him Jared responded, "That's okay. I want to go into town."

Virgil was no fool, and he had been a young boy once, though it had been so long ago he could barely remember. He smiled at his grandson. "Well, maybe they'd like to come with us. Why don't you ask them? That is, if their parents don't mind."

***

Virgil Millhouse pulled into the parking lot of the Crossroads Café on the northeast corner of Highway 50 and Bynum. Giggling with excitement, his three small passengers jumped out of the truck.

"Now, you all run along and have a good time, but be careful. You're not to go across Highway 50. You-all just stay out here, where I can keep an eye on ya, or come inside and have a soda." Scooting to the entrance, Virgil nodded politely to old man Lovelace, who had both hands resting on his cane as he sat in the shade of the overhanging tin roof on a bench next to the door of the greasy spoon restaurant. "Morning, Ned. You're not in there playin' chess today?"

Mr. Lovelace pushed his furry chin out with rock-solid defiance. "Them kooks don't know how to play chess. Might as well be playin' checkers."

Jared tapped Molly on the shoulder. "Come on! Follow me!"

He led the two girls to the side of the building to investigate the many wonders a restaurant had to offer. Discovering the garbage dumpster, the stench sent the kids racing across the sticky pavement. There wasn't much traffic at the restaurant–there seldom was in the sleepy town, and the church crowd had already attended morning services, eaten, and moved on. In the middle of telling the girls one of his favorite jokes, a too-familiar voice rang out, one he'd hoped to hear no more until the following summer. It was Shanks. "Well, looky here. It's Millhouse. I'm surprised you had the guts to come outta that crummy farmhouse today. You cost us the game, you loser!"

Jared's body tightened and his cheeks turned a dark shade of red. He looked over his shoulder, praying it was only his mind playing more tricks on him. As he caught a glimpse of almost the whole team moving closer, he wished he'd stayed at the farmhouse, up in his tree, even if Molly Overkamp wasn't there to keep him company. Pedaling fast through the back alley were Shanks, Beans, Porker, Suds, and Sweets. They'd already seen him and he had no escape. Shanks sped towards Jared and slammed on the brakes, creating a very impressive semicircle skid on the pavement. Had Shanks not rushed at him only to insult, abuse, and possibly harm him, Jared would've complimented him on his maneuver.

"Why don't you crawl back to your hole in the dugout, Millhouse?" Shanks continued his assault. "Nobody wants you around here. When you goin' back to Kansas, anyway?"

"Really," Porker added. "You cost us the game, ya little twerp. I oughtta beat the crap outta you."

As Shanks and Porker dismounted their bikes and headed towards Jared, Suds rode up to block their path. "Lighten up, Shanks. Millhouse is on our team."

"Man, Timmy Brickshaw's got a mustache," Sweets stated from a few yards away. "Nobody coulda caught that ball."

Shanks balled up his hands into tiny fists. "Whatta I done told you, Sweetwater? It ain't no mustache! It looks like his dang lip is dirty, for cryin' out loud!"

"Give it a rest, Shanks," Beans, who offered up the round tripper, said. "That's all you've talked about since last night—his homerun and his mustache."

Shanks pointed and shook his finger at the Stars' hurler. "Millhouse shoulda caught the ball. And if he don't admit to it right now, I'm gonna whoop him!"

No one had even noticed Molly standing nearby, watching the boyish antics, until she marched up and took a firm, protective stance in front of Jared. Several inches taller than both Shanks and Jared, she created a serious obstacle for the fiery shortstop. "Just you hold it right there, Shanks. You won't touch him. If you do, I'll beat you up the same way I did in third grade."

Shanks waved his hands in front of him in a diplomatic, peaceful gesture. "Relax. I don't want to be fightin' no woman. And I gotta warn ya, I was just a kid when you and I went at it. And you attacked me from behind. I didn't never see it comin'."

"She punched you in the nose as you rushed at her, dude," Sweets explained. "Your face exploded like a water balloon. Blood was everywhere."

"Put a sock in it, Sweetwater!" Shanks yelled. "Nobody asked ya!"

Suds glanced at the tall girl and then looked her way again. "Molly Overkamp?" he asked, barely recognizing her as the goofy girl he'd spent the entire fourth grade year sitting next to. "Geez, Molly. You look…different."

"Why don't you just kiss her and get it over with?" Porker teased, earning a firm jab from Suds in his shoulder.

"Yeah," Molly replied and looked away. "Hey, Suds."

Suddenly uncomfortable himself, Suds dropped his eyes and

kicked a rock across the steamy asphalt. "Well, we're gettin' ready to head on down to the creek behind the high school. You-all wanna come with us?"

"Wait a second!" Shanks screeched. "This here's a club. Men only. No girls and sure as heck no Millhouse…who's also a girl in my book!"

"Club?" Jan stepped towards him. "What club?"

"The Crossroads Club," Shanks informed her, incensed by the very thought of explaining himself to the annoying, nosy girl. "It's our club and no girls allowed."

Molly put her hand on her hip. After less than three minutes she'd already had enough of Shanks' childish behavior. "That's no club I've heard of and, if you're in it, it's no club I want to join anyway, you shrimp. What kinda name is the Crossroads Club, anyway? Sounds like a club for old men so they can have a reason to sit around and drink beer. Where did you come up with that stupid name?"

The founding members of the Crossroads Club looked at each other with confusion, trying to figure out where their organization's name originated. "It's a secret," Porker explained in a calculated move to hide their collective ignorance. "If you ain't a member, it's not for you to be knowin'."

Old man Lovelace, who had one good eye and one made of glass, had heard everything the kids had said from his perch on the bench near the entrance of the Crossroads Café. The spooky old man spit on the concrete and laughed with amusement. "You dumb kids are as sharp as mud and as obvious as a coyote in a chicken coop. A pile a dog turds is more of a club than you little gnats."

"Blow it out your hole, Mr. Lovelace," Shanks snapped, but still addressing the man with the respect his parents had taught him to show to adults.

Resembling a bird's nest, the man's tangled dry beard raked across his hands resting on his cane as he leaned forward. "You don't know where the name of your dumb club came from 'cause you're too stupid to learn nothin' in school and have no regard for history. Glad I won't live to see you cowchips runnin' this town someday. Everybody in town talks about the Crossroads all the time and you booger-eatin' morons don't even know what theys talkin' about. Makes me wanna just up and croak."

"Well, why don't ya get to it there, mister?" Shanks shot back. "Don't let us go and stop ya."

Suds calmly approached the unpredictable town crazy and took a seat next to him on the bench. "So, go ahead and tell us what the Crossroads is then, Mr. Lovelace?"

"You really don't know?" Ned asked, shaking his head in disbelief.

"All I know is it's where the roads cross by City Hall," Suds answered. "At least, that's what my dad told me."

"Son, your dad's an idiot," replied the bearded old man coldly.

"You're callin' Keg Davis a liar?" Porker exclaimed.

Mr. Lovelace moved his good eye in a circle, like a helicopter trying to land, ultimately locating his target. "No. I'm sayin' he's an idiot there, tubby. There's way more to it than just two roads that cross by City Hall. There's history involved." Ned scratched his beard as the group moved closer. "See, back when this town was established it had a couple of the very first roads ever to cross Jackson County. One of the roads ran north and south from Lexington to Harrisonville. That road today is this one right here." Mr. Lovelace pointed to his right. "Bynum Road. Now, the other road ran east and west from Westport to Warrensburg, and it does go right by city hall and intersects with Bynum. It's Lone Jack/Lee's Summit Road.

"In 1837 there was a market right there at the Crossroads to the southeast called Beattie's Log Store, which sold and traded goods to everybody in the area. In fact, the Crossroads and the town was boomin' and bringin' in business and folks from all over. And, at one time, Lone Jack had nearly two thousand folks in town. Everybody thought it'd be bigger than Kansas City someday. But that's the story of the Crossroads."

He stared at the faces of his disinterested audience. "I didn't say it was a thrillin' dang story, just that it had history behind it. All right then, who knows how Lone Jack got its name?" All eyes dropped away from the old man as if they were back in school dodging Ms. Ramsey's gaze for fear she might call on them.

"That's what I figured. Dang kids. Well, the Indians, the Osage Indians mainly, were pretty plentiful round these parts, and high on a ridge atop this vast prairie sat one, solitary, humungous blackjack oak tree. The thing had been there for centuries and could be seen for miles in all directions. Once the Indians were forced from the area, the settlers used it as a landmark, too. They'd tell one another'un, 'meet me at the lone jack,' and, as folks started movin' to the area, they eventually made that the town name—Lone Jack.

"Now, the tree is no longer here, obviously, but it sat where the cemetery is now. The tree died in 1861, the same year the Civil War started. Some say that dreadful war turnin' brother against brother tore the life right outta that tree. It just couldn't take it and died. The fact is, so many people used the tree as a meetin' point that all the wagons and livestock tramplin' under it simply destroyed its root system and caused its death. Either way, bein' alive several centuries ain't nothin' to sneeze at. That tree had seen itself a lot." The old man paused, snaking his eye across the youthful faces in disturbing fashion. "What's with the blank stares and dumb looks on your faces? Somebody got a question or somethin'?"

Shanks slowly raised his hand and pointed at Mr. Lovelace's face, completely mesmerized. "When you look out that one eye made of glass, is it like lookin' through the bottom of a Coke bottle?"

Slightly offended and caught off guard, the old man leaned back against the bench. "It's made of glass, son. I don't see nothin' outta it."

"Is it like lookin' through a jar or like with goggles on underwater?" Porker continued.

Mr. Lovelace scowled. "Daggum kids," he huffed. "Can't learn 'em nothin'. Dumber'n all get out. Might as well be talkin' to a herd of goats."

***

The group of fifth graders kicked rocks, laughed and teased each other, and hung out until there was little fun left to be had in the parking lot of the Crossroads Café. Porker, who was sweating like a horse after a ten mile run even with the slightly cooler day, stomped lazily across the pavement. "Man, let's go get some snacks or somethin'. I need some Oreos."

"Geez, Porker. You're always hungry," Shanks criticized. "We can't go nowhere without you havin' to eat."

Porker bumped Shanks with his belly, sending the scrawny kid sailing backwards. "Ram it, Shanks! Mom says my *temabolism* is outta whack. I need food more than most kids."

"Heck with that," Beans responded. "I don't want to sit inside all day playing video games and watchin' you eat. Let's go to the creek."

Suds and the rest of the Crossroads Club members lived east of the cemetery in the newly built and still growing Blue and Gray Estates. As the pack saddled their bikes, a sense of dejection came over Jared. He'd spent the last three summers trying to make friends in Lone Jack, and especially trying to fit in with his teammates, and just as he felt he was breaking into their tightly woven circle, the group was about to sail off towards Blue and Gray Estates. Standing between Molly and Jan, Jared dropped his head.

The five boys maneuvered their bikes around until they were all pointing towards the cemetery. Suds motioned to Jared. "Hey, Millhouse. You comin'?"

A smile exploded across Jared's face. Though he didn't want to appear too eager he blurted out, "Yeah! I'll come!"

Jared and the two girls ran to the bikers. "Hey, wait a minute!" Shanks yelled. "Who said Millhouse could come? And I sure ain't lettin' no girls come along!"

Jared paused. He looked at Suds and then turned towards Molly. "If they can't come, then I can't either."

"Good," Porker exclaimed.

Suds shook his head and slapped Jared on the shoulder. "Don't go listenin' to them. You-all can come. Hop on the bars of Sweetwater's bike. Molly, come on. I'll give you a ride."

Tingling with excitement Jared positioned himself atop Sweets' handlebars, while Beans offered Jan a lift. Once everyone was ready the gang headed out. They gathered at the intersection of Highway 50 and Bynum. Jared had promised his grandpa he wouldn't leave the area around the Crossroads Café, but, as he balanced on the front of the bike and saw all the other kids laughing and having fun, he couldn't help feeling a sense of pride. For the first time in his life, he felt a sense of belonging.

They dashed across the highway like a pack of wild dogs, each peddling, pumping, and churning their legs as fast as they could. Once they reached the other side, they pulled into the gravel entrance of the cemetery a hundred yards south of the highway, cut behind Blue and Gray Estates, and headed towards the high school football field.

Because of the summer drought the creek was almost completely dried up. Only a few inches of stagnant water remained in puddles. Porker hurled a large stone into one of the deeper murky pools, splashing Beans. "You're dead!" Beans hollered and darted after him.

Jared stood close to Suds as if he couldn't let go of his new friend, a boy he admired very much. The two girls picked dandelions and blew away their blooms. Suds threw a rock at an old washing machine that had been dumped along with several other items the Crossroads Club considered 'neat' and claimed as their booty. "Wow. This place is really cool, Suds," Jared marveled, staring at the graveyard of discarded appliances and assorted trash.

Suds scanned the garbage. "Yeah, I suppose," he agreed. "It ain't much, but we used a lot of it to build us a clubhouse for meetin's and such. Come on, I'll show ya."

Shanks leaped to the other side of the creek. "Hey, wait a dang minute," he hollered. "He ain't no member of the club! It's bad enough that Millhouse dropped the darn ball, but now you're gonna take him to our secret hideout? I'm sayin no on that one, Suds! He idn't in the club!"

"Lighten up, would ya, Shanks?" Suds responded. "What's a club if it ain't got new members?"

"Shanks is right," Sweets concluded. "He can't just go into our clubhouse. He has to take an initiation like the rest of us."

"Who says he can be in the club?" Shanks asked, folding his arms in defiance. "We need to vote and I vote no."

"Well, I say yes," Suds replied. "Sweets, what do you say?"

"Well, I guess it's okay," the first baseman responded.

"Porker?" Suds called out.

"Heck, no."

"All right, Beans, it's up to you then. Is Millhouse in or out?" Suds waited for the boy's response.

Jared clasped his hands together and clenched his jaw. Even knowing there probably wasn't much to the club, he wanted in. Beans was jumping from one stone to another, making a game of trying to avoid touching the mud in the creek. "Fine by me, I guess."

"That's three votes to two. You're in, Millhouse!" Suds shot a victorious glance at Shanks.

"Well, he ain't steppin' foot in our clubhouse till he does the initiation," Shanks battled back.

"Shanks is right," Sweets added. "He does have to go through the initiation."

"What do I have to do?" Jared asked, equally excited and nervous about what the gang might force him to do.

The boys gathered in a circle with Jared standing several feet away next to Molly and Jan. They huddled for several minutes, occasionally throwing a glance in his direction and every once in a while letting loose with a nerve-racking snicker. Finally, they adjourned their private meeting and positioned themselves in an official manner. "Okay, Millhouse," Sweets said, "We've decided on your initiation. You have to go to Robber's Cave and stay in it for *ten* minutes."

The dark. Jared cringed like someone had poured ice cold water down his back. He hated the dark. He desperately wanted in the Crossroads Club—why he didn't really know considering its loose affiliation and nonexistent agenda—but was absolutely terrified of the dark. Robber's Cave was an old mining hole used in the 1800s to retrieve rock for building homes, walls, and walkways. Though not a vast network of shafts, the cavern went back several yards and was pitch black. The entrance had been practically covered up over time. Rumor had it that various wanted criminals had used the cave as a hideout and as a place to stash their loot.

Jared bit his lip and pondered his dilemma. He looked at Molly, who shook her head. "Don't do it, Jared. My dad said that cave is dangerous. It could fall in on you at the slightest sound."

"Really, you could get hurt, Jared," Jan added in her nasally monotone. "And there could be wild animals, and spiders, and snakes in there."

"So?" Shanks shouted impatiently. "What? Are you chicken?" The ornery boy danced around like a bird, flapping his arms and sticking out his scrawny backside.

Faced with his own crossroads, Jared shook his head and closed his eyes. "Okay." His face strained as if he'd just gotten a shot at the doctor's office. "I'll do it."

With little time to prepare, Jared followed Sweets over the hill towards the entrance of Robber's Cave, marching like a man going to the gallows. They stopped and Sweets pointed with his long, gangly arm. "That's how you get in. Stay in there till I come get you." Jared hesitated, buttflies dancing in his stomach, and then slowly walked past Sweets. The tall boy planted his hand on Jared's chest, stopping him in his tracks. "Don't worry, Millhouse. I won't let 'em make you stay in there longer than you're supposed to."

With Sweets watching his every move to make sure he didn't try to pull a fast one on the Crossroads Club, Jared inched his way towards the narrow opening of the cave. He stared at the hole for several seconds. He looked back at Sweets, who stood high atop the hill, pointing down at the entrance like a judge condemning a guilty man. There was no turning back. Jared pushed the tall grasses and weeds to the side and tossed away several sticks that blocked his path. He poked his head into the hole and cringed. It was pitch black and suffocating. He took deep breaths to calm his nerves and inspected the narrow passageway again. He'd have to crawl several yards before being able to stand, and had no idea what he would crawl over or run into.

Jared crouched down and grabbed onto both sides of the entrance. "One," he counted and took a deep breath. "Two." He shut his eyes. "Three!" the boy exclaimed and dove in.

"Ahh!" he yelped, reacting to the cold sensation of the dirt. He tried to turn back around, but hit his head on the side of the cave, forcing him to move deeper into the shaft. "Oh my god! Oh my god!" He crawled as fast as he could go. The walls—walls which he could not see—felt as though they were closing in on him. He tried to stand, but hit his head again and returned to the hard ground, scampering as fast as he could—to where, he had no idea. Wrestling his fear and sucking at the cool dusty air, he stopped, praying it would all be over soon. He leaned his back against the side of the cave and pulled his legs towards him, making his body as small as possible. The flutter of flying creatures broke the eerie silence, as his noisy entrance disturbed their rest.

Something crawling up his leg sent him into another panic. He slapped at every portion of his body and leaped to his feet, hitting his head again on a formation above. "Uhhg!" he screamed. "I want out! I wanna go home!"

Trembling, Jared slid back down the cold, bumpy wall. He laid his head on his knees. "I can do this," he mumbled and closed his eyes. "I can do this. I want in the club. I want in the club. I can do this."

Just as he was starting to calm, he heard something rustling at the entrance of the cave. Fearing the worst, a coyote or raccoon coming in unexpectedly for relief from the heat, his body tensed. He held his breath as the noise grew louder and closer, but then he heard the mumbling of voices and a light jumped across the walls. His ten minutes had passed, he concluded with overwhelming joy. "Sweets!" he hollered. "Is that you? Can I come out now?"

"Nah, it's me, Millhouse."

"Suds!" Jared exclaimed.

Suds crawled slowly towards him, clutching a flashlight in his right hand. "Doggone. This here is a bad idear, I'm thinkin'."

"What are you doing here, Suds? Did you come to get me?"

Suds maneuvered his way past Jared. "Nah, man. You barely been in here a minute. She wanted to come."

Suds shined his light towards the entrance so Molly could see. "I came to make sure you were okay," the pretty girl explained. "It's dangerous in here and if you got lost we might never find you."

Overjoyed that he wouldn't have to go through the nightmare alone, Jared breathed a huge sigh of relief. "Thanks, guys. I was okay, but I'm glad you showed up."

"Yeah," Suds said, "we snuck away from the rest of 'em, grabbed the flashlight, and circled around. They think we're off at the pond. They don't know nothin'." Suds turned and began crawling further into the cave.

"Suds, where are you going?" Molly snapped. "We're in far enough. We need to stay close to the entrance."

Ignoring her, Suds continued to move into the shaft until he could stand. He directed the flashlight at the top of the cavern. "Wow. You guys need to check this out."

"No, Suds," Molly ordered. "We need to stay here. This place is creepy."

"Well, since we're in here already, we might as well see what it's all about," Suds reasoned. "I mean, maybe we'll find us some buried treasure or somethin'. We could be rich. They say stagecoach and train robbers used to hide their loot in here. Maybe they left some behind. Who knows, maybe ole Jesse James himself used this here place as a hideout when a posse was breathin' down on him."

Wanting to scamper to freedom, but also not wanting to appear chicken, Jared followed Suds' lead and headed deeper into the cave. "Oh, all right," Molly huffed. "But if I see something that scares me, you-all are on your own. And don't say I didn't warn you."

The two less eager adventurers stood close to Suds as he scanned the far reaches of the mine. The supporting beams of the old shaft were bowed and ready to snap at any moment. The jagged rocks, created during excavation by dynamite, formed unique patterns. Molly crossed her arms, rubbing her shoulders for warmth. "It's too cold in here. Let's just leave. We shouldn't be in here, Suds."

The dancing light disturbed a group of bats in an isolated corner, sending the swarm fluttering around the cave and the three trespassers. "Ahh!" Jared yelped as one of the flying critters buzzed his ear. "Keep the light off them, Suds!"

Another bat crash-landed in Molly's hair. "Ahhhh!" the frightened girl screeched, her scream echoing through the shaft. "Get it off! Get it off!" The young girl danced around like she was walking on hot coals.

"Oh man!" Suds yelled. "It's caught in your hair! Hold tight! I'll brush him off!" Too distraught to calm down, the girl spun in a circle and jumped up and down. "Molly! Hold still! We can't get it off of you if'n ya don't!"

Coming to the realization that the only way to get the bat out of her long flowing hair was to stop her gyrating, Molly froze. Suds shined the light on the little gross fur ball, its beady eyes red and creepy and its pointy ears tracking even the slightest of sounds. Jared inched forward for a closer look. "It's an Indiana bat!"

Suds stared at Jared. "How can ya tell?"

"Who cares! Just get it off of me!" Molly pleaded.

"It's bigger than the little brown bat, which is most common, and the color is different. Indiana bats are more gray. They're endangered species. When they hibernate in caves they cluster together. There can be so many of them they're like carpet."

Molly began to shake. "Geez! Just get it off!"

Suds and Jared exchanged looks, hoping the other would leap into action. Suds ultimately dropped his head. "Oh all right. Hold still Molly. I'll try to get him off of ya." The boy moved the flashlight towards the fury creature, and pressed it gently on its body. Hoping for a reaction, he got one. The bat leaped from its place of refuge and sailed between the two boys, smacking Jared in the face with its rubbery wing.

"I told you not to come in here, darn you, Suds!" Molly smacked the boy on his arm. "I'm leaving!"

Suds clamped onto her wrist before she could escape. "Wait. They all headed for the entrance. You'll just get 'em all worked up again. Come on, let's check this here place out." He moved the flashlight around the cavern again.

"Hey. I know what this is," Jared informed them. "This is a limestone mine. There's a ton of these things all over Missouri and Kansas. They must've closed it off a long time ago."

"Not all of it," Suds replied with a sly grin, locating an opening into another shaft. "Come on. Let's see what's in there."

As Suds headed for the opening, Molly shook her head. "Dang you, Suds. We shouldn't be doing this."

The three explorers stepped into the newly discovered area and marveled at its vast space and magnificent rock formations. Strange, twisting rocks stretched down from the cieling and reached up from the floor. Suds raced forward and clamped onto a stalactite, scaling the massive formation like it was some type of strange obstacle course.

Jared walked further into the cavern. "This is definitely a limestone mine. There's something like 200 million square feet of limestone mines in Kansas and Missouri. There's so much of it, they've started turning the space into businesses. All 'cause they couldn't spread out, or up, as easily as they could simply go down. Some of these mines got railroads and can be used like refrigerators. Mining limestone started in the late 1800s."

Standing triumphantly on the peak of the jagged stalactite, Suds stared at Jared. "How come you know all this, Millhouse?"

"Well, some I learned in books and the rest of it I learned from my dad and grandpa. My dad's an engineer, so he kind of knows a lot about the stuff. He told me…"

"No," Suds interrupted. "I mean *why* do you know all this stuff?"

Remaining close to the entrance, Molly rubbed her bare arms for warmth. "Okay, we've seen it. Can we get out of here now?"

"No," Suds replied, "we have to look for treasure first. Everybody start lookin'." He leaped to the dirt, dropped to his knees, and scanned the floor with his light. "Seriously, start lookin'. There's gotta be somethin' in here—gold or jewels. They say it was hid here all the time. Surely they didn't get all of it. Search everywhere."

Jared dropped to his knees and began raking through the loose dirt on the bottom of the cave. Molly shrugged and joined the two treasure seekers in the hopes that, the sooner they were done, the sooner she could get out of the confined, dangerous shaft.

"Hey, Millhouse," Suds said as he cupped a mound of dirt with both hands and tossed it over his shoulder, "Did you ever get your handlebars back?"

Jared paused and leaned back on his heels. "How did you know about my bike? You didn't take them, did you, Suds? Was it Porker? Or Shanks? They hate me 'cause I didn't catch Timmy Brickshaw's homerun. It wasn't you, was it, Suds?"

Suds stopped and looked at Jared. "No, man. Of course not. Geez. I wouldn't do that. And it wadn't Shanks or Porker, neither. Pittman took 'em dude. I thought you knew that."

Doug 'Dozer' Pittman, a big block of a kid two years older than the Crossroads Club, was the bully, constant tormentor, and nemesis of the gang and most of the younger kids in Lone Jack. He lived northwest of Blue and Gray Estates, across Highway 50, but didn't let the distance prevent him from wreaking havoc on every neighborhood in the town. He ran with two other boys the same age, but much smaller in stature. One was Lathon Greeley, a lanky, zit-faced weasel with a hideous laugh, whose long, greasy red hair hung over his eyes, making it a wonder the boy could see where he was going. Dozer's other accomplice was Colby Shannon, also known as 'the Goat.' The Crossroads Club gave him the name because his blond hair was almost white, his eyes were a strange light blue and bulged from his long protruding face, and he would eat just about anything. The three of them left destruction in their wake anywhere, and everywhere, they went.

"Pittman?" Jared asked. "Who's Pittman?"

Suds shook his head and returned to his disorganized excavation. "You don't want to know, Millhouse. Just stay on your grandpa's farm and pray you don't never come across the Dozer."

"Really," Molly added, "he's the meanest, nastiest boy in town. Stay away from him, Jared. He'll kill you."

"But he stole my handlebars," Jared reasoned. "He can't get away with it."

"Yes, he can," Molly argued.

"Yeah, Millhouse," Suds agreed. "Dozer'll pound ya. Just forget about 'em, man. We'll find ya some new ones. Help me find some treasure in this here cave and we'll buy ya a whole new bike. One made of gold."

Jared took his frustrations out on the layer of dirt in front of him. He grabbed a stick lying next to a stalactite and started poking and digging all around him, motoring like a worker bee. He moved between a pile of rocks and one of the support beams, attacking the ground with all his might. *Clank!* The stick hit what sounded like a solid metal object. "Oh my gosh," Jared exclaimed. "I think I found something."

Suds and Molly rushed to his side and peered over his shoulder. Suds pointed the light on the ground in front of Jared. The boy discarded the stick and began digging with both hands. Like a dog trying to locate a bone, Jared worked the loose dirt until his fingers hit something hard. "Ouch. I think I got it!" Jared put his face close to the ground and blew away the dirt, like he'd seen the archeologists do on *The Discovery Channel*, and meticulously worked his fingers around his find until it was free.

As Jared started to dust off his discovery, Suds leaned in with his light on the boy's nimble hands. "What is it, Millhouse? Is it gold? Is it a jewel or somethin'?"

Jared held his hand flat and raised the object towards the beam of light. A tarnished five-pointed star with rounded tips covered the width of his palm. "That's just junk," Molly concluded disparagingly. "That isn't worth anything."

Suds spit on the floor of the cave. "Aw, shucks. She's right. That's just a dingy piece of nothin'."

As Molly and Suds turned to continue their search Jared started to rub the dirt from the metal. "No, wait. I think it's gold. It's pretty solid. Maybe it's a sheriff's badge?"

"Big deal," Suds stated. "You can get a sack full of 'em in Branson, along with a fake coonskin cap. It's a kid's toy. Keep lookin', Millhouse. There's gotta be somethin' better in here."

Captivated by his find, Jared continued to clean the star, rubbing it earnestly between his fingers. As the friction built up, the metal got hot, so hot he could no longer grasp it, forcing him to drop it to the ground. "Ugh! It burned me!"

"Whatta ya mean, it burned ya?" Suds responded.

"The star. I was trying to clean it by rubbing it between my hands and it got hot. I couldn't hold it any longer." Jared patted the loose earth trying to recover his find. A faint, dull noise rumbled in the dark reaches of the cavern.

In an area where the shaft had been sealed, the sound of moaning and clanking metal echoed through the mine. "What the heck was that?" Suds squealed.

Jared scrambled to his feet, leaving the star where it landed, and darted over to Suds. "What is it? Where is it coming from?"

The disturbance grew louder. The three huddled close together. Molly clasped Jared's shoulders. "Let's get out of here!" she cried.

Suds stepped towards the noise, scanning the far corners of the cave. "They're gettin' louder. I can't tell what it is or where it's comin' from."

"Uhhhh!" a gruesome voiced bellowed. "Uhhh!" Then a thunderous bang sent shock waves through the mine. "Key! Give us key!" The hideous voice was deep and muffled, like a person trying to speak underwater.

"Ahhhh!" Molly screeched.

Suds jerked the flashlight from one area to another, trying to locate the origin of the beastly sounds. And then they saw it. Standing ten feet in front of them was a black man with a pale face and hollow, charcoal-colored eyes, wearing an iron collar around his neck and holding a chain in his left hand. Dangling from the chain was a large iron ball connected to a brace around his leg, yet they could see no foot on the body. "Uhhh!" the being moaned again. The creature's billowing cry swirled through the cave like a cold wind. "Key!" The creature collected the chain in his pale hands, swung the iron ball in a large circle above his ghastly head, and slammed it against the side of the cave. The shockwave rippled across the three trespassers.

"Let's get outta here!" Suds screamed.

The three terrified kids darted for the entrance. As they sprinted through the opening, a second spirit, almost identical in appearance except with a mustache and beard, greeted them on the other side. "Uhhh!" the beast's groan echoed. The demon slammed the ball and chain against the wall above them. Rock fragments exploded through the air. "Key!" he roared and hurled the iron ball again.

Molly covered her ears and screamed. Suds pushed her towards the mine's main entrance. "Come on Molly!" he yelled. "We gotta get outta here!"

The three dropped to their knees and crawled as fast as they could through the narrow passageway to safety. Once in the warm open air they scrambled to their feet and raced towards the top of the hill, racing as far away from the mine as possible. With his long legs and ability to run like a deer, Suds took off, leaving Molly and Jared to fend for themselves. He took the lead by thirty yards, not looking back. Molly motored after him with Jared, who had yet to realize his potential as a runner, falling back, too slow to keep up with Suds or even Molly. Sensing that he was losing his friends, Suds skidded to a halt and turned to locate them.

"Get a move on, Millhouse!" he screamed.

Jared staggered the last few steps to the top of the hill and fell facedown in the weeds. "Okay. What was that?" Molly cried. "I mean, they weren't people. No kinda people I've ever seen. But…but…what were they?"

Panting like a dog, Jared rolled over onto his back. "They're… ghosts," he answered with dejection. "I've seen some before."

"Ghosts?" Suds responded. "Crap. We got ghosts comin' after us. That can't be good."

Molly stuck her hands out in front of her and backed away. "Wait…they can't be ghosts. There's got to be another explanation. I mean…they just can't be."

Jared sat up on the grass and leaned back on his hands. "There isn't. They're ghosts. Trust me." Jared recognized the fear on her face. He had worn that expression when Sirus told him about the spirit of Mrs. Cave. "Might as well accept it, Molly."

"What have you seen, Jared?" Molly begged. "You said you'd seen some before. What have you seen?"

Jared climbed to his feet and placed a reassuring hand on the nervous girl's shoulder, like he'd seen the brave leading man do in the movies when comforting the distraught heroine. "I'm not sure what I saw, really. All I know is I did see something. But you should probably talk to Sirus. All of us. We need to go talk to Sirus."

They tramped down the hill to find the rest of the Crossroads Club. Jared was now a full-fledged member of the group, though the impact of his accomplishment had not sunk in, considering the events of his initiation ritual. They wandered through the dense forest, following the creek west. Visions of the ghosts of Robber's Cave fresh in their heads, they crossed over the dry creek and through the club's stockpile of garbage.

As Suds staggered up the incline, a stern voice called out to him. "Hold it right there, Curren Davis, Jr.!" Sergeant Cliff Kunkle, the thirty-one-year-old member of the Lone Jack Police Force—which consisted of only three officers and two squad cars—stood with his chest out and his thumbs tucked behind the buckle of his shiny black utility belt. Large, reflecting sunglasses hid his ever alert and roaming eyes. "Get on up here, Davis. I need to talk to you."

"Crap!" Suds exclaimed as he froze. "It's Skunkle. What's that turd doin' down here?"

"Who's Skunkle?" Jared asked with trepidation as he crept up behind Suds.

"He's a town cop with one mission: to make our lives miserable," Suds answered. "All 'cause he ain't got nothin' better to do, the worm."

The self-proclaimed protector of Lone Jack pointed forcefully at the ground in front of him. "Get on up here now, boy! You're in big trouble."

Wanting to make a break for it, but realizing he was already busted, Suds cautiously approached the trigger-happy policeman, while Jared and Molly hunkered down in the tall weeds, hoping they wouldn't be spotted next. "I seen you-all, too!" the officer informed them. "You're that Millhouse boy, and Molly Overkamp! You-all get on up here too! Now!"

Jared had never been in trouble with the law before. "Oh no," he sighed. "My Grandpa. He's gonna kill me."

Jared moved from his hiding place and slowly followed Suds up the incline with Molly close behind. The three kept their heads down, not wanting to set off the touchy policeman. Suds kicked at the weeds and put his hands in his pockets. "Yeah, officer," he said sheepishly.

Officer Kunkle pointed in the direction of the mine. "You-all done been in that cave. You know you ain't supposed to be goin' in there. That's tresspassin', son. That's a serious offense."

"I don't know what you're talkin' about," Suds lied. "We been playin' by our clubhouse."

"Don't you lie to me, boy! Your little no–account, hoodlum friends already done told me."

Suds raised his eyes and stared at the officer. "Who told ya?" he asked, not believing his friends would rat on him.

Officer Kunkle placed his hands on his belt and jutted his chest out, very impressed with his system of collecting the evidence, gathering information and confessions, and solving the serious crime. "Well, it was the fat one mainly. He sang like a canary. A fat canary, that is. I think he was hungry and knew he wadn't gettin' no dinner until he told me what was goin' on. He sold you up the river. The rest of 'em, too. They weren't about to take the heat for a troublemaker like you, Davis."

Caught hook, line, and sinker, Suds dropped his head, but he wasn't about to give up that easily. "Well, I don't know what you're talkin' about, officer. We ain't seen them in a good while. We never went in no mine."

A sinister grin ran across the policeman's face. "So, that's how it's gonna be, huh, boy? Fine. But I know the truth. And I already contacted all your parents. They should be here directly to take you-all home. And I will be givin' them citations made out to you-all to appear in court on the serious charge of trespassin'." The long arm of the law pointed sternly at Suds. "I got my eye on you, boy. And I'm gonna be watchin' you like a hawk."

3

Jared woke the next morning with a terrible sense of dread. It had been a long night for the petty criminal, especially considering he'd never been in trouble with the law a day in his life. After their run-in with Officer Kunkle, Molly's parents hustled to the scene of the crime, both casting disapproving glares at Jared and, primarily, Suds. Then his father arrived. Rob snatched Jared by the hand, anger seething through his grip, and thanked the officer. Thanked him for what, Jared really couldn't figure out.

Humiliated, Jared crawled in the truck and made himself as small as possible, hoping his father would not notice him, like he'd done so many other times recently. The boy turned and looked out the back to see Suds standing alone with Officer Kunkle. Suds waved like it was the last time they'd ever see each other, pulling his hand from his pocket, raising it, and bending it to one side as the dust from the Millhouse truck churned from under the wheels and rolled towards him. Rob didn't speak or even look at Jared. Jared tried to believe it was lucky that his father said nothing to him, but it only added to his misery.

Rob was just too angry and, as a person who generally kept all his emotions inside him, he wasn't prepared to scold his son. For Jared, the silence was worse than a thrashing.

Knowing he'd have to face the music eventually and wanting to get it over with, Jared took a deep breath and marched into the kitchen. He pulled a chair out from the table and sat down. His grandfather, whose back was to him, broke an egg on the side of a skillet and dropped it delicately onto the hot surface. Jared's dread grew. He hated being in any kind of trouble, but most of all he hated disappointing his grandfather.

With his arthritic fingers the old man separated the bacon and laid the strips into a pan. "I don't have to tell ya, Jared, that you shouldn't have run off like that," Virgil said without turning from the stove. "I told you three not to cross Highway 50. And if that's not bad enough, then you ran off to Robber's Cave." He turned and looked at his grandson, his wrinkled face stern. "You coulda got yourself killed, kiddo. That mine has been off-limits as long as I can remember, 'cause the roof is collapsing in several spots. Do you know how me and your pop would feel if something happened to you?" He pointed a crooked digit at Jared. "Don't ever disobey me like that again."

"I'm sorry," Jared mumbled, staring at the table as his grandfather set a plate of hot food in front of him.

"Well, your dad went to Kansas to get more clothes and stuff for you two. I told him I would make sure I talked to you about what you pulled yesterday. He also wanted me to tell you that you are grounded." Jared's head dropped. He'd just started to make friends and, because of his actions, he'd never get to see them again. The elder Millhouse sat down next to the boy and began eating. "Look. It's summer and, well, I don't want you moping around here all day. The way I see it, your dad idn't gonna be back till later today, so you got till then to round up your friends and have them come over here."

Jared's eyes brightened and a huge smile ran across his face. He choked down the rest of his breakfast, gulped his milk as fast as he could, and darted off to his room to get changed. His grandpa had given him a reprieve, a stay of execution, but only until his father returned to the farm. The boy threw his clothes on and ran back into the kitchen, where his grandfather was putting dishes into the sink.

"Hey, Grandpa." He hesitated at the door. "I'm sorry about yesterday and the cave and all. I didn't mean to disobey you."

The elder Millhouse smiled and shot a wink at the boy. "I know you didn't, kiddo. You're a good boy. But you're gettin' older and you're meetin' kids your age who aren't always gonna guide you in the right direction. I trust ya, bud. I love ya. Now you go and find your friends and have 'em come here to play. Ya ain't got much longer to see 'em before you head back to Kansas for school."

The tricky screen door slammed behind Jared as he bolted from the farmhouse and up the gravel driveway. His dad was supposed to use the brush hog to cut the growing weeds, but, as they'd come to expect, his headaches had been too bad to perform the chore for his father. As Jared trotted up the long narrow path, something leaped from the weeds, catching him completely off-guard. "Ggrrrr! Rrrrahhh!" it roared.

Jared yelped and leaped to the far side of the driveway. "Suds!" Jared clutched his chest. "Don't do that, Suds. You scared the crap outta me!" Suds slapped his knee as he laughed. "What are ya doin' here? I thought I'd never see ya again, cause you'd still be in jail or something, or worse…your dad grounded ya for life."

With a camera dangling from his neck, Suds pushed his bike out of the weeds. "I seen ya come runnin' outta your grandpap's farmhouse, so I figured I'd give ya a good scare. Especially since we seen them ghosts like we done did." Suds turned his bike in the direction of Bynum Road and the two started walking. "So you ain't in trouble for gettin' the coppers after ya and gettin' caught goin' in Robber's Cave and all?"

"No," Jared responded. "Well, sort of. I'm grounded for who knows how long, but my dad isn't here for most of the day."

Suds stopped and looked at Jared with surprise. "Well, look at you, Millhouse. Get the cops on ya one day and the next you go and break outta jail. I'm kinda impressed."

"Well, it ain't like that," Jared replied, though a sense of pride produced goosebumps on his arms. "But I mean, I'm in trouble and all, but I had to come find ya. That's where I was heading when you saw me coming out the door—to find you. Aren't you in trouble?"

"Oh, I don't know. It's kinda hard to tell with my old man. After you left I had to sit there with that psycho Skunkle for another hour, 'cause my dad had to work late. When he did show up he just smacked me real hard on my head and didn't say much. My old man ain't much into lecturin'. That's kinda how he punishes ya for any kind of a thing, so it's hard to figure out what he's real mad about or just kinda mad. He did make me go to my room without dinner, though, but I think that was just 'cause my mom was working at the church and he didn't wanna cook nothin'. Anyway, he had to be at work early this morning, so I ain't seen him since."

Jared reached out and touched the item hanging from Suds' neck. "What's the camera for?"

"What's the camera for?" Suds repeated. "Geez. Ain't it obvious, Millhouse? We seen us some ghosts. We need to document our findings. We need us some proof. We get us some pictures and we can sell 'em. We'll be rich, man."

Jared shook his head. "We can't go back in that mine, Suds. I promised my grandpa. If we get caught again, I will be in big trouble."

"The ghosts ain't just gonna come outta there so we can take their picture cause we ask 'em to, Millhouse. We have to go back in there to get our proof so we can get rich."

"No, Suds. We can't. We need to go talk to Sirus. He knows what to do."

Suds chewed his lip as he pondered the situation and Jared's objections. "Well, we'll talk to Sirus first, but if he doesn't have no good ideas, I'm goin' back in that cave. And if we're goin' to talk to him, then we need to take Molly with us. She was there, too, and seen the whole thing of them gray-colored black fellas from beyond the grave swingin' them chains and iron balls all over the place."

Suds pedaled his bike slowly as Jared tried to keep up on foot. They went to Molly's neighborhood hoping they could find her house without ever having seen the front of it before. Jared spotted the large oak tree on the edge of his grandfather's property and pointed it out to Suds. They were in luck with the second door they knocked on. Molly answered, surprised to see the uninvited guests who had gotten her in serious trouble the day before.

She glanced into her home, scooted out the front door, and shut it quietly behind her. "What are you doing here?" she whispered. "I'm in trouble because of you two. My dad said I'm never to hang out with you again, Suds. He's says you're an instigator and a juvenile delinquent. Now I'm grounded for the whole week because of you."

"A juve da…what?" Suds asked. "Dad says we're Irish."

"It ain't where you're from," Molly informed the confused boy. "It's what you are when you're young and up to no good."

"Well, is he here?" Jared questioned, hoping he wouldn't have to face the angry man.

Molly folded her arms. "Of course not. He's at work. My sister is watching me. But you two need to get outta here. She'll tell on me if she sees you and she loves to get me in trouble."

"Look, Molly," Suds said, "we didn't come here to cause no trouble. But you can't pretend like we didn't see what we done saw in that cave. Me and Jared are goin' to talk to Sirus and you need to come along. Jared says he can help us. Maybe even capture them ghosts and take pictures of 'em," he held up his camera as if she might not have noticed the large object hanging from his neck, "to make us rich. Ya have to come with us. He'll want to know what we all seen."

"Well, I can't go." Molly tilted her head towards the door. "My sister is right inside there. She'll get me in big trouble. I'll be grounded until school starts."

Jared thought about their dilemma for a moment. Like Suds, he liked having Molly around, though he couldn't understand why. Girls generally were annoying. But Molly was different and his heart skipped a beat when she was around. "Tell your sister you're going to Jan's. Will she let you go to her house?"

"I don't know…maybe."

"Tell her you're going to Jan's and we'll make sure you're back before your dad gets home," Jared suggested. "Seriously, Molly. We need to talk to Sirus. He knows a lot about the ghosts."

Molly hesitated and then reluctantly agreed to the boys' plan, knowing it could add to the trouble she was already in. But it was a risk she was willing to take. She, too, felt frightened, yet captivated, by her run-in with the ghosts of Robber's Cave. She couldn't let the two boys carry on their quest without her.

Because Jan played a part in their cover, the ghost hunters forced her to join them on their mission. She was Molly's alibi, and Molly would have little chance for escape if the adults foiled their plot. The four kids crossed into the cemetery as Mrs. Dottie Morgan led a tour of Japanese visitors through the gates of the old graveyard, snapping photos and speaking peculiarly. Lone Jack didn't receive many outsiders, especially from so far away, so the four youths gawked at the Japanese tourists as if the circus were in town.

Mrs. Morgan opened the cemetery gate, allowing her foreign audience to enter as the fifth graders moved closer to get a better look at them. "Now, children," Mrs. Morgan said with a half-hearted smile, "you don't need to be disturbing our guests. Run along."

"What are they doin' here?" Suds asked rudely.

Mrs. Morgan cleared her throat and glared at the inquisitive boy. "Why they're here to learn the history of the battle of Lone Jack."

"Ain't they got no history in China?" Suds asked.

"Our visitors are Japanese," Mrs. Morgan corrected him uncomfortably.

Suds turned to Jared. "I guess they done ran through theirs so they gotta come learn ours."

"Back off, Curren Davis!" Mrs. Morgan snapped. "It takes contributions to keep this museum going. These people have donated a lot of money to save this battlefield so your dad can have a place to pass out every Fourth of July." Embarrassed by her outburst, the woman collected herself, patted her hair, and turned her focus to her visitors. "Now, folks, if you will gather around these two monuments...."

"Geez. What's her problem?" Suds asked.

Mrs. Morgan pointed to a spot next to the gate. "Right there, where we entered these sacred grounds, is where the blackjack oak tree, which gave the town its name, stood. The Osage orange trees, or hedge apple trees, you see lining the cemetery from east to west were significant to the battle. At that time, the trees were trimmed much lower, as a hedge, and were used as a natural fence to keep cattle away from fields of corn. They were very thick and prickly, almost like barbed wire. During the battle, several soldiers from both sides were severely injured trying to break through them. Some getting their uniforms completely ripped from their bodies as they tried to get away."

She waved her arm towards a tall monument placed in the center of the graveyard. "The battle of Lone Jack was the bloodiest battle fought in Missouri during the Civil War. The United Daughters of the Confederacy erected this monument here in 1869 to pay homage to the Rebel soldiers who died during the fierce battle. It is thirteen feet tall." She motioned to a second structure a few yards away. "William Rooney, who served in the Union army and fought in the historic battle, built this monument, which is eight feet tall.

"For years after the battle, there was an annual tribute to those who fought and died here. Mr. Rooney attended the festivities and felt a little slighted that no monument had been erected for the Union side. He decided to build his own to honor his fallen Union comrades. With a horse-drawn wagon of supplies, he came and built this wonderful structure." Mrs. Morgan moved closer to her captivated audience.

"The battle itself was fought on August 16, 1862, a dreadfully hot day—much like it is now. When the dust settled, over two-hundred-eighty men lay dead or dying, and thirteen homes and businesses had burned to ashes. Though both sides claimed victory, the Union left the ruined town to what remained of the Confederate troops. In the aftermath, the town was riddled with bodies. In the dreadful heat, the townsfolk left to bury the dead decided that they would be put to rest in eighty foot trenches. Union prisoners and Rebel soldiers alike joined the townsfolk and dug the trenches. It took over three days to dig them and, because of the heat, estimated to be over one hundred degrees, the stench was horrendous. The frightened horses that survived that bloody day wouldn't go near the town, so teams of oxen had to be brought in. The men were laid in the trenches, segregated between Union and Confederate, and buried in layers." Mrs. Morgan gestured with both hands to her sacred surroundings. "The brave men who fought, died, and were buried here are cherished by this community for their service, and seen as a reminder of things not to be forgotten—brother against brother."

***

Sirus lived in a small white house on a six-acre lot a half a mile east of Blue and Gray Estates. Though he had enough in savings after he'd retired from Ferrell Gas, he lived conservatively, as if the stock market would implode and the banks would board up their windows and doors at any moment. Because he was particular and neat, his large yard and small home were kept immaculately clean. The grass was mowed to perfection with not a weed in the flower garden. The house was kept tidy with not a single chip on its exterior. In contrast, however, because his thrifty nature kept him from throwing anything away, the garage on the back of his property was filled with old mowers, beat-up tractors, rusty equipment, and other junk that had outlived its time. Sirus kept them all running though, tinkering and cranking a wrench to get a few more years of life out of them. He wasn't about to waste money on new ones.

Surprised by his visitors, the old black man brought the kids through the living room and into the kitchen where they gathered around the table. The air was muggy in the home, as Sirus, again to save money, seldom used his air conditioning. As they sat there, Jared told him about their chilling experience in Robber's Cave, while Suds and Molly chimed in occasionally with their recollection of what had happened. Sirus absorbed it all like a sponge. When Jared finished, Sirus simply nodded, a serious expression on his face. After a few seconds he walked to an antique writing desk in the corner of the living room and retrieved a leather-bound notebook. He turned the pages and began writing, while the four kids stared.

The anticipation was killing Jared. "You believe us, don't you?" he blurted.

Not looking up from the pages, Sirus responded, "Of course I believe you. I just gotta get it all written here in my journal while it's still fresh in my head. My mind don't work like it used to, son. It's one of the disadvantages of gettin' old." He scribbled as much as he could remember and noted the date of the encounter.

"What do you think?" Molly asked. "Will they come after us again? Are they trying to get us?"

"No," Sirus reassured her. "These here ghosts are as confused as we are. They don't know what you are anymore than what they are. They don't want to hurt ya at all. In fact, they can't, 'cause it's like we're both in two separate worlds occupying the same space. There is something happenin', though. These here ghosts you-all ran into… you say you felt the vibrations of them slammin' them metal balls into the sides of the cave, and that you could hear 'em? You say they was saying, '*Key. Give us key*'?"

"Yeah," Suds replied. "That's what it sounded like to me anyway. What do you make of it?"

Sirus rubbed his scruffy gray beard. "I ain't sure. Maybe they're askin' for a key to free 'em from them chains. It really ain't important right now. What I find interestin', though is that you heard 'em and felt the vibrations of them hittin' the sides of the cave with them chains. What I done found is most ghosts you can only hear on a tape recorder and it's generally all mumbled at best. You can barely make out what they're sayin'. And the fact that they were able to make somethin' as solid as the rock in a cave feel their blows is really strange.

"Most ghosts can't really touch stuff in the real world. Most cases, it's hard enough for 'em to turn the page of a real book, blow out a candle, or break a mirror. It's so hard it almost frustrates 'em, 'cause they see the things but can't really do nothin' with 'em. All 'cause they're on one side of life and them items is on another. But these here ghosts were able to make an entire rock cave vibrate. That is most peculiar." Sirus paused. "I'm tellin' ya, somethin fishy is goin' on here. I don't know what it is, but I'm gonna find out. These ghosts of Lone Jack are gettin' stronger and more agitated, like they's fightin' against somethin' or for somethin'. But I will find out what's goin' on, I can promise ya that."

"But who are they?" Jared asked. "Why did they come after us like that?"

"You disturbed their home," Sirus continued. "You say they had chains on their legs and iron collars round their necks? I bet they're slaves. Lone Jack had slaves in them days. When slaves died, they weren't buried with white folk. They were taken and buried away from town. I bet slaves was buried near that old mine and you disturbed their grave and caused them to start actin' out. But don't worry. They wadn't comin' after you. They woulda gone after anybody who done trespassed. They don't know any better. Like I said, they were probably as scared and confused by you-all as you were of them. They just want some peace."

The expressions on his four guests' faces told the old man they were not reassured. "But hey, Jared, I think I got somethin' that you might want. You-all follow me."

He led the kids out the backdoor and along a stone path to the garage, filled to the ceiling with things most folks would've taken to the garbage dump long ago. Sirus maneuvered his way past an old riding lawnmower with two flat tires. Leaning against a rust-covered tractor was Jared's bike. The old man had put a new set of handlebars on it and filled the tires with air.

"My bike!" Jared exclaimed.

Sirus picked it up like it was no heavier than a loaf of bread and carried it to the front of the garage. He set it down in front of Jared. "Yeah. I found me a set of handlebars for ya. They were on a bike my grandson used to ride, but he done got too big and doesn't need it no more. So I'm givin' 'em to ya."

Jared glided his hand across the frame and new set of bars. "Thanks, Sirus."

"No problem. Just don't go lettin' nobody take these ones."

"So, Sirus, do ya think we'll see us some more ghosts?" Suds smiled with dollars signs flashing in his head as he held up his camera. "How long you done been seein' 'em?"

Sirus scratched his chin. "I been seein' these here ghosts off and on for twenty-five troublin' years. Look, son, don't be goin' and messin' with these here spirits. Like I said, they don't mean ya no harm and I can appreciate that you's tryin' to make ya some money and all, but right now I don't know what these ghosts are up to. What you seen in that cave could be a sign. If they keep actin' like they are, who knows what they're able to do and ya might get hurt."

"Well, what are they doing?" Molly asked. "What do they want?"

"Well I ain't never seen them ghosts of slaves you all seen, so I ain't sure about them yet. But I have seen them soldiers. See 'em all the time. See em goin at it in the cemetery, in my back yard, racing on horseback through the middle of town. They're still fightin' that same battle," Sirus informed her. "Ya see, about two-hundred eighty soldiers was killed and they're still tryin' to kill each other. War has a strange effect on a man. Makes him crazy years after it's over. But these are ghosts. They ain't men in the sense that we know of men. Who knows what it's doin' to them. People carry around scars for the rest of their lives." He licked his lips and rubbed his hands together. "You-all ever heard of Wesley Gibson?"

"No. Who's he?" Jared questioned.

"Well, in 1892, thirty years after that famous battle, people were amazed at how far medicine had come and Wesley Gibson was one of them crazy miracles of modern medicine. Modern for back then, mind you, 'cause it wadn't nothin' like it is today. Wesley Gibson fought in the battle of Lone Jack and was shot in the head. The bullet stuck in his skull, but didn't kill the man. Thirty years later, a doctor figured it was puttin' pressure on Gibson's brain, causing him to have a bad stroke and suffer from convulsions, so he removed it, since gettin' the bullet out of Gibson's head was the only way to prevent him from dying. He cut a one inch circle out of the man's skull and removed the bullet." Sirus scanned their youthful faces. "Ya see, kids, like that bullet in that old man's head, men in war carry around stuff. These ghosts here are carryin' around things so intense that they're ready to explode. You-all be careful."

Because the two girls were on foot, the four meandered through Blue and Gray Estates, stopping at each of the Crossroads gangs' houses. Like his grandfather had said he could do, Jared asked his new friends to come over later in the evening so they could play, and everyone said yes, mostly because Suds was with Jared when he asked. Leaving the neighborhood, the four took a shortcut behind the high school and walked along the winding creek towards Bynum. It was a scorching hot August day, with no sign of rain to relieve the area even for a moment, and they all appreciated the shade created by the trees along the edge of the woods. Pushing his bike through the tall weeds, Jared panted and closed his eyes. Inching closer to Bynum, Suds stopped and inspected the heavy brush to their left.

A rustling noise flowed across the creek. "Hold up. Somethin's in there," Suds whispered.

Molly and Jan moved closer to the boy. "Is it the ghosts?" Jan chirped like a baby bird.

"I dunno," he replied with excitement, struggling with the contraption around his neck. "I'm gettin' my camera ready, though, just in case."

Jared froze, not sure if he should stand solidly with his friend or run for cover. Molly had less of a dilemma. "Ta heck with that dumb old camera, Suds! You don't know how to work it anyway!" she whispered forcefully. "You're gonna get us all in a heap of trouble! Let's get outta here! I done seen enough of them ghosts or any others for the rest of my life!"

"Well, well, well," a large block of a boy hollered as he cackled and stomped through the weeds. "If it ain't Crud Davis."

"Oh boy. It's Dozer Pittman," Suds reported with contempt. "This idn't gonna be good."

"I thought it was Scum Davis." Another boy revealed his position in the high grass and leaped across the creek.

"Who's that?" Jared asked.

"That's Colby Shannon," Molly answered with a look of despair. "Those two were the meanest boys in school last year."

"Yeah, everybody calls him the Goat," Suds said, holding his ground and remaining alert as the boys neared.

"I thought he was Crap Davis," a third voice called out with a laugh like nails down a chalkboard.

"And that's Lathon Greeley," Jan informed Jared in her nasally monotone. "They're basically gonna beat you and Suds up. At least, that's all I've ever seen them do to kids, and they hate Suds most of all."

Thinking that maybe it wasn't entirely a treat to be friends with the boy just revealed as the primary target of the school bullies, Jared suddenly recognized the names. "My bike! You said they're the ones that stole my handlebars."

"Forget about it, Millhouse," Suds whispered out of the corner of his mouth. "It ain't like they're here to give 'em back to ya." Suds kept his eyes on the three thugs, studying their every move. "We can't outrun 'em, especially without leavin' the bikes. And if we leave 'em here, we'll never get 'em back."

Like three hyenas stalking an injured antelope, the bullies worked out their attack angles without verbal cues. It was instinct for them, of course, and something they'd done a thousand times. To add confusion to their stressed prey, they intertwined their paths and randomly took turns darting closer and backing away.

"What are we gonna do?" Molly pleaded.

"Keep an eye on 'em," Suds instructed through clenched teeth. "Don't let any of 'em get behind us. Keep your eye on 'em at all costs."

Jared's lip quivered, frightened by both the unknown and what he entirely expected. He didn't make a sound or move. He just waited.

Dozer relished the fear he put into his victims, but soon grew tired of the games and brazenly walked up to them. "So, Crud, what do you have for me today?" Dozer scowled. "That bike looks like it might fit me."

"Bend over and we'll find out," Suds shot back.

"Oh. A wise guy." Dozer clenched a meaty fist and held it up to the boy, showing Suds what the penalty was for disrespecting him. "Maybe you'd like to walk home, Crap Davis."

Greeley and the Goat closed in and flanked their ruthless leader. Dozer scanned the troubled faces. He locked his gaze on Jared. "Who's this little maggot?"

Hoping to diffuse the situation, Jared stammered, "Uhh, uh, uhh, I'm...j...j... Jared. Jared m...m...Millhouse."

"Scared Smallmouse," the Goat repeated in a mocking voice. "Is that what ya said, geek?"

"Millhouse?" Dozer roared. "Your loogie–hockin' grandpa's got that crappy farm down the road."

Jared's demeanor changed as his grandfather became the butt of the bully's jokes. His anger outweighing his fear, he stepped forward. "Leave my grandpa alone! Don't talk about him like that! You stole my handlebars!"

Incensed by the disrespect, the Goat leaped forward and shoved Jared, knocking him to the ground. "Watch who you're talkin' to, shrimp!"

"Hey!" Molly yelled. "Leave him alone! We haven't done anything to you! Just leave us alone!"

"Put a lid on it, girly," Dozer ordered. He towered over Jared, who remained dazed on the ground. "Thanks for the handlebars, geek. They work nicely on my bike. Oh, and nice catch. You're a great outfielder." His two accomplices cackled, while Dozer turned his attention back to Suds. He stood directly in front of the lanky boy, glaring into his eyes, then snickered and grabbed the front of his bicycle. But Suds held tight. The two fought back and forth, each unwilling to let go. Suds' eyes narrowed and his muscles tightened. He couldn't let go. Dozed released his grasp, snickered again, and made a move for the camera.

Both boys fell to the ground, throwing up dirt and grass as they wrestled. When Jared tried to get up, the Goat punched him in the stomach, knocking the wind out of him. He fell to his knees, gasping for air.

Suds battled like a cornered animal. "No! You're not gettin' it!" he hollered.

Dozer raised his large fist and punched Suds in the face, but Suds kept his composure and, more importantly, his hold on the camera straps. "Give it!" Dozer swung again, hitting Suds on the cheek. "Give it now, maggot!" The tyrant unleashed a barrage of powerful blows on the weaker Suds.

Being nimble like a cat, Suds rolled to his right and squirmed out from under Dozer, scampered to his feet and with one flowing motion pulled the camera from around his neck and held it out towards his attacker. "You want it?" he asked, panting. "Here, take it!"

Dozer crawled to his feet and stood in front of Suds. A grotesque, victorious smile grew on his round face. Humiliation was the real spoils of the day. He reached for the camera. As his large hand neared, Suds jerked the camera back and wielded it in a circle like a medieval ball and chain. As Dozer looked up, the camera smashed into his large, freckled face, shattering to pieces with the impact. Dozer dropped to his backside, blood trickling from his nose.

Stunned, the big kid fingered the blood. Dozer's surprise quickly turned to anger. His cheeks reddened. "Get 'em!" he yelled and, like a pack of wolves, the three leaped in for the kill.

"Run!" Suds yelled and the four took off in every direction.

Jared grabbed his bike, but didn't make it far. Greeley tackled him from behind and began pulverizing him. He threw a barrage of punches at Jared, who curled up into a ball, trying to protect his face. He'd been picked on before, but never to this extreme. But, Suds got the worst of it. The Goat and Dozer had him on the ground, thrashing away at him.

Judging the sentence had been carried out, Dozer called a halt to the onslaught. He didn't want to get in trouble, and relished in leaving some of the punishment for later. "That's enough," he ordered, "for now." He stood over Suds as he lay on the ground, his face a bloody and bruised mess. "You try that again, Crud, and I'll beat you even worse next time," he warned and then spit a loogie into his victim's face—a calling card the Crossroads Club had experienced several times, and were all too familiar with, from numerous past run-ins with the tyrannical Dozer.

As Dozer and his accomplices left the field in triumph, the two girls tended to the wounded. Molly rushed to Suds' aid and Jan consoled the bruised and battered Jared. "Sorry you got beat up," she said, though the boy couldn't gauge the girl's sincerity with her nasally monotone. "Dozer Pittman's a mean jerk. Stay away from him, Jared."

Jared's first run-in with the notorious Dozer and his goons was a memorable one. He touched the knot on the side of his head as the four staggered down Bynum to the Millhouse farm. There, they snuck in the backdoor and headed directly to the bathroom to wash and treat their wounds. Jared couldn't let his father or grandfather find out about his confrontation with the older boys, so the four of them concocted a story. A good, old-fashioned bike wreck seemed the perfect explanation, and on the Millhouse farm, too—so Jared could say he never disobeyed his dad's strict orders about not leaving the property. He was grounded after all.

Satisfied that Suds and Jared were well on their way to mending, Molly and Jan left to check-in at their houses, promising to return later. At about four o'clock, Jared's dad returned. He entered the kitchen as Jared and Suds searched one of the cabinets for a snack.

Virgil walked into the kitchen, wiping grease from his stained hands with a rag. "Now, don't go gettin' on the boy, Rob. I said he could have some friends over. It's better than him runnin' off like he done and gettin' into things, and far better than sittin' around here lookin' at the walls by hisself." The man rubbed his hands with the towel. "Darn tractor won't start. It won't turn over."

Rob poured a glass of ice tea. "What do you need it for, Dad?"

"Well, nothin' at the moment. It won't start."

"Well, if you don't need to do anything with it, what does it matter if it won't start?"

"Well, what does it matter if I have anythin' to do with it or not, if the darn thing won't start?"

Rob rolled his eyes. "I give up." He turned to Jared. "You know better than going to that cave, but if you're grandpa said you can have friends over, I'm not gonna stop ya. Who do you have there with ya?"

Surprised by his father's energy and interest, Jared introduced his pal. "Umm, this here is Suds, Dad. He's the best player on our team. Is it okay if him and the rest of the guys stay over tonight? We were gonna camp out in the backyard."

"Oh geez," his father responded. "I just figured it was one kid, Jared. A whole buncha kids here…all night?"

Jared clasped his hands together. "Pleasssse."

"Let him have his friends over, Rob," Virgil advised. "They'll be out back runnin' around. They ain't gonna hurt nothin'. Let the kiddo have some fun."

Rob frowned and placed his hand on his hip. "Well, if your grandpa says it's okay, it's fine with me. But don't do anything stupid or you'll be in big trouble."

Jared rushed his father, hugging him around the waist. "Thank you. Thank you. Thank you."

"Hey what happened to your face?" Rob asked. "You look like you got the crap beat out of ya."

Jared went into rescue mode. He couldn't let his dad know the truth about what happened or he might change his mind. "Oh, it's nothing. Me and Suds were riding our bikes and didn't see this ditch. We both wrecked and smacked our faces on the bank on the other side. It hurt bad, but we're okay."

"Ya see, that's what I'm talkin' about. You can't be having kids over and then one of 'em gets injured or even killed, Jared. I'm not sure about this whole thing. We don't even know these kids or their parents. And you're still in trouble, after all, for going into that mine in the first place. This is like rewarding that type of behavior. I'm none too pleased with your grandpa for even allowing this. You're *my* son and I say you're grounded."

Jared's head dropped. Virgil understood both his son and his grandson—he, too, had been a kid and the parent of a kid, after all. "Rob, it's fine son. They'll be fine. They're boys. Boys get into mischief and stuff, and they get a scratch or bruise here or there. They're just boys—boys being boys. It's fine. He's a good boy. Let him have some fun."

***

The Crossroads Club pitched their tents while Virgil collected wood from the barn for a nice fire. Even in August, no campsite was complete without a fire so everyone could sit around, telling stories and throwing sticks into the coals. As the sun set, Jared and the other kids roasted hotdogs and marshmallows, while Virgil kept a discreet eye on the youngsters from inside the house.

Porker tossed a stick at Suds. "That's bullcrap! You didn't see no ghosts! You're just tryin' to scare us!"

"It's true!" Molly insisted. "Sirus has seen them, too! Just ask him."

"What does that old man know?" Shanks chimed in. "He's nuts! My dad's even said so! Where's your proof, if you-all seen 'em?"

"No seriously," Sweetwater defended. "My mom said one time she was at the Baptist Church across from the cemetery and she went in the basement. She said she felt like something was down there. It made her feel all creepy. She left and swears she turned off the lights, but when she went back down to pick up her keys that she'd forgot...the lights were on. It's true."

"Oh cram it, Sweetwater," Shanks hollered. "Every time we get together you gotta bring up your mom. She's as nutty as Sirus. Make's peach cobbler every picnic that nobody can eat 'cause she burns it! It's like a big gooey brick. That lady can't cook for squat."

Insulted, Sweets stared at Shanks. "What's wrong with her peach cobbler? I like my mom's peach cobbler."

"You would," Shanks continued, driving the knife deeper. "If she ain't smart enough to remember her keys, what's to say she didn't forget to turn off them lights, too? Your old lady can't remember nothin'."

"Well, it happened," Suds stated. "You-all don't have to believe us. But we all seen it. And we know what we seen."

Porker pulled a marshmallow from the flames and jammed the entire crispy cube into his large cheeks. "This one time," he said as he chewed and attempted to blow the heat from his mouth, "this guy and this girl were parked out near Longview Lake and it was real dark and spooky. The guy has to go to the bathroom, so he gets out of the car. He's gone a long time and she gets real scared. Then she hears horrifyin' screams and this hook comes slicing through the top of the convertible. Oh yeah, I forgot to say that the car was a Mustang convertible and that they had the top up 'cause it was rainin'. So she jumps over to the driver's seat and starts the car. She's scared to death. When she turns the car lights on, there's a monster standin' in front of it. So she…"

"She floors the car and runs over whatever was in front of her," Shanks completed the sentence. "We done heard that story a thousand times! You tell it like we ain't never heard it before. She drives all the way home with the monster on the hood of the car and the hook still stuck in the roof of the convertible. When she gets out the car, still frightened and screamin' bloody murder, she realizes the monster was actually her boyfriend and the hook was a fallen tree limb. Come up with a new story, for cryin' out loud, Porker! And that ain't even a true one, no way! It's a *turban math!*"

"No, it's true," Sweets corrected. "My mom…"

Shanks snarled at the large boy. "Don't even go there, Sweetwater."

"Somebody tell a ghost story," Beans demanded. "A real one. Not no phony made-up one."

"No way!" Molly cringed and jumped from her seat. "I'm not sitting here and listening to ghost stories!"

"Well who asked ya to be here anyway?" Shanks snapped back. "This here is a boys' club. No girls allowed. So hit the road, lady."

Beans dug in the bottom of his duffle bag and retrieved a flashlight. "Let's play spotlight tag. One-Potato for who's it."

"I hate spotlight tag!" Porker complained. "I'm always it. I'm bigger'n the rest of you guys, so I can't hide as good or run as fast."

"That's not our fault, man," Beans responded. "Maybe if you'd stop shovin' marshmallows and hotdogs in your face, you'd lose some weight."

"Blow it out your hole, Beans!" Poker retaliated. "I've got me a condition. It's an eatin' disorder thing. My blood sugar gets outta whack."

"Oh it's a condition, all right," Shanks said. "You eat more than my grandpa's hog."

"Back off, ya little twerp!"

Sweetwater lost One-Potato and begrudgingly grabbed the flashlight as the rest of the crew giggled with excitement. He put his forehead on the back of the Millhouse home, closed his eyes, and started counting as the rest of the gang ran in every direction like bugs from under a rock. At first, Jared followed Porker into the cornfield, but then he remembered what the large boy had said about always being caught. He abandoned Porker and broke right across the cornrows and found himself behind Molly and Beans. They ran another fifty yards and stopped as they heard Sweetwater yell, "One hundred! Ready or not, here I come!" The three of them dropped to their knees and hunkered down.

Though Virgil had little energy left in his late years to plant much corn, every year he managed to grow tall stalks about fifty yards behind his house, over a twenty-acre area. He leased the rest of the land to other farmers and cattlemen, making enough money to live on. Though the season had been dry, the corn was still fairly tall, but not like it had been in previous years. It made no difference to the kids, however, as the corn stood much taller than they did and blocked the moonlight.

Sweetwater first checked the barn to the south of the house and then started walking the perimeter of the cornfield. The song of the whippoorwills and thousands of cicadas pierced the silence. Jared could barely make out Beans in the darkness, crouching several feet away. Molly hid behind Jared two rows away, her darkened form vaguely visible and motionless. Suddenly a long, riveting noise tore through the stalks. Jared tensed. Then he could make out someone trying to hold in their laughter.

"Dang it, Porker," Beans whispered. "You're gonna get us all caught and kill all this here corn. He farts louder than my dad when he pees in the morning—and longer, too. I'm outta here." In a flash and with minimal sound the spry young boy disappeared before Jared could even locate the direction he headed.

Porker broke wind again, sending Jared and Molly on the move for a safer, less polluted location. Losing Molly in their escape from Porker, Jared instantly remembered how much he hated the darkness. It wasn't bad when he had his friends next to him, but alone was another story. After what seemed like an eternity, he prayed Sweets would catch someone so the game would be over. Then he thought of giving up, but that would mean he'd be caught and ultimately *it*. He had no choice. He was going to have to wait it out.

In the confusion after his second retreat from Porker and his notorious gas, Jared had lost all sense of direction. He had no idea where he was in the cornfield, and the only thing worse than the darkness for him was being lost. Crouching among the tall stalks, he closed his eyes and took slow, deep breaths to calm his nerves. Just as he started to feel comfortable and wonder why he was ever scared of the dark, he heard something rustling in the distance to his right. He peered between the stalks and squinted. "Beans, is that you?" he whispered. "Porker? Molly?"

"To the right," said a disturbing voice he didn't recognize. "Watch out for our right. They's tryin' to outflank us."

"Suds," Jared called quietly. "Jan?"

"Hunker down, boys," another chilling voice advised. "They's comin'. When they get in range, give it to 'em with both barrels."

Jared quietly got up from the ground and tried to sneak away from the voices. As he tiptoed between the stalks, a louder disturbance came from the direction he was heading. The boy turned around slowly, confused as to what to do next.

"They's spotted us and they're on horseback, sergeant. They'll run right over us," a third strange voice warned.

"Hold your position, Logan," the first voice directed. "Keep cover and hold your fire till I give the order."

The ruckus in front of him grew louder. A horse neighed like brakes squealing. Jared's body tensed. He scanned his surroundings, searching for a way out. The full moon shone on his face as he tried to use its light to see. Then he heard the most horrifying sound of all.

"Let 'em have it, boys!" a demonic voice cried out. Blasts of gunfire, flashing light and sparks from gun muzzles broke the calm. A shrill battle cry sounded across the field followed by return gunfire.

The intensity of the deafening booms and devilish howling sent Jared reeling. He tripped and fell to the ground, but quickly scrambled to his feet. A horse broke through the stalks, the rider pulling back on the reins and stopping beside him. Its fiery eyes glared at him. The head of the beast was grotesque, mostly bone with only pieces of fur covering it. Its body, as well, was patches of bloody hide on top of connected bones and sinewy muscle. Jared screamed, drawing the rider's attention. In a blue uniform with a brimmed, blue hat and gold decal on the front of it, the hellish rider had chunks of skin ripped from his face. Most of his face was human skull. Bugs crawled from his decaying flesh and tattered uniform. A bloodstained beard grew from his jaw. His shredded, decaying lips revealed a skeleton's teeth. In his mangled left hand, he held a large saber and the reins of the hideous beast, while a long-barreled pistol gleamed in his right.

The demon rider stared at Jared for what felt like an eternity, his eyes opaque and morbid. He suddenly turned his attention to the men in front of him and fired a fearsome volley into the stalks.

A second rider appeared out of nowhere, another skeleton in blue with rotted, torn flesh for a face. His bone hand held tightly to a pistol. A large plume pointed backwards from his blue hat and shimmied in the night breeze. His skeleton horse with shredded fur neighed chillingly and bumped into Jared, spinning the boy in a circle. The second rider fired his weapon.

"Run 'em down!" the rider growled.

Trapped in the middle of the chaos, Jared held his position and searched for a way out. The haunting sound of a unified battle cry rang out as, behind him, dozens of skeleton riders on mangled horses galloped forward. In front, the cornstalks shook and snapped eerily, indicating something was charging towards him—and fast.

"They're comin'!" the ghoulish rider to his left roared.

Jared waited in terror as the cornstalks whipped and crackled. Something burst through the stalks and charged the rider on his left. The creature carried a long rifle with a shimmering bayonet. He was dressed in gray with a gray cap; only the beard and mustache on his bloody, flesh-torn face revealed that he was once a man. The rider fired at his attacker, hitting the beast in his chest. The gray uniformed demon's ribcage exploded. Bone fragments hit Jared's face as the creature tumbled to the ground. Blinded by the sparks from the muzzle, Jared frantically wiped the bloody pieces from his face. Despite half of his chest being blown from his body, the attacker miraculously regrouped and charged again as other skeletons in gray entered the fray. The demons howled as they engaged the riders in blue all around him.

Jared held his ground and watched, snapping his head back and forth from one fierce engagement to the next. The blood-curdling screams and blasts of gunfire rippled over his body. One of the gray attackers pulled a blue skeleton rider from his bony steed and wrestled him to the ground only feet away from Jared. His skeleton hands thrashing at the rider, the blue uniformed ghoul pulled a pistol from his belt and fired as his attacker plunged a large knife into his shoulder. The ball ripped through the gray dressed skeleton's jaw, shattering it to pieces. The jawbone, with jagged teeth still intact, hit Jared's stomach. The blue soldier crawled out from under his opponent, only to be cut in two by another shotgun-wielding monster dressed in tattered gray. The two injured ghouls flopped on the ground like fish on the deck of a boat, but, to Jared's surprise, kept moving. They writhed about, trying to locate the portions of their skeletons they'd lost. The gray soldier groped along the ground for the missing segment of his jaw. Jared saw the teeth at his feet and kicked them towards the demon.

The gray pile of bones snatched the jaw fragment from the ground and jammed it back into place on the bottom of his hideous mouth with a loud *crack*. "Tank you," he said politely to Jared, unsettling the boy even further.

As Jared looked around, struggling to find a way out of the center of the strange battle, a figure from the darkness barreled over him, knocking him on his backside. Jared curled up into a ball, fearful of what was to come. "What?! Ya takin' a nap, Millhouse!" Shanks shouted as Suds pulled their fallen comrade to his feet. "Get the lead out! We're bein' invaded!"

The three boys raced through the towering corn, the sharp leaves slicing their arms and faces. "What are they?" Jared asked as a stalk smacked his cheek.

Suds put his arm up to block the barrage of leaves. "I dunno! But they's real mad at each other!"

A monster in gray charged through the corn and blasted a blue enemy in the back. The intensity of the shotgun blast sent the boys scurrying in the opposite direction down the row. A demon dressed in blue cut an attacker in two with a saber before taking a musket ball between the eyes. The fleeing boys leaped over the writhing skeletons and turned right again, running into Beans.

"Ahhh!" the Stars' pitcher screamed. "Run! They're comin' this way!"

Reaching the edge of the field, they burst through the final row of corn. Thinking they had escaped the battling demons, the boys became trapped in a thick hedgerow that appeared out of nowhere. The pointy thorns pierced and scratched their skin. Suspended, like flies in a spider's web, they wrestled and twisted to get out. "What is this?" Suds yelled. "Ahh, it hurts!"

Suds struggled with the prickly thorns. His shirt was torn off his body as he pulled himself free. Deep scratches covered his arms and torso. He grabbed Beans, who was deep in the hedge and pleading for relief. As he tugged on Bean's arm, three ghouls in gray spotted the defenseless boys and marched towards them. "Suds! They're comin'!" Jared screamed. "Help me' Suds! Help me!"

The ghastly soldiers marched closer and closer. The gray skeleton in the lead carried a long saber, his uniform decorated with shiny gold buttons. His gray beard grew below a mouth with disfigured lips, a terrifying row of teeth and no nose.

Suds grunted, desparate to save his friends. "I can't!" Suds hollered. "It's too thick!" He pulled on Beans for as long as he could, trying frantically to dislodge the boy from the grips of the hedge. As the demons reached him, Suds scrambled to his feet and turned to flee. The gray beast snatched him by the back of the neck and lifted him off the ground.

"Give us the key," the creature roared. "Give us the key!"

The demon raised his saber, preparing to slice the frightened boy in two. Shanks fought his way free from the thorns and tried for an escape. One of the dark soldiers clamped a skeletal hand onto the boy's throat, the bones crunched as he tightened his grip. "The key!" the gray monster ordered. "Give us the key!" Shanks struggled for air as the ghoul lifted him off his feet. Jared and Beans screamed.

The horrible stench of the creatures' rotting flesh hit Jared's nostrils, making his stomach crawl. The third ghoul carried a long rifle in his greenish-white, rotting hands. Half of his face was also decayed with bugs feasting on his head and neck. The creature turned towards the corn, the bones in his neck crackling like loose gravel. "Captain Bradley," he groaned, "the Federals is preparin' another charge. We must regroup and counter."

The beast growled and tossed Suds to the ground. "Yes, Lieutenant Cross," the bearded skeleton responded. "Give the orders. We must repel their advance. There is hell to pay."

The second skeleton soldier dropped Shanks, who scampered like a frightened rabbit towards Suds. The three monsters entered the corn and, to the boys' amazement, disappeared. Jared and Beans dropped to the ground. As if it all had been just a bad dream, the boys found themselves lying on the ground: no hedgerow, sounds of gunfire, or bloodcurdling screams. They crawled to their feet and stared at each other. The night was silent and calm as only the whippoorwills and cicadas made their presence known.

Shanks brushed himself off and searched his body for cuts and scrapes. None were found. Suds too had no injuries or open wounds. The shirt that had been torn from his body and shredded by the ghostly hedge lay delicately on the ground, completely intact. He picked the shirt up and put it back on. Jared and Beans, too, were unscathed though the pain of the thorns pricking their bodies remained in their senses.

Staring with dazed eyes at his friends, Shanks shivered. "Okay, Suds. I believe ya. There's ghosts here in Lone Jack."

While they discussed the terrifying encounter, trying to make sense of it all, Sweets jogged up, the anger leaping from his face. "What are you-all doin'?" he yelled. "You weren't supposed to leave the back area! You even promised and said that nobody was to go outside the fence or they'd be *it*! You-all cheated! I know you jumped the fence and hid where ya wasn't supposed to go! I'm not playin' no more!" He slammed the flashlight to the ground.

"What?" Beans asked. "You didn't hear the guns or see the soldiers?"

"Up yours, Beans," Sweets responded. "Don't go playin' your-all's foolish tricks on me. You-all cheated! I've been lookin for almost thirty minutes! You jumped the fence and wadn't supposed to! Admit it!"

"Stick it in your ear, Sweetwater!" Shanks shouted. "He ain't lyin'! We almost got ourselves killed in here! We was attacked by army guys with massacred faces and guns and… swords! You don't have to believe us! But it's true!"

Porker, Jan and Molly appeared from the shadows. "I knew I wouldn't be the first one caught," Porker boasted. "So which one of these turkeys did ya get?"

"None of us, Porker!" Shanks yelled. "Forget about the crummy old game."

The round boy pointed at his tiny friend and laughed. "Ahh, it was Shanks!"

"No," Jared corrected. "He didn't catch any of us. You mean, you guys didn't see it either? Molly?"

"See what?" Molly responded.

Beans threw his arms in the air. "The dang monsters. They was fightin' in the corn and shootin' at each other. Some was on horses and others was on foot."

"You've got to be kidding!" Molly's expression changed. "You better not be messin' with us! You saw more ghosts? Seriously."

"Heck, yeah," Suds screeched. "One of 'em had me by the neck and another'n had Shanks by the throat, nearly chokin' him to dagblang death. You-all was in the corn, too. How could ya not see it or hear it?"

Porker sneered, his fat cheeks shoved to the edge of his face as he smiled. "Oh yeah. Keep it up, Suds. A ghost was chokin' Shanks?

I done heard it all now. For one, any ghost who was to run inta him would surely go ahead and kill the loudmouth and, for two, Molly supposedly seen them ghosts in Robber's Cave, but didn't see these here. Nice try, stinkbreath." As Porker turned and started walking towards the campfire, a blaring siren sent the youngsters' hearts jumping again.

"For cryin' out loud!" Shanks shouted. "I've done had enough of this spooky crap for one night!"

Blue and red flashing lights danced across the side and roof of the farmhouse, flickering off Jared's blackjack oak tree. "It's the police?" Jared asked, fearing the worst. "They're here at my grandpa's farm? What are they doing here?"

"Oh crap!" Suds blurted. "It's Skunkle! Everybody run and hide." Without missing a beat, the Crossroads gang darted for cover, returning to the very cornfield they'd fought so hard to escape. The only thing more terrifying than ghosts with rotting flesh was Officer Kunkle. "Everybody keep'er quiet and nobody move till that nitwit is gone," Suds ordered.

With all eyes fixed on him, Officer Kunkle marched around the side of the farmhouse. The kids huddled together, hoping he wouldn't spot them in the dark of night and cover of the tall cornstalks. The officer looked left and then right. He placed his thumbs behind the buckle of his black utility belt. He looked left and then right once more. He moved his head steadily, scanning every inch of his surroundings like a radar antenna. As his head swiveled, he stopped on the gang's location. Their bodies tensed and they squeezed closer together.

"Well, let me tell ya," Sergeant Kunkle barked, "I done had me enough of you little cow chips! You morons get on out here, front'n center! Now, boy! Come on, Davis! You and that fat kid and that one little turd with the mouth! Out here, now!"

Awakened by the commotion, Virgil and Rob flung open the screen door on the back of the house and raced to the officer. "What's goin' on, Cliff?" Virgil asked, fearing something terrible happened to one of the children. "Has there been an accident? Is everythin' okay?"

"No, everythin' ain't okay," Officer Kunkle exclaimed. "Mr. Millhouse, we got us several calls from the neighbors to the north of ya, complainin' of screamin', whoopin' and hollerin', and somebody lightin' off fireworks. It's my duty to get to the bottom of this ruckus and issue citations for disturbin' the peace, if 'n I must."

"Jared, come out here now," his father ordered.

The boy dropped his head and slowly lurched forward in the direction of his father. Sensing the jig was up, and knowing Jared shouldn't have to face the music alone, the rest of the Crossroads Club traipsed out of the field, dreading what was to come.

Jared stopped in front of his father. "Did you kids light off fireworks?"

"No, Dad," he responded.

"Don't lie to me, son. I'm gonna ask ya again."

"We didn't. I swear."

"The neighbors say otherwise, Mr. Millhouse," Officer Kunkle interjected. "They said there was loud booms and all kinds of screamin' comin' from over here."

"Dad, we didn't. I swear," Jared pleaded. "You and grandpa would've heard if we had."

"Well, me and your grandpa were sleeping. I got another one of my headaches, took some medicine, and was out like a light. I knew I shouldn't have trusted you, Jared. I don't know what has gotten into you. You could've set fire to that entire field, burnt this whole house down, and God only knows what could've happened to the neighborhood next to us. They didn't even allow fireworks for the Fourth of July, but you kids thought you'd just go ahead and have a show of your own. I'm very disappointed in you, Jared. You're grounded. And I mean it this time. Your campout's over. I'm taking your friends home."

"But dad," Jared begged. "We didn't. I swear. It was..." He quickly realized he had no good explanation for the disturbance...at least none his dad, grandfather, and Officer Skunkle would accept without calling him a liar.

"You just can't trust kids these days, Mr. Millhouse. They'll lie to ya as soon as look at ya—'specially these here little wisecrackers. Your son is hangin' with a bad crowd." Officer Kunkle pointed at Suds, staring the boy down. "And that little cowchip right there is the ringleader. You can tell 'cause he's got the most flies swarmin' around him."

"That's quite enough, Cliff," Virgil interrupted. "We can take it from here. We'll take these kids home and put this all to bed. Our apologies for the disturbance." The old man extended his hand to the officer and then offered a sympathetic look to his dejected grandson.

4

Jared spent the rest of the week indoors, where his father kept a watchful eye on him between bouts with migraines and liquor. As time wore away the anger, Rob loosened the reins on the boy and allowed him more freedom. It was not complete forgiveness, however, just parole. Jared had no more chances to screw up. If he did, his father had threatened to send him away to a military school. Jared knew it was only a threat made in the heat of the moment—or, at least, he hoped it was.

It was Friday, August 8th. After his grandfather had had a tough week battling his emphysema, and Jared and his dad were going stir-crazy cooped up in the tiny farmhouse, Rob, who was having one of his better days, decided he'd take his boy out to lunch and let his father get some needed rest. The Crossroads Café was uncommonly busy. Rob searched for a place to sit until a voice in a corner booth called out to him.

"Hello, there," a middle-aged lady said. "Yoo-hoo, hello." Jared and Rob politely walked over to the unknown woman waving to them. "You can join me. I'm about done and, when I leave, you can have the table all to yourselves." Jared's father accepted the woman's invitation gratefully and sat down across the table from her. She smiled and extended her hand to Rob. "I'm Darla Ramsey."

"Very pleased to meet you, Darla," Rob replied as he took the lady's hand. "I'm Rob Millhouse and this is my son, Jared. Thank you very much for letting us join you. It's really nice of you. I wasn't sure we'd ever get a table. This place is packed today."

Darla smiled at Jared. "Hello there, Jared. You're not anyone I've seen before," the slender brunette said as she looked over the boy with her stunning brown eyes. "And I would know 'cause I am a teacher. Ahhh!"

Jared chuckled, slightly embarrassed. "No, I live in Overland Park. I stay summers with my grandpa."

"Well, I teach fourth grade and you look like you're about that age," the attractive lady continued. "You don't know how lucky you are not to have me as a teacher."

"No, Jared's actually going into fifth grade," Rob corrected her. "He's just a little small for his age, but he makes up for it by being one of the brightest in class."

Jared ignored the insult as well as the compliment. "You teach fourth grade here?"

"Yes, I do. In fact I teach summer school to all the bad kids," she joked. "But luckily, yesterday was our last day. Hurray for me. School was supposed to end today, but it's so hot and humid, and the forecasted temperature so dreadful, they actually made yesterday the final day. The building is pretty old and I practically sweat to death in there. What's a girl to do, huh?"

"Then you know Suds and Beans, Molly, Sweetwater, and Jan?" he asked excitedly.

"Yes, I do," she answered, equaling the boy's excitement. "In fact, Molly and Daniel—or Sweetwater, as your crew calls him—were my favorites in class. Daniel is the nicest, most responsible boy I've ever seen. I bet he's gonna be a politician someday, don't you?"

Jared glanced at his father, who dodged the boy's eyes. "Well, we had the boys over a few nights ago and let's just say they got into a little mischief," Rob told her. "The police were called."

"Common criminals?" Darla joked. "I'm sitting here with an outlaw. What will my friends say?"

"So you know Shanks and Porker too?" Jared continued, as if listing everyone they both knew made up a conversation.

Darla leaned back in the booth and folded her arms; her bright smile left her face. "Yes, I do. Let's just say I've had a few sit-downs with those two boys. Shanks has got a mouth on him and, well... Parker...I had to feed that kid every two hours for an entire school year, like a newborn baby, all because his mother insisted he had some kind of condition and required food throughout the day. Not fun. Those two are a little ornery. I've had sit-downs with their parents as well." Rob glanced at Jared, who stared at the table. "But I love 'em all. Just love 'em—even the ornery ones. They sometimes make it the most fun." Ms. Ramsey turned to Rob. "So what's your story, Rob Millhouse? I haven't seen you in these parts before."

Not one who liked talking about himself, Jared's father became tense and bashful. "Well, I'm actually kind of in between things. I'm an electrical engineer by trade, but Jared's mother died some time ago. She had ovarian cancer. And, well…I decided to take a break from work to care for the boy. Jared was six when she passed. It's been tough, I must say—tough on both of us. Jared is an only child. I grew up on my parents' farm, just down the road and then decided to stay in the area after college. But since Sara died…I guess you could say I don't really know what to do, or at least what to do next."

"I'm deeply sorry to hear that. I'm sure your wife is missed and it has been tough. My sympathies," Darla said. "But I guess you and I have a lot in common, then."

"Your husband died?" Rob asked.

"God, I hope so. Did you hear something?" The woman giggled. "No, he left me with two young children four years ago. We barely speak when he comes to pick them up on his weekends. So now I'm the proud forty-one-year-old single mother of two. Isn't that great? All 'cause Mark Ramsey had to run off and trade me in for a newer model. I'm sure that ditz didn't know what she had gotten herself into. I think I won out on that one."

Darla placed her slender hands on the table and exhaled. "Well, I'm off. I think I'll leave the Millhouse boys alone to their lunch. The special's good today. Nice to meet you, Rob." The pretty woman's smile brightened the greasy restaurant. She turned to Jared. "And nice to meet you as well, Jared. Hope you have fun in crummy old Overland Park, you lucky."

With stuffed bellies leading the way, Jared and his dad left the Crossroads Café, working the gaps between their teeth with toothpicks. As the bell dangling from the door handle clanked, Rob hesitated. "Oh, geez. I almost forgot about Dad. I need to grab him a plate of food. Wait here and I'll be right back."

Jared stood in the scorching sun, squinting to block the rays.

"You gonna stand there like a dummy or you gonna find yourself a little shade?" old man Lovelace asked, sitting in his usual spot on the bench under the overhanging roof of the restaurant. "Just like a kid. Too dumb to come in outta the rain."

The gray-bearded town crazy was a little unpredictable, so Jared approached with caution, unable to resist the idea of getting out of the miserable heat. "Hey, Mr. Lovelace," the boy greeted the spooky old-timer and plopped down on the bench next to him.

"What's your name again?"

"I'm Jared. Jared Millhouse. You play chess with my grandpa."

"Oh yeah. Virgil's grandson. I didn't recognize ya. I forget who some folks are sometimes, so don't take it personal."

"I won't."

The old man's hands shook as he draped them across his cane. "That one cop, Kunkle's his name, was sayin' there was a disturbance up at your-all's farm the other night. Been talkin' about it like it was a dagblang bank robbery or somethin'. The moron."

Jared thought back to Monday night's events; the mangled, decaying creatures fresh in his mind. "Well...it was nothin'. We lit us some fireworks and got in trouble for it. I've been grounded all week. It won't happen again. I swear."

"Bull hockey," Mr. Lovelace sneered, seeing through the lie. The cantankerous man pushed his withered face towards the boy's. His good eye protruded freakishly from its socket, the wrinkles in his face deep and telling. "You seen 'em, didn't ya?"

Jared backed away. "Seen what?" he feigned innocence.

"The ghosts, ya little twerp. The ghosts of Lone Jack! You seen 'em fightin' like they do. You did. I know you did. I can see it in your eyes."

Surprised by the grizzled man's directness, Jared stammered, "You mean, you...you... you've seen 'em, too?"

The old man showed his yellow teeth, a disturbing look of excitement beaming from his face. "Shucks, yeah. I seen 'em. I seen more than my share of 'em. Makes for an interestin' day for an old man who ain't got many friends left to talk to." Mr. Lovelace leaned in close again, leading with his good eye. "So what'd ya see?"

Hesitant at first, as Sirus had warned him not to tell a soul, Jared soon disclosed every detail of his run-ins with the ghosts of Lone Jack. He described Mrs. Cave's pale, sunken face and jagged teeth, her long dark dress. Then he moved on to his encounter with the ghosts of Robber's Cave and their chains slamming, making the mine vibrate like an earthquake, and how they asked for a key. He went on to recount his horrifying adventure in the cornfield behind his grandpa's house and all the ghoulish figures, some dressed in blue and others in gray, and the hideous horses he'd seen. He ended with the story of Suds and Shanks nearly getting killed while they were trapped in a hedgerow that wasn't really there. "And they demanded a key from us, too." He paused as he rubbed his hands up and down his thighs. "It was scary. Real scary."

Mr. Lovelace sat motionless for a few seconds. "Wow. Now that was entertainin'. You done good, son. Real good. Added a little spice to an old man's life. Makes me feel young again."

"It wasn't fun at the time," Jared insisted. "I guess you had to be there."

"Oh, them ghosts is harmless enough. This dull town could use a little excitement, let me tell ya, even if it is lost souls from the other side. I like 'em." He turned to Jared and locked his eye on the boy. "How much you know about that historic battle, son?"

"More than I want to, I suppose. Sirus has told me most of it, but not all."

"Well, do you know what you're seein'?"

"I don't know. I mean, I know there was a battle here and all during the Civil War."

Mr. Lovelace raked his wrinkled hand through his beard. "Well, you see, son, the north, or Union soldiers…the ones dressed in blue, entered Lone Jack on the fifteenth of August. They'd had a skirmish with some of the Rebels, or Confederates—the soldiers dressed in gray. They entered the town and overwhelmed the Rebel forces, takin' many prisoners in the process. The Union was led by Major Emory Foster, a brave leader and good strategist." The old man cleared his throat and adjusted his position on the hard bench.

"Now Lone Jack was founded in the early 1830s. In 1843, New Town was built just south of the original settlement. By 1862, it had two stores, a saloon, a post office, a blacksmith shop, and a few scattered homes. About thirteen hundred people lived here, and dang near all of them was rootin' for the Rebels. Foster had a Union force of around eight hundred men, while the Rebels, who regrouped after they was routed on the fifteenth, had them some fifteen hundred soldiers. But what Foster didn't know, didn't hurt him. Ya see, he didn't know he was outnumbered two to one. He also didn't know that half the Confederate army was unarmed. A lot of 'em had just joined the Rebel army and was expectin' to get needed weaponry and supplies once they enlisted, but the Confederates didn't have nothin' to give 'em. So it ended up a pretty even match.

"Now, what I'm g'tting' to is an explanation of what you seen in that cornfield. Ya see, most of the rebels only had shotguns, which meant ya had to get in real close and use surprise to your advantage. The Federals had them better guns, which, coupled with their two cannons—or James Guns, as they was called—gave the Union a definite advantage. Now, a lot of the close fightin' and hand-to-hand combat was in a cornfield. The cornfield was huge and just east of New Town, where Foster and his Union boys were holed up in the buildings they'd taken. Around the perimeter of the field was this thick hedgerow, like a prickly natural fence to keep livestock away from the corn. The thorns on them things were several inches long. Durin' the battle, they tore up more than their share of soldiers on both sides who got trapped in 'em when they was tryin' to escape a charge. When the battle started, most of the Union Calvary had tied their horses to that hedge."

Jared's eyes grew big. "So you're saying that what we got caught in was that hedgerow, and the Union and Confederate soldiers were fighting again in the corn?"

The old man pointed at the boy with a crooked index finger. "Exactly. That same hedgerow. It appeared on your grandpap's farm like it done when them boys fought it out all them years ago. And them loud blasts and sparks, they was from the shotguns and powder rifles that the men used in battle. Worst of all was the close fightin' that was necessary in the cornfield and all in the town. You had to get in close to be deadly with a shotgun. It made for a bloody mess and several hand-to-hand struggles where it wadn't easy to take a man's life. It takes a cold, tough man to take another'n's life like that…when you can see the white of his eyes, right at the end of your arms. Several new Rebel recruits couldn't do it and refused to fight. Simply too scared.

"Even one colonel—a colonel, mind you—with the Rebels named Tracy was bein' carted off the field of battle. When Jackman, one of the Confederate's brave leaders on the battlefield that day, went to check on him, Tracy said he'd been shot all to pieces and that blood was runnin' down his leg. Jackman looked him over and said the colonel was mistaken as to what was runnin' down his leg, if you know what I mean." Mr. Lovelace snickered and waited for Jared's reaction, but Jared didn't get it.

"He'd peed his pants, son. Too scared by the violence and carnage to continue. He wanted outta that gruesome battle, as did many others."

As Jared continued his chat with the strange man, Suds and the rest of the Crossroads Club walked around the corner of the restaurant, each toting a fishing pole and tackle box. "Hey, guys!" Leaping from the hard bench, he greeted his fellow club members.

"Well, if it ain't Millhouse," Shanks responded. "We done thought your dad went and buried ya in the cornfield. Where the heck have you been?"

"Hey there, Millhouse." Beans grinned as he and the rest of the group circled around Jared. "We're goin' to catch us some fish for dinner. You comin'?"

"This here is like watchin' dogs eat their own turds," Mr. Lovelace observed. "You-all oughtta have leashes around your scrawny little necks and be chained in your backyards. What's the matter with your parents?"

"Give it a rest, would ya, Mr. Lovelace?" Shanks sniped. "We ain't done nothin' to you. We're just passin' by. It's a free country, ain't it?"

"Not if you nitwits join the military," the old man returned.

While Jared caught up with his friends, his father came out of the Crossroads Café carrying a Styrofoam box of hot food for his father. The boys quickly put pleading expressions on their faces. "Please, Dad," Jared begged. "Can I go with 'em?"

Rob rolled his eyes. "Oh, all right," he relented, setting the food next to Mr. Lovelace and reaching for his wallet. "Let me give you some money for dinner."

"He won't need no money," Beans informed the man, holding up the fishing pole and tackle box. "We're goin' fishin'. We're just gonna eat what we catch."

Rob continued to look through his wallet. "Oh, I'm sure you're gonna catch a lot. No doubt in my mind. I mean, it's nearly one o'clock in the afternoon and about nine hundred degrees out here today. You're gonna catch a whopper with every cast, of course, but I'd feel better giving him a little money just in case." Jared snatched the money from his dad's hand. Rob pointed at his son. "But hey, Jared,

I don't have to remind you what'll happen if you get in anymore trouble or pull anymore of your stunts. You won't leave my side till school starts. I mean it." The boys raced off before Rob could finish his warning. "Jared, you call me when you need me to come pick you up! I'm not kidding! No screwin' around or gettin' into trouble! I mean it!"

Jared and his pals journeyed north on Bynum Road, stopping occasionally to investigate a dead squirrel or take a needed breather. The historic and famous crossroads, where their club got its name, was the intersection of Bynum Road and Lee's Summit Road. At the northeast corner stood the Lone Jack Public Library. North of the library was City Hall, followed by the tiny police station. A mile further, after a sharp turn in the road, lay the elementary school and Caleb Winfrey Field. A half a mile beyond that, and a quarter of a mile down a grungy gravel road, sat their large fishing hole, hidden behind the tall weeds and trees, completely isolated. The fishermen reached the police station and decided they needed another break. They plopped down in the shade at the west corner of the tiny complex, resting their poles against the building.

While they guzzled water and tore into the snacks they'd brought for their outing, a police squad car raced into the parking lot, tires squealing. Officer Kunkle jumped out of the vehicle, excitement on his face. He adjusted his shiny leather belt and scurried towards the entrance. "You boys get on home! You shouldn't be loiterin' at a police station no way," he hollered.

"Aw, give us a break," Shanks shot back. "We ain't doin' nothin'. We's just takin' a break on our way to go fishin'! Ain't no laws against that, is there?"

Though pressing matters required his immediate attention, the decorated officer stopped in his tracks and pointed at Shanks. "I ain't got time for you little turd-disturbers taday! Now, I'm warnin' ya to get home! We want everybody off the streets! We got us a Code 3!"

"Oh yeah," Porker snickered. "Ain't it obvious? All I ever seen ya do is your Code 7 to eat or Code 8 to take yourself a crap." The large boy's belly rippled as he chuckled.

"I'm warnin' ya, tubby! We got us a serious situation here…a 4537! That's escaped prisoners! They was being transferred to Farmington and goin' down Highway 50, when the bus that was transportin' 'em broke down. They overtook the guard that was watchin' 'em, while the other'n checked the engine, got the keys to their shackles and a couple of 'em stole the guards' clothes, then they all fled on foot! We rounded up most of 'em, but six is still on the loose: two blacks, a Mexican and three whites. This here is serious bidness and nothin' I need to be wastin' my time arguin' with you about, porky! Now I done told ya to beat it, so get your ornery butts on home! Now!"

"It's a 4532," Sweetwater interjected.

"A what?" Officer Kunkle replied. "Don't get smart with me, boy. I done told ya."

"It's a 4532," the lanky boy continued. "An escape. It's a 4532. I've studied all the codes the police use. 4537 isn't a code. You mean 4532."

The desperate, excited officer dropped his head. "Whatever. There's convicts on the loose. Get home till it's safe. This here is a police matter."

A second squad car squealed into the parking lot, slamming on the brakes. Captain Pickering heaved his round body from the driver's seat and adjusted his falling pants. The buttons of his shirt popped open from the strain of trying to support his massive gut. He wore large reflecting sunglasses and his signature matchstick rested between his lips. "Hey, Captain," Shanks yelled. "Why you always got an unlit match in your mouth? You keep it there in case ya need to light somethin'?"

"Daggum it, boys," the Captain barked, "I ain't got time for your foolish games. We got us prisoners on the loose. Didn't ya tell 'em to get their scrawny butts on home, Cliff?"

"Of course, Capt'n. They's just dumb kids. They don't mind. They'll wish they'd've listened once they get caught in the crossfire and mayhem."

"Is it in case ya need to smoke out a fugitive?" Porker asked with serious interest.

"What did I done say? You-all need to get. Go on now. Let us do our job." The two officers, excited to finally see some real action in the one horse town, rushed towards the door. "Do you got the bulletproof vests and shotguns ready, Cliff?"

Officer Kunkle held the door open for his superior. "Well, the vests is still in the plastic bags they was shipped in when we got 'em two years ago. I found one of the shotguns, but can't remember where we done put the other'n. I'll have to move my desk out the other cell, too, just in case we need to separate these lowlifes…" he answered as the door swung closed.

"Well." Suds peeled his body off the hot pavement and reached for his pole. "Let's go do us some fishin'."

"But what about the escaped prisoners?" Jared asked. "They told us to go home."

"Man, them prisoners'll go to one of our homes sooner than stay out in this heat," Suds replied. "They may be dumb, but they can't be that dumb. Besides, if'n we spot 'em we could get us a reward or somethin'. We can track 'em, like cowboys in the old west searchin' for Geronimo, and then let the cops know where they's hidin'. We could be heroes."

***

Sweat beads swelled on Parker's nose and cheeks as he stumbled through the dense brush. His chubby face red from sun and exertion, the boy hadn't stopped complaining since the Crossroads Club had started their important mission. "Suds. Come on, Suds. What do we know about finding escaped prisoners anyway? I'm hot. My feet hurt. I'm tired. Let's just go do us some fishin', like we said we was gonna do. Suds. Come on, Suds."

"Well, how could we find 'em with you makin' all that racket?" Sweetwater pointed out, walking delicately through the thick brush, holding a large stick in his hands. "You can't never be quiet. This is an important operation. It requires the element of surprise, so put a sock in it, Porker, or they's gonna hear us."

"Bite me, Sweetwater," Porker snapped. "We're just kids and shouldn't be up to this foolishness anyway. I'm getting hungry. I quit."

One by one, the Crossroads Club abandoned the mission, until only Jared and Sweetwater remained at Suds' side. As the three started to climb a steep hill, Suds stopped and looked at his comrades. "Aw, shucks. We done searched a couple square miles for them escaped convicts. They ain't nowhere near Lone Jack, I reckon. That Skunkle don't know what he's talkin' about. Dang. I wanted me a reward. Make us heroes. But they's probably halfway to Mexico by now, if they really escaped at all. Let's go do us some fishin'."

For Jared, reluctant to join the posse in the first place, the words were a godsend. "That's a great idea, Suds. Those fellas have got to be by here already, if they'd come this way at all. Let's get the heck outta here and find the rest of the guys."

On the other side of the hill, a sweat-soaked man dressed in a prison security guard uniform tripped and fell, rolling to the bottom. "Damn it! Where in the hell are we?"

"Keep quiet, Jackson," a second man ordered. "We got to get us a car. Just keep movin'. We can't be stoppin'."

The notorious Earl Bridges walked calmly to Jackson. He grabbed the man by his shirt collar, lifted him off the ground, and slammed him against a tree. "I done told you to keep your mouth shut. If I got to tell you again, they's gonna find you easy enough—if the coyotes and vultures don't eat ya down to the bone."

Jackson swatted Bridges' arms off his neck and shoved him away. "Don't be threatenin' me, Earl. You's the one who said you knew a way outta here."

Bridges' evil face developed a sinister grin. "Yeah, I do. And we're doin' it. We run and keep on runnin'. That's how we get outta here." A disfiguring scar ran from the gangster's forehead around the left side of his face to his chin. His cold eyes stared at Jackson, as the rest of the desperate escapees gathered near him. Bridges inspected the group with disgust. Jackson was dressed in a prison guard uniform he'd wrestled off one of the officers during the break. Another had snatched a pair of jeans, a white t-shirt, and hardhat from a construction site they'd passed as they fled. A third hid his true identity with a cowboy outfit he'd taken from an unlocked Chevy truck. "Christ. Look at you idiots. All we need now is a damn Indjun and a biker and we got us The Village People."

Orlando Jackson, a muscular black man with a shaved head, balled up his fist, the muscles in his arm swelling. "I've had about enough outta you, Bridges." He lunged for the scarfaced man, only to be held back by two of his fellow escapees.

"This ain't gonna do us no good." Mitchell Lancaster, who had disguised himself as the cowboy, struggled to hold onto the much larger and stronger Jackson. "We ain't got time to be fightin' one another. We got to get on the move. Time's a-wastin'."

"Yes," Miguel Torez seconded in a thick Hispanic accent. The short man wiped his brow. "We need agua. Water. I tink I pass out soon."

"Get a grip, Torez," Bridges ordered as he approached Jackson who stood with clenched fists at his side. "We keep runnin' till I say otherwise. And if you cross me again, Jackson, I'll kill ya where ya stand."

"Forget this!" Jackson shouted. "We're splittin' up. We look like a circus runnin' around like we's doin'." The large black man turned his sights on his fellow convicts. "Any man wanna run off with this scumbag, then go with him, but I'm makin' my own way outta here. Any man wanna come with me, then come on." Jackson glared at Bridges. "But I'm done with you, Earl. Stay out my way and stay out my sight. If'n I see you again, you can be sure I'm there to kill ya."

Bridges snickered and threw his hands in the air. "Oh, send me shiverin'. Looks like we got us a mutiny, boys. First mate Jackson done turncoated on old Cap'n Bridges. I'll see ya then, Jackson." The large black convict stared at the notorious man for several seconds and then turned to continue his flight for freedom. "But if you boys screw up and get caught and you rat on me," Bridges continued, causing Jackson to stop, "I'll see you in hell when they put me back inside. And that's where I'm a gonna send you, Jackson. Straight to hell."

Torez and Sterling Bishop, the other black escapee, joined Jackson, while the two remaining white prisoners, Lancaster and Johnny Sims, disguised as a cowboy and a construction worker, stayed behind with Bridges, who naturally led the men in the opposite direction Jackson was heading. Without food or water, and with the horrendous temperature of the August day—a scorching one-hundred degrees—the evil, desperate men raced for freedom, ready to destroy anyone who got in their way.

***

The club's secret fishing hole was tucked away in the back corner of a one-hundred-and-fifty-acre property. The boys did not even know the owner, let alone get his permission to frequent the pond. The pond was hidden just off a gravel road, on the other side of a barbed wire fence. Though the pond was rather wide, the weeds, dense vegetation, and tall trees camouflaged the watering hole so well that seldom a person stumbled across it. The boys named it Buck's Pond after the famous Kansas City Monarchs first baseman, John

Jordan 'Buck' O'Neil, who'd visited the boys at school and signed autographs for them when they were in second grade.

Jared, Suds, and Sweets arrived at the pond to find that little fishing had been done, not to mention anyone actually catching a nice bass or catfish. Dinner wasn't going to come easily. Beans, Porker, and Shanks lay at the end of an old wooden dock that stretched thirty feet into the water and suffered from a severe case of dry rot. The dock wobbled and squeaked as Jared stepped carefully on its weather-beaten planks.

"Thanks a lot, Beans," Suds snapped. "I can expect as much outta these two, but you? We gotta catch us some fish for cookin' and it's gettin' late. My stomach's growlin' already."

Beans lifted his ball cap from his face and squinted. "Don't blame me, man. You can't catch no fish with these two hollerin' and whinin' like they do."

Porker struggled to his feet on the rickety planks. "Heck with this, Suds. Why do we gotta always do what you wanna do? None of us knows how to cook fish for squat, no way. Let's just go back to my house and my mom'll cook us up some peanut butter and jelly sandwiches, Oreos, and chips or somethin'. I'm tired."

Suds and Porker argued at the end of the dock until a rustling noise from the tall reeds on the edge of the pond interrupted them.

Jared stared at the dense vegetation. "What was that?" he asked.

The weeds gyrated, then settled. "Do you think it's them prisoners?" Sweetwater mumbled with dread in his eyes.

Suds gulped like he was swallowing a large pill. "I dunno. But somethin's over there. Maybe they ain't seen us. Nobody move."

The boys kept their eyes fixed on the thick vegetation for several tense minutes, but nothing happened. Figuring it was just the wind or a stray dog, the boys started to relax. Then the dock jerked towards the reeds. "What's going on? Is it some more of them dang ghosts?" Shanks whispered. "It could be them prisoners, Suds. We gotta do something."

With eyes glued to the edge of the pond, Beans reached for his fishing pole. "Really. Let's get outta here".

"Go where?" Suds replied. "We'd have to run right past 'em and, whatever they is, they'd hear us, and maybe give chase."

While they analyzed their situation, the dock suddenly jolted towards the rustling weeds again. The boys yelped and braced themselves. His mind racing with thoughts of hatchet-wielding convicts or rotten corpses, Jared spotted a rope stretching from the surface of the water. "Guys," he whispered. "Guys. Guys." His hand shaking, he pointed at the murky pond. "Guys. The…water. There's a ro…"

With a thunderous *crack*, the dock snapped near the shore, sending the boys tumbling into the water. A roar of laughter burst from the weeds, mingling with the submerged boys' terrified screams. They flailed at the murky water, trying to remain afloat. Jared and Beans clawed at the sinking dock, as Porker grabbed the closest thing to him, which was Jared's neck. The weight of the large boy dragging him under, Jared fought for air; smacking at the water with all his might. Just as he feared he would go under for the final time, his feet hit solid ground. He bounded forward, fighting the waves created by the crashing dock. Disoriented, he gagged and slapped the filthy water from his face. He spit the horrible taste from his lips and coughed. In water up to his chin, he bobbed up and down with the rest of his gang hollering all around him. On the dry bank, Dozer Pittman, the Goat, and Greeley exchanged high-fives, laughing with cruel pride.

"Did you clowns have a nice swim?" Greeley jeered. "We followed ya here and, when you was off doin' whatever you was doin', we tied this here rope around the dock and waited for you-all to be on the end of it. We figured this old piece of crap wouldn't be much trouble to break. We was right." The pimple-faced redhead howled.

With no possible escape, the boys stood in the filthy water, waiting for Dozer and his goons to grow tired of their games. Like a cat playing with a mouse, Dozer marched back and forth on the bank, taunting them with every stride. "I told you I was gonna pay you back, Crud. This here is just the beginnin', so don't be thinkin' you're getting' off that easy. I'm gonna beat the daylights outta ya, but right now I think I'll just sit here and watch you-all swim awhile."

The Goat hurled a large rock at the easy targets, splashing Shanks. "Might wanna watch out for snappin' turtles and water moccasins. Water moccasins like to slither around under docks, ya know?"

Wiping away the muddy water and spitting it from his mouth, Suds seethed with anger, while the practical thinking Sweetwater collected all the poles and tackle boxes that floated near him. He cradled them in his arms and waited. Shanks, bouncing on tiptoes to keep from going under, smacked at the water. "This ain't fair! You let us go! We can't be standin' in here all night!"

The water up to his chin, Jared stood shaking in the murky, disgusting pond, never taking his eyes off the evil Dozer. His skin started to shrivel and his shoes felt like cement blocks. "What are we gonna do, Suds?"

Porker's face strained with anger and despair. "Come on, Dozer! Let us outta here! I can't stand no more! I'll drown!"

Not one to waste time when he could be finding his next victim, Dozer walked to the edge of the water. "Well, since you won't come outta there to fight me, Suds, I guess I'll have to beat the crap outta ya some other time. I actually kinda like that. Make you wait. Make you squirm. But I'm bored with this." Dozer folded his arms, posing in victory. "So, if you-all want outta there, then...well, give us them fishin' poles and them lures and we'll let ya go."

"Yeah," the Goat sneered. "Give us them poles. I could use me a new fishin' pole."

Beans grabbed Suds' shoulder. "Don't do it, man. That's my dad's pole. He'll kill me if I don't come home with it."

"Dude, we have to," Sweetwater replied. "I can't stand in here no longer. Porker's about to pass out. We need ta get outta here, man. Just give 'em the poles. I wanna go home."

Jared stared at the rods and then at his friends. He glared at Dozer. The smug, sinister expression on the bully's face sent waves of anger through him. "What should we do, Suds?"

Suds stayed frozen, never taking his narrowed eyes off his nemesis. The boys waited and waited for Suds' decision. He was Dozer's main target, after all, so they left it up to him. Finally he spoke. "Give him...the poles," he instructed with a strange calm. "Go ahead."

Beans tugged on Suds' arm. "We can't, Suds—my dad."

"Just give 'em to him, Sweetwater," Suds continued, ignoring poor Beans.

Sweetwater tromped through the water and cautiously approached the Goat. He glanced at the poles and then extended them towards the boy. "Aw, you wimps!" the Goat mocked, yanking the bundle of fishing rods from the boy's grasp.

"You coward, Suds!" Dozer hollered. "This ain't over. Come on, guys. Let's leaves these sissies to cry."

As the three bullies headed for their bikes parked on the other side of the cattails and thick weeds, Suds leaped from the water and in three graceful strides landed on dry ground. In one flowing motion, he scooped up two rocks resting on the bank, cocked his stellar arm, and hurled a stone at the Goat. As the boys watched in awe and surprise, the rock hit its intended target, hammering the freakish boy in the back of the head and sending him tumbling to the ground. The poles scattered in the air, dropping all around his limp body. After Dozer turned to see his friend writhing in pain with blood gushing from his head, he quickly focused on Suds. The star centerfielder moved the second rock into his throwing hand and hurled it at Dozer. Dozer caught it in his meaty hand, inches from his face, without a whimper.

Stunned by the feat, Suds' eyes bugged out like doorknobs. "You're dead!" Dozer exclaimed.

Suds took off. The chase was on. "Run, Suds! Run!" The boys, waist-deep in the pond, cheered.

As Greeley and Dozer tore through the vegetation racing after the nimble boy, Jared and the rest of the gang quickly waded through the water to shore. "We gotta help him!" Jared yelled. "Dozer's gonna kill him!"

Sweetwater and Beans rushed over to the Goat and collected the fishing gear, leaving the dazed boy bleeding on the ground. Shanks started running along the shoreline waving his hand. "Follow me, guys! Follow me! We'll head him off at the pass!"

Being faster than their three pals, Shanks and Beans quickly left Jared, Sweetwater, and Porker well behind them as they raced off to Suds' aid. His shoes filled with water, Jared stumbled through the brush. Suds ran as fast as a greyhound, even with his whole body soaked with dirty water. Forced to stop and catch his breath, Jared spotted his pal two hundred yards in front of him, hurdling a fallen tree. "Run, Suds. Run," he panted. "Run, man. Don't let him catch you."

A few yards ahead of him, Sweetwater dropped the reels, bent at the waist, and put his hands on his knees, while Porker, who'd run less than thirty yards from the time they'd left the water, tromped through the bushes to Jared. "He'll get away. He's Suds, man. They'll never catch Suds. He's the fastest guy in school."

Realizing that wasn't saying much, considering Suds' classmates, Jared patted the round boy on his shoulder and nodded. "I know. They'll never catch him."

Sweetwater gathered the fishing rods and walked back to Jared and Porker. "Come on, guys. It's gettin' late. Let's get home before dark. We'll call Suds and see if he made it home all right."

The three boys made it to the paved road and decided to take a shortcut behind a row of houses, where they could keep out of sight of Dozer and Greeley, who they figured would be after them if they didn't catch up to Suds. As the sun faded behind the horizon, they entered the woods and headed up a steep embankment. The air was thick and spooky.

***

"It will be good to get to the bottom of this," Sirus said into the phone receiver as he sat on the edge of his bed. "I can't tell ya enough how strange things've been in this town. It will be nice to have experts come and check it out. You'll have to see it for yourselves to believe it." Sirus paused to listen. "Yes. Yes. Lee's Summit's got itself a fair share of hotels to choose from and it's only about ten miles from here. You can call me when you land. You have my number. You also got directions to get to Lone Jack? Good. I'll see you on Monday, then. I can't say enough how much we need to keep this between us. Folks in this town is as spooky as the ghosts. Okay. See ya Monday." The old man hung up the phone and let out a deep sigh.

He walked to the wood dresser in the corner of his room, an antique passed down from his mother. Opening one of the drawers to grab his night clothes, he heard the alarming sound of the front door of his home flying open. Having heard about the escaped convicts on the radio, Sirus scrambled for the shotgun resting next to his bed. His calloused hands like a vise on the old gun, he crept to the bedroom door. Opening it a crack, he peered into his living room, as muffled voices and noises of someone moving about rumbled through the house. Straining his eyes, he caught a glimpse of his intruders. Three ghostly creatures with mangled faces floated past his antique writing table. Dressed in blue, the ghouls started throwing his furniture and cherished possessions in front of the windows and doors.

"Barricade the door," a creature in a blue, brimmed hat ordered in a deep, but muffled voice. "The Rebels is comin'. Shoot the first thing that moves."

"Lieutenant Copeland," one of the beastly soldiers moaned, "when do you think they will attack?"

"Just be ready, Private Barnett!" the ghostly leader shrieked. "Secure the house and make ready for battle!"

The ghost soldier, Barnett, followed orders and glided towards Sirus, while the third sailed out of his line of vision. Sirus shut the door and crept to the entrance leading into the second bedroom. As he reached for the handle, a ghastly voice called out, "Rebel!" and charged the helpless old man, tackling him to the floor.

The figure's eyes were like lit charcoals. He smelled of rotting flesh and blood seeped from his open wounds. Sirus grappled with the ghost, who had him pinned to the ground, as his decaying hand searched for a sheathed knife on his belt. Sirus clamped down on his wrist, the bones crackling as he squeezed. But the ghost was much stronger than the old man had anticipated. The creature grabbed the knife and thrust it towards Sirus' chest. Sirus barely blocked the attack, causing the knife to slice his left bicep.

"The key!" the monster roared. "Give us the key!"

Blood spewing from the deep gash, Sirus gouged the glowing eyes of his attacker. The sensation was like sticking his fingers in boiling water. He punched the demon in the face, and the skin peeled away like wet mud and bugs started crawling from the bloody wounds. Sirus reached for the shotgun resting near his head. The ghoul jabbed the knife at him as the door to the bedroom was kicked open. The ghostly soldier in blue, Barnett, leveled a long rifle at Sirus' face and fired. Sirus winced, believing he was doomed. The blast nearly deafened and blinded the man, but nothing happened. The ball never made impact.

With a burst of adrenaline, the old man shoved the creature off of him and kicked him in the chest. As the beast lunged for him again, Sirus scooped up his shotgun and yanked the trigger. The blue demon's chest exploded, sending bits of bone, thick blood and flesh scattering across the room. The being fell limp to the floor, though the old man didn't know if he could kill what was already dead. The second soldier charged with his bayonet aimed at Sirus' neck. The man rolled to his knees and deflected the sharp blade with the butt of his shotgun. The bayonet glanced off the weapon and lodged deep in his thigh.

Sirus screamed in agony. As the monster jerked the bayonet from his flesh and recoiled to deliver a final blow, the old black man thrust his shoulder into the fiend's chest, sending him sailing backwards. He pulled the shotgun in next to his side and blasted the ghoul in the stomach. The creature's guts dangled over his belt as he dropped to his knees and, ultimately, to the floor. Sirus barreled through the door and plowed into the ghost in the brimmed hat, knocking him into the wall. The old man raced through the living room and out the front door into the terrifying night.

***

The three boys trudged through the woods carrying the rods and tackle from their adventuresome fishing trip. In the distance, an owl's hoot echoed through the forest canopy, signaling the start of another creepy night. Jared held two poles in one hand and a tackle box in the other. The cumbersome objects made walking difficult; the ends of the rods snagging on every bush and smacking every tree as he pressed forward. His head bobbing from exhaustion, he tried for some good news. "Sweetwater," he mumbled. "How much further do we got? I have to rest for a second."

"Me too," Porker chimed in. He'd lagged behind the entire journey, having to rest every ten steps. Porker fumbled with the rods he'd reluctantly offered to carry. The tip of one caught in the weeds, nearly sending the boy to his backside as he fought to pull it loose. "Dang it. Let's leave these poles and come get 'em tomorrow."

"We can't," the responsible Sweetwater pointed out. "We might never find 'em. We ain't got much farther to go. There should be a clearing up ahead, where we can stop for a second. It's that old dirt road some farmers still use to get to the back of them fields. We'll rest for a bit and then we got about a half a mile to go."

With wet, itchy feet the boys stomped up an incline and stopped in the middle of the narrow, overgrown dirt road. Porker closed his eyes and tilted his large head back. Sweets dropped the poles and tackle boxes, and plopped down, completely exhausted. "Do you think he made it?" Jared asked, still concerned about the fate of his friend. "Suds. Do ya think he got away from Dozer?"

Sweets leaned back, supporting his body with his hands and staring at the starry sky. "He made it, Millhouse. I guarantee it. He can run forever, especially when dogs or, even worse, Dozer, is chasin' him. He's probably done ate dinner and hopped in bed."

"Dinner," Porker scoffed. "Don't even talk to me about dinner. I ain't ate nothing since…" The boy stopped and stared down the isolated road. "What was that? I heard somethin'."

Sweets and Jared perked up their ears and inspected the road, which the night's full moon fully illuminated. In the distance, a faint rumble stirred. Sweets crawled to his feet and collected the fishing rods and tackle boxes as the noise intensified. "What is that?"

The ground started to vibrate under their aching feet. The boys stared at each other, each expecting the other to explain what was happening. The rumbling steadily grew louder. Then Jared saw it. "Look!" He pointed down the dim, isolated road.

Like a runaway train, a herd of wild horses rolled towards them. Their piercing screams and thunderous, ground-shattering hooves sent chills through the three boys. Thick plumes of smoke exploded from their nostrils with each breath. As if caught in an earthquake, the boys struggled to keep their balance with the wild herd barreling towards them.

Jared grabbed Porker's arm and pulled him towards the ditch. "Come on! They'll squash us if we don't get outta the way!"

Sweets followed Jared's lead, but his foot slid out from under him in the loose dirt. He fought to get up, but overcome with fear and confusion he squatted on one knee. "Come on, Sweets! Run!" Porker pleaded. "They'll run over ya!" But Sweets couldn't move.

Jared glanced at the coming beasts. Chunks of grass and dust exploded under their hooves. With foggy, dead eyes, shredded fur covering their huge bodies and sinewy muscle, and bones piercing through the missing sections of thick hide, the wild beasts barreled towards them. Their heads were also mangled, bloody flesh and bone, but their manes glistened and flowed in the moonlight, magnificent yet menacing. As the wild herd rumbled closer, Porker and Jared winced, begging Sweets to jump out of the way.

As the ghost herd reached twenty feet, a form tore through the trees and shot across the road. The stranger grabbed Sweetwater around the waist and raced for safety. With the lanky boy securely in his grasp, the rescuer hurled his body into the air, smashing into the ground on the far side of the ditch. The two bodies tumbled into the darkness as Parker and Jared rushed to help them. The ghostly horses continued to swarm past, their shrieking neighs echoing as the ground rocked. Then they disappeared into the darkness.

Jared and Porker stared at the limp bodies until finally one moved. "Ugh." A painful groan came from the stranger.

Jared inched closer, peering at the dark figure. "Sirus!" he exclaimed.

"Help me up, kid," the injured man pleaded. "I'm in some pain here. My leg is hurt, and I think I just separated my shoulder."

Jared and Porker pulled Sirus from the ditch, propped him up on the road, and rushed to check on Sweets. The boy lay motionless for several seconds, then rolled to his back. "What was that? What were they?" he mumbled.

Jared smiled and rubbed Sweetwater's head. "Don't worry about it now. We thought you were dead. Let's just get out of here."

Sweets slowly collected himself and climbed out of the ditch. The three boys sat next to Sirus on the road, the sights and sounds of the ghost herd still running through their minds.

Glancing at the disheveled old man, Jared noticed blood stains on Sirus' clothing. "You're bleeding! We got to get you to a doctor."

Sirus placed his hand gently on the boy's shoulder. "I'm fine…for now. Just let me rest here a bit. This is a lot for an old man like me to be takin' in."

Sweets moved his jaw back and forth to see if it was broken. "What happened?"

"You don't wanna know, kid."

"But what were those things?" Sweetwater continued. "They weren't horses. Not like I know 'em to be. They were… monsters."

Sirus clamped both hands around his throbbing leg and gritted his teeth. "They's creatures from beyond the grave. They're ghosts. Look, boys, I don't wanna scare ya, but there's somethin' you should know. I was attacked by three skeleton creatures dressed in blue uniforms. They tried to kill me. I had to fight for my life. One came at me with a knife and cut me pretty bad on my arm, while another charged me with a bayonet. He caught me in the thigh with it 'fore I was able to fight him off."

"But you said they couldn't really hurt us, right?" Jared pointed out. "That they could barely turn the page of a book or blow out a candle in our world?"

"I know what I said. Things is changin' though. They're becomin' more real—able to do things they weren't able to do before. They broke inta my house, just like they done during the battle of Lone Jack. The Union soldiers took over the town and commandeered the buildin's, using them for their cover and as lookouts. They was simply doin' what they know to do—what they've done hundreds of times. Only this time they're gettin more agitated, more real, and more dangerous."

"And the horses?" Porker asked.

Sirus ran his fingers across the open wound, biting his lip in pain. "Ugh. Them horses is just part of the battle. They're trapped in between worlds same as them soldiers. Ya see, in the battle over one hundred and forty horses was killed. The bluecoat Calvary and Rebels on horseback would charge and the only way to prevent the charge from runnin' clean over ya was to shoot the horses out from under the riders. Dead horses were scattered all over the streets, and the soldiers used 'em as barriers and hid behind 'em. When the battle was over, the gruesome sight of dead horses layin' everywhere, and the stench of 'em, sent many a man, woman, and child to their knees wantin' to vomit. It was hot then, like it is now, and a guy named Tom Roupe was ordered to drag all their dead stinkin' carcasses off the street and put them in a ditch outside of town." Sirus glanced at his surroundings. "Probably even this ditch here. It took him all day to drag them dead horses off."

"So what do we do, Sirus?" Jared asked.

The old man shook his head and scratched his beard. "I dunno. But we's runnin' outta time. One of them demons shot at me, right at my face. There's no way he coulda missed at that range. I think them ghosts is becomin' real, more and more every day. That knife and bayonet was real enough, that's for sure. But luckily their guns ain't changed…yet. If them guns start becomin' as real as the rest of 'em, this town's in a heap of trouble. We ain't got time to find out.

We gotta do somethin'.'"

"But what?" Sweets asked as he rubbed his aching neck.

Sirus hesitated. "I don't know. But I got me two guys comin' in to help out. They're ghost hunters—experts. But I'm sure they ain't never come across nothin' like this. They's in for a surprise." Sirus gestured to the boys to help him to his feet. They tugged and pushed on the large man until he was standing gingerly on one foot. "But that ain't all, too. You know how them ghosts in the mineshaft and them other'ns in the cornfield demanded a key?"

"Yeah," Jared answered. "What about it?"

"Well, their voices were deep and staticky, but I think the one that wrestled me to the ground was wantin' a key from me, too. I couldn't really hear and was pretty much out of it at the time, but I think I remember him demandin' 'the key.' But whatever they wanted, they'd've killed me to get it, that's for sure."

***

Not a man with a diplomatic nature or pleasant disposition, Jackson forced Torez to scout out their situation by threatening him with bodily harm or death if he did not do as he was told. Dressed from head to toe in a bright orange jumpsuit, the nervous Hispanic felt quite vulnerable belly-crawling through the weeds to the edge of the paved road. He parted the vegetation as if it were made of delicate glass and scanned the area in front of him. The low-hanging full moon glistened off the concrete. Several lit houses glimmered in the distance, a half a mile to the south. If they could get to one of the residences they could make good on their escape. They could get transportation, water, food, some needed rest, and maybe even take hostages for bargaining power later.

As the convict was about to the leave the road and return to Jackson to report the good news, bright lights started flickering off the pavement. The escapee strained to see through the tall weeds, searching for the source. Heading in his direction with deliberate speed were four police cars, aiming spotlights into the dense woods. The red and blue strobes on the cars' roofs flashed. Torez pressed his body against the ground and cringed, gritting his teeth as the police vehicles approached. The spotlights danced across the leaves and bushes above him as blue and red flickered in sync with his rapidly beating heart. He pressed his cheek against the ground and shut his eyes. The lead car put on the brakes, hesitated for several seconds, then motored on. Once they passed, Torez let out a huge sigh of relief.

Pacing back and forth on the loose sand of a dry creek bed, Jackson kept close watch on the area around them, while Bishop sat with his back against a tree, smacking at the ground with a large stick. "Somebody's comin'," Jackson warned, sending Bishop to his feet.

"Es me. Es me." Torez stumbled over a honey locust sapling and raced to Jackson. "Cops. Mucho policia. There is house. Many house. Across da road. But no go. Police everywhere. Dey drive by when I look. No way we make it to house wit so far to run."

"Hmm," Jackson grunted. "We gotta find us a place to hide out. We oughtta keep cover in the woods and walk further on up the road. Maybe we can spot us a house or car on this side, so we ain't gotta cross an open field. Let's go."

"Man. Let's just make a break for it," Bishop voiced his frustration. "We can't go back the way we come. We'll run right into 'em. But if we keep goin', they's gonna catch up to us for sure."

Jackson glared at the man, his lust for freedom seeping from his pores. "If you wanna try to get to them houses 'fore somebody spots ya, go ahead, but I say it's better we stay outta sight in these here woods and try to find some farmhouse tucked away back in here somewheres." Bishop shook his head, but knew better than to further anger the crazed man. "Okay, then. Let's get goin'."

Barking hounds in the distance grew louder and closer as a helicopter buzzed overhead with a massive spotlight. Billowing clouds glided in front of the moon, covering the eerie night with a blanket of darkness. The wanted men slowed to nearly a crawl, having to literally feel their way for every step towards freedom.

"Well, if we can't see our hands in front of our faces," Bishop deduced, "then them cops can't neither."

"Wait," Jackson murmured tensely. "What was that?" The three men stopped in their tracks, realizing their next sound could be their last outside the confines of a prison cell.

Jackson struggled to pinpoint the direction the sound was coming from until he realized it was all around them. "Who...who is it?" Bishop stammered to Jackson's displeasure. "Is...is it them? The cops?"

"Shut up," Jackson whispered.

Torez clasped his grimy hands together in front of his heaving chest. "Me no like dis."

A shrilling cry cut through the darkness, sending the escapees scattering. "Run!" Jackson yelled and tore through a sticker bush.

As the moon reappeared in the night sky, a ghastly figure leaped from behind a tree, blocking Jackson's path. Dressed in gray, the demon clamped his hand around the prisoner's neck. Bugs crawled from the beast's tattered sleeve. Jackson tussled with the powerful grip and swung at the ghoul's rotted face. The creature staggered backwards from the blow. A second demon twirled a sword above the dancing plume of his hat, green slime and blood oozing from his eyes and open wounds on his face.

"Ahhh!" the abomination howled. "Dyin' time is here!" The soldier swung his saber, striking Jackson across the chest. The convict dropped to the ground, clutching the open wound. Blood trickling between his fingers, the convict stared into the cold eyes of the gray-clad beast. The creature thrust the sword forward, driving it through Jackson's abdomen and out his back. Jackson collapsed to his side.

Bishop bulled his way past two creatures and tumbled to the ground. As he rolled over, a hideous fiend leveled a shotgun and fired. "Nooo!" Bishop screamed and shut his eyes, the energy of the blast swarming through his weary body. Expecting his chest to be like a jigsaw puzzle, he tore open the front of his orange jumpsuit. Shocked to find he was unscathed by the deadly pellets, the prisoner scrambled to his feet and took off.

A ghoul jumped on his back as he passed, unleashing merciless blows to his head and neck. Bishop fought the beast until the butt of a gun plowed into his jaw. Blood trickling from his lip, the convict dropped to his knees. The gray demons circled around him like a pack of hungry wolves. They moaned and hissed, then in unison let out a screeching, blood-curdling cry. They inched closer and then pounced, tearing the escapee to shreds.

Bishop's screams piercing his ears, Torez dodged a bayonet assault by one soldier and a jab from another's knife. He raced through the dark night, unable to see where he was going and begging for salvation, even if it were behind bars. He tore through the woods, never looking back. When he reached the road, the headlights of a solitary car approached him in the distance. The anxious man waved his arms frantically and sprinted towards the vehicle.

"Hep!" he pleaded. "Hep me! I wanna go home! Take me to prison! Por favor! Take me back to prison! I beg you!"

Unable to avoid the hysterical man, the car screeched to a halt in the road. "Sir." Officer Kunkle exited his police car. "Sir. You need to get on home. We's searching for escaped prisoners. They took flight from a bus takin' 'em to Farmington this afternoon and it ain't safe to be out here joggin'. They could be anywhere right now. Sir." Ignoring the officer, Torez brushed past him, darting for the rear door of the squad car. The hysterical convict fumbled with the handle, unable to open it. "Sir. Sir," the brave policeman continued. "Sir. Please, sir. Don't do that. That's government property. The door's locked, sir. Dang it, sir. What's your problem, sir? I wish you'd stop and talk to me."

Desperate, Torez released the handle and yelled to the officer. "I wanna go! Take me to jail! I beg you. Take me to jail."

Being the thorough investigator that he was, the policeman quickly identified the orange jumpsuit the crazed man was wearing and drew his sidearm. "All right, hold it right there! Get your hands atop your head where I can see 'em!" He pointed the gun at the fugitive, his hands shaking on the grip. "Don't you move nor breathe! I got me one! Daggum it! I done went and captured me an escapee!" He fingered the radio Velcro'd to his shoulder. "Captain! Captain! It's Kunkle, over! I caught me one of them escaped prisoners! Got him right here a starin' at me!"

5

His body covered in sweat, Jared tossed and turned in the night. He thrashed at the surface, struggling to keep his head above water, but something kept pulling on his legs. He eventually lost all strength and will, and plummeted to the depths below. For several moments he floated, suddenly realizing he could breathe under water. The boy stared in all directions. Magnificent formations and fascinating creatures filled the clear blue that surrounded him. As a swordfish raced by, a large manatee-shaped beast glided towards him. The marine creature had large fins and a bull's head with tremendous horns and a saddle. It paused near the boy, floating aimlessly. Jared swam above the mutated animal and hopped on its back, taking the reins in his hands.

The boy and his amphibious steed sailed through brightly colored vegetation swaying in the currents, and through the enormous rock formations. Jared studied the sights with amazement. They came upon a small city chiseled out of the side of a massive rock and, joined by sharks with horses' bodies, attempted to enter. But a large tiger with webbed paws and intimidating claws blocked their path. The large cat roared and showed its incredible fangs. The bull-fish turned in the currents and dove deeper into the unknown.

Then the magical adventure in his mind changed. All alone, Jared fought his way through murky water. Bodies of dead soldiers drifted past him; their faces decaying with fish feasting on their corpses. He struggled to get away, but the bodies kept coming, hitting the boy as they passed and forcing him deeper and deeper. A snake slithered out of the eye socket of one decaying corpse and back through its mouth. As he fought through the wave of death, the bull-headed sea creature joined him once more. Accompanied by large turtles, they forged a path to a tropical island at the bottom of the ocean. On the banks sat a large wooden chest, broken on one side, with magical jewels cascading out the opening. Jared reached for the sparkling treasures. As he did, a raccoon crawled up the beach and bit his hand. Jared pulled away and, as he extended his hand towards the jewels again, they changed. A pile of bright gold stars flowed from the chest. He attempted to grab one of them, but, as he reached, the shimmering object walked away, avoiding his grasp. The mesmerizing objects transformed into unique, brightly colored starfish, crawling through the sand. Several latched onto his legs, tickling the boy as they crept.

He giggled at the strange sensation, but his emotions quickly changed once again as a dark cloud swept over him. He found himself alone in a dim cave with only one way out. He swam towards the light, but a figure appeared before him. It pushed its face through the murky water. It was the ghost of Mrs. Cave. Her gaunt face, chilling cold eyes, and crooked grayish-yellow teeth sneered at him, while her constricting black dress danced in the water. The bundle of hair atop her head was pulled so tightly it raised her wrinkled forehead and eyelids and made Jared wriggle with discomfort. The ghost woman stretched her bony finger towards the boy's face, her nail long and pointy. She dragged the claw down the side of his cheek. A burning sensation sizzled though his body. "Bring us the key!" she hissed through her pale wrinkled lips.

Jared sat up in bed and gasped. He threw the covers off his body and took deep breaths. A layer of sweat covered his face. "It was just a dream," he mumbled. "It was just a dream."

It had been a long night for him. It had been a strange summer. After Sirus had found them on the dirt road, and saved Sweetwater from certain harm, he had accompanied the boys as they crossed Highway 50. In severe pain and limping awkwardly, Sirus escorted Porker and Sweetwater to their homes in Blue and Gray Estates. Jared and the hobbling old man then walked down the secluded road to Sirus' home. A sense of dread clung to them as thick as the humidity while Sirus placed his hand on the door. It creaked as it floated towards the wall. Sirus poked his head into the living room.

The only signs of his ghostly intruders were his belongings, scattered, overturned, and left in disarray. Sirus found his keys and drove Jared to his grandfather's house, promising the boy his next stop would be the emergency room in Lee's Summit to get his leg and gashed arm cleaned and mended.

Jared shook off his dream and walked into the kitchen to find his grandfather sitting at the table drinking coffee. Hoses extended from the old man's nose to a wheeled oxygen tank on the floor next to him. The sight always made the boy cringe; a constant reminder of how fragile and sick his grandfather was. "Hey, Grandpa," he beamed. "Can I get you anything?"

"Hey, kiddo," the man wheezed. "No. I'm fine. You okay, though? I heard ya hollerin' and wrestlin' in your sleep."

"Oh. I'm okay. Just a bad dream. It was nothin'." The boy poured himself a glass of milk and took a seat next to his grandfather at the table.

"Well you're dad's out fetchin' us some breakfast. I woulda cooked, but I'm just not feeling up to it. Sorry, kiddo. I don't know why Rob can't do it. I swear, your grandmother and me never teached that boy nothin'. He can't even scramble eggs or throw bacon into a fryin' pan." The old man coughed into a towel and tossed it onto the table. "You know, son, I ain't gonna be around forever."

"Yeah," Jared replied, the thought making him very uncomfortable.

"Well, your dad…and you, as well…have had it rough since your mom passed. I mean, Rob never mentions her or even talks about it."

"Yeah," Jared mumbled, again the topic too sensitive for him.

"But this morning, your dad got up a' whistlin'. He mentioned yesterday that you and him had met some gal, who was a teacher, at the Crossroads Café. It confused me at first. Rob hadn't mentioned no other woman 'cept your mom for as long as I can remember. He also got up this mornin feelin' pretty chipper. He didn't have none of his usual headaches. He wadn't moanin' or complainin' about his achin' this or that. He didn't even do no drinkin' last night. He woke up in a daggum good mood, which got me to thinkin'."

"About what?"

"You want your pa to be happy, don't ya, kiddo?"

"Of course."

"You want you and him to pick up the pieces and move on, and you wanna have a normal childhood yourself, don't ya?"

"Yeah."

"Well, I can't be watchin' over ya like I used to. I'm old and in bad shape and, heck, you two've been lookin' after me these days, more than I been watchin' after you. My point is, I think your dad kinda liked that gal he bumped into in the café. But I know the stubborn kid. Heck, I raised him and fought with him most of the time. I know how he is. He's too stubborn to admit it and won't go makin' the first move. Lady folk don't like that, by the way. They figure if they gotta chase after the boy, then that boy must not be interested. Remember that."

"Okay."

Virgil let out a loud hack, which sent him reaching for the towel, and then continued. "So let me ask ya this, kiddo, what did you think of the lady in the restaurant?"

Jared thought about Ms. Ramsey for a moment. "Well, she was nice. She made me laugh."

"But did you like her?"

"Yeah," he answered. "Yeah, I did."

"Was she pretty enough?"

Jared's eyes bugged out. "Oh, yeah. Very pretty."

The old man placed his hand on his grandson's wrist. "Well then, what say you and I do us a little matchmakin'? We get these two together and your dad might end up findin' a little excitement in his life once again."

"Sounds okay to me."

"Good." Virgil moved his face closer to the boy. "Now, this here is our secret and we got to have us a plan. You know, one that works so well nobody knows that they's bein' played or used in the action of it. You and I are a couple a spies…kind of a thing. Workin' both sides of the equation and makin 'em do what we want 'em to do, without them knowin' it. Sound good to you?"

Excitement ran across Jared's face. He always liked a good game of espionage and intrigue. "Shoot, yeah. I'm in. Tell me what I have to do."

"We'll work out all the details of our little scheme later. Just be ready when called upon." The old man cleared his throat, initiating another coughing fit. "But what we need to be thinkin' about is how to get these two together because of some innocent reason."

"She said she taught my friends last year in fourth grade. She even said Sweetwater and Molly were her favorites," Jared informed him. "Maybe they would know."

"Hey, that's not bad. See, you're already thinkin' like a seasoned spy, skilled in the art of espionage–collectin' info. But you can't tell them what we're up to. Too many people know a thing and they start talkin' and then the jig is up. This here is strictly top secret, meanin' it stays between us." Virgil staggered to his feet and scooted across the linoleum to the coffee pot.

"I can get that for you, Grandpa."

"No, kiddo, I'll get it. You'd probably pour it right down the front of ya and get yourself third degree burns. Which reminds me—I want you to stay close to home today. No playin' with your friends. I heard on the radio this mornin that some convicts escaped yesterday afternoon. They captured most of 'em, but three's still on the loose."

"Yeah, okay," Jared responded, disappointed, yet understanding the situation. "Hey, Grandpa. What do you know about the battle of Lone Jack?"

"The battle of Lone Jack? Well, look at you—wantin to talk all adult, now. You're growin up faster and faster every day. I don't know if I can keep up with ya. Well, let me think.

"Ya know, at that time, pretty much everyone in town sympathized with the Confederates. The battle began at dawn on August 16, 1862. In fact, the Confederates were goin to fake an attack from the north, led by a pretty seasoned feller named Hays. But just as the sun peeked up in the east, one of the new greenhorn recruits, hiding in the tall weeds with a large force to the southwest, tripped and accidentally fired his weapon, sending the Union soldiers racin' for their guns and for cover. The mistake hurt the Rebels, as the surprise attack wasn't a surprise any longer.

"The rest was a bloody fight, and most of it was hand-to-hand combat across a sixty-foot-wide street. They say it was a dreadfully hot day, with not a cloud in the sky and the temperature well over a hundred. The fight lasted five hours and, in the course of it, the two cannons, or James Guns, that the Union brought from Indiana changed hands four times. Each side fought hard to take and keep them weapons that would give 'em a big advantage.

"Close to three hundred men was killed, about the same number on each side. But the Union troops left the town and the Confederates regained control, which made the townsfolk happy. Like I said, they was rooting for the Rebels. But it was a bloody battle—the bloodiest Civil War battle on Missouri soil."

"Hmm." Jared tried to absorb the information. "Why was the town rooting for the gray side?"

Virgil lowered himself into his seat and stirred his coffee. "Well, people generally do what they gotta do for family and those close to 'em, kiddo. They felt their way of life was threatened. Sometimes people simply don't know no better. But…though the folks here in Lone Jack durin' the war were deeply loyal to the Confederates, they also were people who respected one another. In fact, a man named Martin Rice lived in the town at the time and everybody knew he was a staunch Union supporter. But nobody messed with the man. They respected him 'cause he was a good citizen and would do anything for his neighbors. Rice was a renowned local poet, in fact. So, I guess what I'm sayin is that, even though people have serious disagreements, they can still respect one another. Even in times of war."

"Yeah, I guess so."

"And Rice wasn't the only poet connected with that battle. Frank Trew wrote a poem called *The Battle of Lone Jack*. In it, he honors the brave and fallen soldiers from both sides, equally."

"Who were the heroes of the battle?" the boy asked.

Virgil clutched his chest and coughed. "Well, there were a lot of 'em. In war there's always those who are singled out, while so many others don't get noticed. Just kind of the way it is. Any man who fights bravely in war, fightin' for a cause or country, should be respected. But in this battle, the Union thought they was takin' on Quantrill's Raiders. Bill Quantrill was a tough, mean feller fightin' for the Rebels. Most people don't know that he grew up a Unionist with Unionist beliefs, was a schoolteacher, and tried his hand at bein' a professional gambler. But when the war broke out, he became a soldier. His band skirmished a lot in the beginning with Jayhawkers, or raiders from Kansas who would come into Missouri to cause trouble. But during the battle of Lone Jack, like I said, the Union thought they was fightin' Quantrill, which energized a lot of 'em and put the fear of God into others…but Quantrill didn't get to the battle till late. But one guy who was in the thick of things for the whole battle was Cole Younger. Do you know who he is?"

"No," Jared responded.

"Well, Cole Younger was from Lee's Summit. In fact, he and his brothers are buried in the cemetery there. After the war, them boys were still angered about it and felt the Union had created hardships on those who were loyal to the Confederacy. So him, his brothers, and Frank and Jesse James became famous outlaws, wreakin' havoc and robbin' trains where they could. But Cole was a young man durin' the Battle of Lone Jack. I heard a story about him that the Union leader of the force, Foster, reported. A lot of folks don't know about it.

"The Rebels was pinned down and most of 'em were out of ammunition. Suddenly this lone soldier on horseback came riding to the rescue. He rode the length of the Rebel line passin' out ammo, completely open to fire from the Union soldiers. The bluecoats sent one bullet after another at the rider, but never hit him. The whole time the brave soldier left himself open, just handin' out ammunition. He eventually gave out all the ammunition he had and rode back out of the line of fire. *Both* sides cheered the soldier's amazin' feat. That rider was Cole Younger."

"Wow!" Jared hollered.

"But that ain't even the end of the story. Durin' the final struggle for the James Guns, Major Emory Foster and his brother Melville, who was fightin' beside him, was both shot. First Emory was shot in the back, then Melville ran to drag Emory from the street and took a bullet to his chest. Both men lay in agony. Luckily for them, they were both wounded late in the battle and, after it ended, the Union decided that the injured were better off in the hands of the Confederates than making the dangerous trip back to Lexington.

"The Confederates took the Foster brothers 'prisoner' and put 'em in a house. The two severely wounded men were placed side-by-side in the same bed. As they laid there, the door flew open and one of Quantrill's lieutenants and about a dozen of his loyal guerrillas came into the room. Quantrill's lieutenant told Foster they'd just killed a wounded lieutenant from a Cass County Company and they was there to kill them. The Fosters were horrified. But while Quantrill's man was standin' over 'em with his pistol cocked, a soldier stepped into the room through a second door. Foster recognized the man as the brave soldier who'd distributed ammo to his comrades—Cole

Younger. Cole grabbed the threatenin' Quantrill soldier and wrestled him outta the room. After he got the murderers out of Foster's room, he called for Colonel Cockrell, the man in charge of the entire Rebel force durin' the battle, and told him what had occurred and what he'd done to prevent it."

"So he saved them?" Jared interrupted. "He kept them from being killed?"

"Yes," his grandfather replied, "but that idn't the end of the story either. Foster, who thought he and his brother were surely goners anyway with the wounds they'd suffered, told Cole that he and his brother had a good amount of money on them, totaling about a thousand dollars, which was a fortune in them days. He asked Cole to take the money and their revolvers and have them sent to their mother in Warrensburg. Cole approved and said he'd have it taken care of. Now, you have to remember that these is most likely dyin' men, and Cole definitely coulda used the money and them guns. But bein' an honest man in certain respects, Cole kept his word and had the money and revolvers sent to the Fosters' mother in Warrensburg."

"Wow," Jared responded.

"And you know what else?"

"No, what?"

"All that I just told you about Cole Younger was in a letter written by Emory Foster to Judge George Bennett in Minneapolis where Cole was imprisoned at. He was caught after attemptin' a bank robbery in Northfield in 1876. He was shot several times and ultimately captured along with his brothers, Bob and Jim. He was with Frank and Jesse James at the time, but they got away. Anyway, Foster wrote the letter durin' Cole's parole hearin' and helped the man regain his freedom after spending twenty-five years in Stillwater Prison."

***

Rob arrived with warm food for growling stomachs. After they ate, Virgil winked at Jared and suggested the two of them take a trip into town so the old man could stretch his legs and get out of the house. He kept his ulterior motives secret from his son. Rob was reluctant at first, as there were wanted men on the loose, but Virgil reassured him that he'd keep a watchful eye on Jared at all times. It was another scorching August day. Jared and his grandfather hopped out of the truck in the parking lot of the Crossroads Café with the smell of steamy asphalt burning their nostrils and walked into the restaurant.

Standing deliberately between the counter and a row of booths lining the front glass, Officer Kunkle was in the middle of summarizing the harrowing events of the last twenty-four hours. "So I seen him creepin' in the moonlight, his silhouette like a deer foragin' on the ground for berries. I knew he was dangerous, so I pulled my revolver and snuck up on him."

"That ain't how I heard it," Mr. Lovelace interrupted to Kunkle's chagrin. "I heard he ran right past ya and you offered him a ride, 'cause there was convicts on the loose."

The officer dropped his shoulders, indicating it wasn't the first time Mr. Lovelace had contradicted his story. "Well, ya done heard wrong, Ned. It could've been a trap. I knew who he was, but I needed to outwit him."

"Oh really," the gray-bearded old man replied. "How'd that work out? That's gotta be like watchin' two monkeys try to figure out a crossword puzzle."

"Make jokes if it makes ya feel good, Ned." Officer Kunkle asserted his authority by placing his hands on his shiny leather belt. "The three that are still on the loose killed two of them convicts… sliced 'em to shreds, in fact…so I think I'd be a little more respectful. This here is dangerous business."

"They killed em?" a scraggily man in a Nutrena Feeds hat sitting next to Mr. Lovelace at the counter asked, mashed potatoes stuck to his lips.

"That's right. They did," the officer continued. "We can't get the whole story outta the Mexic'n, 'cause he's a little distraught and don't speak American too good no way, but we went back in the woods a distance and found the bodies of two of them escapees. They'd been sliced up pretty good. We think this one dangerous, no-good scoundrel, Earl Bridges, killed 'em as they fled. They musta got inta some kind of altercation and went ahead and killed them fellers rather than have 'em go in a separate direction, get caught, and turn in old Bridges. That's what they's thinkin' happened, anyway. Like I done said, we can't figure out the story from that Mexic'n."

"Can't ya get an interpreter or somethin'?" Agnes, the food-stained waitress, asked in a deep country twang.

"Well, we got us Mrs. Stemple, the Spanish teacher from the high school to come in," the officer informed his captivated audience, "but all she got outta him was that he liked ice cream and that her shirt was red."

"Well, there's a break in the case," Mr. Lovelace mumbled as he put his coffee cup to his lips.

"But look, folks," Officer Kunkle's voice boomed through the restaurant. "We are on the case and think them other fellers are long gone outta Lone Jack. They wouldn't dare stay around these parts with the police presence we got here now. It's safe. I can assure you of that."

Mr. Lovelace rolled his eye. "Anytime they got you carryin' a loaded gun round town, Kunkle, it ain't never safe. Two summers ago, Agnes had to give that old tub of lard Pickerin' the Heimlich Maneuver cause he went and swallowed a bite of pork steak the size of my fist and that daggum matchstick he's always got in his lips and nearly choked to death on it. You just stood there watchin' him die 'cause ya didn't know squat about savin' nobody. If it's all the same to you, I think I'll leave my life in God's hands. He's got a better track record."

"Yeah, I think I'm with Ned on that one," Virgil said under his breath. He looked down at his grandson. "So is she in here, kiddo?"

"Who?"

"The gal your dad grew a likin' for—the teacher. Walk through the place like you're lost or somethin', and see if you see her."

Jared squeezed by Officer Kunkle, who continued to draw as much attention to himself as possible, and meandered through the tables searching for Ms. Ramsey. He spotted the pretty lady alone in a booth in the far corner of the restaurant, reading a book and sipping a glass of iced tea. Proud of the success of his reconnaissance mission, Jared rushed back to his grandfather to report. He ducked under Officer Kunkle's flailing arms, as the officer detailed his heroics to a second wave of patrons entering the establishment. Turning towards his grandpa, Jared spotted Suds, Beans, and Sweetwater, standing near the cash register. Keg Davis, a quiet, lethargic man with a round belly, looked through his wallet as Agnes waited.

"Hey, guys!" Jared shouted. "What are you doin'?"

Suds turned towards him like his body was made of stiff boards, revealing several abrasions on his cheeks and forehead. His right arm and leg were nicked and bruised and his knee was wrapped with a bandage. "Hey, Millhouse," the injured boy grimaced.

"Whoa!" Jared yelled. "Dozer got you, didn't he? Him and Greeley beat you up!"

Suds glanced at his dad, who fortunately paid little attention to Jared's outburst. "Relax, Millhouse. They didn't catch me."

"They might as well have," Beans said. "He fell into a hole on Howser Farm where an old house musta stood. Dozer and Greeley wouldn't let him outta there and threw rocks at him."

"Yeah," Suds added. "I crashed right through part of the floor that wasn't bulldozed up when they torn down the place. I fell nearly ten feet into part of the cellar that wadn't caved-in! Can't bend my leg. Nearly broke my arm. Got cuts all over me. And Dozer and Greeley just stood up there laughin' at me and tryin' to hit me with rocks. Then when they left, and I finally found a way outta there, mom made my dad whoop me with a belt for bein' late and not tellin' 'em." The boy glared at the older Davis. "Can you believe that? Him and mom thought them prisoners got ahold of me. After she screamed at him to whip me, I said I wished they did catch me 'cause they wouldn't've done that to me. I didn't make it home till almost ten, though, so mom was plenty mad."

"Parents ain't reasonable, dude," Sweets sympathized, shaking his head in disgust. "I don't think they can even whip ya with a belt in jail."

"And that ain't the worst of it," Beans added. "Tell him what ya seen while you was down there."

Suds' nose scrunched and his lips pursed. "I seen that scary old lady ghost in the black dress that you and Sirus been seein'. After Dozer left, I pulled myself to my feet and looked up into the openin' where the light was comin' from and she was floatin' there. I wadn't sure what I was seein' at first, but then her face was right in mine and she hissed at me. She scratched down my face with her sharp claws and looked like she wanted to take a bite outta me with her gray-yeller fangs." He pushed his cheek out with his tongue, showing Jared the long scratch down his cheek. "She left me bleedin' and it hurt bad. It was almost like it sizzled. I didn't know what to do. I was terrified, I gotta tell ya. Then she asked for a dang key and disappeared. I got the heck on up and outta there after that. I ran all the way home even with my leg as banged up as it was. I was too scared to feel no pain."

Jared stared at Suds. "That's the exact dream I had last night," he said. "She was floatin' above me, scratched my face, and asked for a key while I was trapped in this cave under water. Are you sure it was Mrs. Cave?"

Suds rolled his eyes. "I didn't get her name, Millhouse. She didn't seem like a real chatty lady. Heck, yeah, I'm sure it was her! She had a black dress on, coverin' her arms and legs, and all ya could see was her pale bony face and her thin gross hands with them long fingernails. Her hair was pulled up in a tight ball on her creepy head. It was her. If there's more than one of them floatin' around Lone Jack, we're in bigger trouble than I reckoned."

"So what are you doin' here, Millhouse?" Beans asked.

Jared glanced at his grandfather sitting next to Mr. Lovelace, both men talking with Keg Davis and listening to Officer Kunkle's boisterous story. "Well, I ain't supposed to say nothin'," Jared whispered, leaning in closer to his pals, "but we're all part of the Crossroads Club, so I figure I can trust ya. My grandpa wants to help my dad meet Ms. Ramsey, but he doesn't want either one of them to know about it. It's top secret and you can't tell anybody."

Suds shrugged his shoulders. "Oh geez, Millhouse. We can't be helpin' nobody do a buncha datin' and smoochin' and the like. Our club ain't to be used for that kinda nonsense, even if it is your old man."

"Yeah, man," Beans chimed in. "That's gross."

Embarrassed, Jared lowered his head. "But...but... my dad. He's...my mom...I just want him...my mom's gone...and...I just..."

"Oh golly, Millhouse." Suds shook his head. "That lady is a tyrant. You'd be better off hookin' your old man up with that snaggle-toothed ghost in the black dress. Just ask Shanks and Porker. She had me and them in the corner or at the principal's office more than we was at our own desks. Especially them two. And we didn't learn nothin' from her. She don't know nothin' to learn, if ya ask me."

Jared felt himself shrinking in front his friend. Suds recognized his discomfort and sighed.

"But, heck, if ya gotta do it—I mean, it is for your old man and all—just invite her to a barbeque or somethin'. That's what my old man does when he wants to drink beer and my mom won't let him. He has hisself a barbeque and my mom can't say nothin'. Have Sweetwater go ask her. She loves him for some daggum reason. If he asks her, she'll come for sure."

Duty called and Sweets trotted towards the back of the restaurant. Moments later the lanky boy slid past Officer Kunkle with a huge smile on his face. "She's in," he exclaimed. "She said she wouldn't miss it for the world. I guess her kids are gone with their dad for a couple of weeks and she's been bored stiff, tryin' to find stuff to do until they get back from Disneyland. She gave me her phone number and everythin'." The boy pulled a crumpled piece of paper from his front pocket. "Said all we needed to do was call her."

"Geez," Suds snarled. "Maybe you oughtta date the cranky witch."

Beans grabbed Jared's arm, twirling the boy towards him. "You need to get the barbeque goin' for tonight. It's the only way any of us'll be able to leave the house and hang out together with our parents all spooked about them escaped prisoners. It's important you talk your grandpa into doin' it tonight, Millhouse. We ain't got many nights left of summer and none of us wanna spend one cooped up inside with our parents. You gotta get it done, Millhouse. We's countin' on you."

As the boys went over the intricate details of their plan—their plan within a plan—Keg Davis, with his customary wild hair and unshaven face, lumbered lazily up behind his son. Getting impatient with the kids' childish antics and hyper chatter, he bumped his belly into Suds and smacked him on the back of his head. "Ouch!" Suds hollered. "I guess we're takin' off. Talk to your grandpa, Millhouse, and call one of us as soon as ya can. But whatever ya do, don't take no for an answer."

Jared watched the other boys march out of the restaurant, then shifted his focus to his grandpa with narrowed eyes. Virgil sipped his coffee and nodded his head up and down in agreement to something Mr. Lovelace had said. Calculating the situation, Jared took a seat on the stool next to Virgil at the counter. His game of espionage had just taken an interesting turn. He was now a secret double agent with two important missions on his plate. Sly as a fox, he tugged on his grandfather's shirt to gain his attention.

"Hey, kiddo. Did you have fun with your friends?" Virgil wheezed and moved his oxygen tank closer to his legs to give Jared some room.

"Yes, I did." His grandpa returned to Mr. Lovelace, forcing Jared to yank harder on the old man's sleeve.

"What is it, son? This shirt is dang near fifty years old. You're gonna rip the arm off the daggum thing."

Jared leaned in close and scanned the area behind him to make sure he wasn't being watched or listened to. "I think I just got us a way for dad to meet Ms. Ramsey without them knowing it."

"Is that so?"

"Yeah. But we gotta do it tonight. We asked her over for a barbeque. She won't suspect a thing 'cause my friends'll be there and so will their parents."

"Geez, kiddo, that's a lotta work in a short period of time. Today ain't one of my better days. I'd have to push this dang tank around in the hot sun. I'll drop dead."

"No. You can sit inside. Me and Dad will clean up the house and everybody'll be outside most the time anyway. And Beans said his dad knows how to cook real good. Come on, Grandpa. It's our only shot. She said she would come if we asked her."

"Oh, why not?" Virgil relented. "I'm too old to give a hoot about a house and who's runnin' through it, anyway. Besides, I've got about sixty pounds of meat left from a steer I had butchered dang near two years ago. This'll be one way to clean out my freezer. Go ahead and tell your friends we'll have us a barbeque when the sun goes down a little. We'll provide the meat and they can bring whatever else."

"Awesome!" Jared leaped from the stool to give his grandpa a hug. "Thanks. You won't be sorry! I promise."

"Yeah, yeah. We'll see. Aw, dang. I gotta go take a leak. I hate draggin' this daggum thing around and peein' ain't no easy task like it used to be."

"Why's that?" the naïve boy asked.

"It just idn't. When ya get old nothin's easy—even peein'. I'll see ya in about a daggum hour." Virgil stepped away from the counter, rolling his oxygen tank behind him. "Just stay here with Ned. Keep an eye on the boy, would ya, Ned?"

The bearded fellow cocked his eye in Jared's direction. "All I got me is one good eye, but I'll keep it on him. Good luck with the peein'. Pull your pants down around your ankles and try bendin' at the knees a little. That's what works for me." As Virgil crept through the crowded café, Mr. Lovelace patted Jared on his thin shoulder. "We may not see your grandpa again till mornin'. Order yourself a soda or somethin'. Tell Agnes." Jared accepted the offer and asked for a Coke. He immediately started blowing bubbles through the straw, irritating the surly old man. "Can't you kids just sit still like a loyal dog or somethin'? Makes me wanna ram that straw up your nose."

"Sorry," Jared whispered.

"So, tell me what you done seen or got your dumb self into lately."

"Well, last night a herd of ghost horses almost ran us over while we were walking home. Their bodies were bone and bloody fur. They were scary. Luckily, Sirus showed up. He told us that so many horses died during the battle that they were laying all over the streets."

"I've seen 'em," Mr. Lovelace said. "They're some hideous gross beasts."

"But why don't more people see the ghosts? Why just you, Sirus, and my friends?"

Mr. Lovelace pushed his cup across the counter for a refill. "Heck, kid, Lone Jack *is* a ghost town. It's as dead as them ghosts, or at least it was until recently. But back durin' the time of the battle, the town was growin'. Like I told ya before, it was figurin' to be as big as Kansas City, but when the war broke out it nearly killed the town along with many young men on both sides of the conflict.

"Ya see, Missouri had the third most battles of any state durin' the Civil War and it was town to town. The Union had a foothold pretty much all north and west of here, but Kansas City and the towns all around it were strong with the Confederacy. The Union knew they had to take over this area to win in Missouri, so it was bloody in these parts. Kansas Jayhawkers would come in and raid a town. Then the guerillas, like Quantrill and Bloody Bill Anderson, would raid inta Kansas and kill the heck outta folks. It was bad. Everythin' was about revenge. The Union rounded up women kinfolk of known Rebel guerillas and kept 'em in jail as a way to flush out the marauders and keep the gals from givin' information to the enemy. This one buildin' they was held in was considered unsafe and, sure enough, it collapsed and killed several women bein' held there. Women kin to Quantrill, Cole Younger, and several other Confederate fighters died. In retaliation, Quantrill's Bushwackers went to Lawrence, Kansas and killed every man they saw, one hundred and fifty in all. The scene was abominable."

"Wow," Jared muttered.

"After that, Order Number 11 came inta action, approved by President Abraham Lincoln himself. Ya see, it was said that about two-thirds of the families in the area were kin to the guerillas. General Schofield, the head Union general out west, figured if he could force these people out of the area, the Rebel guerilla forces would have no support and he could squash them. So that's what he did. What he didn't estimate was the dreadful lastin' consequences of his actions.

"People were forced from their homes with no belongings. Their houses and crops were burned to the ground. Their cattle was slaughtered and left to rot. Anybody who fought back or resisted was killed. It was bad. In fact, there was this one farmer named John Hunter who was forced from his home because of Order Number 11. Before he left, he had to bury two sons, his son-in-law, a grandson, and two of his neighbors killed by the bluecoats. And that's just one case. Jackson County became known as 'the land of the chimneys' as a result of that Order. The town of Lone Jack was reduced to nothin', as so many of the citizens, who'd made this place their home, were forced out of the area and never returned. This town has never recovered since. Its population is a third of what it was at the time— a goshdarn ghost town."

***

Rob was less than enthusiastic when his father informed him of his plans to have a barbeque for Jared's friends. In fact, he was dead set against it, which he forcefully illustrated by shaking his head and waving his hands in defiance. That was, until he found out Ms. Darla Ramsey would be in attendance. Then he dropped his chin to his chest and reflected on the work to be done before the festivities. "Well, I guess it's okay," he responded, lacking the acting skills to hide his delight. "In fact, it might be fun. I'll get the meat out of the freezer to thaw and then Jared and I will get to work straightening up the house."

Grinning like a fox in a chicken coop, Virgil winked at his grandson. After he cleaned up his room by throwing everything into his closet, Jared went to work calling all the members of the Crossroads Club, informing them that the barbeque was a go. Sweets then called Ms. Ramsey, who accepted the invitation and said she'd arrive promptly at seven. Excited, Jared bounced throughout the house on tiptoe. The Millhouses hadn't entertained guests for as long as the boy could remember. He threw open the back door and scurried out to help his dad set up tables and chairs and roll the large barbeque grill out of the fescue on the south side of the farmhouse. Rob dumped an entire bag of coals into the large grill and doused them with lighter fluid. Concerned about his dad's cooking ability, not to mention the man lighting himself on fire, Jared readied himself near the garden hose. Fortunately, Rob set the grill ablaze without a hitch.

Shanks and his hyperactive family arrived first and, after introductions, the two boys raced to the blackjack oak on the property line and scaled the mighty tree. A half an hour later the oak was ornamented oddly with kids dangling from one branch or another from top to bottom. Suds, still rather sore and hobbled, and Porker rested with their backs against the tree's base, while Sweets dangled his long legs just above their heads. Higher up, Jared, Molly, and Jan straddled smaller branches, while Beans stood above, beyond their reach. Within feet of the very top, disobeying his mother's warning in the process, Shanks swung from one limb to another like a wild spider monkey. Jared was in heaven, laughing and joking with his friends. He looked at each with pride.

As the sun got lower in the sky and the nagging heat subsided, Ms. Ramsey pulled her car down the gravel drive. She walked erectly, with impressive strides, around the house towards the backyard. In her hands she carried a pan with a dishtowel draped over the top. Porker leaped to his feet. Though he'd been one of Ms. Ramsey's constant annoyances throughout the school year and was always slightly uncomfortable around the lady, the fact that she'd shown up offering food meant a truce was in order.

"Hey, Ms. Ramsey," the chunky boy greeted her as he shoved his freckled face into the pan. "What ya got there?"

"Well, good evening, Russ," the teacher replied with a bright smile. "I made *brownies*! But you can't have any until after dinner, so get your mug out of the pan." Like a dog persistently sniffing another one's butt, Porker followed the tasty treat with his head glued to the pan. "Seriously, Russ. Russ Parker…stop. You're dripping sweat all over my towel. You have to wait. Russ. Stop, Russ."

Perched in the oak, Molly waited for Ms. Ramsey to disappear around the corner of the house. "So what are you gonna do? How are you going to get Ms. Ramsey and your dad to kiss?"

"Kiss!" Beans yelped from above. "What do they gotta go and do that for?"

"Yeah," Jared agreed. "Why would they wanna do something like that?"

"To date," Jan answered with no inflection. "When a boy and a girl like each other they kiss."

Molly put her delicate hand to her chin. "We have to come up with something. A plan. There's too many people around. We need to somehow get them alone. Then they can kiss."

Still disturbed by the thought, Beans wrinkled his forehead. "Can't they just play video games or somethin'?"

"Oh, that's just great, Millhouse," Suds grumbled. "Next thing ya know, they'll be fartin' in front of each other like my parents do."

Excited about the role they'd adopted for themselves as matchmakers, Jan and Molly whispered back and forth, working out the details of the right moment for *the kiss*, while Jared and the rest of the boys fought to get the vision out of their simpler minds. Finally, Molly leaped from her perch and landed with the grace of a ballerina on the ground. "We've got it!" she exclaimed.

As she started to disclose her brilliant plan, the snapping of branches interrupted her, followed by a shattering scream from the canopy. Like a strange game of pinball, Shanks hurtled through the tree, smacking nearly every limb as he tumbled. His friends watched in horror as he hit the ground below with a *thud*.

Shanks sprang to his feet; his eyes protruding from their sockets. "I'm all right!"

"Man, I swear that boy's made of rubber," Beans stated in disbelief.

"And his head's made of concrete," Sweets added.

"Eat crap, Sweetwater!" Shanks balled up his little fists.

"Guys," Molly pleaded, "guys, listen. I know what we can do to get Mr. Millhouse and Ms. Ramsey alone so they can kiss. Everybody has to leave as soon as we're done eating. Tell your parents you're tired or you're not feeling good. Whatever. Just make sure you leave as soon as we get done eating."

"Aw, shucks," Shanks sniped. "We done had enough of this girly stuff. We come here to play. We don't care about no lovey-dovey crap."

"You're gonna do it," the girl demanded, "or else. Jared, get your grandpa to go to bed."

Using the solid oak for support, Suds pulled himself to his feet. "Heck, Molly that old man done went to bed an hour before we got here. That's what old people do. They go to bed when the sun sets so they can get up and watch it rise in the mornin'. Besides, my old man ain't gonna budge till all the beer's gone."

"Suds! We're leavin'!" Keg Davis hollered from the back of the house.

Suds' eyebrows jumped. "I guess all the beer's gone."

Jared climbed from the arms of his oak tree and looked at his lanky pal. "But you haven't eaten yet."

"Oh, that's okay, Millhouse. I ain't feelin' too good no way. My knee aches and my head hurts. I'll grab some cereal or somethin' when I get home. I don't wanna be around here, anyway, when your old man and mean ole Ms. Ramsey start smoochin'. I think I'd rather see them ghosts again than have to see that."

***

Eating dinner at such a late hour worked out nicely for Molly's scheme, as everyone devoured their food like a ravenous pack of wolves. Luckily Mr. Wilder, Beans' father, took control of the grill before Rob could burn any more of the steaks and burgers, and he churned out a hearty pile of succulent beef. Once the last of the brownies were consumed, Porker even collecting the crumbs and stuffing them into his chubby cheeks, Molly scurried about, forcing the rest of the kids into complaining about tummy aches and sleepiness. Within minutes, like a school fire drill, the backyard was vacant. Only Ms. Ramsey, Rob, Jan, Molly, and Jared stayed behind to clean up the mess. The dog-day cicadas buzzed as the sun set over the horizon and the glowing full moon brought on the night. Though the air was muggy, the clear sky and swollen moon made the perfect backdrop for Molly's plan. As she gathered paper plates and tossed crumpled napkins into the trash can, she smiled at Jan. The two girls giggled.

As observant as any boy, Jared stared with confusion at the young ladies. "What's so funny?"

"We have to get them alone," Molly whispered. "That's how it works."

Ms. Ramsey returned from the kitchen, where she'd put several dishes and utensils in the washer, and walked out of the back of the house. She stood with her hands on her hips and inspected the area. "Well, I guess that's about it. Do you need me to help you with anything else?"

A 'red alert' sounded in the girls' heads and they rushed to Ms. Ramsey's side. "No, wait," Molly said. "You, uhh…you haven't seen the farm."

"Uhh, yeah," Jan agreed, "Mr. Millhouse hasn't showed you around his farm. It's pretty neat."

Rob stopped in the middle of stacking plastic chairs. "Well, yeah. I guess I could show you around the place. It isn't much to see though. I wouldn't call it *neat*. But I could take you around the place. Maybe a night ride on the tractor would be fun?"

A sly grin slid across Molly's pretty face as she glanced at Jan. Being sharper than the two girls put together, Ms. Ramsey intercepted the look. "Okay, what are you-all up to?"

"Nothing," Molly responded quickly, her every motive written on her face. "We just know that you're probably sad that your kids are gone for awhile and figured you're probably bored at home, just sitting around with your mother."

The elementary school teacher folded her arms. "My mom's in Maryville visiting her sister. And I actually kind of like having some peace and quiet for a change—even if it is only for a couple of weeks."

Molly grabbed the lady by her arm. "You can have peace and quiet tomorrow. You should go with Mr. Millhouse and have some fun."

Rob's cheeks reddened from shyness and he dropped his head. "I guess I should fire up the tractor."

Ms. Ramsey sat behind Rob on the tiny seat of the rusty old machine, placing her arms around his waist to keep from sliding right off. The tractor bucked as he got it in gear, then rolled forward with its large wheels digging into the dry ground. As the two adults rumbled down the south edge of the ghostly cornfield, Molly and Jan watched with their hands clasped to their chests, captivated by the scene, their faces beaming with pride. Jared, on the other hand, glanced at the stalks of corn and then at the tractor as it motored in the distance. "I sure hope he doesn't try to take her in the cornfield to kiss her. He might end up getting her head chopped off. I don't see why he don't just lay one on her and get it over with."

"This is perfect." Molly stated with a delicate sigh. "This is just perfect."

"What's perfect?" he asked.

"The night," Jan answered. "It's romantic."

"What's romantic?" the boy continued, perplexed by the ways of love.

"The night, Jared," Molly snapped, irritated that the boy was ruining the moment. "It's magical."

"It is?" He shook his head in frustration. "What, is he gonna doin' a card trick or somethin'? How can you even see 'em from here? How the heck do you-all know?"

"We just do, Jared." Molly smiled. "We just do."

6

Museum curator, Mrs. Dottie Morgan, opened the gate and led a group of five visitors into the Lone Jack Civil War Cemetery. Shanks, Sweets, and Jared leaned against the fence, gawking at the strangers like they were in front of the gorilla pit at the Kansas City Zoo. Mrs. Morgan gave the boys a threatening stare and then immediately put on a delightful expression for her cherished guests. As the group gathered round, the woman went into her well-rehearsed presentation of the surroundings, explaining the monuments, burial trenches, and location of the famous blackjack oak tree that stood so steadily atop the ridge many years ago.

Shanks spit across the fence. "Geez, lady, don't you never say nothin' new?"

Ignoring the annoying boy she continued, "Now you are standing on part of the actual battlefield. Several buildings were erected in the area, called New Town by the citizens, including the Cave Hotel, the blacksmith shop, a saloon, a post office, and several residences. To the east of town, an Osage orange hedgerow kept the livestock away from the neighboring cornfield. Now, the Confederate forces had used the high dense grass and weeds for cover and snuck in very close to the Federal soldiers, who occupied the town. They had the element of surprise on their side. That is, until a new recruit tripped on some weeds and accidentally fired his weapon. After that, the Union soldiers mustered, scurried to their positions, and readied themselves for battle. Then the chaos of close range and hand-to-hand fighting ensued."

"Geez, lady," Shanks hollered, "you're borin' them people to death. Tell 'em somethin' we ain't all heard before."

"Back off, you little brat!" Mrs. Morgan exploded. She quickly collected herself and, with a very ladylike motion, pushed her hair up in back. "Now, the Union forces were outnumbered, but they did have two large cannons, or James Guns—named after inventor and former senator, Charles T. James. The six-pound cannons were handled by the 3rd Indiana Light Artillery, who had arrived in Lexington days before and joined Major Foster for the engagement. During the battle, the Rebels knew they were in serious trouble if they didn't nullify those cannons. In the five-hour battle, the cannons changed hands four times in close fighting and again many soldiers being killed in hand-to-hand combat. Ultimately, the guns remained in Union control, but cost the Federals dearly as they lost Major Emory Foster, Major Foster's brother, and Lieutenant Long who were badly wounded. Though the Fosters ended up surviving, Lieutenant Long died a few days later."

"Oh, come on!" Shanks shouted. "You say the same stuff every time. She does. Every time."

Boiling with desire to scream at the irritating boy, Mrs. Morgan found the strength to ignore him. "Maybe I should pause to take some questions?" From across the fence, like he was still sitting in the back right corner of his fourth grade classroom, Sweetwater raised his hand. Noting the lanky arm pointing straight in the air, Mrs. Morgan huffed. "Does anyone *from the tour* have a question?"

"You gotta be kidding me, lady!" Shanks hollered. "Sweetwater's got his hand up. He's got himself a question. Go on and call on him."

"What is your question, child?" she asked, biting her lip.

Sweets lowered his hand and stood up straight and poised. "Do you think Lone Jack'll ever get a movie theatre or a video game store? It sucks always havin' to drive all the way to Lee's Summit just to see a movie or buy a new game."

"All right, I've had it with you little freaks!" Mrs. Morgan screamed. "Your parents should be behind bars and you should be in a boys' home for disrespectful and misbehaving children." She quickly stopped and collected herself. "Shall we go to the south side of the property, so I can show you where some of the buildings stood during the famous battle?" The lady led the cemetery visitors through the gate, allowing them to exit first. "Now, I hope you folks will attend our annual celebration commemorating the battle of Lone Jack. It is this Saturday, August 16-the very day and anniversary of the battle. There will be all kinds of festivities, and Civil War reenactors will be playing out the tragic and deadly events of that day." The group walked across Bynum Road and gathered around Mrs. Morgan.

"Dang," Shanks murmured as he draped his arm across the fence. "I thought it was a good question, Sweetwater."

The boys goofed around in the front area of the cemetery, waiting for Suds, Beans, and Parker to arrive. It was Sunday afternoon and, because the authorities had determined that the three fugitives still on the loose had left the area, the citizens could breathe a huge sigh of relief and allow their children to travel more freely. Sweets wielded a large stick he'd found near one of the Osage orange trees and swatted at the ground, while Jared and Shanks threw rocks in the circular gravel drive leading to the museum. Growing restless, they started piling up as many fallen branches as they could when Officer Kunkle squealed into the entrance, throwing rocks and dust as he slammed on the brakes.

The officer vaulted from his police car. "Just what do you little gnats think you're doin'?"

Instantly nervous whenever Officer Skunkle showed up, the three froze, feeling guilty, though they couldn't figure out why. "We're just...we ain't doin' nothin'," Sweets answered.

"Ain't doin' nothin', huh? Well, it looks like you're destroyin' public property to me."

"Somebody owns these sticks?" Jared asked, confused.

The officer pointed at Jared. "Don't you sass me, boy. I've done had me about enough of you little crackerjacks. What do you think that old codger, Sirus, is gonna say when he comes here to clean up the place?"

The boys stared at each other with blank expressions on their faces. "Thanks for puttin' all them sticks in a pile?" Jared guessed.

Officer Kunkle dropped his head and placed his hands on his sides. "Look, this here is a public museum and they don't need three wiseacres loiterin' around." He gestured towards the road with a thrust of his thumb. "Now, scram. If'n ya don't, I'll be writin' up citations on the serious charge of trespassin'. So I need you to vacate the premises immediately."

Shanks threw his hands in the air, illustrating he'd given up. "First ya get on us for pickin' up sticks. Then ya tell us to leave. Now you want us to dig up the place? That don't make no sense."

Losing his patience, the officer wiped the sweat from his forehead. "Not *excavate*, ya little moron. *Vacate*. Ya don't look like no archeologists to me."

"No," Sweets replied. "I'm Baptist."

"Leave, daggum it! Get your little scrawny butts on outta here!"

Fearing ultimate incarceration, the three boys picked up their bikes and headed behind the museum towards Blue and Gray Estates. As they pushed their bicycles through the backyards and between the houses, they spotted Suds limping in their direction with Beans and Porker flanking him.

Shanks hopped on his bike and motored down the street, putting an impressive tire burn on the cement as he slid in front of the three boys. "Don't go thatta way. Skunkle's over there and he done run us off."

The boys looked at each other, searching for something to do. "Let's go to the clubhouse," Beans suggested. "Might as well have us a Crossroads Club meeting."

Meetings for the club generally resulted from nothing better to do. Suds tossed his head to the side. "Might as well." He turned to Jared, Sweets, and Shanks. "You guys can leave your bikes at my house, so we can cut across the back of the high school."

The Crossroads gang journeyed through the open field of tall grass and reached the tree line. They jumped across the creek and headed up the hill towards their secret clubhouse, constructed from dilapidated boards and dented metal siding they'd found dumped in the creek, loosely nailed, taped, and screwed together. Though it wasn't an architectural wonder or pleasing to the eye, the club was very proud of their base of operation. It had several chairs, a table, a broken microwave someone had tossed, and several other cherished items most people would label as 'garbage.' A grown man could stand almost upright inside, and the roof worked surprisingly well during the rain. The door even closed tightly and soiled carpet pieces made the tiny structure homey. Pictures of athletes ripped from magazines and various artistic contributions from the members decorated the walls. In the corner, a wooden chest contained the club's valuables, consisting mainly of shiny rocks, a couple of arrowheads found in the creek, Pokemon cards, baseball and football cards, and anything and everything the members deemed as 'neat' or 'cool.'

But as the boys reached their beloved clubhouse, their hearts sank. It lay in a heap with several pieces scattered across the hill; the tiny meeting place they so cherished torn to pieces. They gawked at the devastation in utter disbelief. "It musta been the wind, or even a tornado," Sweets reasoned as he picked up an old boxing glove from the wreckage.

Porker rummaged through the debris and located one of his *Star Wars* light sabers, now bent, cracked, and useless. "I got this for Christmas," the boy whined.

Digging through the grass, Beans gathered up some baseball and football cards that were scattered all about. "This sucks. Everything is trashed."

Suds' anger boiled over. He kicked a lawn chair and flung a board through the air. "Dang that Dozer Pittman! And Lathon Greeley! And that Colby Shannon…the ugly goat!"

"Dozer?" Jared asked as he picked through the destruction. "You think he did this?"

"Of course he done did it, Millhouse!" Shanks screamed. "This ain't no wind or tornado! They destroyed our clubhouse!"

Suds bent down and started to unwrap the bandage from his knee. "I've done had me enough of them creeps! I mean it! I've had all I can stand! I've had it with Dozer! Greeley! The Goat! And I ain't takin' it no more! And I've had it with them ghosts! They're all gonna get outta here and leave us alone! I mean it!"

"Come on, dude." Sweets tossed an old license plate onto the toppled pile of what used to be their clubhouse. "You can't go makin' Dozer mad, let alone them ghosts. He'll kill you, man."

Suds wadded up the bandage in his hands and threw it. "Yes I can, Sweets. I ain't gonna take it no more. They chase us down to tease us and beat us up. I've had me enough. And them ghosts, too. We're gonna figure us out a way and get them the heck on outta Lone Jack."

Jared looked at Suds. "What are you gonna do, man? Sweets is right. Dozer will just hurt you again. And them ghosts…how are we gonna do anything to them?"

Suds stormed past Jared, bumping the smaller boy's shoulder. "I don't know, Millhouse. But we're gonna do somethin'. We just can't sit back and take it no more."

The boys looked at each other, not knowing what to do and concerned about what the angry Suds might do. "Well, come on," Sweets finally ordered and headed off after Suds. "What are you guys waitin' for? We have to help him."

Laying belly down in the tall grass a short distance away, completely hidden, Earl Bridges and his fellow escapees watched as the boys, one by one, left the hilltop. "Maybe we oughtta go after 'em. They could have 'em a car and we could steal it from 'em and get on outta this crazy place," Johnny Sims whispered.

"Yeah, Sims. They're a buncha forty-year-old dwarfs wandering through the woods… looking for their Cadillac so they can pick up Snow White." Earl Bridges grabbed the back of the man's head and rammed his face into the hard ground. "Shut up. Don't say another word until you're spoken to. Next time you say somethin' stupid, I'm gonna break your neck."

Feeling the coast was clear, the wanted men crawled to their feet and scanned the area around them. "This here is ridiculous," Lancaster snapped. "How do we get outta this town? I don't like it, Earl. This place is haunted, man. We been trottin' around this place for days. We're goin' in circles. We gotta get outta this town. I'm tellin' ya, it's haunted. Let's just turn ourselves in."

Bridges grabbed Lancaster by the collar of his soiled cowboy outfit and flung him to the ground. "Shut your mouth! You wanna go back to prison? I've spent all the time I'm goin' to in there and I've killed before…and I'll kill again. You mention givin' ourselves up again, Lancaster, and I swear I will kill you."

"But what we gonna do, Earl?" Sims begged. "Mitchell's right, man. I've seen me things in here. I can feel it like somebody's got their hands around my neck and is chokin' me. I can't breathe. I keep lookin' over my shoulder like somebody's watchin' me. This town is haunted, man. Like somebody's comin' after us."

"You idiot," Bridges snarled. "You're both idiots and cowards. Of course, somebody's comin' after us. We're escaped cons. Now are you gonna buck up like men or curl up like cowards?"

Lancaster crawled to his feet, his beady little eyes angry. He pointed at their psychotic leader. "That ain't right, Earl! We want outta here same as you, but somethin's strange about this place. How do you explain us walkin' and walkin' and endin' up in the same spot we started from? And what about them hedgerows that seem to appear outta nowhere, like they's fencin' us in like dang cattle? Every time we get to the edge of this crazy town we run into them thick thorny things that we can't climb over nor get around, no matter how hard we try. We get stuck in 'em like flies in flypaper. You really don't see nothin' strange or spooky about that? I got cuts and scrapes all over my body from the thorns on them thangs. This town is haunted!"

***

Suds plowed across the field behind Lone Jack High School, his aching body tilted forward with determination. Even with his injured knee slowing him a bit, the rest of the gang lagged behind him, calling out for him to rethink his decision and reflect on the dangerous consequences. As he started to cross the street that ran between the high school and Blue and Gray Estates, Suds spotted Dozer and his two cohorts straddling ATVs at the end of the road, where it ran into Bynum. He stopped and stared at the goons. Dozer soon noticed Suds and stared back. The big kid hit the gas on his ATV, letting the machine buck and jerk like a bull ready to charge, but the determined Suds held his ground. Like two wild west gunslingers preparing for a deadly draw in the middle of town, the boys stared each other down, neither blinking.

"How's your clubhouse, Scum?" Dozer hollered with a sinister grin.

About to drop from running so far, Jared sucked at the thick air like a vacuum. Nearing the curb, he realized Beans, Shanks, and Sweets had stopped. They stood like statues, staring down the road. Moving closer, Jared spotted Dozer in the middle of the street revving the ATV engine. "Oh, no," he mumbled.

Like the townsfolk of the old west, they'd come out to watch the showdown—Suds in a shiny, white ten-gallon hat, and a dark black hat atop the head of the notorious Dozer. Their spirits were low, however, anticipating doom for the brave fighter standing alone in the street.

Dozer sneered and jerked the machine again. Then he floored the ATV, with Greeley and Shannon following fast behind, jeering like wild outlaws. "Suds!" Jared exclaimed. "Suds! Run! Get out of the way! They're gonna run you over!"

The boys yelled for Suds to move, but the stubborn kid refused to budge. He stood in the middle of the street with fierce eyes, his chest heaving as he clenched his fists and tightened his muscles. Jared glanced at Dozer, who barreled forward, roaring towards Suds.

Their ATVs hummed like wicked chainsaws. He turned back to Suds, then again to Dozer.

The ATVs reached twenty yards. Jared and the others screamed. "Noooo! Sudssss! Noooo!"

At the last second, Dozer slammed on the brakes and skidded straight towards his target. Still, Suds didn't back away. As the vehicle stopped with a sudden jolt, Suds slammed his hands down and clamped onto the handlebars. His nose within inches of Dozer's, his intense eyes held only anger. The game of chicken was over. Suds had called the kid's bluff. "Ha!" he blurted. "You guys destroyed our clubhouse!"

Dozer bashed Suds away from his ATV with a straight-arm to the chest, sending Suds flying backwards. But Suds kept his composure and his footing. "Who do you think you are?" Dozer yelled. "Ain't you sick of g'tting' whooped yet, Crud? You touch my ATV again and I'll break both your arms!"

Suds shook his finger at the mountainous boy. "You destroyed our clubhouse!"

"Yeah," Greeley snarled, "so what? What are you and these wimps gonna do about it?"

"I'll tell ya what I'm gonna do about it, moron," Suds shot back. "I challenge Dozer to a race!"

"A race?" Greeley cackled. "Just kick the crap out of him, Dozer."

Dozer leaped from his quad and headed towards Suds, who instinctively retreated a few steps. Dozer clenched his fists and scowled. "You challengin' me? You stupid or somethin'? What kinda race?"

"A bike race!" Suds shot back. "Winner gets the other'ns bike!"

"Ha!" Dozer blurted. "I'd kill you! Heck, yeah, I'll race ya, Crap Davis!"

Silently witnessing the showdown with the rest of the Crossroads Club and trying to stay out of harm's way, Sweets nonetheless scratched his head and spoke up. "Man, you can't ride your bike, Suds. Your knee is screwed up."

Suds thought for a moment, then offered with blistering defiance, "Okay, then…an ATV race! Just me and you! Winner gets the other ones' ATV!"

"Are you nuts?" Beans screeched. "Dozer races ATVs! He nearly won the Junior Missouri title! He'll kill you, Suds! And your dad'll put a whoopin' on you if you lose his ATV!"

Dozer marched towards Suds and shoved the skinny boy again. "You're on, creampuff! Name your time and place!"

Suds pushed back at the solid lug of a boy with no effect. "Tuesday! We'll take off when the sun goes down, so nobody'll spot us. Just me and you. *Me* and you. The winner gets the ATVs."

A seedy grin spread across Dozer's piggish face. He rubbed his stomach with both hands and started laughing. "Spud Davis the racer! I've seen it all now!" Without warning, he punched Suds in the gut, knocking the wind out of him. The meaty boy put his lips next to Suds' ear. "You're on, chump. And you ain't g'tting' outta this one. You better show up. Just name the time and place. Don't go chickenin' outta this Suds, or I'll beat ya to a bloody pulp. If you don't show up, I'll be comin' to get your ATV. You better be there." With a final push to the side of Suds' head, Dozer turned, hopped on his ATV, and sped off down the street with his goons, catcalling and teasing the gang as they went.

Once the coast was clear, the boys rushed to Suds' side. "What are ya thinkin', man?" Shanks asked. "You don't know squat about racin' no quads. He's gonna kill ya. Then your dad's gonna kill ya."

His stomach stinging, Suds gasped for air. "Just get me to my house. We gotta get that ATV runnin'."

"It don't run, Suds?" Porker asked. "Why would ya go and challenge Dozer Pittman to a race when your ATV ain't even runnin'? We're in big trouble, man."

Suds put his arms around Beans and Sweets' shoulders for support and the gang headed into Blue and Gray Estates. Once they reached the Davis house, Shanks and Beans pulled the tarp off the ATV sitting in the corner of the garage. The machine hadn't run in a couple of years; Keg Davis having promised he'd 'get to that' and predictably adding it to the long list of numerous things he'd left unattended to throughout the home. The boys stood in a half-circle around the vehicle and simply gawked at it. They had no idea what to do.

Suds rubbed his sensitive belly. "I don't know what I was thinkin'. I lost it. I completely lost it. We can't never get this thing to run. And if we do, Dozer's just gonna beat the pants off me anyway. I'm in big trouble. How could you guys let me get that mad and get all this stirred up, anyway? How could ya let me get inta this mess?"

Shanks reached above his greasy head and put his finger in Suds' face. "Hey! Whatta ya mean us gettin' ya inta this? We tried to stop ya. We warned ya, Suds."

"Well, what are we gonna do, man?" Beans sighed. "You heard Dozer. If Suds don't show up, he's gonna beat the heck outta him, and they'll beat the tar outta all of us, too,…and he's gonna take the ATV anyway. We're all doomed. We ain't gonna be able to leave our houses for years after Tuesday."

Jared looked down the line of troubled faces standing next to him. He desperately wanted to find a way out of the mess they'd fallen into, and he was more worried about his friends' disappointment than his own safety. Then his eyes twinkled as an idea flickered in his head. "Hey! I know what to do! Sirus! We'll take it down the road to Sirus. He's always fixin' old junk. He can fix it! He'll fix it good as new! I just know it!"

***

Sirus studied the ATV and kicked one of the tires, which was flat as a pancake. "You guys've gotta be kiddin' me. What the heck did ya do to it?"

Because Beans' grandmother had come to visit and Shanks' mom had barked at him to get his chores done, they had gone home, leaving Jared, Suds, Porker, and Sweetwater to push the ATV from the Davis garage down the gravel road to Sirus' in the blazing afternoon sun. Hoping for better news, Suds dropped his head. "Well, I turned 'er over a couple of times, ran inta a tree once, and my dad drove er inta a lake one other time. Then there was the time my dad went headfirst over the handlebars and slammed it inta a ditch. Then my dad took her up this steep hill…"

"Okay. Okay." Sirus waved his hands in front of him. "I get the point. I'm thinkin' that you and your pa really shouldn't be operatin' ATVs—or any other kinda vehicle, for that matter. Look. The fact is, son, if you're gonna wanna ride this thing by Tuesday, I don't know if can be much help to ya." He turned the key and pressed on the gas. The beat-up ATV coughed and sputtered. The engine tried to turn over, but to no avail. "I can't even get it started. It's leakin' oil. Somethin's wrong with the transmission…and them's just the problems with it I'm noticin' right off."

Porker lay on his side with dirt sticking to his large, sweaty body from head to toe. Pushing the ATV to Sirus' had exhausted the lazy kid, who never willingly volunteered for laborious tasks. He raised his large head off the ground. "But we have to have it fixed by Tuesday. You can't do nothin'?"

Sirus looked at the boys' anxious faces. "Okay. What's goin' on? You boys in some kinda trouble?"

Jared glanced at Suds and then lowered his eyes. "Big trouble," he sighed. "Suds challenged Dozer Pittman to a race on ATVs and they're supposed to do it Tuesday evening."

"Daggum it," Sirus responded. "You could get yourselves hurt or even killed. This is a big machine. Not one boys should be messin' with and get inta trouble on. I can't let you-all do this."

"But Dozer'll kill us if we don't," Sweets exclaimed. "They'll never let us live it down."

"That big Pittman kid and them two boys he hangs with been pickin' on you-all?" the old man asked.

"Yeah," Jared answered. "They beat us up. Dumped us in Buck's Pond. Threw rocks at Suds. Then they trashed our clubhouse. Tore it completely to the ground."

Sirus wiped his hands with a rag that seemed to add more grime to his fingers than it removed. He tossed the greasy cloth on the seat of the ATV. "Well, shucks. If there's one thing I can't stand, it's bigger boys pickin' on littler ones. Aw, heck. Okay, then…if it helps y'all keep them boys from teasin' and pickin' on ya, then I'm in. But here's the deal: even if I had me a month I couldn't get this thing to run good, let alone beat that Pittman kid. His old man, who's as nasty and irritatin' as that kid is, is always up at the Crossroads Café talkin' about how his son races ATVs. The kid is good. He wins all the time. Their whole goshdarn house is filled with trophies and medals that boy done won in one race or another."

"So what are we gonna do?" Jared begged.

"Well, the kid is stupid, ain't he?" Sirus pointed out. "I mean, his old man is a dumb ole mouthy bird, so I gotta figure the apple didn't fall too far from the tree. You're gonna have to outsmart him, 'cause he's gonna be better on the ATV. He's simply better and that's all there is to it. Outsmartin' him is the only way ya got a chance."

"How do we do that?" Porker responded.

"That ugly boy rides an ATV that's 400cc's, if I heard his old man right. That's a pretty big machine for a kid and he's gonna have more power and speed."

"But wait a second," Jared interrupted. "You already said you couldn't fix Suds', so what does it matter? We don't have an ATV for him to race with anyway."

"Wrong," Sirus said. "Follow me." The gray-haired old man squeezed past his rusty tractor and led the boys to the back of his garage. He pulled a tarp off something sitting near the wall in a dark corner, uncovering a dingy ATV with several rust spots and a torn leather seat.

"You want Suds to ride that?" Porker, never accused of being polite, said in disbelief. "That thing's more trashed and broken than the one we done got. How's he ever gonna beat Dozer on that?"

"Don't judge a book by its cover," Sirus replied. "I got this here from a farmer in Harrisonville two years ago. It might not look like much, but I've fixed and worked on this machine till it's runnin' like new. I had a couple fellers help me bring 'er back to life, and they done several upgrades on her so she's more powerful than she looks. Now, she still might not have the power to keep up with that Pittman kid's quad, but she'll help ya stay in the race and give ya a shot." He folded the dusty tarp neatly and dropped it on a hay bail. "I'll let ya use it, but if anybody asks, I don't got no idea where you got it. You know what I mean?"

"But if it ain't gonna keep up, how can I beat him?" Suds asked.

"I done told ya," the old man answered. "That boy's dumber than a post. You gotta outsmart him. Use your wits. Them morons'll be putty in your hands if you play your cards right." The boys looked at each other with blank, confused stares, not feeling much confidence in their collective smarts. Sirus put his weathered hand on his hip. "Ya make the race on your terms. If his quad is bigger and faster, then you make that work against him. Pick a course that's got a lotta turns in between straightaways. Make him work hard to keep in front of ya. Then make sure you got a couple sharp turns near the end before a final straightaway. That's when ya take him."

Feeling a little more confident the boys nodded and giggled with excitement. Jared quickly calmed down, remembering the agreement of the challenge. "Wait," he hollered, attempting to quiet down his friends. "Wait a second." The other three stopped and focused on him. "We can't take this ATV."

"Why not?" Porker objected. "What are ya talkin' about, Millhouse?"

"It's Sirus'. Suds and Dozer agreed that the winner of the race got to keep the other one's ATV. If Suds loses, Dozer gets this one."

The ever-responsible Sweets, shook his head. "Millhouse is right," he said. "We can't use this ATV. We can't do that to Sirus."

Sirus looked at the dejected faces. "Well, I guess you-all better win then."

7

Waiting for his fresh cup of coffee to cool, Sirus tapped on the counter, checking his watch every twenty seconds. His paranormal experts from Connecticut were supposed to arrive at Kansas City International at ten, but due to 'mechanical failures' their plane had been delayed by over an hour. Sirus would have to wait patiently, something he normally did quite easily.

Ned Lovelace eyed the jumpy man sitting next to him, studying his every move. "What...do ya got ants crawlin' all over ya? What the heck's the matter with you, Sirus? I think you might want to slow down on the coffee a tad. You're bouncin' around so much it's makin' me nervous. My glass eye's about to shoot outta my head."

"Sorry." Sirus picked up his cup and blew across the top.

Disturbing no one except Ned, Sirus glanced over his shoulder to find Officer Kunkle standing close behind him with his thumbs tucked behind the buckle of his police belt. Mr. Lovelace felt the man's presence as well and turned on his stool. "Crapper's back and to the left," Ned said. "Light a match."

"Mind your own business, Ned," the officer snapped. "This ain't got nothin' to do with you." Confused by Kunkle's behavior, Sirus stared at him until Captain Pickering walked into the restaurant, the bell clanking off the glass as the door swung shut. "I got him right here, cap'n." Officer Kunkle pointed at Sirus who sat no more than three feet in front of him, as if his superior wouldn't recognize a man he'd known for more than twenty years. "This is him. I tracked him down for ya."

"Tracked him down," Ned repeated with a snicker. "Nice work, detective. He lives barely more than a mile from here, ya idiot."

"Daggum it, Cliff," the rotund captain huffed, heaving his massive frame onto a stool next to Sirus. "I know who he is. Don't have to act like you just apprehended Lee Harvey Oswald or somethin'. How 'bout a cup a coffee, Agnes?"

"What's this all about, Cecil?" Sirus asked. "Why you come looking for me?"

Agnes poured a cup of coffee for the captain, who waited for her to move away before he answered. "Well, look, Sirus, I've known you a long daggum time. And the folks in this town know ya and you're liked by everybody." He pulled his large sunglasses from his round face and rolled his signature matchstick around in his mouth with his tongue. "But I also know you can be a little quirky…in fact, you act completely bizarre a lotta the goshdarn time. A few people say ya got yourself a mental problem. That you's a tad crazy. You went around town talkin' about ghosts and goblins and the like, freakin' the whole town out. People started avoid'n ya and some parents wouldn't even let their kids around ya."

Incensed by the officer's callous comments, Sirus cocked his head and raised his chin. "You ain't gettin' to the point."

"Well, I'm gettin' there. What I'm sayin' is, that was quite awhile back. Several years, in fact, and since then ya've kept to yourself and stopped talkin' crazy about ghosts and creatures from the dead. You ain't stirred up no trouble. You've been a model citizen of Lone Jack since them days. Help out with the cemetery. Do work for farmers like Virgil Millhouse and Andy Cuthbert. But the last few months, you've changed a lot. You're actin' all fidgety and spookin' everybody out again. Now, I don't know if you need medication or not. I ain't no psycho…whatever…doctor."

"I'll keep that in mind. Are you finished?"

"No," Captain Pickering barked with authority. "No, I ain't. Ya see, your strange behavior is all fine and good, 'cept I got me the bodies of two dead runaway convicts sittin' at the morgue in Lee's Summit."

"What's that gotta do with me?"

"They was killed west of Jack Parsons' farm Friday evening. Jack said you was doing some work for him. He said he seen you until around five, then ya disappeared. Now we got one of them convicts in custody, a Mexican feller who don't speak good American. At first, we figured they was killed by the other escapees, who're still on the loose, assumin' the savages got inta a quarrel and bein' diabolical criminals like they is, the ones hacked up the other'ns. The problem with that is that it ain't what that Mexican is sayin'. He tells a different story—one that involves monsters and demons and the livin' dead."

Sirus scratched his beard. "What exactly are you sayin', Cecil?"

"Well, it's like this, Sirus, you're gonna have to hear me out, 'cause I'm gonna need ya to answer me some questions. I think, and the Federal authorities think as well, that you was involved in them prisoners' deaths. You took a knife and an axe from Parsons' place and hacked them boys to pieces. And just 'cause they's criminals, don't mean we ain't gonna investigate what happened fully, get to the bottom of it, and prosecute anybody involved in their killin's. Now, you was at Jack's workin' around the time they died. You also got crazy notions in your head that Lone Jack is overrun with ghosts. I'm guessin' ya killed them two boys and, while tryin' to get the Mexican, ya caused him to think it was ghostly monsters—the same way your disturbed mind keeps trickin' you."

"And how would I do that? This here is completely absurd. I'm an old man, for Pete's sake."

Captain Pickering pulled the matchstick from his lips and gestured with it. "Well…I believe your crazy mind is so twisted that you actually believe your own bullcrap. And everybody knows a man who's a bit insane is strong as an ox. I truly believe that you really think you're seein' these ghosts that your mind is actually creatin'. You probably acted on that, started makin' strange noises and howling like a daggum ghost or somethin', and then when you had them boys good and spooked, you attacked."

"Now, that is crazy. Crazy as all get out."

"Well, answer me this, Sirus." The captain ran the matchstick across the greasy counter. "How did ya get them scratches and bruises on your face? Why are ya limpin'? And how come, when I checked into it, you had to go by the emergency room in Lee's Summit for stitches? The doctor that worked on ya said your wounds looked like cuts from a knife."

The seriousness of the situation hit Sirus like a punch in the gut. He had no logical answers–not logical by the police captain's standards anyway. "Look, Cecil. I did some work at Parsons' farm. That, I'll give you. But I didn't kill nobody. That's ridiculous. I ain't never hurt nobody my whole life. And I got these bruises and cuts fallin' over an offset farmin' disc I got parked behind my garage. I forgot I had it back there and it was dark. One of the discs sliced my arm, and a sharp metal rod stickin' off it went inta my leg. That's it. That's what happened."

Mr. Lovelace slid his coffee cup forward and swiveled around on the stool. "This here is the dumbest buncha bull malarkey I ever done heard, and I can't sit here and listen to it with my mouth shut no more. Sirus, a murderer? Have you two boobs lost your minds? Are your brains so tiny that they went and fell outta your heads through your ears when you was sleepin', or they shot outta your noses when ya sneezed? This is daggum ridiculous. This is Sirus you're talkin' about. He helps everybody in town. Everybody loves 'im, and you got the nerve to come to him with this load of crap. Do us all a favor and go back to playin' rummy in the jail cell ole Dirty Harry here uses as his dang office and leave all of us alone."

Captain Pickering pinched the matchstick between his chubby fingers and shook it at Mr. Lovelace. "You just hold it there, Ned. Things here just don't add up."

"Well, nobody accused you and Officer Nitwit of bein' able to learn simple arithmetic."

"Enough!" the captain shouted. "All I know is, I got two dead convicts. Sirus was in the area at the time of the murders. He's got bruises and knife wounds all over him. And I just got off the phone with the FBI and they said they traced his phone calls to two daggum ghost hunters!" Ned swiveled back around in his seat and slouched over the counter. "Yeah, ya ain't got nothin' to say on that one, do ya, Ned? How 'bout you, Sirus? Ya wanna explain why ghost hunters are comin' to Lone Jack to visit ya? I mean, if ya ain't seen no ghosts in several years, why would ya need to contact ghost hunters and have them come check out the town?"

Frustrated by his inability to defend himself, Sirus glared at Captain Pickering for several seconds. Realizing that all he could do was ignore the policeman and his disparaging accusations, the old man turned in his seat and grabbed his coffee.

Captain Pickering returned the matchstick to his lips and put on his oversized reflective sunglasses. He slapped the counter lightly, then pulled his round body from the stool. "So, that's how it's gonna be, huh, Sirus? Okay, then. But I'm here to tell ya, I'm stayin' on top of this. I'm gonna figure out what is goin' on. And I'm gonna figure out what happened to them two dead convicts. I'm also gonna warn ya. Call it friendly advice. I don't know what you're up to with them ghost hunter fruitcakes from Connecticut. You probably got them fooled the same way ya fooled them dead convicts, but I'm gonna be watchin' you. Watchin' ya like a hawk.

"Now we got the Battle of Lone Jack Commemoration this Saturday. If I catch you stirrin' up trouble or spookin' the folks, I'm gonna arrest you and them two Yankees on the spot. No questions asked. Mrs. Morgan estimates we're gonna have us as many as a thousand visitors from around the area on Saturday. She's got the high school band playin', museum tours, and the reenactment of the battle itself. She's a nervous wreck 'cause it's all on her shoulders—she done planned the whole thing herself. The mayor don't want no problems, neither. I told him I'd see to it personally that the whole day's festivities go off without a hitch.

"Now, I can't arrest ya. All I've talked to ya about is just speculation, but, if my hunch is correct, we'll be talkin' to ya again. In the meantime, go see a psych… whatever they is…a doctor. Get yourself some help. I'm sayin' that as a friend. We've known each other a long time, Sirus. No matter what, I don't want to see nothin' bad happen to ya. I mean that. Do yourself a favor. Do Mrs. Morgan and the mayor a favor. Do me a favor. Do Lone Jack a favor and stay away from the commemoration come Saturday. Take them Yankee ghost chasers to a Royals' game or somethin'. I think they's playin' the Mariners. But whatever ya do, don't go and do nothin' foolish."

Captain Pickering turned towards the door and motioned to his subordinate. "Come on, Cliff. Fifty cars done sped down Highway 50 goin' about a hun'rd miles an hour while we was talkin', and you just stood there with that dumb look on your face, like a baby looks when it's crappin its diapers." The bell, dangling from the entrance, rang behind them as they left.

Sirus plunked his elbows down on the counter and buried his face in his hands. "Uhh, this is a nightmare—a nightmare that just keeps g'tting' worse."

Ned's eye focused on the distraught man next to him. "What in tarnation is goin' on, Sirus? How did ya get them bruises and knife wounds?"

Sirus dropped his hands from his face. "You wouldn't believe it if'n I told ya."

"Try me. It ain't like I can't figure it out. Don't forget, I was the strange bird of Lone Jack way before you come along. You mighta stole my thunder as of late, but I'm crazy old man number one, and you're crazy number two."

Sirus swiveled towards the old man. "The ghosts of Lone Jack ain't like they used to be. They ain't like they was when me and you was the only ones in town seein' 'em—or, at least, admittin' to it. These ghosts are changin'. Used to be they'd appear a split second and be as scared and confused of you as you were of them. This summer, though, somethin's come over 'em, and it's dangerous, real dangerous."

He took a deep breath. "Friday night, I was in my room gettin ready for bed, when I hear a loud commotion comin' from my livin' room. I got up to see what the heck it was, and three ghosts of Union soldiers was in there overturnin' my furniture. One of their names was Lieutenant Copeland. I looked the feller up and he was a Union officer killed in the battle of Lone Jack. Normally, if I'd've come outta my room and shouted at 'em pretty good it would've spooked 'em off, but these ghosts was different—more real. I knew somthin' wadn't right, so I figured I'd just hide till they was gone. I mean, normally they turn a page in my journal when I ain't lookin'. These here demons was throwin' my furniture around like it was nothin'. I went to shut the door that runs inta the spare bedroom and one of them Union creatures tackled me to the ground. He sliced my arm and I shot him with my shotgun. The next thing I know, a second one is comin' at me with a bayoneted rifle. I block it with the butt of my gun, but it catches my thigh. He drove it into the meat of my leg. He wanted to kill me, Ned. I was lucky to get outta there. I swear that's what happened." Sirus paused for some type of response, but Mr. Lovelace just sat hunched over, drinking his coffee. "You don't believe me? Then I am screwed. If I can't make you, of all people, believe it, nobody's goin' to."

Sirus started to move back around in his seat when Mr. Lovelace grabbed his arm. "No. Now, hold on. I'm just lettin' 'er all sink in. They was Union ghosts, and the one's name was Copeland. And they come in to take over your home."

"Yeah, that's right."

Mr. Lovelace shook his head from side to side and grunted. "Hmm. It makes sense. The Federal troops commandeered many a house to use as cover in the battle." He trained his eye on Sirus, a serious, intense expression on his face. "I believe ya."

Not really understanding why, since Ned Lovelace was no more respected or admired in the small town than an unwanted possum with rabies, Sirus closed his eyes and sighed in relief. "Thank you, Ned. For a second there I thought I *was* goin' crazy."

"Don't mention it." Ned continued to sit tensely atop the stool with his wiry beard buried in his chest.

"Hey. Wait a minute. You's actin' awful funny. I was wonderin' what you was doin'. I thought you was just intimidated by Pickerin'. You seen them ghosts actin' funny lately, too, ain't ya?"

Mr. Lovelace's crippled body jerked and he spun towards Sirus. "Oh, all right. Yes, I have! In fact, I was gonna tell ya all about it till Capt. Nose Pickerin' came in here and accused you of murder. If I'd've said somethin' then, as dumb as that gorilla is, he'd probably have us both arrested for conspiring with John Wilkes Booth or somethin'. So I figured it best to keep my mouth shut."

"What did ya see, Ned? Tell me. It might help me out and, I don't have to tell ya, I'm in big trouble here. I wanted them ghost hunters to come help me get them creatures outta our town before they hurt or even kill somebody. Now they have killed and I'm gettin' the blame for it. You gotta help me, Ned. If them ghost chasers don't see firsthand what is goin' on in this spooky town, I'm gonna end up in prison for the rest of my life for somethin' I didn't do. Now, more than ever, them Yankee ghost hunters got to film them soldier beasts and what they's capable of doin', or I'm cooked."

"Well, ain't nobody gonna believe us two, that's for sure," Mr. Lovelace responded. "Everybody in Lone Jack thinks we're completely nuts. Of course, I'll help ya Sirus. I couldn't let ya go to prison for somethin' ya didn't do. But you're right. With everybody thinkin' we's more than a couple cards short of a full deck, we gotta get them ghosts to show up for them Yankee ghost seekers ya called in. How is the question, though. Them fickle ghosts don't show themselves to everybody. All I know of is me, you, that Millhouse kid and them little snot-nosed punks he runs with. We're in big trouble." Ned patted Sirus on the shoulder. "I mean, you are."

"I'm well aware of that," Sirus mumbled. "Thanks." He downed the rest of his coffee and motioned to Agnes for a refill. "So, tell me what you done saw, Ned."

Mr. Lovelace locked his good eye on Sirus and stroked his long beard. "It was Injun's. Osage Injun's. *Dead* Osage Injun's. Ya see, ever since last winter when we got that awful ice storm and it knocked down trees and limbs and even broke trees in half, I been meanin' to get some of them branches away from my fence line. So last night, I took me a big metal garbage can—and I know I ain't supposed to be doin' this, as dry as it is—but I took that metal can to the middle of the field behind my house and gathered up as many of them loose sticks as I could carry, which weren't many, since I'm too old to be doin' it in the first place. 'Cause it was so daggum hot, I didn't start pickin' up the debris till right at sunset. When the garbage can was good and full, I tossed a little gasoline and a match on it. It went to blazin' quick, too, let me tell ya. So I stand there, watchin' it burn for about thirty minutes, makin' sure no cinders hop outta the can and set the whole field on fire. The fire was makin' me so hot I thought I was about to pass out, but it was well contained in the can, so I figured I'd go inside to cool off as best I could, and check on it a little later ."

He paused, petting his beard and reflecting on the prior night's bizarre events. "Anyway, I end up fallin' asleep in my recliner, I ain't sure how long I slept, but then I get startled awake by the low beatin' of drums and folks cryin' out and singin'. I figure it's some kids playin' a prank and messin' with me, but I ain't none too careful, so I grab my two Colt revolvers, which were handed down to me over the years. I peek out the window as I'm loadin' to see what the ruckus is, but I can't see much with it so dark out and only havin' one dang eye and all. All I can see is shadows movin' past the light of the fire. I hustle out my back door and march towards 'em with my revolvers in both hands.

"I get about halfway to 'em and am about to scream at 'em, when I make out who—or what—they is. Dancin' around my fire and stompin' to the beat of the drum was four Injun's from beyond the daggum grave. They was beastly creatures, too. Each one of 'em had two faces on a single head. One face was human, or human like, but the skin was rotted away, showin' bone. The other face was of an animal. One was a deer with a huge antler stickin' out of the side of his head. Another had an elk snout and one large antler. Then there was this Injun with a bone fleshy face and the face of a bear. Another'n had a rabbit face with a solitary long ear stickin up. The Injun creature beatin the drum had himself a buffalo face with a short horn curling up. I froze.

"I generally like and actually appreciate them ghosts I see. In fact, they kinda make a lonely old man's life a little more entertainin'. But these beasts had me scared. Real scared. As I was about to turn and sneak back inta my house, they spotted me. The deer-faced ghoul howled, sendin' chills up my spine. I started to run, but I ain't ran in fifty years. They was headin' straight for me with tomahawks, spears, war clubs, and bows and arrows, all raised and ready for combat. Their heads was shaved into tall, flowin' mohawks with parts of the skull showin' through. Long magnificent feathers decorated the mohawks and the parts of their human faces that weren't bone was colored with warpaint. Their bodies were grotesque, as well. The deer-faced Injun had a deer leg. The buffalo one had a hump and a thick hide on his chest and stomach. The elk had a hoofed arm, while the bear one's arm was a gigantic paw.

"They were movin' on me fast and I didn't have much time to react. The bear stopped and let an arrow fly straight for me. Knowin' I couldn't get out the way, I flinched, but it disappeared like it simply disintegrated in the air. The rest of 'em was still comin' fast, so I raised my Colts; my hands, which shake much of the time anyway, was tremblin' so bad I didn't think I could pull the dawggone triggers. But, *whack!* I nailed the rabbit Indian high in the chest. The bullet exploded through him and sent him reelin' to the ground. With no time to spare, I shot at the elk. *Bam!* I caught him in the cheek of his human face and the bullet came out the top of his elk one. I wheeled around and headed for the backdoor again and made it, just as one of 'em hurled a tomahawk at me. It smashed into the wood just inches from my face. I rushed inside and bolted the door.

"I couldn't hardly breathe and thought I was gonna have me a heart attack. I barricaded the door and scurried to the window. I peeked out cautiously, holdin' onto my Colts as tight as I could, and they was gone. Completely disappeared. I dropped down in my recliner and put my head in my hands. I was shakin' uncontrollably. After a while, I started thinkin' it was just my senile mind playin' a terribly mean trick on me, and that it was all somethin' I made up in my head. I don't know what to think anymore."

Sirus shook his head and patted Lovelace on the shoulder. "It wadn't your mind playin' tricks on you, Ned. I wish it were. They was aimin' to kill ya and take a scalp. I can assure you of that. We gotta do somethin'. If we don't, they could kill again. This town's in big danger and they don't even know it."

Mr. Lovelace leaned towards Sirus with his one eye sizzling. "Whatever you and them Yankee ghost chasers come up with, I'm in. You can count on that."

The two men sat quietly, alone in their thoughts, struggling with events they were helpless to control. Keeping watch atop his stool at the counter, Sirus spotted a car with two men turning into the parking lot. The old man jumped from his seat and threw some money onto the greasy counter. "I think that's them—my ghost hunters. Stay around where I can find ya, Ned. We's gonna have to stir up some crazy critters tonight, or these fellas is gonna think I'm just as crazy as everybody else done does around here, and then I'm gonna be in big trouble. I'm gonna need your help."

"Will do," Lovelace responded with a confident wink. "We'll give them boys a show they won't never forget."

Weary from their travels, the two men got out of the car and stretched as Sirus hurried towards them. One of the men, short and skinny and appearing to be in his early forties, wore a Union Jack bandana on his head. On his face, he had a scraggly goatee and thick glasses. He wore a gray shirt with no sleeves, displaying his lack of muscle and aversion to the sun, and long dark green shorts with large pockets on the sides. Leather sandals scarcely covered his sunburned feet.

"Hello. You must be Mr. Payne." The short man spoke rapidly with a distinct Eastern accent. "Sorry we're late." He extended his hand to Sirus. "I'm Jerry Finnell."

On the opposite side of the vehicle, a bald man with a thick mustache nodded. He was slightly taller and thicker than his partner, though similarly lacking muscle and sunburned just as bad. "And I'm Louis Steadman," he said as he walked around the car to meet Sirus.

"Nice to meet ya. I'm real darn glad you-all decided to come. Things is gettin' a little crazy round here." Sirus put his hands on his hips. "I hope ya don't mind the heat. We ain't had a good rain in these parts for quite awhile. Did you find Lone Jack okay?"

"Actually we did," Jerry answered. "Our only trouble was gettin' a bus to take us to the car rental location."

Sirus gestured to the Crossroads Café. "You guys must be thirsty. Wanna go inside and get some lemonade or ice tea or somethin'?"

"If it's all the same to you, Mr. Payne," Louis responded. "We'd like to get started. We'd kind of like to check out the town…get our bearings, if you will, and then go check into our hotel. We'll probably sleep a bit, get our equipment ready, and then get out here to do our research when the sun goes down. We'll be working late, that's for sure, so I hope you're up for a long, exhausting night."

Sirus grinned. "I don't mind. I don't mind at all. Actually, that was exactly what I was hopin' to hear."

Jerry pulled the keys to his rental car from one of the many pockets on his shorts and tossed them to the old man. "Then you drive. You're the one who knows where to go around this town to encounter paranormal activity. Show us what you got."

Sirus' grin turned into a large smile from ear to ear. "I'll see what I can do."

He drove the two men north on Bynum until he passed Jack Parsons' farm and the spot where the escaped convicts had been killed, though he thought it best to keep that to himself for the time being. "I'm gonna circle back around here when I can and then I'll drive kinda slow so you can understand where we're at. The ghosts don't seem to move any further than about right here." Not sure if he was intriguing or boring his guests, Sirus tried to think up general topics of conversation. "So, you guys are from Connecticut? What parts?"

"We're from New Haven," Jerry answered from the passenger side of the back seat, speaking so fast Sirus could barely understand him. "We're both college professors in the physics department."

"Wow!" Sirus exclaimed. "I got me a couple regular brainiacs here. New Haven, huh? You-all both teach at Yale? Yale teachers! Ain't that somethin'?"

The two professors quickly turned their attention from Sirus to the passing scenery. "Umm, no," Louis corrected him. "We're actually at Southern Connecticut State University, a fine institution in its own right."

Afraid he might have insulted the out-of-towners, Sirus quickly recovered. "Oh I'm sure it is, sir. Bein' a professor is a mighty impressive accomplishment, no matter where's you doin' it."

"I guess we should apologize, Mr. Payne," Jerry added from the backseat. "We're a little travel weary, to say the least, and slightly agitated. Call it stir crazy or something. You see, ghost hunting is a passion of ours and we've been able to put more time into it recently. We hope to document several cases of ghost sightings and paranormal activity across the country. Then we can transform ghost hunting from our passion to a core discipline of higher learning. So far, we haven't gotten a lot of backing from the university, and even less funding. They seem to think we're just thrill seekers trying to use their funds to tour the world and see 'cool' stuff."

Louis nodded in agreement as he pulled a pair of large prescription sunglasses from a case and put them on. "My colleague is right, Mr. Payne. These phenomena are incredible, but few people see the connection between paranormal activity and physics. It's frustrating. We see that connection and understand its potential, but we're running out of time. It's going to be hard enough to convince the higher-ups with real data and undeniable evidence, let alone with what we've got—several illuminated floating orbs, photographs that are arguably of ghosts in complete form, and several recordings of mumbo–jumbo. All of which are absolutely open to pessimism and debate. Time is running out on our little project of love.

"Right now, it's a hobby that will probably stay that way, but we haven't given up. In fact, when you called we weren't in Connecticut. We got your message while we were in southern Arizona. We called you right away so we could fit you into our schedule. If what you told us is true, this place would be a remarkable find, but I have to admit that, thus far, we've been disappointed and, in a couple instances, mislead by either slightly disturbed people or people hoping to get a name for themselves by pulling a fast one. This has been our fourth summer of endless travel and preparation with few results. In fact, it has started to make me more of a skeptic. I don't have to tell you…"

"What my colleague is saying, Mr. Payne," Jerry interrupted, earning in a stern look from his fellow professor, "is, and this is no offense to you, we are losing our patience a little, and the thought of sitting in this humidity and dreadful heat with mosquitoes sucking pints of needed blood from our bodies doesn't leave us too excited." Jerry pushed his thick glasses up on his nose. "We've been on this mission for four weeks now. We started in New Haven at Albertus Magnus College, where several buildings and locations have confirmed paranormal activity. We spent a week working out of a hot, smelly girls' dorm and got very little of significance. In fact, I felt we should have left days before we did, but, of course, I was ignored." Jerry shot a disapproving glance of his own at Louis. "Then we traveled to Gettysburg. The air was thick and you could just feel that something abnormal and real was there. You could smell it. We got several wonderful pictures of orbs, but that was it. And Gettysburg is one of the most haunted places on the planet, but it just wasn't our night."

"You mean our two weeks, Jerry," Louis interrupted, more like he was hurling a rock than correcting a fact. "Let's not forget we were there for two weeks. After that, we went to Tombstone Cemetery in Arizona. Again, you could feel it in the air. Shivers went up your spine 'cause you just knew you were being watched, but nothing but orbs again. Next we went to Tucson, where there's a theatre with several confirmed sightings of a known ghost. We didn't get much of anything there and even our equipment picked up very little."

"Of course not. I told you that one was a waste of time." Jerry returned fire. "And that's when we flew to Kansas City. We'll spend a couple of days following up on your sightings, then we're off to investigate the Lemp Mansion for two days in St. Louis and then head back east. We have a stop planned at Mammoth Cave National Park in Kentucky. Civil War-era slaves guided many people through those caves, and there've been over one hundred and fifty sightings of the slaves still roaming the various recesses, just as they did in the 1800s. Finally, we'll investigate the Chesapeake and Ohio Canal National Historic Park in Maryland. In 1906, a miner was killed by an explosion there and, since then, spirits known as 'Tommy Knockers,' are said to haunt every shaft of the mine. Two years later, the mine closed for good because a security guard encountered a ghost that appeared human, but with eyes glowing red, like fire, and a ten-foot-long tail."

Louis cleared his throat loudly, covering his mouth politely, though the other two knew his real intention was to drown out Jerry. "Now, Mr. Payne, we will want to get as much information as we can about the historic battle that took place here. Then we'll want to get as much detail as we can about the various sightings that have occurred and their general locations. After that, Jerry and I will drive to Lee's Summit, check into our hotel, charge up the batteries for our equipment, double-check to make sure everything is in working order, and then catch a few winks before we get started tonight."

"Right," Sirus responded. "It's gonna be a full moon and still no rain. Them conditions seem to get 'em all worked up, so I'm crossin' my fingers. We should have ya talk to Mrs. Morgan first, though. She runs the museum and cemetery, and she knows the battle frontwards and backwards, every slight detail. But you can't go tellin' her you're ghost hunters. She'll freak out and probably get you run on outta town. They got the anniversary of the battle on Saturday. She's expectin' about a thousand folks from all around. She won't want you-all stirrin' up trouble and scarin' people off. But she's the best for tellin' what happened and where duri'n the battle. After ya talk to her, you can go back to Lee's Summit and then come to my place about eight o'clock. Me and another feller who's had hisself a few run-ins with the ghosts of Lone Jack will tell ya everythin' ya want to know about them creatures from beyond the grave."

***

Sirus sat in his living room, in a chair next to his fireplace, fidgeting like a caged animal. Jerry sat on the couch taking notes on a legal pad, hanging on to the old man's every word. "So these Union soldiers attacked you? Stabbed you in the leg and sliced your bicep?"

"That's right," he answered, showing less and less emotion as the interrogation dragged on.

Louis, pacing back and forth behind the couch with an overabundance of energy, stopped and stared at his colleague. "You've asked him that ten times now, Jerry. He answers 'yes' every time."

"Back off, Louis!" Jerry shouted. "Just back off! I'm not going to tell you again." The distressed ghost hunter pushed his glasses up onto his forehead and rubbed his eyes. "My god, it's hot in here. I'm sweating all over the paper. Now, Mr. Payne, do you take any medication?"

"Just some pills for arthritis and cholesterol. They's prescribed by my doctor and don't cause a person to hallucinate, if that's what you's askin'."

"And the ghosts that attacked you...the one named Copeland had a long white beard and rotting human face?"

"Yes." Sirus sighed.

Louis scurried over to the equipment lying next to the front door and checked it for the hundredth time. It appeared ready and operating perfectly. He buzzed over to the window. "Holy cow! I think there's one in the yard! Get the camera! He's walking towards the door!"

As the two men leaped into action Sirus put his head in his hands. "That's just Ned Lovelace. I asked him to join us 'cause he's seen some weird stuff in these parts, same as me. He ain't no ghost. He's a hundred percent human." The frustrated old man dropped his hands away from his face. "Well, he does got him a glass eye, so I guess he's just ninety-nine percent human. He's gonna get a kick outta you guys. I think this town is better off with them ghosts."

Jerry banged the camera back on the floor after the false-alarm sighting. "Come on, Louis. You can't distinguish between a flipping ghost and a real person?"

"Careful with that!" Louis shouted in response to his colleague's treatment of the expensive and vital equipment. "It was a false sighting! I apologize! Like you've never had one! The guy has got a long gray beard and he looks half dead! It was an honest mistake!"

When Ned entered the home, Sirus made the necessary introductions with waning enthusiasm. The gray-bearded man took a seat on the couch and politely took off his hat. His hair was combed and greased to perfection, while his Sunday best attire adorned his crippled body. "What you all dressed up for, Ned?" Sirus asked.

"This here is like a night out for me. Ain't had me one of them in as long as I can remember. I figured I'd look my best, especially if I'm gonna die."

"So Mr. Lovelace," Jerry continued, flipping to a new page in his legal pad, "you've seen some of the same apparitions as Mr. Payne? Could you tell me what you've seen?"

Ned waved the question off as if he were swatting a fly. "Na. I'll just show you when we get out there, if it's all the same to you. It's already about six hours past my bedtime, so I'd kinda like to get this show on the road. But if you ain't sure if you'll be able to identify the ghosts, they'll be the monsters with hideous dead faces that'll be tryin' to kill ya."

"Well, sir," Jerry countered, tapping his pen on his note pad, "I kind of have some questions I need answered here, just to know what we are dealing with."

"Like what?" Ned asked.

"Like, have either of you been diagnosed with the beginning stages of Alzheimer's? Or have you had a catscan recently, or suffered from sleep disorders? Do you have severe mood swings or suffer

from depression? How about tense, severe headaches? Have either
of you seen a therapist or psychiatrist?"

Louis threw his hands in the air. "Well, if you're going to ask
them fifteen questions without allowing either man to answer, why
even bother, Jerry?"

"I made the list of questions, Louis!" the ghost hunter retaliated.
"You never even thought of using a list of questions to sort out which
sightings were real and which were induced by paranoia or mental
deficiency!"

"You made up the questions?" the bald ghost chaser replied. "You
thought up the list? You, you, you. That's all you talk about. What
you did. What about me?"

"I'm thinkin' maybe you two're the ones that should be seein'
a therapist," Ned stated. "You oughtta try ya one of them couples'
counselors."

"Enough already." Sirus jumped up out of his chair. "This is
ridiculous. All you two do is argue. I suggest that, when ya get back
to Connecticut, you take a break from each other. This here trip of
yours, with you-all cooped up in hotels, and cars, and planes together,
is gonna make ya end up killin' each other. You's givin' me a headache.
The fact is, I'm relyin' on you two and, so far, all I've seen ya do is
bicker. Neither one of ya has actually ever seen a ghost, just orbs. I've
done my share of readin'. A lot of folks say orbs can be reasonably
explained. Are you guys really as good as you said you was when I
called? Do ya know what you're doin'?"

Louis crossed his arms, sweat rolling from his bald head and
stinging his eyes. "Well, okay then. Now we can be honest. The fact
is, Mr. Payne, we don't trust you anymore than you trust us. No,
neither one of us has actually seen a ghost, only the orbs. That's
actually not uncommon. What you have encountered, however,
is completely out of the norm and, to be quite frank, totally
unbelievable. I mean, come on. Ghosts that make contact with
humans, and not just for a split second, but long-lasting contact?
Heck, according to you they even attacked you and tried to kill
you! That's completely absurd, if you ask me, and I think you're
making this whole thing up, whether it's in your own mind or an
attempt to make us look stupid. You could be taking us on a wild
goose chase."

Sirus shook his head as he listened. "Okay. I'll give ya that. But now I'm gonna say somethin'. I'm depending on you two more than ya know. We'll show ya the ghosts, but you guys better hold up your end of the bargain."

Jerry adjusted the bandana on his head and put his hands out, hoping to calm the situation. "Let's just take it easy here. We're all in this together. I just want to get through these questions. It won't take more than another hour."

Ned slowly climbed out of his seat. "Aw, to heck with your dumb questions, ghostboy. Grab them daggum cameras and crap and let's go chase us down some ghosts."

***

The cemetery—without having to say a word to one another, Sirus and Ned knew the best ghost-hunting grounds would be the Lone Jack Cemetery. They drove the Connecticut men's rental car there, just a mile from Sirus' home, and parked in front of the museum. Bursting at the seams with excitement, the two ghost chasers dug through the trunk, gathering their overwhelming supply of equipment. Sirus and Ned, in contrast, brought only one thing each…weapons. Ned belted a fancy leather two-gun holster around his waist and loaded his prized Colt revolvers, while Sirus placed a handful of shells in his pocket, loaded his twelve-gauge, and *clicked* the barrel shut. As Jerry worked the strap of his night vision goggles over his bandana, he stared uneasily at the old men.

"Come on. You can't seriously be taking loaded guns into a public historical site. I am not comfortable with this at all. It's bad enough that—no offense here, but I feel I need to be brutally honest—I have an aversion to guns, but–again, no offense—you two are a little old to be driving, let alone waving firearms around. And, Mr. Lovelace, you, sir, have two pistols and only one eye. How does that work? What if you were to accidentally shoot someone? And when I say 'someone', I mean *me*."

Ned ran the cylinder across his wrinkled hand, causing the old pistol to buzz like a large bumblebee. Feeling confident that the gun's action was operating properly, he dropped it into the holster. "Hey, you boys brought what ya felt you needed, and we brought what we felt. And, to answer your question, I actually shoot better with the pistol on the side of my glass eye. But enough with all this messin' around. Let's get down to business."

Louis placed a large, cumbersome movie camera with a long round lens on his shoulder. He pointed at a spot in the darkest corner of the property, just north of the cemetery and the third trench of buried soldiers. "Mrs. Morgan told us earlier this afternoon that the blacksmith shop was located there. The Union leader, Major Foster, I believe she said his name was, used the blacksmith shop as his headquarters after the Cave Hotel came under heavy fire and forced him to find a more secure location." The professor moved his hand southwest. "That's where Mrs. Morgan said the Cave Hotel sat. And then north of there, on the same side of the street, is Dr. Winfrey's house, which used to be right where that Baptist Church is now. The hedgerow that was so important during the battle is probably these same trees and you can see that they ran north and south here in front of the cemetery."

"Get to your point, Louis," Jerry demanded. "I'm already getting chewed to death by these carnivorous bugs they have out here. Get through your irritating monologue and let's get set up."

Louis glared at his colleague and continued his drawn-out soliloquy mostly out of spite. "The blackjack oak tree that gave the town its name stood just on the other side of the fence as you head through the gates of the cemetery, according to Ms. Morgan. Major Foster positioned the two James Cannons he had with him near the blacksmith shop and placed them so they controlled both ends of the street, an intimidating and frightening presence, I am sure. And finally, all the fighting was done at close range across Bynum Road, right here. The Confederates were mainly armed with shotguns, which have limited range. The soldiers were positioned no more than sixty feet from each other across that road and, more often than not, the fighting was intense and bloody hand-to-hand combat."

"Thanks for the history lesson," Mr. Lovelace sneered. "I've been waitin' for some Yankee to come here and tell me what happened in the battle of Lone Jack—the place I done lived my whole life. Now I can die a happy man."

Jerry tossed the straps to a Nikon camera around his neck and shoved a sound recorder into one of his many pockets. Sirus stared at the man completely bogged down with electronic devices and gadgets. "You look like a Radioshack done fell down on top of ya. How the heck you know what all that is, and where it's located on your body?"

"Easy." Jerry beamed with pride. "I drew an exact picture of my body to scale and indicated on the drawing exactly where everything goes. Then I memorized it, and tested my reflexes and reaction time for retrieving any item I have with me. Anything I need, I can get to within .21 seconds. Trust me; I've tested it."

"You still live at home with your mother, don't ya, son?" Ned deduced.

Shocked and embarrassed by Ned's assessment, Jerry studied the perceptive man. "How did you know that?"

"Ya don't gotta have you a doctorate and a buncha data to figure out some things, son," the old man responded. "Some things is kinda obvious."

"Come on," Louis instructed. "Let's get into position where the blacksmith shop used to be. We'll hide next to the steps in front of that covered ceremonial stand."

With the same enthusiasm of the scout, Bloody Knife, who tried to warn General Custer at The Little Big Horn, Sirus shook his head. "So ya want us to take a position about where them Union James Guns was at durin' the battle? Okay…"

***

The full moon illuminated the acres of neatly cut grass. The four men felt like spectators sitting in the shadows, looking out across a football field, waiting for the game to start. An owl's hoot echoed in the distance as Jerry swatted his neck. "Dang these bugs are everywhere. They're eating me alive. Hand me that bug repellent."

The men had held their position in the shadows for nearly three hours without sight or sound of the spirits. "This is ridiculous. I knew it," Louis fussed. "This is going nowhere." He raised his voice and called out to the unkown. "If something's out there, show yourself. Give us a sign. Talk to us and let us know who you are." The air was silent. A bat fluttered its wings above them and disappeared. The professor shouted out again. "If there is someone, a spirit in this cemetery, show yourself. Break a branch. Show us some sign. Tell us your name."

As Jerry covered his scrawny, sunburned body with insect repellent, a rustling sound drifted from the dense vegetation east of the museum. "I heard me a noise," Sirus whispered. "What was it?"

"I heard it too," Jerry crowed.

Louis checked his camera for the thousandth time. "If someone's out there, show yourself. Give us a sign. Tell us who you are." There was nothing.

Twenty more minutes passed. The men scanned their perimeter, waiting for a sign, but the field remained eerily quiet. Jerry jumped to his feet. "I've had it. These bugs are driving me crazy. Give me the bug spray again."

"Will you shut up?" his irritated colleague begged. "You're like a little kid. Can't sit still for a second."

Declaring a war of his own on the bloodsucking critters, Jerry attacked his limbs with the spray, the hissing of the can and powerful odor of the chemical penetrating the air. Instantly, the ruckus in the tall grass next the museum returned. "It's there again!" Jerry whispered.

Knowing what he did about the nature of the ghosts of Lone Jack, Sirus raised his shotgun to the ready position. "Wait a minute. Spray that repellent again."

"Right," Louis agreed. "Keep spraying the repellent, Jerry. Ghosts often react to strong odors. It makes them agitated."

"Agitated?" Mr. Lovelace repeated with a chuckle. "Oh, boy. We're in big trouble."

Jerry quickly grabbed a second can and, with one in each hand, sprayed them in front of him. Sirus felt his hair stand up on his arms and legs, not sure if it was caused by the electricity in the air or his own fear. As the professor continued to empty the cans into the open, the disturbance in the grass returned, only this time louder, more chaotic and nerve-racking.

With his camera locked securely to his shoulder and a device in his left hand, Louis stood up and walked slowly in the direction of the noise. "I'm getting some good readings," he said. "It's saying there is a strong source of heat coming from the vegetation."

Jerry grabbed a contraption dangling from his side and joined his comrade. "Me, too. The air is charged. It's magnetized! Serious electrical readings!"

As Ned reached for his pistols, Sirus moved to one knee. "I would sit back down if I was you two."

The noise intensified as the ghost chasers inched closer with light, deliberate steps. A chilling voice sliced through the balmy air. "We go for the guns," it moaned. "Take the guns."

"Did you get that on tape?" Louis squealed.

Jerry quickly dropped the gauge he was holding and searched through the various items dangling from his body. Like a desperate man fumbling for his keys in a horror movie, the professor scrambled from one gadget to the next. "Yeah…I don't know! Wait! It's here! No! I don't know!"

Sirus and Ned looked at each other and shook their heads in frustration. "So much for his .21 seconds to find any of that crap. Might wanna try Plan B," Ned reasoned.

"I don't know," Sirus said. "I don't like this. Them fellas is gonna get themselves killed. Be ready."

"Come on, Jerry," Louis scolded. "I told you we don't need all of those instruments. I asked you to leave half of them in the car. In fact, I don't know why you bring any of them along anyway. You should've left them in Connecticut. Most of them are completely unnecessary and just get us strip-searched at every airport. It's ridiculous."

"Hey," Jerry shot back, continuing his helpless search for the recorder, "Don't get snippy with me, Louis! I'm the one who has to do everything. You hold the camera and heat senser. That's it. I'm in charge of this stuff. I do the interviews. I make our travel arrangements. I do the reports. I'm in charge of the publications, the findings, and the files. It's all me, Louis! You don't do anything!"

"Just get the voice recorder going, Jerry!" Louis pressed his eye against the camera and aimed it at the tall weeds. "Roll sound! Roll sound! Do it, Jerry! And shut up about it!"

"Oh, man," Ned chuckled in the shadows. "The strangest thing up in this here cemetery is these two arguin' Yankees."

"Oh, no." Louis jerked the cumbersome camera from his shoulder and held it in front of him. Frantic, he started pressing buttons and whacked it on the side. "Aw, man! The battery is dead. I have to get my spare."

Jerry, who'd finally located the recorder and had it stretched out in front of him, dropped his hand to his side. "You've got to be kidding me, Louis! You're an idiot! The battery died because you can't stop tinkering with that thing. Turning it on. Turning it off. Turning it back on again. Because of your obsessive-compulsive behavior, you caused the very outcome you were hoping to avoid!"

"Don't talk down to me, Jerry, with your psychoanalytical babble," Louis retaliated. "I don't live with my mother. I think you might be the one in need of psychiatric therapy. You can't leave the slightest thing…"

Sirus placed his hand on his forehead and sighed. He returned his gaze to the nagging, useless ghost hunters, concluding they were more of a hindrance than help in getting rid of the ghosts of Lone Jack. Shaking his head in frustration, he spotted something moving in the tall grass. Before he could shout a warning, the being leaped from the brush and raced for the unsuspecting ghost hunters. With glowing red eyes under the bill of his gray cap, the creature charged with frightening determination, a glistening bayonet aimed right at Louis' chest. His legs stinging from his uncomfortable position on the ground, Sirus stumbled to his feet.

A bloodcurdling battle cry shattered the silence and brought the professors' argument to a complete halt. The soldier ghost raced across the grass with the bayonet headed straight for Louis' sternum. Sirus leveled his shotgun. "Get down!" he yelled and fired. The heavy load caught the demon in the face, scattering chunks of his skull across the ground.

The impact and sound of the blast sent Jerry tumbling. "What was that?" Jerry cried as Sirus grabbed the overloaded pack mule by the arm and yanked him off the grass.

"They's ghosts of the Rebels!" Sirus hollered. "Come on! We need to take cover!"

"Get them cannons!" a demonic voice howled from the shadows. "Take them James Guns!"

Louis cradled the camera to his chest and sprinted after Sirus and Jerry. A phantom with eyes like smoldering coal and bloody green goo seeping from open wounds on his face blocked the terrified man's escape. The beast's gray cap sat low on his skull and a brown goatee covered his rotted mouth. The creature pulled a knife from his belt, his skeleton hand crackling like cinders, and reached for a pistol with the other. Sparks exploded from the muzzle. Louis jumped in the air. With eyes like saucers, he scanned his torso for a bullet hole. Shocked that he wasn't mortally wounded, Louis turned to flee. The demon Rebel raised his knife and lunged. Hidden in the shadows, Ned cocked his revolvers and pelted the soldier with rapid fire. The bullets tore through the creature's gray uniform. The soldier gyrated with the impact of each connecting shot before collapsing to the ground.

Panic racing through him like an ice-cold shower, Louis cradled his camera as if it were a child's teddy bear. A gray soldier pounced on his back, driving the professor to his knees. As Jerry and Sirus rushed to Louis' aid, three more Rebel ghouls attacked. A beast with its cheek and nose ripped from its face swung a sword at Jerry, who jumped out of the way just before being sliced in two. The soldier whirled back around and grabbed the professor by the throat. "Give us the key!" he growled, squeezing the man's thin neck.

Another soldier thrust his bayonet at Sirus' face. The old man bashed the deadly weapon away with his forearm and rammed the butt of his shotgun into the creature's skull. The ghoul shook off the blow and lunged forward again. Sirus kicked him in the chest, shattering his ribcage like an ancient ceramic pot and getting his foot caught in the phantom's grisly torso. The old man hopped up and down on one leg until ultimately falling to the ground.

Jerry hacked at the skeleton's arms, struggling to get the creature off his neck. He punched the beast's face and pried at his grip. The soldier raised his sword high above his head, ready to deliver the death blow. The professor's eyes rolled back as he lost conciousness. With his foot still caught in the dead soldier's ribcage, Sirus steadied his shotgun. The blast caught the creature in the side of the face as he brought the sword down, sending his skull tumbling through the air. As the creature's headless body fell, Jerry dropped to his backside, sucking at the air.

Sirus kicked the gruesome torso from his foot with one final thrust of his leg and scrambled to his feet. A few yards away, Louis battled his attacker, using the camera to block a bayonet aimed at his face. The desperate professor screamed in horror, realizing he wasn't going to fend off the blows for much longer. As Ned leveled his revolver on the beast with a trembling hand, a ghastly, chilling voice echoed across the field. "They's g'tting the James Guns! Attack! Keep 'em from gettin' the cannons!"

A force of blue-uniformed creatures appeared out of the darkness from the location of the blacksmith shop. The monsters flooded the field like a wave and engaged the Rebel beasts. As the demons collided in the middle of the battlefield, Sirus loaded his shotgun and crouched in preparation for the coming attack. With one barrel he cut a charging

Union monster in two, and with the other, a Union ghoul who was about to run Jerry through with a bayonet.

As the Rebel demon continued to pin Louis to the ground and bash the poor man with merciless blows, a blue-clad soldier drove a knife through the right side of the zombie's breast. The creature collapsed on top of the helpless man. Unable to reach the professor through the chaos all around them Sirus, Ned, and Jerry retreated to the edge of the cemetery, staying alert as they watched the chaos unfold. A Rebel tore Louis' camera from his grasp and sprinted for cover in the dense vegetation east of the museum. Two Union soldiers gave chase and blasted the gray-uniformed creature with their powerful muskets, ripping his back apart and sending the camera skidding across the grass. One of the Union creatures snatched it from the ground and darted back with the device locked in his arms.

To their right, a Union soldier, with one human eye and the other a hollow socket, charged towards the hiding men. Ned hammered the beast in the forehead, sending his blue cap scooting across the ground. Two officers, one Union and one Rebel, squared off in the middle of the conflict, each holding a pistol and saber. The Union creature swung his mighty sword, missing his mark as the Rebel leaped backwards. The gray officer countered, his saber narrowly missing separating the Union officer's head from his body. The Rebel fired his pistol with a dark plume of smoke and bright sparks hurling from the barrel. The shot caught the Union officer in the thigh, sending him to his knees. The Rebel fired again; the shot hit the Union officer in the left arm and ripped it to pieces. His body shredded from his wounds, the Union creature aimed his pistol and fired as the gray demon raised his saber to smash his foe's exposed collarbone. The bullet struck the Rebel officer in the stomach, splattering blood and rotten guts onto the trunks of the Osage orange trees behind him. The Rebel staggered backwards and then collapsed. Realizing he'd won the duel, the wounded Union officer released his grip on his saber and pistol. The weapons floated to the ground. The beast let out a final bloodcurdling gasp and fell to his back.

"The Rebels killed Captain Long!" a voice hissed through the smoke. "Them boys done killed Captain Long!" The fierce hand-to-hand fighting raged on, until one by one, the ghosts faded, eventually disappearing into the night as if it were all just a treacherous nightmare.

Only the body of the fallen Captain Long remained, opaque, but still visible on the battlefield.

Laying flat on the ground with his hands clamped to his chest, Louis inhaled like a man who'd just run a marathon, his body soaked with sweat. Sirus, Ned, and Jerry crawled from their hiding place in the shadows next to the cemetery fence and approached the body of the Union officer. "Louis," Sirus whispered, "are you okay? Are ya hurt bad?"

Louis checked his body. "I'm fine," he answered with a trembling voice. "Just think I crapped my pants." The professor crawled to his feet and started towards the body of Captain Long.

When the four disheveled men reached the corpse, Sirus poked the beast's left shoulder with the barrel of his loaded shotgun, checking to see if he had any fight left in him. A foul odor drifted from his body. Torn and rotting flesh covered the left side of his face. The human-looking portions of his body and face were covered in blood and smeared with black gunpowder. The soldier beast's shirt was open. Bugs sprinted along his ribs and feasted on his lungs. On the other side of his chest, blood dried on human skin, resembling any injured man the four had ever seen. One of the soldier's eyes was recognizable as that of a man as well, but the other was a ghastly red ball. His tattered leg hung by loose skin where the Rebel officer had shot him.

As the four men circled around the ghost, the Union officer coughed. Blood squirted through his clenched, jagged teeth and trickled down his chin. The beast raised his head and inspected his situation. "My leg must be amputated," he moaned. "Take me off this battlefield." The four men stared at each other, paralyzed by the tragic scene and devilish voice of the ghoul. "Give us the key," the ghost of Captain Long begged. "Give us the key." The creature let out a long, steady moan and gradually disappeared into the deadly night, returning to his perpetual hell.

With only the smell of gunpowder and smoke from the muskets lingering in the field, the four men stood quietly, trying to make sense of it all. "Okay," Jerry said, wiping the grime and sweat from his face. "I believe you, gentlemen. There are ghosts here in Lone Jack."

Ned chuckled with a sharp grin. "Well, if it makes ya feel any better, I don't think them ghosts liked you boys any better than you liked them."

8

Jared ran through the living room and out the back door of the house, letting the screen door slam behind him. He had slept very little, tossing, turning and fighting through intense nightmares; most of them involving Suds. The boy's race with Dozer was to take place in the evening. Jared had little hope Suds would make it to the finish line in one piece, let alone actually beat Dozer, but he planned on sticking by his friend's side to the bitter end. Still in his pajamas, he walked through the grass and looked around the yard.

"Mornin', kiddo." Virgil came out of the barn and greeted his grandson. "Need me to get ya some breakfast?"

"Na," the boy answered, "I already ate some cereal." He continued to search the area. "Where's Dad?"

"Him and Ms. Ramsey went to the Farmer's Market in Lee's Summit to get some fresh vegetables and fruit. They wanted to get there early before it got too hot. Then I think they was gonna head down to The Plaza to eat lunch. Don't expect him back till late this evenin'."

"We've got all kinds of vegetables," Jared wondered. "Why does he have to go to Lee's Summit to buy 'em?"

Walking by the boy, Virgil patted him gently on the head. "Sometimes gettin' vegetables ain't exactly gettin' vegetables, if you know what I mean." He stopped and smiled at Jared. "We did all right, didn't we, kiddo? This here is their third meetin' in four days. I'd call that a case of puppy love, but I'm just an old man. I ain't sure how it works these days."

"Shoot," Jared snapped. "I was hoping to ask him if I could stay over at my friend Suds' house tonight."

"Is he the tall skinny kid who's a tad country dumb? Keg Davis' boy? The good baseball player?"

"Yeah. Can I stay at his house tonight? Please."

"Well, we'll call your dad on his cell phone and ask, but it's fine by me. Just don't go gettin' inta any mischief, and I want to hear it from his mom's lips that it's okay with them that ya stay over, so I wanna talk to her first."

"Thanks, Grandpa." Jared hugged the frail man around the waist, feeling as though he was squeezing a pile of thin sticks. "Are you feeling okay, Grandpa? I'll stay here tonight if you need me to help take care of you."

Virgil pursed his lips and crinkled his nose. "Gosh, no. I'm fine. I'm feelin' pretty good today, breathin' a little better. You're ten years old, kiddo. You need to live like a ten-year-old boy, and not have all this stress and worry in your life. Ya worry about me. Ya worry about your dad. Life's too short for all that, and too new for you to be growin' up before you're supposed to. Go and have fun, but don't be doin' nothin' foolish. I mean it."

The two Millhouse men walked to the back steps and sat down. They rested with their elbows on their knees, staring out across the sprawling acreage of Millhouse land. "Hey, Grandpa, what was it like in the war?"

Surprised by the boy's question, Virgil hesitated and looked at his grandson. "Cold. Miserable. Fight for inches. Every foot seeming a big waste of time and life, but that ain't what you's really fightin' for." He ran his wrinkled hand through the boy's hair. "Ya fight for family, things closest and most important to ya. What you believe in. It's all worth it in the end, though sometimes it don't seem so at the time. But, in life, you always want to do what's right, even if it's hard and slightly scary. And you don't want to let people push you around, neither, 'cause they'll keep pushin' and you'll just keep on gettin' pushed around."

***

Jerry sat at the table in Sirus' kitchen, typing on his laptop like a beat reporter with a looming deadline. Scattered bumps, cuts, and bruises all over his face and body testified to his ghostly encounter. Occasionally he'd apply a pack of frozen vegetables to his cheekbone as he stopped to think about what to document next. There was so much to remember and get recorded. Across the table, Louis held a pile of ice cubes wrapped in a hand towel pressed against his mouth and nose. Both men wore only their underwear, as the temperature in Sirus' home was unbearable even in the early morning hours.

Too excited to sleep, the men had gone there after their harrowing engagement with the ghosts of Lone Jack to recount the course of events over and over until they passed out from exhaustion barely an hour before sunrise.

Sirus rolled out of bed and limped into the kitchen, surprised to find his guests already awake. "I reopened the wound on my thigh. Didn't know it till I woke up. There's a big bloodstain on my sheets." The old man slapped Louis on his shoulder. "How's the nose?" He limped to the kitchen counter before the battered ghost hunter could respond. "I'll make us some coffee."

As Sirus poured the grounds into the filter, Ned shuffled out of the spare bedroom and through the living room to join the others. "Mornin', everybody." He took a seat between the two Connecticut professors. "Figured you fellers would already be on your way to St. Louis by now, or straight back east, for that matter."

"Common sense would suggest that, yes," Louis mumbled like he'd just gotten a shot of Novacaine at the dentist's office, unable to breathe through his swollen nose or to work his throbbing lips. "In fact, it would demand it. But one thing's for sure about professors… they're a dumb bunch."

"That's right," Jerry confirmed, continuing to attack the keyboard like an expert pianist, "We're staying. We've cancelled the rest of our trip and will be here in Lone Jack until next Sunday. You work your whole life to stumble across a phenomenon like this. What we've seen and encountered is like discovering the Dead Sea Scrolls, or the very Ark of the Covenant. I wouldn't leave now if my life depended on it."

"It just might," Ned pointed out.

Sirus grabbed four cups from the kitchen cabinet and set three in front of his guests. "So, Louis, how did we make out?"

Louis removed the wrapped ice from his nose and pulled his head upright. "We didn't," he responded. "The battery died on the camera and before I could change it, they were on us. I don't think it would've mattered much, though. The camera is all beat up. It even has three holes in it where the zombie ran a bayonet clean through the side of it. It's toast. But luckily we brought a spare video camera. Not as good, but it will work."

The corners of Jerry's mouth dropped. "*Wouldn't have mattered.* Come on, Louis. You could drop that camera from a thirty-story building and still be able to recover the footage as long as the tape was rolling. Admit it. You screwed up. You blew it. Our first real experience with paranormal activity—in fact, the most amazing encounter ever in the history of paranormal phenomena—and you run the battery dry before we even get set up. It's ridiculous."

"Well, what about you, Jerry?" Louis countered. "You were in charge of the EVP equipment and the EMF detector. You never even got the voice recorder going. You had it clutched in your hand and yet... we got nothing."

"I'm sorry, Louis," Jerry sniped sarcastically. "Please forgive me. It's just that it's kind off hard to ask for an interview with a soldier zombie when it's crushing your windpipe with one hand —a hand consisting solely of bone—and trying to slice you in half with the three-foot-long saber he's holding in the other! Not to mention that we had a guy with a glass eye shooting anything and everything that moved in the area!"

"Man, you guys don't ever ease off, do ya?" Ned chuckled.

"So that's what they is?" Sirus asked as he joined the team at the table and started pouring coffee into their cups. "Zombies?"

Jerry adjusted his glasses on his face and tossed his hands in the air. "Mr. Payne, I don't know how to classify any of this. This is all foreign to me—foreign to the whole paranormal community, for that matter. I mean, from what I can tell, these demons aren't occupying their former bodies in the sense that a zombie would. There'd be collapsed graves and open caskets all over the area. But they are not ghosts, either. They aren't spirits or apparitions. They're real. At least, what had me by the throat was real. Very real. But they're not human. These ghosts have transformed into something you can touch and feel, and they're touching and feeling in return... violently."

"Let's talk about what we do know," Louis suggested. "That might help us understand what they are doing and what they want, and might help us get them out of your town.

"First, we know that the creatures responded to the strong odor of the bug spray. It got them agitated. We also know that they reenacted part of the battle where the Rebels try to take the James Guns. The zombie that attacked me wanted my camera, as if it were one of the guns. The Union soldiers that appeared in response shot the Rebel as he was taking off with the video camera and brought it back. I was of little consequence at that moment. They never attacked me."

"Tell me about the fight for the James Guns again," Jerry requested.

Ned cleared his throat and stroked his scraggly beard. "Well, as you've done been told, the guns changed hands four times during the five-hour fight. At first Major Emory Foster, the leader of the Union Army during the battle, had 'em stationed near his headquarters at the Cave Hotel. But when that buildin' came under heavy fire, he moved to the blacksmith shop. He positioned the cannons—let's call 'em cannons for now—in front of the blacksmith shop, aimed so they could control both ends of Bynum Road. Bodies of dead soldiers and horses lay scattered and piled all over the place. Many of 'em died trying to get possession of them cannons.

"From inside the blacksmith shop, Major Foster watched as the Rebels regained control of the cannons, killing several Union soldiers and losing several of their own in order to do it, and started rolling them to the other side of the street. Foster knew losing the cannons meant losing the battle. He called on Captain Long to help him retake the mighty guns. The captain was already injured, covered in blood and gunpowder, but, without hesitation, he mustered sixty of his men. With Major Foster and Captain Long leading the charge, the Union regained the cannons, holding them for the rest of the battle.

"But it was costly, as Major Foster and Captain Long were gunned down in the struggle. The major was hit in the back and fell helplessly to the ground, though he didn't die. Forty-eight of Long's sixty men were either killed or wounded in the effort. And, of course, Captain Long had a musket round tear through his leg, crippling the man. Major Foster's brother, Melville, seein' that his brother was hit, ran through the gunfire and attempted to drag the major to safety. Though brave, he too was struck in the chest." Mr. Lovelace paused and sipped his coffee.

"A lotta death and destruction for control of a couple of guns. The ironic thing about it is…after all them dead soldiers on both sides, each one of 'em tryin' to get them James Guns, when the Union left town they rolled the cannons south past the hedgerow. Once they got east of the cornfield, they spiked 'em, makin' the James Guns completely useless, and left 'em hidden in the brush. Ain't that somethin'?"

Jerry typed away, trying to get every intricate detail on record, and paused when he reached the end. "Now, tell us more about Captain Long."

Sirus pushed his coffee mug forward and placed his elbows on the table. "Well, Captain William Long was a brave and respected officer in the Union Army. Before the war started, he commanded the Federal forces in Pleasant Hill, a town about twelve miles southeast of Lone Jack. Pleasant Hill was a town with deep Confederate leanings, but the folks seemed to like and admire Captain Long. He treated them with respect and the town, in turn, respected the captain.

"He befriended a family called Henley, whose farm was across from the Federal garrison. Now, a few days prior to the battle, Vard Cockrell recruited the Henley boys into the Confederate army. When the battle of Lone Jack commenced, the Henley boys rushed to get them a crack at the bluecoats. When the battle was over, James Henley walked through the field completely covered with dead soldiers and horse carcasses. While James stared at the horrific scene, he heard someone call out his name. It was a wounded bluecoat soldier. At first, James couldn't recognize the man lying there with bodies scattered all around him. The wounded soldier's face was too bloody and smeared with gunpowder. He studied the man pretty good until he finally recognized him. It was Captain Long, and he was hurt bad—his leg needed amputating.

"Though Henley was a Rebel, his heart went out to his Union friend—a man he'd known for some time. He had his father, Joseph Henley, bring a wagon from Pleasant Hill and carry Captain Long to his farm. The Henleys cared for Captain Long in their very home. When another'n of the Henley boys, Andrew, made his return home, he'd been wounded in the battle of Lone Jack fightin' for the Confederates, Captain Long asked to see the boy who was recuperating in the room next to his. Andrew limped into the room and the two friends, who were enemies only days before, shook hands and told each other how glad they each was that the other'n was all right. Captain William Long took a turn for the worse and died soon after, still in the care of the Henleys. He spent his last moments of life comfortably in the home of the Rebel sympathizers."

"Well, that would explain his exit last night," Louis stated. "He's probably fought for those James Guns a thousand times since he died. They're caught in a loop and we have to find someway to get them snapped out of it."

"Right," Jerry agreed with his colleague, "but how? What is this key? The monster that choked me demanded one. Captain Long pleaded for a key before he disappeared. Sirus has told us other instances where these demons demanded a key. The key has to have some significance, but what?"

"That's what I done been goin' over in my head a thousand times." Sirus scratched his scruffy beard. "But there ain't no key. Nobody who's ever done studied that battle has said nothin' about a key. It don't make no sense."

"That's the point though, Mr. Payne," Louis explained. "The key might not be part of the battle, unlike the James Guns, or Dr. Winfrey's home, or the Cave Hotel. That's where we need to think beyond the facts and events of the battle."

"Then what is it?" Sirus asked, feeling a bit overwhelmed. "If that's the case, it could be anythin'."

Jerry shook his finger in the air and then put it to his chin. "Then let's narrow it down. Let's think about it logically. When the ghosts ask for the key, it's like they forget they are fighting a battle and realize they are spirits trapped between worlds. If you're locked in a prison, or locked out of a car, what do you need? A key. Let's take what they are wanting for what it is. Let's make it simple. They want a key. And why do they want a key?"

"'Cause they's trapped," Ned answered, impressed with himself for being able to follow the conversation.

"Right," Louis responded. "Let's look at more of the facts. Until recently, according to your accounts, these ghosts appeared briefly and not nearly as often. Now they're transforming into…zombies, for lack of a better term, and attacking anything and everything that gets in their way. They're desperate for something. The key they want may just be that. The key to open a door to the other side. We can't look at their transformation as a freak occurrence. It's my belief that it is leading up to something."

"But that still leads us back to the same question," Sirus stated. "What is the key? It could be anythin'. It could be anywhere."

"True," Jerry agreed. "But you're missing a very important point. They want the key. They want the key just as bad as we want to get it for them. They want out of here just as bad as you want them out of here. Right now, they are trapped in…purgatory. The ghosts obviously don't have the key, or they wouldn't be demanding it from us. Maybe they'll give us a clue to its location. Regardless, this key is of great importance. I'll keep reading up on it, but we'll need to be ready at a moment's notice. If they get more aggressive and more agitated, they could tear this town to pieces. We have to do everything in our power to prevent that from happening."

"Can you call for help?" Sirus pleaded.

Jerry shook his head. "Who would believe us? In the field of paranormal phenomena this is without a doubt the most bizarre and spectacular case ever recorded. I don't even believe it. And I saw it with my own two eyes."

***

The ATV buzzed along the bumpy terrain as Suds drove it towards the starting line. The Crossroads Club had stayed steadfastly with him most of the afternoon, doing their best to endure the August heat. Suds cut the engine and pried off the Kansas City Chiefs' football helmet he hadn't worn since he was seven. Unable to find protective headgear suitable for a racer at short notice, the pit crew had come up with the Chiefs' helmet. The boy had taken several practice laps around the recently marked track to be fully prepared for the feat in front of him.

A practical thinker and superior to the rest of the gang when it came to games of logic and geometry, Sweets had laid out the course, scribbling a blueprint with every intricate detail on notebook paper. He had incorporated several of Sirus' suggestions, strategically placing the course in a location with sharp turns and rugged terrain. He hoped to slow Dozer down in certain sections of the track, thus allowing Suds to catch up on the lighter, more agile machine.

Jared spent most of the afternoon sweating and biting his fingernails. The group's nervousness was palpable. Each desperately wanting Suds to win and shut up the mean-spirited Dozer once and for all.

As Suds handed his helmet to Sweets and wiped the dirt from his upper lip on his sleeve, Molly and Jan marched towards the racing crew. "Suds Davis!" Molly yelled as she folded her arms. "Just what do you think you're doing?"

"What does it look like?" Shanks quipped. "Back off, lady! This here is men's stuff."

"I ain't doin' nothin'," Suds fibbed. "I wanted to ride this here ATV, so I did."

"Everybody in class knows you're gonna race Dozer," Jan informed the boys. "The phone's been ringin' off the hook at Molly's house. Her sister was plenty mad, too, 'cause she had to click over every time in case it was their mom. Everybody says Dozer's gonna kill ya."

"What does everybody know?" Porker snapped. "They don't know squat."

Molly looked the round boy up and down. "More than you, Porker. You were the only one in our class who ate the gingerbread house at Christmas last year. That thing sat on the corner of Ms. Ramsey's desk for over a month, and you were sick for a week."

"It was made of bread and candy," the large boy defended himself. "It had icing and everything."

"Ya don't eat everythin' made of food, Porker," Jan explained. "Some stuff is just for lookin' at."

Porker threw his hands in the air, pleading his case. "If ya can't eat it, why would ya make it with food? What's the point of that?"

Though Suds knew little about mechanics, he crouched and inspected the engine, hoping Molly would stop her attack. Jared bent over next to him, staring through the dense stack of metal and wires. "You sure you wanna go through with this, Suds? You don't have to. We could tell Dozer you were sick, or maybe even grounded."

Suds thought about the idea and then shook his head. "Na, I'll do it. I've done had all I can take from that guy. He'd just make it worser on me, and all of us. I gotta do it, Millhouse. I can't back out now."

Sweets wiped dirt from the gas tank and handed Suds the map of the course. "Look at it again, Suds. Memorize it. I got all the holes, fallen trees, and bumpy places marked. I even put a reminder in red ink where we piled fallen limbs and trash we found. Dozer's been all over this area with his ATV, so I'm hopin' he won't figure there's much in the way. Know the course, Suds, know it like the back of your hand. If we start the race just before sunset, the sun will be in Dozer's eyes…and yours, too. If he don't know the course like you do, he'll have to slow down to make out where he's goin', while you can keep on motorin', 'cause you know the course."

Suds snatched the piece of paper from Sweets' hand and studied it briefly. "Geez, man. You done had me look over that thing ten times. I got it. You're as annoyin' as my mother." He returned the map to his pit chief. "Thanks though, Sweetwater."

Feeling as though he would never see his good pal again, Sweets clamped his hand onto Suds' shoulder. "Don't mention it, man."

Wishing their doomed hero a safe voyage and fond farewell, the gang gathered around Suds as he straddled the large ATV. A couple of minutes later, Beans arrived, walking backwards through the grass dragging a large plastic gas can. The skinny boy's body was soaked with sweat from heaving the cumbersome, heavy container through the dense woods. "Here's the can ya wanted, Suds," he said, fighting to catch his breath.

"Thanks, Beans," replied Suds. "Set 'er over there, where the other one is and bring that other can over here, so we can fill this baby up."

Jared paced while Sweets put the final drops of gasoline from the plastic container into the tank. The tall boy looked at his friends, their faces riddled with worry. "Well, all we gotta do now is…wait," Sweets commented with a shrug.

As the seconds ticked by, and the sun dropped lower in the distance, Jared nibbled on his fingers, hoping with all his might that Dozer would be a 'no-show.' Molly grabbed him by his arm and spun him around. "You have to stop him, Jared. He's gonna be in big trouble if he wins or not. What if he gets hurt? Dozer's gonna pound him into hamburger, no matter what."

Jared put his hands out, indicating he'd done all he could do. "I… I…I tried Molly. He wants to go through with it. He's not gonna let anybody talk him out of it, either."

Squatting in the tall grass, picking at the ground, Beans looked over at Sweets. "You told them where we was gonna be, didn't ya, Sweetwater?"

The lean boy continued to clean and tinker with the ATV. "I called him last night at seven, just like Suds told me to. He said he'd be here."

The minutes ticked by with no sign of Dozer. "He ain't showin' up," Porker exclaimed. "I knew he was chicken. You won, Suds! You won by forfeit!"

Jared and the rest of the gang started laughing and cheering, slapping each other on the backs for a job well done, and sighing in relief. As they celebrated, Jared relaxed...until the thunderous roar of a motor in the distance reached his ears.

"Wait a second," Jared hollered, having little effect on the celebration. "Wait a second! I hear something."

Their hearts, overjoyed moments before, sank as the noise intensified and grew closer. "It's them!" Beans shouted, spotting Greeley running through the woods towards the clearing.

The group huddled near their rider. Suds turned to Sweets. "Grab that gas can again and bring it over here." Sweetwater did as ordered and returned to Suds' side. "Make like you's gettin' ready to pour gas in the tank when I tell ya to."

Standing upright as he drove, Dozer entered the arena like a champion gladiator atop a golden chariot drawn by white stallions. Once he spotted his prey, a grin spread across his face. He hit the gas and raced towards them, throwing dust all over the Crossroads gang as he hit the brake and spun out. The large boy glared at Suds and then inspected his ATV. "Well, if it ain't Sucks Davis! Didn't figure you'd show up. Where did you get that piece of crap? I won't even be able to sell that hunk of junk for a nickel."

The Goat jogged into view, carrying a gas can and cackling like a hyena. "Look at that thing! You might as well be on a tricycle! Dozer's gonna bury you on that ridin' lawnmower! Hey, Dozer, when ya win it from Crud, I'll give ya a used stick of gum for it!" The odd-looking boy's laugh rained down like hail.

"You oughtta just leave that thing here and run, Crap!" Greeley chimed in. "That rust bucket's just gonna slow ya down!"

Jared stood sheepishly behind Sweets, his emotions running between extreme fear and anger. As Suds revved the engine to drown out the boys' taunts, Sweets grabbed a second map he'd drawn (one that didn't show the numerous hazards and booby-traps the Crossroads Club had added to the course) from his pocket and approached Dozer as if he were about to feed a hungry bear.

He extended the piece of paper to the boy, who snagged it rudely from his hand. "What the heck is this, geek?" Dozer asked.

"That's the…the…map of the…the course," Sweets stammered in response. "Three laps from…from here, followin' the cleared roads the…the farmers use to get to the back of their fields. You…you start here, follow the path runnin' on the edge of Howser Farm, all the way back around behind Caleb Winfrey Field to here. You… you do that three times. Three laps, then you head back to Howser Farm and race to the far corner. The first one to…to reach the corner entrance to Howser Farm wins. In all, it's about six miles."

Taking a quick glance at the map, Dozer snickered, crumpled up the piece of paper, and chucked it at Sweets. The paper wad hit Sweets' large forehead and bounced to the ground. "Whatever, nerd. It don't matter where we race to or how far. I'm gonna crush you, Scab Davis. You and the rest of these dorks'll be walking home cryin', while I go and throw that pile of crap you call an ATV in the garbage."

"Well, ain't ya gonna even really look at the map of the racetrack?" Porker asked.

"Ha," the Goat barked. "Dozer don't need no map. He's done rode that lap you nerds spent all day drawin' a thousand times. We all know these backwoods roads like the back of our hands. And Dozer knows 'em best of all. He's gonna have Puke Davis beggin' for his mommy halfway around the first lap."

Suds' face flushed with anger as he stared at his opponent. He nodded to Sweets. "Put some more gas in this thing. I don't wanna lose 'cause I ran out."

Sweets picked the can up and held it near his chest. "This here is dang near empty, Suds. You want me to get that other can?"

Suds shook his head. "I can't. If I come home with no gas in that other can, my dad's gonna be mad and I'll get in big trouble. He'll think I was playin' with fire or somethin' and whoop me good." The boy leaned forward and peered into the tank. "I got me enough to get through the race. Plenty, in fact. I won't need to use that other can and get in trouble."

Paying close attention to the conversation, Dozer eyed Suds and then the gas can sitting on the ground near Jared's feet. The boy's face produced a sly grin. "I think I could use me some gas. Greeley, grab that gas can and bring it over here."

Not a bright kid who caught on quickly, Greeley soon developed a sinister smile of his own. "Yeah, Dozer. I'll get ya some gas. I'll get ya some right over here." Salivating like a wild dog, the ugly redhead jogged towards Jared and the can.

Suds and his team sprang into action. Suds leaped from his ATV and attempted to block Greeley's path with Shanks, Beans, and Sweets forming a rearguard next to Jared. "No," Suds yelled. "That's my can! I'll get in trouble! No!"

"Come on, man!" Shanks shouted. "You-all got your own gas!"

"This idn't cool, man!" Porker yelled.

With his cruel leader only a few yards away, Greeley bullied his way past the younger boys, knocking Shanks to the ground and pushing Sweets easily out of his way. The freckled kid reached Jared and stood practically on top of him, towering over him and smiling, meanness seeping through his teeth. Jared shrank inside his body, but managed to hold his ground.

"Don't let him get it, Millhouse!" Shanks screamed, lying in a defeated pile on the ground.

The grin faded from Greeley's face as it turned to utter cruelty. The boy punched Jared in the stomach, causing him to buckle and collapse. Greeley calmly picked up the gas can, while the Goat jeered.

Molly and Jan rushed to Jared. The wind knocked out of him, he clutched his abdomen with both hands. "Leave us alone!" Molly shouted. "Do your stupid race and just leave!"

Shanks peeled his little body off the ground. "The lady's right! Time's a–wastin'! We gonna race or what?"

Adding to the humiliation, Greeley untwisted the cap and carried the plastic container to Dozer's ATV. Suds cried out, "Seriously, man. Don't use that can. It's mine." In stubborn, joyful defiance Dozer unscrewed the cap to his tank, allowing Greeley to pour the newly stolen gasoline into his ATV.

"I'm warnin' ya," Suds continued his plea. "Don't use that can! I'm warnin' ya, Dozer, and everybody here done heard me, you do not want to use that can!" The can chugged and burped as the redhead filled Dozer's machine with cynical satisfaction and triumph. "I'm warnin' ya!"

The Goat stepped around Dozer's ATV and pushed his face towards Suds'. He held his arms out, inviting an attack from Suds or any of the Crossroads gang who dared. "Or what? Huh? Whatta ya gonna do about it, Scum? What are any of ya gonna do? I'll kick the crap outta every last one of y'all!" The Goat pushed Suds, launching him into his rickety ATV.

Suds crawled to his feet, dusted himself off, and boldly returned to his opponent. "That ain't right, man. That's my gas can. I warned ya, Dozer. You shouldn't've used that can."

"That's right, man!" Shanks screamed. "You shouldn't've taken that can!"

Dozer jerked forward on the leather seat as if he was going to punch Shanks in his annoying nose. "Shut it, mouth, or I'll pound your head down like a jackhammer!"

***

The two competitors revved their engines at the starting line while Sweets stood a few feet in front of them holding a red flag, consisting of an old rag tied to a stick, high above his head. The spectators held their breath in anticipation, waiting for the dust to fly. His gut still stinging from getting punched by the pimply-faced Greeley, Jared stood next to Molly and rubbed his stomach.

Desperately hoping Suds would exact revenge, Jared murmured. "Come on, Suds. Beat Dozer. Just this once. Beat him and shut him up for good. Come on, Suds."

"Challenger Suds Davis, are you ready?" Sweets shouted over the noise of the engines. Suds winked through the facemask of his Chief's helmet and nodded. Sweets turned to Dozer. "Challenger Dozer Pittman, are you ready?"

"Just get on with it, geek!" the boy hollered. "Drop the flag already!"

Sweets inhaled, expanding his lungs to full capacity. "On your marks!" He paused. "Get set!" He paused again. "*Go!*"

The larger, experienced rider peeled out in a cloud of dust and quickly moved in front of Suds, whose engine grinded like a rickety chainsaw. The rest of the kids cheered and ran after the ATVs. By the first turn, Dozer had a sizable lead of nearly twenty yards. Things were already looking bad for the inexperienced Suds and his rusty machine, but it was a long race.

Dozer veered to his left to avoid a large limb hidden in the weeds, while Suds hit the gas. He closed the distance between them and attempted to pass on Dozer's inside. Dozer slammed his ATV into Suds', hammering his opponent's fender and making the tires squeal as they rubbed together. Suds fought the front end of his quad, turning the wheels towards the contact to avoid being forced into the woods.

"Back off, loser!" Dozer screamed. "You can't win, doofus! I'll crash ya into a tree!" The large boy turned his machine into Suds again.

The ATV started to wobble, forcing Suds to retreat and attempt to pass on the outside. Dozer countered the move by kicking Suds in the thigh as he sped forward. He took his hand off of the brake and punched at Suds, clobbering the boy's chest and front of his Chiefs' helmet. "You ain't g'tting' around me, Crud! I'll break your neck! You can't beat me!"

Suds dodged the blows while trying to push forward and not lose control. Determination filled his eyes. His body tensed and his jaw tightened; he would not back down. "Cheat all ya want, Dozer! I ain't gonna quit!"

Beans, Greeley, the Goat, and Shanks cut through the woods to get a glimpse of the racers when they reached the backstretch of the first lap, leaving Sweets, Porker, Jared, and the two girls to watch and judge the participants as they came back around. With the track as long as it was, they'd have to wait for some time, nervously hoping Suds would make up ground. In the distance they could make out the faint sound of the two quads as they hummed around the oval.

"I think they reached the one snaking turn with ruts and fallen trees!" Sweets informed them. "It sounds like Suds is right there with him!"

Porker plopped down in the tall grass, and attempted to cross his meaty legs. "You can't tell nothin', Sweetwater! Put a lid on it! You're makin' me nervous!"

Jared clasped his hands together and mumbled a quick prayer, pleading for Suds to come barreling down the long straightaway towards them with an insurmountable lead. Molly stood next to him with her arms folded, biting her lower lip.

"We need to go home, Molly," Jan insisted. "It's getting dark."

"Wait, please, Jan," the anxious girl begged. "I wanna make sure Suds is okay."

As the steady sound of the engines got closer, the tension mounted. Shading their eyes with their hands, they stared down the track, searching for the riders. To their disappointment, Dozer motored around the turn first, but to their surprise, Suds had closed the gap, only a few yards separating him from his challenger.

"Come on, Suds!" the youngsters yelled. "Come on! You can do it!" Leaning forward on the vehicle like a jockey urging on his mount, Suds gritted his teeth, fighting to keep a good line and avoid the thick dirt kicked up by Dozer. He pushed the ATV to its limits.

The riders passed the cheering spectators at the starting line and motored around the turn. Reaching the end of the first turn, Dozer slammed on the brakes. With no time to react, Suds smashed into the back of Dozer's ATV, nearly flying headfirst over the handlebars. Dozer hit the gas and quickly extended his lead. Suds coaxed the old quad to make up ground. As he caught up to Dozer, the bully reached once again into his bag of dirty tricks. Purposely allowing Suds to inch past him on the outside, the goon floored his more powerful ATV, forcing Suds off the track and down a steep ravine. Heading full steam and bouncing like he was atop a bucking bronco, Suds zigzagged through the trees, until he crashed into an elm tree. A look of horror and shock exploded across Suds' face. He was doomed.

Dozer turned his ATV around in the middle of the course and rumbled to the high ground above Suds. "I told you not to race me, clown! That oughtta teach ya not to mess with me! See ya at the finish line—if you ever get outta there!" Dozer hollered. The big kid turned his ATV around and pulled away with victory flowing through his veins.

Defeated, Suds leaned against the handlebars and laid his head on top of his arms. He exhaled as if the life had been sucked out of his body. Then he heard Dozer's engine start to knock and pop in the distance. He raised his head as a rush of adrenaline hit him like a club. Snickering to himself, he put the ATV in reverse.

Dozer pressed the gas as far as it would go, but his ATV still lost speed. The engine grinded and hacked like it had smoker's cough. Up the track, the Goat, Shanks, Beans, and Greeley watched as the perplexed rider punched the front of his quad. "What the heck is the matter with this thing?" he yelled. "The engine's dyin'! Come on! I done won me twenty-two races on this thing! What's goin' on?"

Shanks and Beans exchanged sly grins, enjoying the creep's tantrum. Shanks chuckled, slapping his hand on his thigh with delight and then gave Beans a high-five. "Next time somebody tells ya not to use a can to fill your dumb ATV, ya might wanna listen!" Shanks chided. "Gasoline mixed with water don't work! Maybe ya shoulda used your own gas instead of stealin' ours!"

"Stealin' our can full of water, ya mean!" Beans chimed in.

"Wh…wh…what?" Dozer stammered as his ATV gave one last loud gasp and died in the middle of the track. Like a bull ready to charge, he stared at the two taunting boys. He unscrewed the gas cap and leaped off the machine. "Whatta ya mean, twerp?"

"That gas can ya took from us," Beans explained. "We warned ya not to use it! It had water mixed in it!"

Dozer, Greeley, and the Goat danced around the machine like it was on fire and they needed to find something to douse the flames. "Do somethin'!" Dozer demanded as the Goat bumped into him. He grabbed the strange-looking kid by the shoulders and threw him to the ground. "My ATV…they's ruined it! Get…get…get the gas can we brought! We need to run the water out…hurry!"

As Shanks and Beans continued to laugh uncontrollably, Dozer snarled, his face as red as a ripe tomato. "Get 'em! Kill those two little creeps!" With clenched fists, he and Greeley rushed towards the two agitators, only to be reminded they had a race to finish. As the Goat hustled to the broken-down quad with the gas container, Suds cruised past them, smiling like the cat that'd just eaten the canary through the bars of his facemask.

"Dang it!" Dozer cried and hustled back to his hobbled machine. "Get the water out, Colby! Get a tube! Hurry! I'm gonna kill that Suds Davis! He's a dead man!"

Victory within his reach, Suds cruised down the straightaway with Beans and Shanks running alongside him, cheering. Unable to keep up on foot, the boys soon tired and stopped as Suds reached the far turn. *Nothin' can stop me now!* he thought. Joy spread through his lean body, and a smile spread across his face. Putting distance between himself and Dozer on the isolated far turn of the track, he felt the front end of his ATV coming loose. Just looking at it, he could see nothing physically wrong with the machine. He checked the road in front of him. It was rather flat and manageable, yet his

ATV continued to bounce and gyrate like an old washing machine. Suds slowed down, praying he didn't have mechanical problems of his own. Over the dull roar of his motor the sound of thunderous stomping rolled past him. He turned in his seat and looked behind him, hoping Dozer hadn't already fixed his problem and reentered the race.

Suds' jaw dropped and his eyes shot out of their sockets. "Oooh.... crap," he muttered and hit the gas. Five ghostly riders on painted horses charged towards him.

A chilling battle cry echoed through the trees as the Indian ghouls raced after the boy. Flames burst from the flaring nostrils of their appaloosas. The horses' eyes were morbid gray, their flowing manes and tails, slithering snakes. Suds hit the gas, begging the junky ATV to go faster. A warrior beast charged forward, pulling alongside the boy's outside shoulder. A large antler from the creature's gory head glanced off the side of Suds' helmet as a deer-faced demon tried to skewer the defenseless boy. Blood flowed from the Indian's mohawk, trickling down his decaying face. The snakes from the horse's mane slithered in the breeze, hissing and striking at Suds as the monster's head bobbed next to his ATV. Suds leaned away as far as he could while desperately trying to speed up and keep his machine moving.

"Ahhh!" the frightened boy screamed. "Get outta here! I'm in the middle of a race here! I ain't got time for this! Leave me alone!"

The ghostly, deer-faced warrior raised his war club and swung it at Suds. The boy ducked; the club nicked his Chiefs' helmet. The buffalo-headed creature leaped from his fire-breathing appaloosa and pounced on Suds' back. The beast went for Suds' neck with his hoofed arm. As the creature unsheathed his knife, Suds bounded over a fallen tree, bouncing the mutant into the air so he hovered above the seat with his wooly arm still draped around the terrified boy. Suds ran under a low-hanging limb, catching the Indian demon in the chest and sending him crashing to the ground behind the motoring ATV.

***

With darkness settling, Jared stood next to Sweets, rocking back and forth. Molly clutched her hands underneath her chin, while Jan and Porker sat next to each other in the weeds. Around the far turn, a headlight appeared in the distance. "Is it Suds?" Jared asked. "Who is it? There's only one light! Is it him?"

Porker and Jan scrambled to their feet, each trying to identify which rider was barreling towards them. Then the beasts came into view. "Ohhh, nooo," Jan muttered.

"What...what are they?" Molly exclaimed

"Hide!" Jared yelled. "Everybody hide!"

The terrified kids smacked into each other as they scampered for cover. Porker dove into the brush with Jared, Sweets, and the frightened girls close behind him. Jared peered through the thick vegetation. Suds raced by them with four Indian creatures hot on his heels. Porker was about to scream when Jared slapped his hand across the boy's chubby cheeks.

One of the ghostly riders pulled his fire-breathing steed to an abrupt halt. The demon twisted his two hideous faces towards the weeds where the kids clung together like a nest of exposed baby birds. Its bloody mohawk jerked back and forth as the Indian beast scanned the thick brush. Bones poking through its shredded hide, the demon's appaloosa whinnied like screeching brakes before a crash. The creature's bear face roared and showed its fangs. He sniffed wildly at the air, catching the scent of human flesh. The kids hunkered down, clasping onto each other. The bear continued to sniff the air to locate his prey. Tugging on the reins, the creature turned the demon horse in a circle again, and then took off.

"Get off of me. You-all are squashing me." Porker pushed himself to his knees with bodies rolling all around him. "Man, let's get outta here," he whimpered. "I wanna go home."

"Me, too," Molly cried. "I want out of these woods." She smacked Jared on his back. "Dang you, Jared Millhouse. Dang that Suds Davis. The two of you—this is all you're good for. Trouble."

Jared rolled to his back and put his hands out in an apologetic, pleading gesture. "We can't leave. Who knows where those creepy ghosts are going. We have to help Suds. Let's get to the finish line. Suds'll surely head that way and hopefully those... whatever they are...Indian monsters'll stop chasing him."

Figuring his best chance at escape was in the dense woods, Suds veered off the track, caroming over the bumpy terrain and zigzagging, once again, through the trees. The rabbit-faced demon hurled a large spear with bloody feathers and human scalps dangling from its shaft. The lance hit above Suds' right knee, ricocheting off the gas tank and floating into the darkness. The Indian beasts exploded into a thunderous, bloodcurdling battle cry, causing Suds to scream in return. Then his pursuers were swallowed up by the night.

Suds brought his ATV to a stop and scanned the darkness. His engine grumbled underneath him. Close to collapsing from exhaustion and fear, the boy took deep breaths, trying to calm his nerves. Then in the distance he heard another disturbing sound—an ATV.

Suds bounded onto the course with Dozer a mere hundred yards behind him. While he'd rambled through the woods trying to lose his gruesome pursuers, Dozer had gotten the water siphoned out of the tank, leaving Greeley and the Goat nauseated and dizzy as a result. Once he'd refilled his ATV, Dozer got the vehicle churning and maneuvering around the track at top speed. Suds barreled forward, peering over his shoulder every ten yards to locate his newest predator. The seasoned racer was gaining on him.

Suds motored past Shanks and Beans, who were cheering wildly, with a lead of only fifty yards. The riders were halfway done with the final lap. Only one half to go and then a final sprint to the finish line located at the far corner of Howser Farm. But Suds knew he had too far to go to fend off Dozer.

Jared, Porker, Sweets, and the two girls crept along the fence on the property line of Howser Farm, keeping a watchful eye on their surroundings. There was little light to guide them with only a sliver of the moon in the night sky. As they started to make a run for the finish line, Beans hurtled over the barbed wire fence and tumbled to the ground.

"Ahhh!" Molly screamed. "Beans! What are you doing? You scared me to death!"

The boy scrambled to his feet. "Come on! They're gonna be headin' for the finish line any second!"

As Beans turned, Jared grabbed the boy by the arm. "Wait! Did you see anything weird in there? Was anything chasing you?"

"No," the tall boy responded. "Come on, Millhouse! We didn't put enough water in the gas can! Suds is in the lead, but Dozer was gainin' on him fast! It's gonna be close! Let's go!"

Shanks burst through the brush, and the kids darted across the field to wait for Suds' hopefully victorious arrival. Minutes ticked by with no sign of the racers, only the dull roar of engines in the distance. They paced nervously at the finish line, where the back entrance to the farm linked up with Lone Jack/Lee's Summit Road. Soon Greeley and the Goat arrived, panting like dogs with sickly green faces—the effect of inhaling toxic fumes while siphoning the water from Dozer's tank. The two hoodlums collapsed in the weeds and moaned, too ill to avenge the dastardly trick played on them.

Sweetwater paced back and forth at the finish line. Two solitary lights flickered in the distance as the rumbling of engines intensified. Sweets extended his lanky arm and pointed. "There they are! Suds is in the lead, but Dozer's just behind him!"

The Crossroads gang gasped in unison. Suds made a sharp turn into the field, cutting Dozer off and preventing the boy from passing on his inside. The racers charged across the bumpy terrain. Dozer feigned another pass on Suds' left. As the boy countered the deceptive move, Dozer hurled his ATV to Suds' right and hit the gas. The two riders were neck and neck with three hundred yards to the finish line.

The veteran racer smiled at Suds. "So long, Crud!" he gloated. "You shoulda known you could never beat me! You're done, boy!" Dozer zoomed past his competitor, laughing as his ATV pulled away.

With two hundred yards to go and an insurmountable lead, Dozer basked in his glory, a vicious grin on his large evil face. Gritting his teeth with determination, Suds leaned forward on his quad, desperately fighting to the bitter end. Dozer turned around and gave Suds one last insulting wink, a final insult. Just as he was about to raise his hand in victory, his ATV hit a pile of loose bricks and boards, launching him three feet into the air. Dozer's expression transformed from cruel pleasure to extreme fear. The machine sailed through the air like a slow motion scene from a movie, as the spectators at the finish line gave a collective gasp. The ATV dropped, nose first, through broken boards overgrown with weeds and crashed into a deep dark hole. Dazed and bruised, the big kid lay on his side with his ATV upside down on his legs.

Witnessing Dozer's ill-fated trip from several yards behind him, Suds hit the brakes and decreased his speed. He slowly circled the wreckage, peering over his facemask into the dark hole.

Dozer clutched his nose with both hands, blood spewing between his fingers. "My nwose is bwoken!" he whined. "Gwet me outta hwere!"

Suds laughed heartily, with no sympathy for his tormentor and nemesis. "I guess ya forgot about the old house that used to be here. You know the one…the one that I fell into when you threw rocks at me instead of helping me get out."

"Cwome on, mwan!" Dozer pleaded. "Hwelp mwe! Cwome on, Suds! I tink my arm is bwoken!"

Cruelty not a trait in Suds Davis' nature, unlike Dozer's, the boy rolled his eyes and dropped his head. "Oh, all right. Let me go and cross the dagblang finish line, and win this here race…and then I'll come back and help ya out. Geez."

Triumphant, Suds slowly rolled across the finish line, taking the checkered flag, though it was merely a blue checkered hand towel Sweets had stolen from his mom's kitchen tied to a stick. Sweets waved the victory flag as if it was the Daytona 500 as Suds pulled his ATV to a stop and removed his football helmet.

The group rushed to their gallant hero, cheering the rider's miraculous feat. Jared slapped Suds on the back. "You won, man! You did it! You beat Dozer!"

***

Sirus stared at his guest's dirty, tired faces as they stood on his porch. "What the heck're you young'ns doin' here? Ain't it past your-all's bedtime?"

"Suds done it, Sirus," Shanks stated flatly. "He beat ole Dozer. We come by to tell ya and to return your ATV. We ran outta gas and had to push it all the way from the cemetery."

Sirus placed his hands on his hips; a pleasant smile grew on his wrinkled face. "Man, ain't that somethin'? Good for you boys. Put that mean ornery cuss in his place."

"But that wadn't all," Jared explained, leaning his weary body against the frame of the door. "As if it wasn't bad enough to go up against Dozer, Suds nearly got chased down and killed by scary Indian creatures with two faces. One of 'em had a bear face connecting to a face of bloody, mangled skin. He had a mohawk, too, and his left arm was all wooly with a huge bear paw for a hand. Two others had antlers coming out the sides of their heads. They rode horses that breathed fire and had snakes for manes. It was scary."

Hearing the wild tale from his seat on Sirus' couch, Jerry sprang to his feet and rushed to the door. "You say you saw the Osage Indian mutants?" Too exhausted to answer, the boys simply nodded in reply. "Those sound like the ones Mr. Lovelace was talking about. Please come in."

Understanding that the boys needed rest and having gone through the torture of the Yankee ghost chaser's litany of ridiculous questions, Sirus reluctantly moved to the side and invited the three in. "Kids, this here is Louis and Jerry. They's ghost hunters I asked to come in to help us with our little ghost situation here in Lone Jack. Come on in and sit down. They's gonna ask ya some questions, so try to recollect as best ya can and tell em everythin' ya know and done seen. Give 'em every detail…'cause they'll hound ya to death if'n ya don't. I'll see if can't stir me up some lemonade or sweet tea. I'm sure you-all is thirsty."

"Wow!" Suds exclaimed, taking a seat on the floor between the coffee table and fireplace. "Ghost hunters! That's cool!"

Embarrassed but flattered by the attention, Louis blushed. "Well, it's a job. In fact, it's an adventure and a job. Not for the faint of heart."

"They ain't seen squat until they come to Lone Jack," Mr. Lovelace, who was perched in front of Sirus' antique writing table in the corner, informed the boys. "Them dogs don't hunt, if'n ya know what I mean."

While Sirus delivered needed refreshments for the boys' dry mouths and hungry bellies, Jerry and Louis interrogated them thoroughly, assaulting them with a barrage of questions that went on for what seemed like hours. Between the professors' intellectual minds and the boys' simple answers, little progress was made, causing frustration for both parties.

"I'm going to ask you again," Jerry said, revealing his lack of patience in his tone. "Did it seem like the bear portion of the demon's head was in control of the…being's actions, or was it the rotting, bloody Indian part of the creature that was in control?"

"Who gives a crap?" Shanks snapped. "They was tryin' to kill Suds!"

Mr. Lovelace chuckled and slapped his knee. "Doggone, sonny. That's the same thing I told him."

"Really," Sirus added. "This is ridiculous…no offense. You keep askin' all the same stuff over and over. We's focusing on the past, but we need to be worryin' about the present…like how we gonna get these dangerous beasts outta our town. They coulda killed these boys tonight."

Louis removed his reading glasses and rubbed his eyes. "That's what we are trying to get at, Mr. Payne. We know what they're capable of, but what we need to find out is how they operate. We know we can't kill them. They're already dead. But how do we get them out of your town? This situation is pretty serious, in my expert opinion." Louis threw a sharp glance at his colleague.

Sirus intercepted the professors' looks. "Wait a second. There's somethin' you ain't tellin' us. What's goin' on? What have ya done found out?"

Jerry moved to the edge of the couch and placed his elbows on his knees. "Look this is hypothetical, but I've done some research and made some phone calls. What I found out is quite telling and a little disturbing."

"What exactly did ya go and find out?" Ned asked.

"Well," Jerry continued, "I think there may be a reason why these apparitions aren't your ordinary, everyday ghosts. You see, a few weeks before the battle of Lone Jack there was a solar eclipse. The effects of eclipses are unknown, and scientists often argue the points. However, there is no doubt that there's some effect on our planet with every eclipse, and we're not just talking about waves in the ocean. There's also an effect on humans. Days before—and after—an eclipse people are often stressed and agitated. I'm talking living humans. The effects on the paranormal could be much worse. But there was an eclipse before the bloody battle. There's also another eclipse in the Saros cycle to take place very soon."

"An eclipse?" Sirus asked. "I don't understand. These ghosts are agitated because of an eclipse?"

"There's more to it than that even, Mr. Payne," Louis stated. "This eclipse is in a cycle—the Saros cycle, which happens every eighteen years."

Jerry nodded. "Right, every eighteen years. The Saros cycle." The professor grabbed his notepad from the coffee table and flipped to one of the pages. "There's something else that is very telling. 144. The number 144 comes up a lot in relation to this battle. Several reports say 144 Rebels were killed during the conflict. Other reports say 144 Union soldiers died as well. The numbers for the killed horses vary, but several sources say that 144 horses died–144 again. So I did some research on the number. I looked to see if the number had any hidden, spiritual meaning. It appears only once in The Bible. In the Book of Revelations, the seventh angel shows the wall of New Jerusalem, which measures 144 cubits. The Rosicrucians think there are 144 different types of atoms in the universe. In numerology, 144 means 'All Possibilities.' But the most relevant meaning I found was the Gematrian value for *light*. In that system, 144 means light." Jerry turned to Sirus with a serious expression on his face. "144 means light," he repeated. "The date of the next eclipse in the Saros cycle is this coming Saturday."

Sirus let out a sigh. "The anniversary of the battle of Lone Jack. They's searchin' for a portal."

"A portal?" Shanks interjected as he sat with his legs crossed on the floor. "What the heck's a portal?"

Louis cleared his throat. "It's a door. These ghosts are looking for a door to pass through to the other side. They're looking for the light. Jerry and I think that they're trapped in one of the Saros solar eclipse cycles."

"The good news is," Jerry interrupted his colleague, "we think we know when we will have the best chance to get them to, or lead them to, this portal. It's going to be this weekend, on the anniversary of the battle of Lone Jack. When the eclipse comes, we think the door will open."

"What's the bad news?" Sirus asked.

"If we can't get them to the portal," Louis responded, "and they end up trapped here, they may destroy everything in their path. By all accounts, these demons are becoming more and more real. You all have said so. As each day goes by, they change. By the day of the commemoration, they could very well be as real as you or me, and very dangerous."

Sirus scratched his head and reflected on the situation. "So we got from now till Saturday to find the portal, which could be anywhere, and if we don't…"

"They could end up killing a great number of people," Jerry finished the sentence. "And it would actually be helpful to have the portal's location figured out before then. The battle was over by around ten o'clock on the morning of the sixteenth. And guess what time the eclipse is scheduled for? Ten o'clock…this Saturday. If we go past that time, and past the eclipse, it may be too late. We'll have to put something in motion as soon as possible. I've looked into Saturday morning. The weather forecast calls for a good chance of a powerful thunderstorm. There will be a high electrical charge, which ghosts like. They will be extremely active and agitated just before the storm comes. It's our best chance."

"We been needin' us some rain around here," Ned pointed out. "The farmers'll be pretty happy to hear that."

"There won't be much to cheer about if everyone in town is killed by a swarm of angry creatures from beyond the grave, Mr. Lovelace," Jerry replied bluntly. "If we can't get these spirits out of your town, there may not be any one left, including farmers, to appreciate the rain. I think the dry conditions are the least of our worries."

"Hey," Ned snapped, "just tryin' to focus on the positive for once. Everythin' don't have to be gloom and doom all the time, does it?"

Ignoring the old man, Jerry continued, "This Saturday is it. It's our best chance to rid your town of these demons. It might be our only chance. The charged atmosphere will be ripe for paranormal activity."

"But what about the portal?" Sirus asked. "We don't know where it is or how to find it."

Louis crossed his legs and rubbed his bald head. "Well, we're just going to have to wait. Now I know this sounds a little crazy, but we think we can replicate the battle. If we can do that, the ghosts will surely respond. Hopefully, as the battle unfolds, the portal will show itself to us. Then we can lead them to the light."

"Simulate the battle?" Ned blurted out in apparent disbelief. "What are ya talkin' about?"

"You have a commemoration scheduled for this Saturday," Jerry stated. "You have reenactors coming in Thursday who are going to set up camp right in the middle of the battlefield. They're going to be dressed from head to toe in Civil War uniforms; representing both sides of the conflict. They'll have muskets, shotguns, knives, bayonets, they'll even have cannons—all for the reenactment scheduled for Saturday morning. I know it's crazy, but if we can get them going as early as possible in their mock battle, I think the ghosts will respond. It's scary and a little dangerous I know, but we have few options and are running out of time."

Sirus dropped his head into his hands. "This is crazy. We gonna get arrested for inciting a riot. And what if somebody gets killed?"

"It's our only option, Mr. Payne," Jerry informed him. "We're running out of time. That portal is going to show itself this weekend, just before the solar eclipse. We have to do whatever we can to lead these creatures to it." The professor paused, rubbing his tired neck. "That brings us to the last and most troubling of our problems: the key."

Sirus threw his hands up and chuckled. "We might as well give up and head on outta town before we all end up killed. We done told ya. None of us know nothin' about no key. And now you're tellin' us we got three days to find one."

"We have to try, Mr. Payne," Jerry responded. "There's going to be a lot of people in this town come Saturday. There could be multiples of 144 dead people to carry on the pattern and live out the curse."

"These ghosts are in…a type of purgatory," Louis added. "Trapped between worlds in their own prison. It's as if each spirit, because of the Saros eclipse cycle has been sentenced to a purgatory. They're desperate, too, Mr. Payne. They need that key. They've told us as much on more than one occasion. Jerry and I think that key opens the portal. Without it, there's no chance of unlocking the door and finding the light that takes them to the other side."

"Wait a second," Sirus said, "you're saying that the ghosts from the battle are trapped here because of this eclipse cycle. The Saros cycle. But that don't explain why them Indian creatures and slaves the boys done seen are in this town."

"The eclipse is in a cycle, remember," Louis explained. "Who knows, maybe they met their demise in the same cycle, years before the soldiers died in their bloody battle, and are trapped as well. That's are best guess." The professor took his glasses off and cleaned them on his shirt. "But we need that key."

Jerry leaned forward on the sofa and stared at the kids. "None of us can figure out what this key is that these ghosts keep demanding. I want you to think as hard as you can. There are no wrong answers. Think about every tiny detail of your encounters with these apparitions. Do any of you have any idea what this key might be, or where we might find it? You have to think. This is urgent. Without it, we could be in big trouble."

The boys looked at each other, shaking their weary heads. "I don't know," Jared answered. "I'm sorry. I just don't know. They never say what the key is."

Sitting next to Jared, Suds nodded. "Millhouse is right. They ain't a real talkative bunch, if ya know what I mean. How do we know? You-all is the ghost chasers. If you-all don't know, then how are we gonna? We're just kids."

Jerry fell back into the couch. "Then like I said…we're in big trouble."

Sirus shook his head solemnly. "Ya mean Lone Jack's in big trouble. Come Saturday, these ghosts are gonna tear through here like a volcano."

"Yeah," Ned agreed with a smile. "But what a way to go! It's gonna be somethin' to see. This here commemoration Mrs. Morgan's puttin' on is gonna be one for the ages. Hold on to your britches!"

9

Walking the perimeter of the house, Rob and Darla held hands, giggling like teenagers. "This is ridiculous," he said. "We're sneaking out to get some alone time, like my dad's watching me with disapproving eyes or something."

Darla playfully pushed him away and retreated to the shade of the blackjack oak. "He's just concerned for me. He's gonna make sure you treat me like a lady. Call it chivalry. Only old men know anything about it anymore."

"Chivalry? Sounds like I have to slay a dragon or lead an army in your honor or something. That's not pressure, I suppose."

The energetic Darla leaped off the ground, reaching up and grabbing one of the low-hanging limbs. "Come on," she said, swinging her leg over the branch. "Let's climb this tree. If we're gonna act like goofy kids, let's do it all out."

While Rob watched in disbelief and admiration, she pulled herself onto a branch and sat perched in the large tree. "Climb a tree?" he asked. "Are you crazy? I haven't climbed a tree since I was Jared's age."

Darla rolled her eyes and headed for the limb above her head. "Oh come on, Rob, live a little. Geez. You can either sit in the weeds fighting off chiggers, or you can sit high in the tree and enjoy the breeze. Call it metaphor for life. A baby step in your rehabilitation. Besides, it's a beautiful day. And I bet you can see all the way to Howser Farm from up top."

Rob placed his hands on his hips and chuckled. "Oh, all right. I know you're not taking 'no' for an answer." He heaved his body into the arms of the oak, following Darla as she scaled higher. "Talk about playing hard to get."

"I just want you to show me how strong and manly you are. Let's go to the top. Besides, I have to act like the responsible adult for nine months out of the year. I want to feel what it's like to be the child for once, before I have to go back to sitting kids in the corner and cracking them over the head with a ruler."

The two wended their way through the heavy branches until they were only a few yards from the top of the oak. They each straddled a branch and stared across the town of Lone Jack. "Well, I have to admit, it is nice up here this morning."

Darla reached over and pinched Rob on the cheek. "Where's the trust, Mr. Millhouse?"

"You like adventure…that's for sure."

"Does that scare you, Mr. Millhouse? Am I too wild and daring for you? Are you up for the challenge?"

The bashful man chuckled as his cheeks became a rosy shade of red. "If I make it out of this tree without falling and breaking my neck, I'll let ya know." He patted the limb between his legs and rubbed its rough bark.

"You know, there was a dendrochronologist from Iowa University running around here about twenty-five years ago, studying trees. I was visiting dad when the guy stopped by to ask about this tree. It was huge even then. He wanted to know if we planned on cutting it down and selling it for lumber some time. You get a real good price for oak and this tree alone would've been some good money for my dad. The guy wanted to take a sample of the rings for study, but dad loves this old tree. It's kind of part of the family. We got to watch it grow and it got to watch us grow, so he told the dendrochronologist 'no' and offered him some sweet tea. The guy stayed for awhile and told us that this oak was well over one hundred years old. That was twenty-five years ago."

Rob shook his head and exhaled the fresh, soothing air generated by the massive oak. "Man, that's old." He moved his hand to Darla's knee. "You ever been to the Redwood Forest? It's amazing. They get as tall as 350 feet. In fact, California has three species of the tallest trees in the world. Some of the sequoias and bristlecone pines are over 4,500 years old. The sequoias are massive. It makes you feel awfully small and unimportant when you walk around the base of those trees. You just stand there in awe."

"My gosh," Darla giggled. "Rob Millhouse. You do get out of the house. You've actually traveled beyond the suburbs of Kansas City. Maybe you are adventurous."

***

Knocking. Sirus stumbled through the door of his bedroom, stubbing his toe on the writing table. Groggy from a night of restless sleep, battling his own demons in his mind, he limped through the living room. His two Connecticut guests, again in their underwear thanks to the heat, sat in the kitchen, working in their own little world with their minds completely focused on the ghosts of Lone Jack. The old man unlocked the door and opened it.

"Mornin'," Captain Pickering said, moving his trademark matchstick around in his mouth with his tongue. "Looks like you had yourself a rough night."

Catching his reflection in the officer's round sunglasses, Sirus responded, "Man, you are some kinda detective, ain't ya? What do you think? I got you thinkin' crazy things about me. Would you be able to sleep? What do ya want anyway?"

The round policeman glanced at Officer Kunkle. "Can we come in?"

"You got a warrant?" Sirus asked. "Besides, I got me some company."

"No," Captain Pickering snapped, "we ain't got no warrant, but I can get me one, if that's how you wanna play it. I can call me the judge right here and right now."

Realizing the morning interruption wasn't going to end until he let Pickering get on with his business, Sirus moved out of the doorway so his unwanted guests could enter. "What's this all about? I got things to do today."

Captain Pickering looked past the old man and into the kitchen. "Mornin', fellas. You must be them Yankee ghost chasers."

"Hello." Louis greeted him cautiously. The two professors pushed their chairs away from the table.

"Oh, you boys don't have to get up," the captain informed them. "In fact, we'll just all come on in there and join ya, since this has to do with you fellas, too. Let's go sit down and have us a chat." Sirus and Officer Kunkle sat down at the table, allowing Captain Pickering to move his large, sweaty body around the tiny kitchen, expressing his authority with every calculated motion. The officer pulled on the belt of his pants in a feeble attempt to work them over his gut and large rump. "Well, I been meanin' to meet up with you boys since you been in town. Unfortunately, duty called me to other pressin' matters, so I wadn't able to stop by till now."

"Well, thanks for stopping by," Jerry replied sarcastically.

"Ya see, this is a simple town. We got us a lot of hospitality. The folks is real nice and will do anythin' for ya. But what I got a problem with is a couple fellers from outta town comin' in here makin' us look foolish—scarin' people, and g'tting' everybody all worked up. I find that insultin'."

Glaring at the two professors, Officer Kunkle leaned forward on the table. "We got us a major celebration comin' up this weekend. I'm the man in charge of security." He thrust his thumb towards his chest to emphasize his point. "We don't need no Yankee ghost chasers comin' in here creatin' havoc."

"Daggum it, Cliff," Officer Pickering interrupted. "I done told you, boy, that I would do all the talkin'. We was gonna do good cop-bad cop and you done went and screwed it all up." The large captain wiped the sweat from his brow, and slung the perspiration to the floor. "Now, where was I? Anyway…you're to cease and desist your little ghost chasin' crap immediately. I also recommend you make your way on outta town. Feel free to catch a Royals' game on your way to the airport. They's playin' the Red Sox, so it should be an excitin' event for ya. But to put it simply, your work here is done."

Not one to tolerate being pushed around—or to think before speaking, Jerry jerked in his seat. "Now you just hold on, sheriff."

"I ain't elected, boy. I'm a captain on the police force." Pickering corrected him as if he were a child. "I ain't no sheriff."

"Captain, then. Excuse me, but the last time I checked, this is a free country. We aren't doing anything wrong. We're breaking no laws. I can assure you we won't get in the way of the commemoration planned for this weekend."

Captain Pickering tugged at his belt again in vain. "That ain't the point. Listen. I didn't want to bring this up, but, when this is all said and done, you might find yourselves in the middle of a serious criminal case. Just take my advice, pack up your junk, and leave."

Sirus shook his head. "Come on, Cecil. That ain't right."

"You didn't tell 'em, did ya, Sirus?" the captain asked.

"Tell us what?" Louis demanded.

"While you weirdoes was sittin' around in your underwear," Officer Kunkle announced, "Sirus here is the prime suspect in a murder case."

"Daggum it, Cliff! Shut your pie hole!" Captain Pickering ordered. "But, since the dang cat is outta the bag... yeah...we had us some fugitives runnin' around in town and two of 'em got hacked to pieces. Sirus is our main suspect. I'm tellin' you boys, you might find yourselves as witnesses for the prosecution or worse... accessories."

"Accessories?" Jerry shouted. "To what? This is absurd!"

The chunky captain pulled the toothpick from his lips. "Absurd? He's settin' you boys up. Playin' with your minds and makin' ya think you're seein' things you ain't really seein'. He's playin' ya. All so he can use you as an alibi. He's got you on a wild goose chase to save his own neck. A wild *ghost* chase, to be exact. Don't get sucked into this baloney. Just take my advice and get on outta town."

Sirus jumped out of his chair. "This ain't right! You got no business tellin' people that! I know what you're doin', Cecil! It ain't right and I got my rights!"

Captain Pickering studied the old man's thigh. "Well, how's the leg Sirus? Looks pretty bad. Seems to have been torn open a tad. Ya told us you got it stabbed on some equipment behind your garage. You mind if we check that out? I mean, if you got nothin' to do with them convicts' murders, then you shouldn't mind if we take a look, right?"

"Do what ya want. I ain't got nothin' to do with them boys' murders! You'll see!"

The captain replaced the matchstick between his teeth and gestured with a jerk of his flabby neck to Officer Kunkle. "Let's go, boy. We need to check out the garage." The junior officer did as he was told and marched from the table.

"I hope I'm wrong, Sirus. I seriously do. I don't want to think you're a delusional maniac. I've always liked you. I'm just doin' my job. We'll leave ya to sit around here, doin' whatever it is you-all ghost nut jobs do. Obviously it don't require alotta clothes. I'll be watchin' ya, though. Just remember that. Come on, Cliff."

As the two policemen shuffled to the door Sirus fell back in his seat and threw his hands over his face. "Oh crap. I'm in big trouble, man."

Louis crossed his arms. "Men were killed? Do you know how unprofessional and unethical it is to withhold that vital information?

These ghosts have killed! One of us could've met the same fate."

"I'm sorry, Louis," Sirus muttered. "I was desperate. Everybody thinks I'm crazy. Now they think I'm a murderer. If you wouldn't've believed me…I don't know…I am in a bad spot here."

Jerry crossed his legs and rubbed his scruffy chin. "Dang. Well, we're in it now. We can't turn back, even if we wanted to. I know what I saw. It wasn't mirrors and smoke screens. It was real. Just one more reason to get these ghosts out of your town. As a professional and a man of principle, I'll go to the wall for you, Sirus. I'll put my reputation on the line, even if it means my career and I'm labeled the next 'crazy' along with you." He extended his hand towards Sirus. "Just…no more lies. We're all in this together."

***

Mrs. Morgan had a case of nervous butterflies as she led her small group of tourists through the Lone Jack Cemetery gate. The woman had spent weeks planning and managing the weekend's approaching commemoration, and the stress of the responsibility overwhelmed her. The celebration was Lone Jack's time to shine, as visitors from all around would come to the sleepy town to rejoice in its historical significance and pay homage to those lost during the bloody battle. But, with the weekend forecast calling for a severe thunderstorm, several venders canceling at the last moment, and numerous other small fires to put out, Mrs. Morgan was ruffled.

Barely taller than the iron fence surrounding the cemetery, Shanks grabbed the bars with both hands and pressed his face against the rail.

"Aw, geez," the tiny boy groaned, "I just can't get me a break from that lady. She must live here or somethin'."

"Who?" Jared asked.

"Mrs. Morgan. She must not got nothin' better to do than walk people around starin' at them cement pillars."

"I think it's her job," Jared explained.

Shanks' face scrunched. "You get paid for that?"

Shooting a cold stare in the boys' direction, the curator allowed her guests to settle and then gestured to the towering Confederate Monument. "This stands at the head of the Confederate trench, which runs north. The trench bends slightly because the ground was so hard at the time that they had to dig where they could. The bodies were then buried in layers. Now, the old blackjack oak, which gave the town its name, stood here in the corner of the cemetery. It died in 1861, the year the war started." The woman paused and smiled. "Again, I do want to invite you all to this weekend's festivities. I can proudly say that the celebration grows and becomes more popular each year, and it really brings to light the conditions and struggles of the participants of the day. There's an exciting reenactment of the battle, music, lots of great food, and tons of fun activities for the whole family."

"Aw, heck, lady," Shanks hollered, "you call that music? Every year it's two guys on banjos that don't play no better than us, and the food ain't no good neither. I got me a hotdog last year that tasted like a frog. How can ya screw up a hotdog?"

"Then just go eat a frog, then, Jeremiah Shanks, you little hoodlum!" Mrs. Morgan snapped. "What normal child would know what a frog tastes like, anyway? I try my hardest to make this celebration memorable and enjoyable for all, each and every year! And I do it with little or no help from anyone!" The stressed woman pointed sternly at the boys. "Now just shut your evil, filthy little mouths and give me a break for just one day! My nerves are shot! The venders are trying my patience, it's calling for a terrible thunderstorm and I can't take much more! Back off!"

Suds leaned his chin on the top of the fence, mesmerized by the curator's explosion. "Wow. Look how red her face is. I think smoke might start comin' out her ears. Nice goin', Shanks."

The distraught woman regained her composure and patted her hair with a very ladylike motion. She cleared her throat. "Now, where was I?" Mrs. Morgan smiled, hiding her embarrassment, and led her group to the Union monument. "Now, this is a very special memorial with a very interesting story. Originally, only the Confederate monument was erected in the cemetery by the United Daughters of the Confederacy in 1869. Lone Jack was a strong Confederate town, you must understand, so the Federal troops were shown little respect. But as the yearly commemoration of the battle started, tensions eased. In fact, a few Union soldiers who participated in the battle actually started attending the celebration.

"One of the bluecoats who fought in the bloody battle was William Rooney. Though he enjoyed the commemoration, he was slightly insulted by the fact that no monument paid homage to the fallen Union soldiers. There are twice as many bluecoats as Rebels buried in the cemetery, after all. So Mr. Rooney took matters into his own hands…literally. In 1912, he brought bricks and mortar and erected this monument himself. It is eight feet tall. As a special and personal tribute to his fallen Union brothers, Mr. Rooney placed a gold star in the middle of his special creation. He locked it firmly in the cement.

"The building of the monument had taken the elderly man and war hero all day, ending with his addition of the beautiful gold star. So Mr. Rooney went to get something to eat, allowing the monument to harden. When he came back to check on it, an hour later, the star was gone." Mrs. Morgan paused for effect. "If you look closely, you can still see the indentation of the star in the cement. It completely outraged Mr. Rooney that someone would desecrate his creation and be so low as to steal his star…and only minutes after he'd worked so hard to make a lasting monument to his fallen comrades.

"Some say the theft of that star has haunted the battlefield. Others say Mr. Rooney put a curse on this place as he left, outraged—a curse that has remained hovering over this town to this day." The woman paused again to catch her breath. "Now, follow me and I can show you the location of the trenches where the soldiers from both sides are buried."

"Daggum robbers," Suds said under his breath and spit across the fence. "Stealin' a goshdarn star meant for dead folks. That thief had to been related to Dozer."

Jared nodded in agreement, then his body jerked and his eyes twinkled. "That's it!"

"What is?" Suds asked.

Jared smacked Suds on the arm. "The star! That's it!"

"What the heck you talkin about Millhouse?" Shanks hollered.

"The star! That's the key! I had it in my hands when we went into Robbers' Cave! Remember? I found it in the cave and dropped it when those ghosts with chains came after us! It's the key! It's the star Mrs. Morgan was talking about!"

Suds raised his upper lip and squinted as if thinking hard made for a painful practice. "Ya sure? I remember you findin' a star, but I never really seen it. I thought it was a toy."

"It got hot! I had to drop it, it got so hot! That's it! It has to be the star Mrs. Morgan is talking about! In fact, I bet it's the key the ghost chasers want—the key to open the door to the other side!"

"A star?" Shanks rebuffed. "How's a star gonna open a door, Millhouse? That don't make no sense! A star ain't no key! A key's got ridges on it!"

Jared turned and faced him. "It is the key, Shanks! Didn't you hear what she said? The star was stolen. The guy who put it there put a curse on this town. A curse! Lone Jack's haunted 'cause of that stolen star!" He grabbed Suds' arm. "We have to get it back. We have to go and get the star! It's the key, I just know it!"

Suds stared at the ground, thinking about the danger. "Go back inta Robbers' Cave. Have them ghosts crush our skulls with them huge iron bowlin' balls. An adventure. A mission. We could end up heroes. We could save this here town. But we'll probably end up dead. Okay…I'm in. I'll help ya get the star." Jared's eyes lit up. "But we oughtta get Molly. She was in there with us, so she'll be able to help us find it. Shanks'll keep watch outside the cave in case somethin' goes wrong."

"Me!" Shanks exclaimed. "Why me? I wanna go in there, too! I wanna be a hero!"

Suds placed his hands on the boy's shoulders in an apologetic gesture. "Dude, them ghosts are real nasty. Your mouth'll just make 'em madder and you can't shut up for nothin'. This here mission takes quiet. That's somethin' that ain't in your nature. You kinda get on everybody's nerves. You drive my dad crazy. Imagine what you'd do to a buncha mad ghosts."

***

Suds and Shanks rummaged through the Davis garage, gathering up as much equipment and supplies as they could. Anything they thought might be useful they'd toss in a pile for later inspection. As the two boys continued slinging items all over the place, Mr. Davis pulled into the driveway. The round man got out of his truck and stared at them. "What do you think you are a' doin'? The garage is a mess."

"Oh. Hey, Dad," Suds said with a smile. "We's just goin' through stuff. We got us a mission that might save this here town and we need to be prepared. Just gettin' together some supplies."

Keg Davis picked up an axe with a broken handle from the concrete. He inspected the dangerous object and then smacked Suds on the back of his head. "Are you an idiot or somethin'? I ain't gonna let you go off with no axe. Now put that thing away." He let it fall from his hand; the item clanking on the cement. "I'll be glad when school starts. You and them friends of yours just keep g'tting' inta things. What mission ya got? Your mission should be to do your daggum chores, so your mom don't crawl down my back and make me get on ya all the time."

"We's goin' after ghosts, Mr. Davis," Shanks informed him. "We need to get us a star so we can open the door for them to get on outta Lone Jack. We's gonna be heroes."

Keg stared at the annoying boy. "Is stupid contagious or somethin'? You two, goin' after ghosts? Look. I had me a hard day at work and I just want some peace and quiet. I ain't got time for you-all's disturbed imaginations. Put all this crap back where ya found it, and then get your scrawny butt on home, Shanks. I need me a nap and don't want to hear your screechin'."

"But, Dad, you don't understand. We gotta get these ghosts outta Lone Jack by Saturday or this here town'll be destroyed. There'll be bodies and burnin' buildings all over the place. Complete carnage. We're gonna save the town and beat them ghosts on outta here. We'll probably get us a medal."

"Stop your dang antics, Suds," his dad ordered. "Ghosts gonna destroy Lone Jack? Sounds like a job for the armed forces, not two little twerps with wild stories. Now get all this crap back where ya found it and stop actin' like a possum with daggum rabies." Keg brushed past his boy and headed towards the door. "And get your dang chores done." As the man stepped into the house, Jared bumped into his belly on his way out the door. "Good golly. Got little termites comin' outta the woodwork round here. Outta my way, boy."

"What's wrong with your dad?" Jared asked as the door shut. "Is he mad or something?"

"Man, he's always mad," Shanks explained. "He's as grumpy as a dang bear."

"Oh, he'll be all right," Suds stated. "That's just my old man. He'll forget about it once he starts snorin' and he's got dribble runnin' down his face. What did Molly say? Did ya talk to her?"

Jared studied the pile of items behind Suds. "Yeah. I asked her to come over and she said she'd have to ask her mom when she got home. She said her mom would be home in a few minutes and she'd call us back."

Suds rubbed his hands together greedily. "Good. Right on schedule. Let's go through this stuff and get our supplies together. Then we'll work out a plan and, after we eat dinner, we'll head on down to Robbers' Cave. Go back in and call your grandpa, Millhouse. See if we can stay over at your house tonight. Once we get that star, we're gonna have to keep it safe. Your place is better for that than mine. Go call and then we'll jot us down a good plan for the mission."

Not wanting to reenter the home where Suds' grumpy father would scrutinize his every move, Jared shook his head and slowly returned to the door.

***

"Robbers' Cave!" Molly pushed her chin in the air and folded her arms. "You two conjured up a plan to get me over here so I'll go back in that creepy cave? How could you? And you, too, Jared? I could expect as much outta Suds."

"Ya have to, Molly," Suds stated. "You was in there before and you know the cave. We'll be in and out in less than thirty seconds if we do it right. I got flashlights and weapons. Them ghosts'll never see us, we'll be in and out so fast, and, if they do come, we'll fight em off. Everythin'll be fine. I promise."

"You should just let me go!" Shanks shouted. "I'm with her. This ain't no job for no lady. Let me at them ghosts. I'll go to town on 'em."

Jared reached up and placed his hand on the tall girl's shoulder. "Come on, Molly. I don't want to go back in there anymore than you do. But we have to. If we don't get the ghosts outta Lone Jack, they're gonna destroy this town. It's our only hope. I swear. Sirus even thinks so."

"Let her stay behind!" Shanks interjected again. "She's chicken and ain't gonna do nothin', but need to be protected anyway. It ain't good for the mission. Ya can't have no weak link. I'll go instead of her. She's just gonna cry and complain like women do. This here is serious business and she's just gonna screw it all up."

Molly stepped towards Shanks. "I'm not scared, you little worm. I'm just cautious. There's a difference. Okay…I'll go. You're far better off having me in there than Shanks and his mouth. The only thing he'd be good for is that the ghosts would definitely go after him first."

***

Jared pulled the overloaded backpack from his bony shoulders and dropped it to the ground. "Geez," he huffed, "why we taking all this again? Hopefully we'll just be in there a couple of minutes."

"Hey, man," Suds replied. "We need to be prepared for anything, Millhouse. It might come in handy. You can never take too much stuff."

"Yeah, actually ya can, Suds." Jared wiped the sweat from his brow. "Do we really need a compass? None of us can even read one. And toilet paper? Are we gonna be in there that long? And what's this string of Christmas lights for? This stuff is just gonna slow us down."

Molly scanned the woods and then stared at the cave's entrance. "I don't know about this, guys. I'm getting a bad feelin'. You-all shouldn't've spent so much time figuring out a dumb plan. All you ended up writing down was 'Go to Robbers' Cave. Get the star. Look out for ghosts. Don't get killed.' And, before Jared rewrote it, you spelled half the words wrong, Suds. What kinda plan is that anyway? Now it's gonna be dark soon. Let's just go back. We can have Sirus and his ghost hunters come and get it."

Shanks threw his hands in the air. "Well, I done told ya so. You can't never count on no woman. She's a scaredy-cat. I done knew she'd back out. Just run on home cryin', girly. We'll ha…"

Before Shanks could finish Molly shoved him, sending the boy head over heels across the ground. "Come on! If we're gonna do this then let's get it over with!" She yanked the flashlight from Suds' hand and marched towards the narrow, overgrown opening.

"You done heard the lady," Suds stated. "Let's get this mission goin'. Wait out here, Shanks. If we ain't out in an hour…call the mayor."

The lanky boy slapped Jared in the middle of his back and grinned with excitement. "Let's go get that daggum star, Millhouse."

Approaching the cave, the entrance appeared to widen like the gaping mouth of a snoozing alligator, ready to snap anything that dared step across his long pointy teeth. A lump formed in Jared's throat. Molly stared at each member of the team. "At the count of three, we're goin' in. And we all stay together. Ready. One. Two. *Three.*"

Crouching to avoid banging their heads, the three raced through the entrance. Once in the first open area, Molly whipped the flashlight from right to left, scanning the darkness. Jared leveled a second light in front of him and located the doorway into the shaft where he had discovered the star.

"This way. Hurry." They scampered through the passage and immediately stopped. "Oh my god," Jared mumbled and slowly crept forward. The small, confined area of the mine that they had explored the first time they entered the cave was now wide open, a vast shaft that traveled as far as their lights reached. Magnificent, wild formations stretched from both ceiling and floor, made of various stalagmites and stalactites of all shapes and sizes. Though shockingly unlike what they expected, the amazing beauty captivated the three. They stepped forward, investigating their surroundings.

"Did we go in the wrong one or somethin'?" Suds asked.

"No," Jared whispered. "The star was through the first passage on our right side as we entered the cave. I'm sure of it. I even double-checked when we came in."

Molly shook her head. "But…but what is going on? What happened?"

Jared stopped. "Wait! I hear something!"

Suds pointed. "There's lights up ahead! Keep the flashlights at your feet and we'll sneak up and see what's goin' on! Follow me."

Molly tugged on Suds' arm. "No. Let's just get out of here. I don't like this."

Jared shook his head in agreement. "I think Molly's right, Suds. Let's just try again some other time."

"There ain't no other time Millhouse," Suds stated. "We got to get that star. We'll go check it out and then, when we know what's goin' on, come back and start looking for it. We have to do it now. It could be our only shot. Drop the supplies here. They'll make too much of a ruckus as we go. When we find out what's down there and what's goin' on, we'll come back and start searchin'. But we ain't leavin' without that star."

Hiding behind the jagged formations the three crawled towards the light. Where the shaft bent to the left, the clanking of metal hitting rock vibrated past them. A muffled sound of something heavy rolling over the hard floor pounded in their chests. Concealed in the darkness, Suds peeked around the side of a large stalagmite. The flicker of lantern light fluttered across the far wall as the rumbling of the rolling metal wheels grew louder. "Stay down. Something's comin'."

The three kids huddled together, gripping each other in anticipation. A large metal cart pushed by the ghosts of bearded miners, squeaked as it passed by. The faces of the ghosts were black and gruesome, dirt smeared over pale, scabby flesh. Their dark gray eyes looked as if they'd been blinded long ago by an eternity in the purgatory of the black mine. Their teeth were as yellow as the gold they sought and as jagged as the rocks that imprisoned them.

"They didn't see us," Jared whispered.

"I don't know if they could see," Molly stated. "Did you get a look at their eyes?"

Suds nudged Jared on the leg. "Come on. Let's move further down the tunnel. I think there's more of 'em down thatta way."

The lights from the ghostly lanterns danced across the wall, growing brighter as Jared crawled. A pale fiend raised a pickaxe high above his head and slammed it against the wall, sending sparks shooting out in all directions. Several feet away, two other gray-eyed ghosts picked up large pieces of limestone and tossed them into another cart, the large rocks banged against the metal as they tumbled. The three watched for some time, in complete awe of the world beyond the grave. Finally, Jared spoke up. "We have to find that star. Let's go."

"No. Follow me," Suds insisted. "I wanna investigate a little further and then we'll go back." Though their minds told them otherwise, Jared and Molly followed Suds' lead and headed further into the shaft.

As they traveled deeper, the shaft curved back to the right and returned to pitch black. "This is getting crazy, Suds," Molly said. "The star is closer to the front entrance. Let's just go back and get it. I'm getting a little scared here."

Having hated the dark his entire life, Jared seconded Molly's suggestion. "Really, Suds. This idn't a good idea. I'm not good in the dark and even worse in tight spaces. Let's go get the star and get out of here."

Ignoring their pleas, Suds pressed further into the passage. The walls heaved in and out like giant lungs, as if they were in the belly of some giant earthworm. Jared panted heavily, fighting for air, as the mine closed in around him. Sensing Jared's struggle, Suds grabbed his friend's shirt and pulled him forward. "Hang on, Jared. It looks like it gets wider up ahead. Relax, man."

At the end of the narrow passageway, Molly stretched her neck through the hole and peered into the darkness. "It drops off." She inched her head further into the unknown. "Oh, no. There… there are…creatures below. They're around a campfire."

"Let me see." Suds let go of Jared and scooted to the edge of the opening. Below, several apparitions moved wearily about. Their clothes were tattered and their faces were gaunt and pale. Three of the ghosts were injured Rebel soldiers with bandages on various parts of their bodies. One Confederate, with a bloodstained dressing wrapped around his head and long wooden crutch under his left arm, hobbled towards the wall and lowered himself to the cold floor, taking a seat next to a fellow soldier smoking a pipe. Several women and children also huddled in the confined area, their pale ghostly faces smeared with dirt and long with dread. "Wow," Suds mumbled. "It's some gray-uniformed Rebel demons. They seem pretty harmless. They got their wives and kids with 'em. You need to take a look at this, Millhouse."

Jared reluctantly crawled past Molly and positioned himself next to Suds. Studying the pit of floating spirits, his fear changed to unexpected sympathy. "It's like they're trapped down there. They know there's a hole here, but they can't get to it. They can't get out. Look at their faces. They look so sad and confused."

"That's fine by me," Molly replied. "I don't want them to get out. But I do want to get out of here myself. Let's go back and get the star and get out of here."

Jared stared past Molly down the dark tunnel. They'd have to go back the way they had come. Jared counted to three, took a last deep breath, and darted through the narrow passage. The walls tightened around him, swallowing him whole. He kept his eyes focused straight ahead and sang *The Star Spangled Banner*—the only song he knew most of the words to—to himself to keep his mind off of the moving walls. The three reached the exit and dropped to the cold floor. Jared leaned against the wall of the cave and sucked at the cool, dusty air.

Suds patted Jared on the shoulder. "Man that there was a tad hair-raisin'. This here cave I think has got a mind of its own. It's like were inside the stomach of a whale or giant snake or somethin'."

"I know," Molly stressed. "Did you feel the ground and the walls? They were hard and bumpy and then they changed. They were like soft, slimy skin." The girl cringed. "I'm done with this. I want outta here Suds."

Jared stared at his hands. They were covered with a cold slimy substance. He wiped them off on his shirt, climbed to his feet, and marched past Suds, leading the way to the chamber where he'd first grasped the precious star.

Taking control of the mission without Suds realizing it, Jared stood tall next to the bags of supplies and turned towards his comrades. The boy had had enough and wasn't about to go following Suds on another one of his expeditions. With unchallenged authority, he placed his hands on his hips. "Okay, the last time I had the star it was in the corner to the right. Molly, come with me and help search where I last saw it. Suds, you look on the other side and, most importantly, keep watch for anything coming after us. Let's get goin' and get the heck outta here."

Jared hustled to the spot between two contorted stalagmites and dropped to his knees. Over his shoulder, Molly pointed the light at the area in front of him. Like a dog trying to uncover a bone, Jared tore through the loose dirt. He assumed he'd uncover the star within seconds, but his optimism turned to desperation as he flailed away. "It's not here! It should be right here!"

Suds grabbed a small hand shovel from one of the backpacks and took it to Jared. "Are you sure you're in the right spot? I mean, this here cave has changed a lot since we was last in it. It's like it's cursed by witch's magic or somethin'."

"Yes. I'm positive. This is the spot. It should be right here."

"There's something!" Molly shoved Jared out of the way and drove her hand into the ground.

"Is it the star?" Jared asked, straining his neck to get a glimpse of her discovery. "Did you find it, Molly?"

She dropped the flashlight to the ground. "Grab the light, Jared, and shine it on my hands."

The three huddled in a circle. Molly released her grip and held her palm out. The dirt trickled between her fingers, revealing two round metallic pieces. "That ain't no star," Suds snapped.

Molly played with the objects between her fingers. "Then what are they?"

"I know," Jared answered. "They're gold buttons from a soldier's uniform."

"Did you say gold?" Suds snatched the artifacts from Molly's hand and studied them with greedy eyes. "We found us some treasure! Keep diggin'! There's probably more jewels around here and we still need to find that star!"

Energized by the impressive find, they covered as much of the ground as they could and, in no time, accumulated a considerable pile of loot. Jared found wire frames from a pair of old spectacles, while Suds uncovered a cap pouch, five bone buttons, and three marbles. Molly located a leather calvary soldier's glove, a belt buckle, and a metal piece from a horse's bridle. But the increasingly important gold star eluded them.

Starting to get a headache from squinting in the dark for so long, Jared rested with his back against a limestone formation. Dirt piles where the three had dug like a pack of zealous gophers were scattered across the floor. "I give up. Where is it? It's got to be in here."

Suds rose to his feet and stretched his back. "We gotta keep lookin', Millhouse. Besides, if we keep findin' all these treasures, we's gonna be millionaires. Don't give up, man. It's in here somewhere and we's gonna find it."

"Right," Molly stated. "You guys dragged me in here and I'm not leaving until we get that star. This is the last time I'm ever coming into this creepy cave." The girl grabbed a large rock and moved it out of her way. Lighter than she expected, the object rolled towards her and bumped into her foot. "Ahhh! It's a skull! I just touched a skull!" She ran to Suds and threw her arms around his neck.

"Quiet, Molly!" Jared whispered as he rushed to her. "Quiet. What was it?"

"It's a skull!" She turned and pointed in the darkness to the spot where she had made her gruesome discovery.

The two boys tiptoed towards the round object, praying Molly was mistaken. Inching closer, Suds shone the light in front of them. A few feet away, the unmistakable features of a human skull stared back at them, grinning. The boys jumped and darted to Molly. Jared's body shook as if bugs were crawling all over him. "Ugghh!" he yelled. "It is a skull! Let's get out of here!"

The three adventurers scooped up the backpacks and supplies, and headed towards the exit. His light on the ground directly in front of him, Jared bumped into something, jolting him backwards into Suds. Jared slowly raised the beam of light. A slave ghost blocked the exit.

"Ahhhh!" Molly shrieked.

Gathering the chains in his hands, the demon roared. He swung the iron ball at Jared, crushing a stalagmite into dust. The force of the blow sent shock waves through the cavern. The ghost wielded the ball again. Suds leaped for Jared. The boys tumbled across the ground as the solid metal sent up a cloud of dirt behind them. The boys scrambled to their feet and raced for the exit.

The second fiend appeared out of the darkness and slung his iron ball and chain at Molly's head. The frightened girl ducked. The iron smashed into the wall. The *boom* of the impact sounded like a bomb as chunks of stone exploded through the air.

The beasts bellowed, piercing the kids' ears. Jared's ghostly attacker twirled the ball above his head. Jared scrambled between the demon's legs, while Suds retreated for cover behind a rock formation. Jared whipped his light across the walls, hoping to relocate the exit, but instead found Molly. The girl cowered on the cave floor with her arm shielding her face, while the second ghost hovered above her. The ghost behind Jared collected the chains in his devilish hands. The boy dodged the blow, aimed for his face, and rushed the phantom hovering above Molly. The ghost held the chain with both hands high above his head, preparing to hammer the iron ball down on the helpless girl. As the metal came down, Jared slammed into the back of the angry spirit. The creature flew past Molly, turned, and roared at the intruders. Jared grabbed Molly's arm and headed towards the exit.

Suds feigned a break to his right and bolted in the opposite direction as the ball hurled towards him. Reaching the exit, he tripped and fell to the dirt. Molly and Jared stumbled past Suds and raced through the passageway. Suds scrambled to his knees and looked behind him. The chained ghoul raised the iron and flung it at him.

"Noooo!" Molly screamed. "Suds!"

Suds rolled to his right. The ball smashed into the ground where he had been, a thick cloud of dust engulfing his lanky frame. The demon hurled the ball into the side of the exit. Large stones crumbled on top of Suds. In desperation, he threw his hands up; shielding his face from the deadly barrage of rock. Jared and Molly grabbed his wrists, dragging him through the opening as the passage started to collapse. The rickety, unstable mine shook like an earthquake. The beams buckled. Dust spread throughout the shaft. "We gotta get outta here!" Molly screamed as she coughed. She ran for the main exit. "It's gonna cave in on top of us! Run!"

The three whisked through the narrow entrance with the thunderous sound of collapsing rock rumbling behind them and dust tumbling over their bodies. Molly leaped to safety and rolled to her feet. Staring at the passage, waiting nervously for Jared and Suds to crawl from the destruction, she clasped her hands under her chin and backed away. "Suds!" she begged. "Jared!"

Two forms staggered through the billowing dust as the distinct sound of coughing reached her ears. She gave a grateful sigh of relief. Then something clamped onto her shoulders and spun her around. The coldest, most evil set of eyes she'd ever seen stared through her like sharp needles, suffocating her like hands around her throat. "Ahhh!" she screeched before a hand knifed through the darkness and clamped onto her mouth.

The beast pressed his lips against her ear, his foul breath making her skin crawl. "You make one more sound, missy, and I'll bite your throat right out of your neck. Go get those two little morons. We're gettin' outta this town tonight."

***

Darla studied the letter tiles stretched out in front of her, then inspected the board. The couple was in the middle of a long game of *Scrabble*. She gathered the tiles and set them on the board for a triple word score. Rob rolled his eyes, defeated, and leaned on the kitchen table. "How do you use the letter 'z' on a triple word score every time? You're killing me."

"Sore loser," Darla quipped. "I know. I'm a teacher. I told you not to challenge me at *Scrabble*."

"I'm fully aware that you are a teacher. I just figured your vocabulary was limited to what you teach to fourth and fifth graders. That's about as far as mine stretches, so I assumed the match would be even." Rob glanced at his watch. "Where is that boy? He said he'd be home by nine. He's got twenty more minutes and, if he's not home by then, he's grounded until school starts. If he's not home in forty, I'm shipping him off to military school."

"Oh, relax. He's playing with his friends. Mrs. Davis said they were gonna play in the woods and then come home. They're fine. You can't play too long in the woods when it's dark." Darla picked up her pen and tallied her score. "This game is over. There's no way you can catch up. Oh, what a wonderful day I'm having."

"Yeah, great day," Rob huffed. "You took me horseback riding, which I haven't done since I was a kid, and I got bucked off in the first thirty seconds by an old swayback nag. Then you beat the tar out of me in *Scrabble*. I don't think *my* day can get much worse."

Bridges raised his boot and rammed his heel into the door, shattering the glass as it crashed into the wall. With his arm around Jared's throat, the convict rushed into the kitchen, and flung the boy across the linoleum. "Howdy, folks!"

Rob sprang to his feet and stepped towards the intruder. "Now, don't try anythin' foolish there, chief. Bring in them other kids, Lancaster." The convict walked into the house with Suds' arm wrenched behind his back. Bridges snatched a butcher knife from a wood block next to the stove. The evil man grabbed Suds by the hair, yanked him from Lancaster's grasp, and put the shiny blade to the boy's throat. "Like I done said, you try anythin' stupid, I slice his head clean off."

Shards of glass crunching under his boots, Sims shoved Molly through the door and shut it behind them. His mind racing, Rob put his hands out in a calming manner. "Take whatever you want. Take the truck. Whatever. Just don't hurt the kids. Please. We'll do what ya want. I won't cause you any trouble."

"Oh," Bridges chided. "You won't cause us any trouble? This whole stinkin' town has been nothin' but trouble! I should kill every last one of ya outta spite! Because of *your* filthy little town!"

Darla slowly backed away from the man's tirade. "Calm down. Please. Like he said. We'll do what you want. Just please take the knife from the boy's neck. He's just a boy. He's innocent. Please."

Pushing the blade deeper into Suds' flesh, Bridges snickered. The boy wriggled in fear. "Who else is in the house?"

"Just my father," Rob cried. "He's very sick. He wont bother anyone or cause any trouble. You can just let him stay in bed. He's no threat to you."

"Sims," Bridges hollered. "Go find gramps and get him out here. Check every room and make sure there's nobody else."

Sims rushed through the kitchen to search the house. "Don't hurt my grandpa!" Jared screamed as he got up from the kitchen floor. "He's sick."

"Well, boo-hoo for gramps!" Bridges returned his gaze to Rob. "Where's the weaponry in the house? The guns?"

"What? We don't have any guns."

"Don't play games with me! This here's a farmhouse! Farmers always got guns! Tell Lancaster where they are! Now!"

Not wanting to anger the crazed man further, Rob pointed into the living room. "They're locked in the closet…in there."

"Where's the key to the closet?" Bridges barked.

Rob nodded towards the kitchen cabinets. "It's in a coffee can on the top shelf of that cabinet."

With the key in hand, Lancaster sprinted into the living room to get the guns as Sims forced Virgil into the kitchen. Jared rushed over to protect his ailing grandfather. "Leave him alone! He's sick! Don't hurt him!"

With his sticky arms filled with as much as he could carry, Lancaster returned and scattered the guns and boxes of ammunition across the kitchen table. "I got 'em. This old bird's got a heck of a collection. These here are the only ones I could find any ammo for. We oughtta take the rest of 'em to sell when we get outta here, Earl."

Bridges studied the weapons and grinned with evil delight. "Load 'em up."

The fugitive emptied the boxes onto the table and started ramming the shells into the firearms. From Virgil's impressive gun collection, he had acquired a double-barreled shotgun, a lever-action Winchester 30-30, and a prized army issue .45-caliber semiautomatic pistol. He filled the clip, jammed it into the .45-caliber, and tossed the pistol to Bridges.

The scar-faced leader snatched the handgun out of the air and gripped it with the relief of a starving man given a meal. He tossed the butcher knife into the sink, moved the pistol to his right hand, and shoved Suds with the gun's barrel. The boy stumbled across the room, falling into Ms. Ramsey's arms. Bridges smiled with greedy eyes. "Now. We're gettin' outta this freakin' cursed town. Let's see what else ya got in this little farmhouse."

While Bridges and Sims ransacked the tiny home, searching every nook and cranny for anything of value, Lancaster sat casually at the kitchen table with the shotgun aimed at his victims. The filthy convict, dressed in his dirt-stained cowboy outfit, forced the group to huddle close together next to the refrigerator so he could keep a watchful eye on them all at once. The three adults had their backs pressed against the wall, not wanting to provoke the intruder, while the frightened children packed themselves tightly in front. Rob stood with his hands on Jared's shoulders, the only reassurance that he could offer to his son. Ms. Ramsey draped her arms around Molly's neck, while Virgil held tight onto Suds.

Mumbling under his stale breath, Lancaster reached into his pocket, retrieved a wadded up blue handkerchief and set it on the table. The convict unfolded the cloth carefully, as if the contents might jump up and bite him. When Lancaster set the final corner of the handkerchief neatly across the table, Jared's eyes lit up. In the middle of the soiled rag sat a dingy, five-pointed, metal star. "Where did you get that?"

Lancaster glared at the boy. "Shut up!" He moved the shotgun across his leg until it pointed at Jared.

Rob tightened his grip on his son's shoulders. "Relax, Jared," he murmured. "Don't get him worked up."

Disobeying his father, Jared tested the desperate escapee again, "I said, where did you get that?"

"What's it to you, kid? You won't be asking anymore questions about things that ain't none of your business with a hole in your gut." Lancaster fingered the star gently. "I finded it in that cave. We been hidin' in there for a couple days now. This town's like a puzzle. Every time we tried to leave this godforsaken place, somethin' held us back. We was about to go crazy when we came across that cave. Bridges said we'd wait it out until this no good town would let us go."

The grungy man flicked the star, spinning it in a circle. "I've had it. I'm tired. I'm hungry. This here town is haunted, if ya ask me—we was being watched by things that weren't there. That cave was worst of all. Every time we went in, the rocks had changed, like they's alive. Then we kept hearin' strange spooky noises. I can't take it no more. Bridges wants to burn this whole rotten place to the daggum ground. I don't blame him, neither. Send this place and them demons straight to hell."

Lancaster moved his eyes back to Jared and snickered. "You dumb kids didn't know what you was g'tting' into when ya went into that cave, did ya? Dumb little monkeys. But your bad luck is our good'n. You little insects is our way outta here now."

"That star doesn't belong to you," Jared declared, causing Rob to try more forcefully to coral his son.

"*That star don't belong to you*," Lancaster mimicked. "Whatta ya gonna do about it? We hold all the cards now. Besides, this here star is magical. I could use me a little magic. I'm gonna make me a small fortune sellin' this thing, when we get outta here."

"Magical?" Molly mumbled. "What do you mean?"

Lancaster leaned forward in his chair and relaxed his hold on the shotgun. "The way I figure it, girly, I stole this here star from them ghosts. It ain't no ordinary piece of metal, neither. It's bewitched by them demons. When you rub on it, it gets hot. So hot, it'll burn ya. That's why I got it folded up in this handkerchief, because ya can't hold it if'n ya don't. It's got some powers, that's for darn sure. And I'm takin' it with me." The convict pulled the gun from his lap and steadied it on the frightened girl. "Now, enough talk. You-all just shut your pie holes for awhile."

Sweat trickling down his head and Sims trailing close behind him, Bridges returned to the kitchen after loading everything of value into Virgil's truck. Bridges scratched his scarred cheek with the barrel of the gun. In his other hand, he jingled Virgil's keys. "Thanks for the loan of the truck, old-timer. But you ain't gonna be needin' it no more. This town can burn in hell. And you all can go down with it." The notorious villain turned his attention to Lancaster. "Stop playin' with that dumb star and get to grabbin' all the food you can carry outta the refrigerator." He aimed the pistol at the man's face. "If I have to tell ya again, I'm gonna blow your brains all over the floor."

Lancaster rose from his seat. "Ya done told me to watch them while you-all loaded the car."

"Well, now I'm tellin' ya to get the food...*now get the food!*"

While Lancaster rummaged through the refrigerator, Sims scanned the troubled faces. "So, who we takin' with us, Earl? You said we needed us a hostage."

The murderer studied the terrified group briefly and gestured with his chin. "Him." The word still hovering in the air, Sims snatched Jared by the arm, prying him away from Rob's desperate hands.

Jared wrestled with the convict. "No. Please!" he begged.

Rob stepped away from the wall. "No! Take me! He's my son! I'll go! I won't cause you any trouble. I promise."

"Shut up!" Bridges yelled; his eyes narrow and cold. "You ain't in no position to negotiate! One more word outta you...or any of ya...and the kid dies! Take him to the truck, Sims."

Rob's heart pounded in his chest as he watched Sims drag Jared towards the door. The boy's face turned pale with dread. Rob stared at Bridges, the blood boiling in his veins. Every muscle in his body tensed, then the fear changed to rage. Like a bull bursting from a rodeo shoot, Rob pounced. He dove across the kitchen table and grabbed Bridge's around the waist. He punched the convict in the face with a right and clamped his left hand onto Bridge's wrist, wrestling for control of the pistol. Taken by surprise by the bold, desperate move Lancaster and Sims simply stood back and watched. With superhuman strength, Rob overpowered Bridges, slamming the con against the kitchen counter and wrestling him to the floor.

Lancaster dropped his bag of food and quickly leveled the shotgun and took aim. As he got Rob in his sights, both men struggling and jostling for position, Bridges moved into his line of fire. Lancaster took his finger off the trigger and looked to Sims, neither man sure what to do. With the convicts' attention focused on the scuffle in front of them, Virgil seized the moment. He pushed Suds from behind. "Run! Out the back! Run!"

Heeding the man's order, Darla yanked Molly's arm and pulled her through the living room, while Virgil reached for his grandson.

"Dad!" Jared yelled.

Virgil grabbed Jared by the neck and pushed the boy, forcing him towards the back of the house. "Leave him, Jared! Run!"

"They's gettin' away!" Lancaster screamed and fired his weapon, the shotgun blast blowing a ceramic lamp to bits as they fled. "Get 'em, Sims! Don't let 'em get away! They'll call the cops!" Sims kicked a chair out of his way and ran for the back door.

Rob punched Bridges squarely in the jaw, forcing the convict's hand off the gun. The two fumbled for control of the pistol, until Rob scooped it from the floor. He pressed the cold steel against Bridges' scarred cheek. The convict froze. His sinister laugh sizzled in Rob's face. Bridges slowly put his hands next to his ears with his palms up. Rob grabbed the front of Bridges' musty shirt and started to pull the criminal to his feet, when Lancaster bashed the back of his skull with the butt of the shotgun, sending Rob crashing facedown into the linoleum.

***

"Get in the corn!" Virgil ordered as Jared helped to steady him. A shot rang out and whizzed past them. Sims stood on the steps leading to the backdoor, working the lever of the 30-30. "Hurry! Get deep in the corn and hide!"

***

Bridges strained to get the limp body off of him. He squirmed out from under the dead weight and climbed to his feet. Rob was facedown on the linoleum with blood trickling from the back of his head. The convict clinched his teeth and stomped on Rob's back with the heel of his boot. "You idiot!" he screamed. "Just couldn't let me get outta this town, could ya? Now you're all gonna get it!" Bridges grabbed the pistol from the floor and ran towards the back of the house. "Come on, Lancaster!" Boiling with rage, he kicked the screen door open, nearly knocking Sims off the steps.

"They ran into the corn!" Sims hollered.

"Kill 'em!" Bridges screamed. "Kill 'em all!"

Lancaster stumbled down the stairs, chasing after his crazed leader. "Wait, Earl! We gotta think about this! That guy in the kitchen ain't dead!"

Bridges stopped and turned to Lancaster, his eyes blazing. "Kill him," he ordered coldly. "Go kill him and come back out to help us take care of the rest of 'em."

Lancaster nodded and darted back into the house. He kicked over a table in the living room and marched towards the lifeless body. "You just had to go and be a dang hero, didn't ya? Now you's a dead man! And the rest of 'em, includin that mouthy son of yours, will be joinin' ya directly!" He stood tall above Rob, straddling the defenseless man. "You shoulda known not to go aggravatin' Earl. That was your death sentence, hoss. He's a mean man. Not gentle like me." Lancaster closed his left eye and raised the shotgun to his chin. "By the way, you's got a nice home. Thanks for the hospitality."

Wham! Sirus burst through the kitchen door. The startled criminal spun to his right and fired, blowing a hole in the drywall over Sirus' right shoulder. The old man crouched and returned fire, catching the convict in the stomach and sending him reeling backwards into the living room. Lancaster fell into the back of the recliner and staggered to his left, clutching his stomach with one hand, the shotgun dangling in the other. He let the heavy weapon fall with a hollow thud. Lancaster's eyes rolled back his head as the blood flowed between his fingers. He collapsed to his knees and, with an eerie groan, hit the floor.

Shanks put his hand on the doorframe and stepped lightly across the broken glass. He stared at the convict's lifeless body. "Is he dead? Did you go and kill him, Sirus?"

"Yeah," the old man responded as he rushed over to Rob. He crouched down and checked for a pulse, while Shanks crept inside. "He's still alive! Thank God."

Shanks inched forward through the kitchen, his eyes glued to the fallen criminal. "Is this guy really dead?"

"Don't go near him," Sirus warned. "That ain't nothin' for no boy to be seein'."

"Does he got tattoos on him? Like on his face? I bet he's missing some teeth or a finger or something."

"Get away from him, Shanks," Sirus insisted as the boy nudged the criminal's limp body with his foot.

The nosy boy spotted a handkerchief sticking out of the dead man's pocket. His curiosity outweighing Sirus' orders, he reached for the cloth and pulled it from the pocket. As he tugged, a metal star fell from the wad and slid across the floor. "A star," he mumbled.

"What?"

"Nothin', Sirus." Shanks scooped up the star, wrapped it in the handkerchief, and shoved it into his pocket.

The old man stepped over to the boy and placed his large hand on Shanks' shoulder. "Rob's gonna be okay, but this here is worse than I thought. We gotta find the rest of 'em and them convicts that are missin'. I need you to call the police and tell 'em to get here soon as possible." Sirus reloaded his shotgun and headed towards the backdoor. "I'm gonna go find 'em. Make the call and then go wait in my truck. If you see anybody you don't recognize, take off. Run off and get far away from here. Go as fast as ya can and don't look back. Now get goin'."

***

Like two booms from a bass drum, the echo of the shots soared past Bridges as he stalked the perimeter of the cornfield. He chuckled. "Shot him twice. One for good measure. I taught that idiot well."

"Well, if we don't find the rest of 'em, you can tell him how good he done when we's back in prison," Sims scoffed. "They musta took off and ran inta the field back yonder."

Bridges pressed the side of his pistol against Sims' shoulder, listening intently. The muffled, soft sound of thick dry leaves bending and crunching drifted from the corn. "No. Wait," Bridges grinned. "They's in the corn. Hidin'. Go to the back, Johnny and start up through the cornstalks. I'll head in from here. We'll push 'em up and force 'em back towards the house. Any of 'em give ya any trouble or try to run, kill 'em. Blow their heads off. I've had enough of this."

His legs trembling, Suds stepped softly across the dirt. "They're comin' up behind us."

Rubbing his worn, wrinkled hands together, Virgil stared through the tall stalks. In the distance, coyotes began howling as the thin moon shone in the night sky. "Darla, take the kids and try to get around 'em. Stay outta sight. If they spot ya, run. This is life or death here, and there's no tellin' what they'll do."

Ms. Ramsey nodded, showing she understood the instructions and seriousness of the situation. "Wait. What are you gonna do,

Virgil? You're in bad shape. You can't outrun them. They'll kill you. Let me do it."

Virgil grabbed a cornstalk in each of his hands and started shaking them. "What are you doin'?" Molly asked. "They'll hear you. They'll know where we are."

"No time to explain, little lady. Just take 'em, Darla. Sneak around behind them." The noise of the dancing corn grew louder. "Now go."

Jared grabbed his grandfather's arm. "Grandpa. Stop. You don't understand. Those bad men aren't the only…things…in this field. Just come with us."

"I know what I'm doin', kiddo." Virgil winked confidently, though the gesture was faint reassurance for Jared. "Now follow Darla."

"No. I'm stayin' with you."

"Jared, come on," Ms. Ramsey urged. "I think they're getting closer."

"Go, boy," Virgil insisted. "I mean it."

Jared stood his ground. "No. I'm staying with you." With Sims and Bridges closing in around them, Darla darted into the darkness, leading Suds and Molly south across the stalks, while Jared and Virgil crept to the north. "Grandpa. Seriously. You don't understand. That noise. We'll all be in big trouble."

Virgil turned and smiled at his grandson. "Relax, boy. This is my farm, remember? I know all there is to know about it. Now keep quiet and stay down. If they catch up to us, I want you to run. Whatever happens to me, you do everything you can to get away. I'm old and have had a good life. It's time to stop worryin' about me. Worry about yourself for once. Promise me."

"I…promise," the boy replied, though he was not sure if he could keep his word. Jared heard a noise. "It's them. They're getting closer."

"Hide-and-seek is over!" Bridges voice sailed eerily through the darkness. "Come out, come out wherever you are! We know you're in here. Come to us and I promise not to kill ya." The wicked man's voice subsided. Jared looked at his grandfather and then scanned the stalks. "*Show yourselves!*"

"Good," Virgil whispered. "They're talkin'. That should get things heated up." He grabbed Jared by the hand. "Let's go." As the deadly convicts inched closer, Virgil yanked Jared towards the ground. "Get down. Don't move."

Jared tugged on his grandfather's arm. "They're gonna find us. We have to get out of here."

A horse's whinny knifed through the still night, making Jared jump. Virgil grinned; relief spread across his wrinkled face. "Thank God. I didn't think they'd ever show up." He turned to his grandson. "Whatever happens, kiddo, don't move. Stay still no matter what. The calvary has arrived."

"The calvary?" Jared mumbled. "You know…"

"Quiet. It's coming."

Sims shuffled through the sharp corn leaves, smacking himself in the face with a thick stalk. "Ahhh! I've had it with this town! I'm gonna kill these…" A rustling in the darkness stopped the convict in his tracks. "What was that? Somethin's behind us."

"It's them," Bridges hollered. "Go get 'em, Johnny! Let's get this over with!"

In rapid sucession one, two, and three horses neighed. "What the…?" Sims shouted. "It…it… sounds like…horses, Earl. A whole herd of 'em."

"Get 'em!" Bridges screamed. "They're just messin' with ya! They're a buncha kids, a woman, and an old man, for Pete's sake! Stop screwin' around and get 'em! I've had me enough of this crap!"

Sims tiptoed through the tall corn, his eyes focused and gun ready. A disturbance to his left caused him to swivel and level his rifle. "The Rebels is comin'," a deep, gruesome voice broke through the night. "Cap'n Plumb, the Rebels is chargin' towards us!"

Sims stood very still with the Winchester pressed against his shoulder and sweat dripping from his forehead. He slowly raised his foot and stepped backwards, hoping to retreat quietly from whatever it was in the field, but a voice behind him called out, "When I give the order we charge them bluecoats. Cut 'em down, boys."

"They's comin', Cap'n Bradley," another ghoulish voice groaned.

Dull rustling noises closed in all around him. Sims whipped his head back and forth, scanning the stalks to locate the origins of the haunted voices. The frantic con turned in a circle until a ghostly horse charged him, with flames exploding from under its hooves. The demon rider leaned to the side of his steed and swung his saber at Sims' head;

the terrified man dropped to the ground. "Ahhh!" he screamed. "Help me, Earl!"

A thunderous volley of blasts rang out as ghouls on both sides of the conflict collided in the middle of the cornfield. Smoke from the powdered rifles hovered at the top of the stalks; the smell of battle and animalistic carnage swarmed over Sims. Hearing an attacker knifing through the sharp leaves, the convict scrambled to his feet. Sims raised his rifle and fired, working the lever-action and returning fire over and over as he continued to dance in a circle of confusion. Atop his mangled steed the Union warrior, Captain Plumb, hurtled towards the doomed man. Sims rotated and pulled the trigger, but the bullet missed its mark. He jammed his shaking hand into his pocket for more shells. As he fumbled to reload the 30-30, Captain Plumb struck him with his saber, slicing the convict's right arm in two.

His hand dropped to the ground with blood spraying from the stump. "Ahhh!" Sims cried. "Nooo!"

The demon worked the reins of his grizzly steed, spinning the beast around to charge the injured man again. With a fearsome blow, the demon sliced through Sims' neck, sending his head rolling up the cornrow. Plumb yanked the reins, forcing his mount onto its hind legs, neighing triumphantly with smoke surging from its nostrils.

Virgil shooed Jared forward as a screaming bluecoat charged. The old man pulled his grandson close to him, shielding the boy with his crippled body. The demon lunged with his bayonet, stabbing Virgil in his left side. Virgil dropped to the ground, writhing in pain. "Nooo!" Jared screamed. His grandfather extended his arms in a feeble attempt to block the coming final blow.

The evil spirit hovered above the helpless man and thrust his bayonet forward, narrowly missing Virgil's face and stabbing the dry dirt. "Run, Jared! Get out of here!"

"Nooo!" he yelled as the ghoul thrashed away at his grandfather. Jared jumped in the air, throwing his foot forward. He kicked the demon in the chest, sending the bluecoat sailing backwards. He grabbed Virgil's arm and strained to pull the man to his feet, but Virgil was too battered and worn-out to move. The demon charged again. Jared winced and covered his grandfather with his small frame.

"Rahhhh!" the bogey roared, racing towards them with the bayonet aimed at Jared.

The boy shut his eyes; then his body jolted from a powerful blast. "Look out!" Sirus' familiar voice hollered. Jared lifted his head from Virgil's chest. The headless ghoul writhed, then collapsed in a heap upon the ground. The old man aimed and fired again, separating a second demon bluecoat's torso from the lower half of its body. Sirus grabbed Jared's arm and jerked the boy to his feet.

"Come on! Help me get Virgil outta here!" The two lifted the old man from the dirt, and Sirus pulled Virgil's arm around his neck. "We ain't got much time! Let's go! These beasts is everywhere in here and they's out for blood!"

Bridges fired the pistol, hammering a charging Rebel between its ghostly eyes. The creature crashed into the dirt at Bridges' feet while the man scanned the area around him for his next target. "Come on...you devils! I'll send ya all to hell!" A second beast leaped onto the convict's back. Bridges pounded the demon with his elbows. He grabbed the Rebel's arm, completely ripping it from its decaying body as he tried to toss the creature over his shoulder. A pistol shot to its worm-infested skull sent the soldier crashing to the ground. Two more shots sent another pair of Rebels reeling and body parts flying.

"You can't kill me! I was blessed by Lucipher himself!" Bridges pelted one fiend after another until his pistol clicked and clicked... empty. The criminal dug in his pocket for a new clip. He retrieved the ammo, shoved it into the handle of the .45, and cranked the barrel to load the chamber. Then the man froze. A moist, foul stench hit the back of his neck. The odor of rotting flesh hit his nose. Bridges spun to his left. A bearded creature with gooey saliva dripping from his mangled lips and jagged teeth stared at the convict with blazing red eyes. His right cheek had been eaten away from his eye socket to his jaw. Bloody chunks of skin had been torn from his forehead. Insects and worms crawled from the open wounds. The soldier beast grinned. His brimmed hat touched Bridges' brow. "Oh, no," Bridges mumbled.

The bluecoat raised his saber and, with a mighty blow, separated Bridges' head from the rest of his evil body. The convict dropped to the dirt, while his scarred face tumbled down the path between the stalks. With the convict's gory demise, the ghost of Captain Plumb wheeled to his right and disappeared into the darkness.

***

"This don't make no sense," Captain Pickering stated as Virgil was lifted into an ambulance by paramedics. "I gotta get to the bottom of this."

Resting on the bumper of the ambulance, Rob held an icepack to the back of his head. "I told you all I know. They kicked in the door and held us hostage. Our lives were in danger."

"I understand that." The heavy policeman, who had come straight from home and wore civilian clothes, tugged on his sagging pants. "But I got a dead ole boy in your livin' room, and two bodies in the corn with their heads bouncin' around like bowlin' balls. How can you explain that?"

"I told ya," Officer Kunkle said, standing with his thumbs latched onto the belt buckle of his police uniform. "None of 'em seen nothin'."

Captain Pickering glared at Sirus. "They ain't seen nothin'. And I don't suppose you is gonna explain any of this, either."

"I done told ya," Sirus replied, "the boy ran to my house sayin' there was trouble. When I got here, the one feller was about to shoot Rob in the back of the head. I did what I had to do to stop him. Ask the boy."

"That's how it happened," Shanks exclaimed. "Happened just like he done said."

"Well, if you didn't kill them boys in the corn, who did?" the frustrated captain continued. "Maybe you can help me understand all this, Darla?"

Ms. Ramsey, rubbing her arms nervously, glanced at Sirus and Rob. "We didn't hear anything. I'm sorry. We were hiding in the corn and got separated. Molly and Suds were with me, but we lost track of Virgil and Jared. We hid in the corn until Sirus came and shouted that everything was safe. We didn't hear or see anything. In fact, it was completely quiet."

"Look." Irritated by the questioning, Rob put his hand out towards the officer. "I have to get my dad to the hospital. We've told you already that none of us know how the two convicts were killed. We don't know. We didn't see what happened. Shouldn't the fact that they came in to do us harm, and that we're lucky to make it out alive, be what's important here?"

"Well, you'd think so, wouldn't ya?" Officer Kunkle answered. "But we's investigators. We got to get the facts."

Rob rolled his eyes and grabbed the handle on the inside of the ambulance door. "I've had enough of this. You two would sit here and watch my dad bleed to death, while ya count the rows of corn and reenacted the events of the crime." He hoisted his body into the back of the vehicle and called out to his son. "Jared. Stay here with Darla. She's gonna take you to her house for the night. I'll come get ya in the morning."

Jared stepped towards him. "No. I want to come with you. I want to make sure Grandpa is all right."

Rob smiled lovingly at his son. "You've had a hard night. You need to rest. Dad's fine and you can see him in the morning. Stay with Darla and try to get some sleep."

As the ambulance rumbled down the driveway with lights flashing, Captain Pickering pulled a matchstick from his pocket and set it in his lips. To get the information he needed, he would have to take a more authoritative approach.

"Now I've about had it. You-all ain't tellin' me all that ya know and I ain't leavin' till I get me some answers. Them fellers got their heads hacked off with sharp objects, but there ain't no weapons nowhere to be found. There ain't no footprints in the dirt that I can tell, neither. Who sliced them boys up?"

Intrigued by the chubby man's strange obsession with matchsticks Shanks studied his every move. "Do you suck on that match so it'll keep ya from eatin' everythin' in sight? That's what my mom said you got it in your mouth for. 'Cause ya can't stop eatin' otherwise."

"Will they sew them convicts' heads back on their bodies, or just bury 'em in separate caskets?" Suds asked.

Captain Pickering gritted his teeth and placed his hands on his round hips. "Daggum kids."

"Enough!" Officer Kunkle ordered. "You little dumb squirrels. This here is a serious matter. We need ya to pay attention."

"Well, they are children," Ms. Ramsey pointed out as she started ushering the kids towards her car. "This is a traumatic experience for them. They don't need to be interrogated like this. They've done nothing wrong and told ya everything you need to know. I'm getting them outta here. You can ask them your dumb, pointless questions some other time." The perturbed lady approached the hefty captain. "They could be scarred for life because of this experience."

"Do you think their heads seen their bodies as they went flyin' off, sailing through the air?" Suds continued. Captain Pickering glanced at the inquisitive boy and then stared at Ms. Ramsey. "Scarred? Yeah, I'm thinkin' probably not."

As the exhausted lady packed the kids in her car, Sirus leaned against the side of the house, his face concealed in the shadows. "Can I go now, too? I told ya everythin' I know. I didn't do nothin' wrong…no matter what you might think."

The large officer put his head down and stepped closer to the weary man. "I can't do nothin' to ya on this one, Sirus. You acted in self-defense and saved Rob Millhouse's life. They'd all testify to that.

"I don't know what else went on. I don't know who killed them other two in the corn. If you ain't tellin' me everythin', or if you's workin' with some nut jobs you brainwashed with your nutty ghost stories, I'll find out. I promise ya that. Somebody killed them boys and they may've helped kill them other ones too. Maybe them two Yankee ghost chasers ya got roamin' with ya is more than just ghost chasers. Maybe they's ghost creators, too.

"I still got my eye on ya, and you might want to know that we didn't find no traces of blood on that equipment in back of your garage. You know, the one you said ya injured your leg and arm on. I find that a little troublin', Sirus." Pickering rolled the match in his lips, sneering at the old man. "I can't hold ya on this here. You're free to go. But I wouldn't try leavin' town anytime soon. We's gonna keep a close eye on ya, if ya know what I mean."

10

Jared scooted to the edge of Virgil's hospital bed, disturbed by his condition. Barely able to keep his eyes open, the old man sat in his bed with a tube stuck in his nose and needles in his arms. The emergency room doctor at the hospital in Lee's Summit, decided it was best that the elderly man, whose trauma might affect the rest of his weak body, stay overnight for evaluation. Luckily, the stab wound missed Virgil's kidney, but did puncture his left lung, which coupled with his emphysema only compounded his problems. Groggy but awake, the old man smiled at Jared and patted the bed next to his bruised legs. "Hey, kiddo," he wheezed. "Take a seat next to your gramps so I can get a good look at ya."

"I'm gonna go grab us somethin' to drink and leave you two alone for a bit," Rob said and left the room.

Virgil grabbed the remote and turned the TV off. "Our little encounter's been on the news all day—even made the newspaper. I just wanna get things back to normal. Don't need to be bothered with such nonsense."

"Me, either," Jared mumbled. "Are you gonna be okay?"

The old man lifted his head from the pillow. "Heck, yeah, kiddo." He patted the boy on his leg. "I'm gonna be fine. Don't you go worryin' about it."

Jared stared at his hands as he played with his fingers. "Hey, Grandpa, how did you know the ghosts would come after them?"

"I didn't. I just hoped that they'd come. We didn't have us alotta options at the time, and I was crossin' my fingers that they wouldn't come after us, too, but...well, you know how that ended up. We was lucky to make it outta there alive, Jared. If somethin' woulda happened to you, I never would've forgiven myself, but I figured the ghosts was our only chance."

"But how long have you known? You know...how long have you known about the ghosts? I just didn't know you'd seen 'em, too."

"And I didn't know you'd seen 'em. I really wish I woulda told ya about 'em now. I hoped I was the only one, anyway. But, well… when your dad was a little tike, runnin' around in diapers still, he got real sick. He had a fever and couldn't hold nothin' down. Doctors couldn't figure out what was wrong with him and it went on for several days. Then the docs said Rob mighta had polio, which several people was still contractin' at that time. He coulda died from it. I really lost it then."

Virgil stared at the ceiling, the weight of the experience coming back to him. "I was a wreck. They say men are the strong ones, but it's really the women. Your grandma had to be strong. Strong for me and for her. I always regretted that. But, like I said, your dad was gravely sick. I thought we were gonna lose him. The thought of it tore me up. But somethin' about that experience triggered somethin' in me. I started seein' things. Ghostly, haunted things. I thought I was goin' crazy. I was scared for Rob, and then I was scared for Rob and me.

"I seriously didn't think I was gonna make it through the whole ordeal, and my mind was seein' the most horrifyin', gruesome things—too scary even to tell ya now. It brought back memories of Korea, and the visions wouldn't stop. One day I was at the old coffee shop on Main Street that ain't there no more. I overheard some folks tellin' stories about the battle of Lone Jack. I wasn't from here and I really didn't know much about it. I knew about the cemetery, but I never really connected what I was seein' with what happened at that battle. That was, till I heard them folks in that coffee shop. One of 'em was telling a story about some of the treacheries of the war.

"Three Confederates got cut off from their regiment. They tried to sneak south, traveling at night and hiding in the thick brush during the daylight. At the time, this area was swarmin' with Federal troops. The bluecoats ended up trackin' the Rebels because one of 'em had taken some grain for his horse and left an easy trail leadin' to their location. When the three Rebels was sleepin', the Federals shot 'em, killin' two of the boys…and they were just boys…and severely woundin' a third.

"A widow, whose farm was nearby, heard the shots. I'll never forget her name, either. It was Everett—Ann Everett. The Federal troops approached her and her two young children and bragged about what they'd done, sayin' two of the boys wouldn't cause no more trouble and would make good food for the hogs. Mrs. Everett couldn't allow that and nervously asked to see the Union captain. Reluctantly, the officer gave the woman permission to bury the dead and see to the wounded boy. But when the woman reached out to the local townsfolk, no one would help, and she fully understood why. A man caught helpin' dead or injured Rebel soldiers would end up dead himself.

"Finally, Mrs. Everett's brother and a local black man dragged the dead soldiers and the injured lad into her very home. She and her two young'ns spent the night alone with the dead bodies of them killed Confederate boys. Mrs. Everett didn't get much sleep, tendin' to the wounded feller and, of course, having two corpses laying stiff in her home. A short time after that, Mrs. Everett's brother was dragged from her home and killed by Federal soldiers right in front of her very eyes."

Virgil wiped his dry mouth with the back of his wrinkled hand and reached for a cup of water; his hand trembling while he drank. Returning the cup to the table, he shook his head. "After I heard that story, that's when the ghost sightings and nightmares really started. Ever since, I've had a recurring dream where I am locked in my home with two dead bodies. Both corpses…bloody soldiers dressed in gray."

***

The old truck rumbled over the dry dirt and gravel of the Millhouse driveway and stopped in front of the home. Sitting on the steps were Porker and Sweets. Suds, Shanks, and Beans stood, waiting for the final piece of the Crossroads gang puzzle to arrive. Rob threw the vehicle in park, as Jared leaped from the passenger seat and trotted away to meet his friends. "Hey, Millhouse," Sweetwater said. "How's your grandpa?"

"He's okay," Jared replied. "The doctor said he can come home tomorrow."

Rob gathered up bags of groceries from the back of the truck and walked past the boys. "Hey, fellas," he said and then looked at his son. "I don't want you runnin' off today. It's been crazy and you just need to relax. Stay around here."

"Geez, Mr. Millhouse," Shanks blurted out. "If you'd've said that a couple days ago, Jared wouldn't've got hisself inta all this mess in the first place!"

Slightly annoyed by the boy's perspective, Rob grinned. "Good point. Be home before dark and not a minute later." The man fumbled for his keys, trying not to drop any of the bags, and opened the door. "Thanks for makin' me feel better, Shanks."

"Yeah, thanks Shanks," Jared added.

Beans walked up behind Shanks and slammed his hands down on the mouthy boy's shoulders. "Well… show him what ya got."

A curious expression crossed Jared's face. "What?"

Sweets pushed himself off of the steps. "Go on. Show him. Ya can't keep it. Him and Suds nearly got killed tryin' to find it."

"I'm gonna," Shanks snapped as he dug in his pocket. "Hold your horses, Sweetwater." The boy clutched the handkerchief in his hands and began unwrapping it. "I finded it on the dead guy in your grandpa's livin' room." He revealed the dingy star and extended it to Jared.

Jared squinted at the sun reflecting off the object until he finally realized what was in front of him. "The star! You got the star!" He snatched the cloth from Shanks' hand. "Thanks, Shanks!"

***

Sirus stirred a large pot of homemade chicken noodle soup, while Louis and Jerry worked on their computers at the kitchen table. Ned scratched his scruffy beard, studying the men as if he were doing research of his own. The two professors had spent much of the night collecting data and taking measurements throughout Lone Jack. In their estimation, the situation was more urgent than ever after Sirus' encounter with the ghosts in the Millhouse cornfield.

Louis went through several pictures he downloaded onto his computer. "We've got paranormal activity everywhere in this town. All we had to do was put our camera out the window and click as we drove by and we'd get something. This isn't good."

"The data shows high heat and strong electrical charges in several pockets," Jerry added. "It's off the charts. The barometer showed increases in pressure and the EMF had disruptions in electrical fields everywhere we went. This town is overflowing with a flood of paranormal activity."

"Still not sure this here town's got itself some nasty ghosts, huh?" Ned asked sarcastically. "I figured we pretty much settled that debate when that one ugly ghoul had ya by the throat and was trying to slice ya in two."

Jerry pulled his fingers away from his computer and glanced at Mr. Lovelace. "We need to know just what we're dealing with here. Of course, we believe there is activity in Lone Jack, but we need to get our hands around exactly what we are dealing with."

Sirus set the spoon down on the counter. "I'm with Ned on this one. We ain't got time to take a roll call and count how many of them ghosts is floatin' around this town. We need to focus on how we get 'em outta here. You done said Saturday morning is our best shot and, if we can't get em outta here, we probably never will. That don't make me too comfortable about livin' here, especially if they keep transformin' and eventually overtake this town. We still don't know where the portal is and we got even less of an idea about the daggum key they keep askin' for."

"Well, Jerry is supposed to be working on that," Louis sniped.

Jerry slammed his hands down on the table. "I am! You know I'm working on it! Don't you think I have enough pressure without having you remind me constantly that we have to find the portal?"

"Well, it's kind of important, Jerry, considering it is the doorway for these ghosts to reach the other side!"

Ned chuckled. "Man, you two just never ease off. I don't think ya like each other much."

"Well, what have ya got so far?" Sirus asked. "Where are ya thinkin' the portal might be?"

Jerry took a deep breath and clicked onto another file on his computer. "I've narrowed it down. Unfortunately for us, this isn't an exact science, which isn't the way I like to work, but it's the best we've got at the moment. I'm taking an educated guess here, but I think that the portal is probably in one of three locations. I'm guessing it's something significant to the history of this town or the battle itself. Someplace like the Cave Hotel, the site of Dr. Caleb Winfrey's home, which is where the Baptist church is now, or the location near the cemetery where the blackjack oak tree stood for hundreds of years before it died just before the Civil War started. I just feel that the portal has to be something of significance for the spirits. They must've been very distressed by the violent battle and these three locations were vital to the town and the battle. But, like I said, it's not an exact science. It's just a hunch."

"No," Sirus responded, reflecting on the information. "It's the blackjack oak tree. I'd bet my life on it." He turned from the stove and stared at the ghost hunters. "That blackjack oak was the reason this town was founded. It was more than just a reference point for folks to meet. It was almost like a security blanket for this town. A life source. People held parties and festivals there. Had themselves picnics and reunions…all under that tree. But it was more than just a tree. It was an important part of the community. It was the heart of this town. Once the heart died, the town died with it. It's the tree. I guarantee it."

"Well, that settles that, then," Louis concluded. "Now we just need to figure out what this key is. That should be easy enough. And if we do identify it, then we have to find out where it is and how to get it." The professor shook his head in frustration.

Ned raised his hands and crossed his crooked arthritic fingers. "Captain Levin Lewis."

Sirus repeated the action, crossing his fingers and saying, "Captain Levin Lewis."

"Come again?" Jerry looked baffled. "What…what are you doing?"

"Captain Levin Lewis," Sirus replied. "He was a Confederate officer in the battle. He was also a Methodist minister. Durin' the battle he was shot in the head and fell to the ground. Lieutenant Colonlel Jackman rushed to his aid, assumin' the man was most assuredly dead, only to find that the bullet had embedded in his skin, but hadn't penetrated his skull. When Lewis started explorin' the injury to take the bullet out, he was struck by a second shot in the hand. After witnessin' this, Jackman said he'd hoped to convert the man, but since Yankee bullets couldn't get through his head, there was no use tryin'.

"Captain Levin Lewis." The old man lifted his hands and crossed his fingers again. "When ya need some good fortune for somethin' that seems is gonna take a miracle, folks in this town often do that. Cross they's fingers and say 'Captain Levin Lewis.'"

"Captain Levin Lewis," Jerry worked his hands into position and stated.

"Captain Levin Lewis," his colleague followed suite, as someone knocked at the front door.

"We got it!" Jared exclaimed with the rest of the Crossroads gang crowded around him.

Sirus stared at the boys with a peculiar expression on his face. "You got what?"

"The star!" Jared dug in his pocket and retrieved the soiled handkerchief. "The key!"

"Holy crap!" Jerry yelled. "Captain Levin Lewis!"

The boy extended the cloth to Sirus. "You can't touch it for too long. It gets real hot and glows. But it's the key! We just know it!"

Louis rushed through the living room. "But how? How do you know it's the key?"

"It belonged to the one soldier, Richard or somebody," Suds explained. "It got stole when he was gluing it to that one brick thing in the cemetery and he cursed Lone Jack 'cause of it."

"You mean Rooney?" Jerry exclaimed. "The Rooney star? I've read about that."

Louis snatched the object and handkerchief from Sirus' hand. "Let us examine it."

"Be careful with that thing, mister!" Shanks hollered, rubbing his tender, red hands gently together. "It'll burn ya. It ain't no toy. Trust me on that one."

"You boys come on in," Sirus instructed. "I got me some soup brewin' in the pot. You can help us eat while we study that star."

Noodles flopping and soup dripping onto the table, the gang smacked their lips as they ate and the two professors investigated the metal object. "It's definitely got a story to it," Jerry informed the group. "It's…very strange. Something is very abnormal and powerful about it."

Sirus leaned back in his chair and sighed. "Look. It's the best we got. If it ain't the key, it ain't gonna matter much no way. We got nothin' else."

With his cheeks filled and noodles seeping through his lips, Porker pushed his bowl towards the old man. "Can I have some more?"

"Geez, Porker," Beans said, "You've done had three bowls. He oughtta just set the pot in front of ya."

The round boy elbowed Beans. "I didn't eat much for lunch! Back off, man!"

Louis put his hands behind his bald head. "If it is the key... then what do we do with it? What does it unlock and where's the keyhole?"

The men thought about that question for some time. Frustrated, they tapped the table and scratched their heads with no answer. "I think I know," Jared mumbled. All eyes focused on the boy. "If it's a key and, if Rooney cursed this town 'cause it was stolen from that thing he built, wouldn't the place where it goes to unlock what we're needing to, be the place on the bricks where he put it and it was taken from?"

Slightly embarrassed by the revelation, Jerry stared at Louis. "Now why didn't we think of that? It makes perfect sense. I guess we're too analytical on this. So much so that we overlook the obvious."

"Ya think?" Ned added. "Makes complete sense to me," Louis replied. "Where did you boys find this thing anyway?"

"Robbers' Cave," Suds answered. "We went in to get it 'cause Millhouse figured it might be the key. It wadn't easy, neither. Got attacked by ghosts in chains and then ran inta them convicts when we finally got out."

Jerry wrinkled his forehead. "Robbers' Cave? I'm not familiar."

"It's a cave south of here," Sirus explained. "Used to be a limestone mine at one time. Older folks call it Bartlet Cave. When the Federal troops were all over this area trackin' down Rebels and Confederate sympathizers, the wanted graycoats often had to hide and even live in caves. Bartlet Cave was one of 'em that they hid out in. You can find lots of neat stuff in there—treasures from the past."

"Well," Jerry replied with a nod. "If we make it out alive Saturday morning, you can take me there. I'd like to see it." He wrapped the star neatly in the handkerchief. "This will stay with us for safekeeping. No offense, but I feel a little less nervous having us hold on to it."

"Yeah," Shanks blurted, "that makes sense. Millhouse here figured out it was the key and then he had to tell ya where to put it, to unlock whatever it is we're unlockin'."

Louis lowered his eyes and dropped his head. "Good point."

As the boys rustled out of their chairs, Sirus glanced into the living room. "I done almost forgot. I got somethin' for you boys, and Molly and that girl who talks all nasally, too." He led the gang into his spare bedroom where a box sat on the mattress. He unfolded the top and pulled several plastic covered items from it. "Here ya go. I got one for each of ya. Be sure to give Molly and that other girl theirs for me, too, Jared."

Sweets stared at the package. "But what is it?"

"They's uniforms. I got four gray and four blue. I figured if'n we's gonna lure these ghosts out to do battle, we might as well go all out. Wear 'em Saturday and folks'll just think you're helpin' celebrate." The old man extended one of the uniforms to Porker. "I even found me one in your size, big boy."

"Hey, I'm just big-boned."

Sirus grinned. "Yeah, right." He tossed the empty box to the corner of the room. "Now, look. This here ain't no game. You all keep your eyes peeled and your heads down. We need ya there to help out. We need ya to let us know what's goin' on, but we'll do all the heavy liftin'. I don't want nothin' to happen to you–all, so stay outta the way once...whatever's gonna happen...happens. We'll take them ghosts on if they get rowdy. It could get real crazy and even scary. But we're gonna have to lead 'em to the portal. Keep us informed and stay outta the way. We'll do the rest."

11

Rubbing the crust from his eyes, Jared climbed out of bed and staggered through the bedroom door. He walked into the kitchen and found his grandfather sitting at the table drinking coffee. "Grandpa? You're home?"

"Well, yeah, kiddo," he replied, extending his arms for a hug. "Your dad came and got me this mornin'. He figured you needed your rest, so he asked Darla to come watch ya while he drove to Lee's Summit." Jared pulled a chair from the table and sat down next to the weary man. "I think them nurses was sad to see me go too. A couple of 'em had their eye on your old grandpa. But, man, I hate hospitals. Got tubes and machines all hooked up to ya. Ya don't even feel human. More like a science project or somethin'. It was good to get outta there. So how are you, kiddo? Everythin' okay?"

Jared hesitated, thinking about the commemoration and the ghosts. "Oh, I'm fine."

"You still havin' bad dreams or somethin'?"

"No. I slept great. But I did dream. It started out kinda scary, but then it ended up kinda cool. It was real dark and creepy. I was standing at the base of this huge mountain and the wind was blowing like crazy, 'cause this terrible storm was coming. Then this horse-like creature comes up, but it wasn't completely a horse. It had a horse's head, but it walked upright and had huge furry hands like a person's. It grabs me with one of its enormous hands and puts me on its shoulder. We're walking up the mountain when the ground starts shaking. Then there's this huge explosion and the top of the mountain blows up, sending dust and tiny rocks all over us. Then this river of bright, fiery lava comes sizzling down. It's pouring out like a river and its racing towards us. We can't escape, but when it finally reaches us it's not hot, just a glowing wave. It doesn't burn us at all. We ride down it like a ride at a carnival. Then it all disappears, the horse creature and the mountain and everything, and I'm standing on the top of a hot air balloon that is sailing towards space. I'm just floating. It all seemed so real. The balloon stops and I'm still on top of it, and there are bright stars spinning and shooting out sparks of light all around me. The stars drop right out of the sky and come racing towards me. I have to duck and dodge them before they hit me and knock me off the balloon. Then the scene changed again and I was in a building with nothin' in it and its walls were as tall as skyscrapers, and then I woke up before I could finish it."

Jared paused and looked to his grandfather, waiting for a response. The old man blew gently on his coffee. "A boy's incredible, adventurous imagination—cherish it, kiddo. It don't last forever."

***

Dressed in his elaborate gray officer's uniform with the insignia and medals of a distinguished colonel, Dave Davenport from Maryville inspected the stack of firewood that had been delivered to the battlefield that morning. He had bestowed on himself the role of Confederate Colonel Upton Hays, the highest-ranking Rebel commander on the battlefield that infamous day, something that was not overlooked by his fellow reenactors. But Davenport felt he was the glue that held the group together, even if his leadership went unrecognized and unendorsed by his comrades. He studied the battles, scheduled the reenactments, made all the plans, and oversaw the procurement of supplies and the logistics of horses. The fact that his efforts were unappreciated only added fuel to his fire. Scorned and chastised or not, he'd ride proudly and bravely across the battlefield that fateful *next* morning adorned in that magnificent uniform; wielding his shiny saber as the legendary Rebel leader, Colonel Upton Hays.

"So, Mr. Davenport." Mrs. Morgan walked briskly through the sweltering heat of the August day and approached the strange reenactor. "Have you everything you need?"

The man in his fancy, thick wool uniform turned around. "Call me Colonel Hays, if ya would, ma'am, especially in front of the men." He pulled off his leather gloves and slapped them against the palm of his hand. "Well, the wood could've been chopped into quarters instead of halves, but we'll make do. I also would've liked the water to have been poured into canteens instead of stacked out here in cases of plastic bottles, and the electric generator to run the fans should've been concealed in a tent, instead of just sittin' out here in the open. I don't need my men goin' soft on me, especially the day before a fierce battle. I need my troops hardened and ready come tomorrow."

Mrs. Morgan stared at the man, looked away, and then stared at him again. "Right...I...apologize."

The officer patted Mrs. Morgan on her shoulder. "It's okay, ma'am. We'll make do." A paper bucket shot from one of the soldier's tents and bounced across the ground. "Okay, who brought Kentucky Fried Chicken? How many times do I have to tell you men? We eat as they did in the 1860s. This is insubordination."

"Oh, we're sorry, *Colonel Hays*," one mouth full of the greasy bird sneered.

"Get a life," Bobby Hicks from Odessa quipped.

Davenport pulled a notepad from his pants. "I'm puttin' you on report, MacDonald! You, too, Hicks! See if you're invited to Centralia to ride along side me when I mount my trusty steed as the notorious Bloody Bill Anderson."

Munching on a chicken leg, MacDonald snickered with grease and crumbs sticking to his lips and chin. "Give it a rest, Davenport. You don't even own a horse. The last time we was in Centralia, ya tried to borrow one from the locals and they couldn't find ya none. You ended up riding gallantly inta town in the back of a pickup with signs that read 'stead' taped to both sides of the truck. Ya even spelled *steed* wrong."

Swatting away the flap covering the entrance, two more reenactors stormed out of their tent. "To hell with this," one of them growled. "I'm gettin' a motel room. I ain't sittin' out here sweatin' all daggum day, just to get eaten alive by mosquitoes and chiggers all night."

"Deserters!" Davenport yelled. "Where is your spirit, lads? Where is your loyalty to the Stars and Bars?"

"Bite me!" Taylor MacDonald hollered. The man jumped from his seat and started to tear off his uniform. "This wool is scratchin' me all over! I've had it with this crap! We shoulda just joined the real Armed Forces. Ya get better food, a better place to sleep, and we wouldn't have to put up with ole Colonel *Uptight* Hays."

A young private approached the colonel, saluted and stood at attention. "At ease, Cuthbert," Davenport ordered.

"Sir," the young man said, "I think the men are growin' restless. Probably stressed over tomorrow's fierce battle. Shall I play on my mandolin to ease the tension?"

"Well, finally, a soldier with his heart in the right place. Very admirable, Private Cuthbert. Yes. Play your song and allow the men to dance around the camp. Ease their suffering and nerves, lad," Davenport directed.

"Cuthbert, you get that mandolin out and I'm gonna crack ya over the head with it and then smash it inta splinters under my boot," a voice from inside a tent warned.

"Daggum volunteers," Davenport mumbled.

"Yes." Feeling uncomfortable, Mrs. Morgan smiled at the odd man. "Well, if there's nothing else ya need, I'm off to get everything ready for the pie-eating contest and the raffle. We've sold thousands of raffle tickets for two shotguns at twenty dollars a piece. We'll announce the first winner tommorow at eight in the morning, and the second one after the reenactment is over. There's still time to buy raffle tickets if you and your men are interested, um…Colonel…Hays.

"By the way, as we discussed, in the event of rain–and the forecast says there will be a terrible thunderstorm tonight—if it carries over into tomorrow morning and cancels the reenactment of the battle, we'll perform it on Sunday afternoon after church, as planned. I think you might want to get your men into safer quarters tonight. It's just a suggestion, but I'd hate for one of them to have to sleep out here in the rain in these loosely constructed tents or, even worse, be struck by lightening."

Davenport pushed out his chest and raised his chin. "We'll be fine, ma'am. These are tough men. They're used to having to adapt to inhumane conditions and live without the comforts of home. We'll be ready when duty calls."

"Did anyone bring sun block and a radio?" one of the camped Rebels asked.

Decked out in their uniforms, the Crossroads Club marched through the morning fog from the Davis garage down the streets of Blue and Gray Estates. They kept in an orderly, single file line with the gray-clad troops on one side and the blue on the other. Wearing the gray and stepping proudly on the left were Suds, Shanks, Porker, and Molly. Jared, Sweets, Beans, and Jan donned the blue colors of the Union. The young soldiers turned crisply, cutting between two houses, and stomped through the dew-covered grass, heading for the cemetery and battlefield. "Company, halt!" Sweets commanded as they reached the gate to the sacred burial ground. "At ease, men."

Holding hands and enjoying the festivities, Rob and Darla wandered through the crowd of visitors who were munching on funnel cakes, turkey legs, and barbequed ribs, playing games, and shopping at the many booths for cheap jewelry and other souvenirs. Rob spotted the kids eating snacks in the shade of the Osage orange trees near the entrance of the cemetery. "Rob Millhouse, reporting for duty," he proclaimed with a joking salute. "What are you-all doin' all dressed up in these fancy uniforms?"

Jared scrambled to his feet. "What are you doin' here? I thought you weren't coming to the festival."

"I'm beginning to feel a little unwelcome here, Rob," Darla joked. "I think we're cramping someone's style with our presence."

The man nodded. "Really. I came to keep an eye on ya, but I guess you're doin' just fine." Turning to leave, he hesitated. "You're actin' weird. You-all better not be up to any funny business."

Shanks smiled innocently, a move he'd already mastered in his brief lifespan, and patted Jared on the back. "We're fine, Mr. Millhouse. Just enjoyin' the fun. We ain't up to no nonsense."

Parking in the lot next to the Baptist Church where Dr. Caleb Winfrey's house once stood, Sirus pulled his shotgun from the bed of the truck and held it discreetly to his side, while the ghost hunters collected some of their more inconspicuous equipment, concealing it in their uniforms. Sirus and Louis wore Federal uniforms, while Ned and Jerry dressed as Rebel soldiers. They scanned the area and stepped slowly towards the crowd, hoping they wouldn't be seen or draw too much attention to themselves. As the four crossed Bynum Road, Officer Kunkle pulled up in his police vehicle and jettisoned himself from the driver's seat.

"Just what do ya think you're doin'?" the protector of Lone Jack asked.

"We's takin' a rocket ship to the moon," Ned chided. "What the heck does it look like we're doin'?"

The officer shook a stern finger at the men. "I don't want any monkey business outta you. I'm in charge of security and, so far, every time you show up there's complete chaos and somebody gets their head chopped off. If you-all go ruinin' Mrs. Morgan's celebration and scarin' folks half to death, you're gonna be in big trouble and a world of hurt, let me tell ya. We's had news people from all over comin' here the last week, makin' us look stupid and actin' like we can't keep the peace in this here town."

Not wanting to further excite the dutiful policeman, Sirus and the ghost chasers remained cautiously quiet, while Ned was less covert. "Well, them news folks get a bad wrap, but they generally tell the facts as they see 'em."

"I'm warnin' you, boys," the officer continued, "you pull any of your crap today—in fact, if'n ya even act like you's gonna do anything foolish—I'm hauling ya in." He placed his hands on his belt and spit on the sticky pavement. "Captain Pickerin's at the doctor's g'tting' a boil lanced, so I'm in charge till he gets back. He has instructed me to keep a close eye on you troublemakers. I plan on followin' my orders to the letter."

"A boil lanced?" Ned repeated. "Does that mean he finally came to his senses and you're gettin' fired? Is it like one of them codes you morons like to use?"

"Ha, ha," Officer Kunkle hollered as he returned to the squad car and hopped in. "Laugh it up, Ned. Keep laughin', all of y'all, and I'll just arrest ya and keep ya locked up till these here festivities is over. You can laugh and make your funnies while you's sittin' in a jail cell. Got any more jokes now?"

Illustrating his unadulterated power, the officer glared at the men for several seconds, then slammed the door and sped off down the road.

"None I want to say while you's still standin' here," Ned mumbled.

Jerry dropped his head and slapped his thigh. "That guy is going to birddog us to death. He's going to scrutinize our every move. He has no idea what will happen to this town if we aren't able to get these ghosts corralled and sent back to the spirit world."

"Kunkle?" Ned grunted. "That dog don't hunt. He's a boob."

Watching the officer's car turn into the parking lot by the water tower, Sirus nodded in agreement. "Ned's right. He ain't no problem, as long as we don't do nothin' to bring attention to ourselves. When we do, there ain't gonna be no time for him to mess with us while he's runnin' for his life." Sirus studied the crowd, looking for a secluded area to stay out of the way and wait. "Let's go."

Louis studied the clouds as thunder rolled above their heads. "Look at that sky. It's almost as dark as night out here. Look how thick and black the clouds are." He turned to the other three. "I don't like this."

***

Suds pulled a handful of loose change from his pocket and dropped it next to the register, while Molly grabbed the messy stick of cotton candy from the vender and bit into the light, sugary treat. As they turned from the counter, a large, meaty hand struck Suds in the chest and latched onto his throat. "Did ya think I'd forget about the race, Scab?" Dozer hissed, a bandage spread across his nose and his left arm was set in a cast. "You dangnear ruined my ATV!"

"Snap his head off, man," Greeley cheered with his red bangs sticking to his head like tape. "Kill the cheater. He made ya break your nose and arm and trashed your ATV. Do it man. Beat the crap out of him."

Suds pried at the boy's powerful grip, trying to breathe and looking for an escape. "Can't we talk about this?"

"Leave him alone!" Molly shouted. "He beat you fair and square!"

The Goat snatched the cotton candy from Molly's hand and pushed her away. "Stay outta this, girly. Scumbag's a cheater and now he's gonna pay."

Walking through the crowd, Beans and Jared spotted their pal's dilemma, and rushed over to the scene. "Lay off, man!" Beans yelled. "You're just bent outta shape 'cause he beat you. And you was supposed to give him your ATV, but ya didn't, and Suds never said nothin' about it."

"Oh, a hero," Greeley huffed. The red-haired punk charged the boys and socked Jared in the face, sending him tumbling to the ground.

The Goat's evil cackle cut through the air like an annoying chainsaw. "Look at 'em! They's dressed in soldiers' uniforms! What, ya goin' to war there, general?"

"Hey! Cut that crap out!" the vender hollered. "You're scarin' off customers! Go do your calisthenics someplace else!"

Dozer released Suds from his viselike grip. "This ain't over, Scum. You's gonna pay. I'll be lookin' for you and your wimpy pals later. When you-all least expect it, we're gonna beat the tar outta you and all them little friends of yours. You ain't gonna get away with destroyin' my ATV. My old man was all fired up about it. You're gonna pay. You's definitely gonna pay."

With an icepack, donated by a charitable lady at a barbeque tent, pressed against his cheek, Jared sighed and shook his head. His dad had shown up, unaware of the seriousness of the situation in Lone Jack, and Lathon Greeley had put a welt, the size of a quarter, on his face. Thinking things couldn't get much worse, Jared spotted his grandfather shuffling through the crowd. "What is he doin' here?"

"Who?" Molly asked.

"My grandpa. His emphysema is acting up and he was stabbed by the ghosts. He shouldn't be here. He should be resting." The two kids wandered through the throng of people to rescue the old man.

"Hey, kiddo," Virgil smiled. "Wow, you're lookin' quite stylish in them uniforms. I guess you're goin' all out to celebrate. How ya enjoyin' it so far? Played any of the games?"

"Grandpa!" Jared grabbed the man's fragile hand. "What are you doin' here? You should be in bed."

"I ain't missed the commemoration in twenty years."

Molly took the old man's other hand in hers. "But you don't understand, Mr. Millhouse. This one here isn't gonna be like the other ones. This…this…could be…scary and…dangerous."

The two kids dragged the old man, against his will, into the shade of the Osage orange trees lining the cemetery. Virgil pulled his hands free. "Hey, you two. Watch yourselves. Who's the adult here? I know what I'm doin'. You don't think I know what's goin' on? I'm old, but I ain't catatonic. I'm here to help out. Besides, I practically know them ghosts by name. And I know what they's capable of. If there's a way to get 'em outta here, I wanna make sure it happens. And if they get violent, I ain't gonna have my grandson mangled by spirits from the land of the dead, while I'm sittin at home drinkin' sweet tea. You-all go about your business and leave me in peace. I can take care of myself, and you-all can't. So I'm here to watch over ya and be ready for whatever might happen."

"Pssst. Jared. Come here," a voice whispered.

Peeking around one of the Osage orange trees, Sirus glanced at the boy and pulled his head back behind the trunk. Confused by the odd behavior, Jared looked over both shoulders and approached him. "What are you doing? Who are you hiding from?"

"Oh, I don't know. I feel like I'm bein' watched. Never mind that." The old man extended the star-concealing handkerchief to the boy and placed it delicately in his hands. "I want you to take care of this. I mean, you's the one who finded it, and you was the one who figured it might be the key and all. Besides, I got more faith in you in all of this than I do them two Yankee ghost chasers. They's a little green and ain't too dependable thus far."

The old man's face grew serious. "The fact is, I trust you. I trust you more than I do them, if you can believe it. I've got me a bad feelin' about this. A lotta people here. I've seen me a lot these past couple of days and it's all comin' to an explosive end. Even my dreams is so real and intense I can barely breathe when I wake up. A couple nights ago I dreamed I was ridin' a wave of lava down a volcano."

Jared gawked at the man. "I had a dream about a volcano! I was on top of a man with a horse's head, and he carried me on his shoulder!"

Sirus hesitated and licked his dry lips. "We had the same dream, boy. Only I was carryin' a child on my shoulder—a child whose head was a ball of fire." The two stared at one another, disturbed by the shared vision.

"Keep close. When whatever happens starts happenin', I want you in the cemetery near the Union Monument. When the portal reveals itself and I give you the word, put the star in the place on the bricks where it was stolen from. That should unlock the door and release ole Rooney's curse and cool his fire. But be careful, son. For some reason these ghosts have sought me and you out more than the others. We're the chosen ones and at their mercy till they's gone. But they'll kill ya just the same. Be sure of that, 'cause they's confused and crazed from their imprisonment between worlds. But they've chosen us, even if they don't know it, and we got to get them outta Lone Jack and over to the other side." He looked to the sky, where black clouds and tracks of lightening rumbled in the distance. "Be ready...it's gonna get some kinda crazy on this here battlefield. I can just feel it."

***

The event she'd spent months planning hanging in the balance at the mercy of Mother Nature, Mrs. Morgan tapped the microphone with a pathetic look on her face. It was seven-forty-five in the morning and the sun had been blanketed by billowing clouds since it rose. "It looks like the rain will be on us a little earlier than predicted, so I am going to announce the winner of our first raffle a little early as well. In case you hadn't heard, we are giving away two shotguns. One now and another one after the reenactment is over around ten...that is, if the weather doesn't cancel the spectacular event. But, yes, well... without further ado," she reached her hand into the jar and twirled her arm in a circle, "the first winner is..." The curator plucked a ticket from the container and unfolded it. "Trigger Hargrave!"

"Holy crap! I think I just won me a gun!" exclaimed a skinny, unshaven man in a white tank top as he darted through the crowd.

"Okay." Standing between Sirus and Louis, Jerry hooted. "Did a guy named 'Trigger' just win a shotgun?" Chuckling, the professor shook his head. "Man, only in America."

Louis checked his watch and then retrieved two dousing rods and an infrared thermal scanner concealed in his uniform. The ghost hunter pointed the scanner towards the trees and thick brush behind him. "Man, I'm getting serious readings here. The whole area is one giant cold spot, like a refrigerator. This is too creepy."

Jerry snatched one of the rods from Louis' hand and aimed it at the eerie shadows. "Then where are they?" He studied the sky above. "The air is thick. Magnetic. Charged. Why don't they show themselves?"

Sirus clutched the shotgun hanging at his side, beads of sweat—from humidity and stress—swelling on his forehead. "Be careful what you wish for." He glanced at Jared standing anxiously near the gate of the cemetery and offered a reassuring wink. "Maybe it isn't right? The battle was started at sunrise and here it is almost eight. Maybe we's already missed our chance?"

Discouraged, Jerry shook his head. "No. This has got to be it. As long as they show themselves before the solar eclipse we should be fine. It's coming. I can feel it." He checked one of his gauges. "They're all around us. But what are they waiting for?"

Ned's good eye spun around like a fly landing on a meal. "They's waitin' for the daggum battle to begin, don't ya know? It started when a green Rebel recruit stumbled on some grass and accidentally fired his weapon." The bearded man drew one of his precious revolvers from the holster resting low on his hips, and slid his wrinkled hand across the cylinder. "Ya want this here grand finale of a battle these boys been fightin since 1862 to get goin'…then here ya go." The brittle old-timer waddled across the lawn and stepped into the thick vegetation under the trees.

Sirus and the ghost hunters waited with hands at the ready. The leaves crunched and twigs snapped as Ned stepped through the brush. The glass-eyed man cocked his revolver and pointed it at the ground. The echo of the shot bounced through the trees and across the battlefield. Startled by the unexpected blast, the crowd, wandering through the reenactors' campsite and various souvenir and game stations, stopped and stared into the woods.

Sirus grabbed his shotgun and held it near his chest. "Nothin's happenin'. What's goin' on?"

Mrs. Morgan returned to the steps of the museum and collected the microphone. "Not to panic. We have reenactors here and I'm sure it was just one of them accidentally discharging their weapon. Please enjoy the festival."

In the dense vegetation, a frustrated Ned fumbled to cock his pistol again. "Daggum ghosts. They's a fickle bunch." The old man sent a second shot exploding into the ground.

As if an alarm clock woke them from their daze in the land of the spirits, fiery sets of red eyes lit up the perimeter of the battlefield. Jerry turned in a circle, taking in the glowing eyes of hundreds of demons cutting through the thick, charged air in every direction. "Oh nooo," he uttered. "This isn't gonna be good."

A thunderous howl ripped through the woods, as the people danced around in confusion. Realizing the danger, Sirus charged the reenactor campsite. "Get outta here! Go on home! It ain't safe!" In a panic the crowd shuffled around the battlefield, gathering their loved ones. Sirus stopped near a reenactor's tent with his shotgun at his side. "Get goin'! Get on outta here!"

Ducking between the tents, Officer Kunkle rushed the cause of the mayhem. He grabbed Sirus' arm, ready to slap on his handcuffs. "I warned ya, Sirus! I knew you would be up to no good! You's creatin' a goshdarn riot!" He thrust the cuffs at Sirus, but the old man yanked his wrist out of the way. "Don't you fight with me! That's resistin' arrest!"

As he tussled with the ignorant public servant, Sirus glanced at the woods east of the museum. The howl of the demon soldiers intensified. The beasts broke across the field, like a wave of fiery death. "Kunkle! You don't understand! Look! Look, man!"

The charge of the demons hit Kunkle like a powerful gust of wind. The officer tossed the cuffs in the air and backed away. A swarm of mutilated soldiers sailed towards them. "Oh my God!" he yelled and took off.

The bluecoat ghouls charged from the north and west while their hideous foe rushed the battlefield from the south and east, with Sirus and the ghost hunters caught in the middle. The old man raised his shotgun, blasting the arm of a Rebel banshee, tearing the skeletal appendage from its devilish body.

"What in tarnation is goin' on, mister?" the graycoat reenactor, Taylor MacDonald, screeched.

Sirus ejected the spent shells from his gun and reloaded. "They's ghosts of the dead soldiers from the battle…and they's comin' for one last bloody fight. Get on outta here. They'll kill ya."

"Forget that!" Bobby Hicks yelled. "You need help, mister!" The reenactor rushed to his gang of confused comrades. "Grab your patches, powder, and balls! Get 'em and start firin'! This here is real, boys! These beasts is lookin' to massacre the whole town!"

With his newly won shotgun in hand, Trigger Hargrave grinned in anticipation. "Give me a handful of them shells ya got!" he hollered to Sirus, "and I'll give them freaks a go with this here new gun!"

Sirus wheeled to his left and pelted a charging bluecoat in the breast, sending the monster flying into the side of one of the tents. Reaching into his pocket, the old man grabbed a handful of shells. "Here! Get to firin'! We got to fend these creatures off till we can get the portal open!"

The demons clashed on all sides of the battlefield, fighting with evil ferocity. His limbs trembling, "Colonel" Davenport backed away to safety behind his line of brave fighting men. He staggered towards an opening on their left flank. "I don't think this was in the schedule of events! I'm goin' for reinforcements' lads!" With his knee-high shiny leather boots practically hitting him in the chin, the terrified man high-stepped it to the parking lot.

"Colonel *Hays*," Hicks grunted as he pulled the ramrod from his musket. "More like Tracy, the daggum coward. He's peein' down his leg."

Using a pile of wood as cover, MacDonald jumped forward and fired, smoke and sparks exploding from the muzzle. "Daggum blackpowder!" he yelled. "These beasts is more armed than we are! We oughtta have us M16s and grenade launchers!" The soldier scanned the battlefield as he reached for his powder bag and poured generously into his musket. Across the grass, he spotted a force of Rebel fiends charging the Union reenactors' cannons sitting in the northeast corner of the field. "Look! They's goin' for the cannons!"

Sirus crushed the skull of a Union ghoul with the butt of his shotgun and hammered the creature's chest with his boot. "Let's hope they slaughter each other, like they done in the real battle! We's in trouble here!"

Tires squealing and engines roaring, the people raced in both directions down Bynum, searching for safety. Through the smoke and haze, the herd of ghastly horses stampeded down the street, their heads thrusting and nostrils blazing with fire, forcing the cars into the ditches lining the road.

Jerry and Louis rushed through a hail of bullets and leaped to safety on the opposite side of the wood pile. "I don't think we planned this out well," Louis deduced, brushing the dirt from his uniform.

"Is that a derogatory comment meant for me, Louis?" Jerry raged. "We're fighting possessed demons here! There's no cookbook or reference manual for that!"

Near the Union cannons, a Rebel ball tore through the rotted face of a Union ghoul, ripping off the demon's jaw. Closeby to the wounded ghoul, a second bluecoat warrior was shot in the head, sending half his skull flying through the air. Both monsters held their positions and continued to return fire at their enemy. In another section of the battlefield, two Union soldiers, each missing an arm as a result of deadly Confederate gunfire, worked together to load, fire, and reload a single musket. In the middle of the field, Bradley and Plumb squared off, each with sabers in one deadly hand and pistols in the other. The plumes on the officers' hats danced like sinister marionettes as they battled.

Ned crept along the treeline at the edge of the battlefield. Heading towards him, with two Rebels hot on their tails, were Porker and Jan. The old-timer ducked behind the trunk of a tree. As Porker stumbled and dropped to his knee, Ned leaped into the kids' path with both hands gripping his trusty revolvers. The cantankerous, tough old man fired over their heads, dropping one ghoul in his tracks. The other he hammered with rapid fire until he, too, tumbled to the ground. Steaming dark green slime flowed from the demon's body with the stench of fresh roadkill hovering in the air. Ned put his arm around the frightened girl. "Come on, li'l lady! You-all need to take cover!"

Shaken by the hair-raising encounter, Porker fingered the barrel of the pistol in Ned's leathery hand. "You…you…you're allowed to shoot them things?"

"Call the cops, porky," Ned replied, pushing the two kids into the taller grass. "I ain't as old and useless as ya think. Saved your butt, didn't I? Besides, them cops got more important things to be worryin' about at the moment."

Near the gate of the cemetery, Virgil crouched with a broken two-by-four gripped tightly in his hands. "Get behind them monuments and keep your heads down and eyes peeled!" he ordered. Jared, Molly, and Suds ducked behind a tombstone next to the Union Monument. "I'll fend 'em off if they come for us!"

"Where's Sirus and them ghost chasers?" Molly screamed with her hands over her ears to muffle the terrifying howls and intense gunfire. "We need to unlock the portal thing!"

Beans leaped across the grass and dove through the gate. "They're chasin' us! A whole gang of 'em!"

The slow-footed Sweets broke through the brush with a ghoul clawing his uniform. The monster thrust his gory head forward, clamping onto the boy's shoulder with his jagged teeth. Virgil raised the board and smashed the creature in the back, knocking the beast and the boy to the ground. The zombie released his bite and reared his ugly head. Virgil hammered the demon across the face, separating his skull from his body. A second Rebel charged. The old man blocked the creature's bayonet and plunged the broken, pointy end of the lumber through his chest.

"Come on!" Virgil yelled to Sweets, tugging on the boy's arm as he lay pinned under the headless corpse. "Get inside the cemetery!" Sweets squirmed out from under the insect-infested creature and scrambled to his feet. Blood seeped through the shoulder of his uniform as he rushed for safety inside the gates.

Watching from their vulnerable position in the middle of the heated battle, Sirus fired his weapon and called out to the ghost chasers. "They's goin' after the kids! What are we waitin' for? We need to open the portal!"

"Why isn't the boy putting the star in the indentation on the monument?" Louis yelled. "We're all going to die!"

Sirus rose from cover, blasting a demon bluecoat in the shoulder. "I told the boy we'd tell him when to unlock the portal! You said the portal would show itself! Where is it?" The man hastened to reload his shotgun. "Why ain't it showing itself?"

With his knees tucked under his chin, Jerry's body jerked with every explosion of gunfire. The ghost chaser pushed his glasses up the bridge of his nose. "Well, crap! Maybe he needs to unlock the portal and then it will show us the location of the passageway!"

Sirus dove for cover and patted Jerry on the shoulder as he scrambled to his knees. "That's good to know now. Thanks." He swiveled his tired body in the direction of the cemetery, fifty yards to the east of the reenactors' overrun campsite. "Cover me."

"With what?" Louis cried out. "What…are we going to throw scanners and EMF detectors at them? We don't have weapons!"

Jerry rolled forward and knelt next to Sirus. "Aw, heck! Louis is right! I'll go! But if I die, Louis, this one time, try to get the ghosts that do it on film! I'm sure you'll watch it over and over with pleasure, and probably win an award at my expense!"

Louis fumbled with his camera. "Try to stay in frame."

"Thanks. I was joking. But I'm glad you've finally shown the discipline of a dedicated researcher, going for the historical significance rather than worrying about your colleague's safety. You're all heart." Like a sprinter in starting blocks, Jerry sprang forward and raced towards the cemetery, gritting his teeth and slapping his sandals on the ground. Unfortunately, the effort resulted in little speed for the professor who'd spent most of his life in the science lab rather than on any playing field. Twenty yards into his jaunt, a musket ball dropped the ghost chaser in his tracks.

"Oh no," Sirus gasped and raced across the field with Louis lagging behind, keeping the camera as still as possible.

Sirus slid across the grass and rolled the professor to his back. Jerry's face writhed in pain. "Their bullets…they're real now. They…can…hit their target."

"Where you hit?" Sirus yelled.

"The leg." Sirus spotted the hole on Jerry's uniform and tore open his pants. Blood flowed across his thigh as the fallen man winced. With a hail of musket fire racing over their heads and smoke hovering above the chaotic scene, Jerry reached up and grabbed Sirus' collar. "I think it's time to go now. Get me off of this battlefield or we're all going to be lying dead on top of each other." He moved his arm around Sirus' neck. "Hold me."

"What?"

"I'm kidding! Get me up and get me to the cemetery! We have to unlock the portal!" A force of bluecoats collected and charged at them, howling like a pack of wild animals with their bayonets fixed. "Yeah, it's time to go! Now!"

Rob guided Darla through the gate of the cemetery and tumbled to the ground. "Jared!" he yelled. "We need to get out of here, son!"

Darla ran to Beans and Sweets. The lady threw her arms around their shoulders, protecting them as best she could. "What are these things? We need to get everyone to safety!"

Sirus appeared through the dense smoke, carrying Jerry on his back with Louis following close behind, filming the carnage all around them. He bucked the small ghost hunter from his shoulders, sending him crashing into the fence. "Jared!" Sirus yelled. "Place the star in the lock! Put it in the indentation! Now! I'll hold 'em off!" He spun around with his shotgun and took aim.

His head whirling, Jared shook off the madness and focused on the stones in front of him. He nodded to Sirus and dug in his pants for the precious object. He pulled the handkerchief from his pocket and unwrapped the star. To his surprise, the dingy, tarnished star was sparkling and glowing like a hot coal. Its beauty was captivating. Spanning the width of his palm, it began to vibrate. The vibration gradually slowed and the magical object started beating, a heartbeat Jared could feel through his entire body.

Molly shoved the hypnotized boy towards the Union monument. "Come on, Jared! What are you waiting for?"

The beat of the star intensified, making it jump in his hand. Then blood started flowing from it, trickling between his fingers. "Ahhh!" he screamed.

Sirus ducked a volley of gunfire. The shots ricocheted off the tombstones. "Now, Jared! Unlock the portal!"

Molly smacked Jared across his cheek, jolting him back to his world. "Unlock it, Jared! Put it in the stone!"

Jared shook the cobwebs from his head and reached towards the indentation on the monument. As he leaned forward something slammed into him, sending the star spiraling through the air. "These ghosts is gonna kill us!" Dozer cried as Greeley and the Goat huddled behind him. The large boy spotted the star and plucked it from the grass. "What is this thing?" Dozer wiped the blood from its surface; the star began beating and glowing in his palm. "This is witchcraft! You-all done this! You're why these here monsters is tryin' to kill everybody! Everybody in town says Sirus is a witchdoctor and inta voodoo! You-all is in it too! He's put a hex on ya!"

Jared rushed forward, pounding Dozer's chest with his fists. "Give it back! You don't understand! Give it now!"

Dozer blocked Jared's assault with the cast on his arm and backed away, protecting the star. "You's in cahoots with the devil! You're Sirus' pupil! That crazy old man done brainwashed ya!"

Jerry rolled to his side and screamed through the bars of the fence. "Jared! We're all going to die! Do it!"

Squeezing the star in his hand, Dozer and his two cohorts backed away and stopped next to the towering Confederate monument. The ground started to rumble like an earthquake. His large frame shaking, Dozer's eyes bugged out of his head. The ground suddenly crumbled beneath their feet, plummeting the three boys into a deep, dark trench, and sending the star flying through the air once again. Dozer and Greeley clung to the grass on the side of the hole that rippled through the graveyard like a line of falling dominoes, while the Goat clamped onto Dozer's belt.

Dangling from Dozer's pants, the Goat stared down into the bottomless pit. "The ground! I think it's movin'! Get me outta here!"

Bursting from the darkness, the skeleton of a decomposed Rebel buried in the trench came to life. Hissing like a cobra, the rotted corpse latched onto the Goat's legs as the entire pit seethed with bodies of the walking dead. In their tattered uniforms, the skeletons scratched at the sides of the deep grave and clawed at the three helpless boys.

"Oh my god!" Greeley cried. "Help me! Please! Somebody!"

"Come on!" Rob yelled to Darla. "They're in trouble!"

Rob raced past the monument and dove across the grass to where Dozer was quickly losing his grip. He clamped onto the boy's cast on his left arm and heaved, but the weight of the kids and the attacking zombies was too great. Darla rammed her foot onto the demon Virgil had impaled, and plucked the broken two-by-four from the flopping zombie's chest. The frantic woman started beating back the attacking corpses. "Get outta here!" she screamed, as if the gruesome skeletons would respect her teacher's authority. "Suds! Help!"

Suds and Sweets rushed across the grass and locked onto Greeley. His muscles straining, Suds gripped the boy's wrist. "Are ya sure we should be helpin' these guys, Ms. Ramsey?" he groaned. "We probably oughtta just save ourselves. Some kids is just meant to get eaten by the walkin' dead, don't ya think? No sense messin' with God's will!"

Darla wielded the board, smashing one of the possessed skeletons in its face and shattering it to pieces. "We don't have time for your nonsense, Suds Davis! Just pull!"

Rob held tight to Dozer's arm. His muscles trembling and starting to lose strength, he stared into the depths of the ungodly trench. Steam rose from its bowels and the temperature swelled. The pit gradually started to glow until its bottom was a flowing river of boiling lava. "Ahhh!" Rob screamed, his skin sizzling from the intense heat.

"I've had enough of you ugly stinkin' creeps!" With one final blow, Darla pummeled the attackers, casting them into the bubbling river of death. Rob and the boys pulled Dozer, the Goat, and Greeley from the pit, collapsing in a heap of relief and exhaustion.

Molly and Jared scratched and clawed at the ground, searching for the sacred star. "I got it!" Jared exclaimed and plucked it from the grass.

Virgil grabbed his grandson by the back of his collar and jerked him to his feet. He ushered Jared towards the Union monument as a musket round hammered a chunk out of one of the bricks and richochetted through the air. "Stop screwin' around!" Virgil hollered.

Jared put his left hand onto the monument and braced himself. With the star between his thumb and index finger, he thrust the glowing, throbbing object into the indentation. The star plunged into the cement like it was soft mud. The battlefield immediately jolted, as if Lone Jack was a bus that slammed on its brakes, and an eerie buzzing sound filled the air.

Clinging to the fence, Jerry climbed to his feet. "That's it!" As the ghosts of Lone Jack continued their generations-old battle mere yards away, the ghost chaser stared at the spot where the blackjack oak tree once stood, waiting for the portal to reveal itself. "Come on! Anytime now, if you will!"

"It's not happenin'!" Sirus hollered over the disturbing humming sound. "It ain't it!"

Louis pulled the camera from his shoulder and held it near his chest. "Nice goin', Jerry. Wrong again. We're all dead men."

"Wait!" Molly pointed towards the sky. The clouds to the southwest of the cemetery parted, and a large ball of light appeared in the heavens. "It's there! It's a light!"

"We have to get to that light!" Jerry exclaimed.

Jared dropped his eyes from the heavens and glanced at the battling demons. "Wait! What if the ghosts don't go to the light? We have to get them to go to it!"

"That's easy," Ned replied as he snuck up on the group, guiding Jan and Porker through the brush behind the graveyard. "All we need is one of them James Guns. Keep your heads down and follow me."

While the ghosts continued their wretched clash in the middle of the battlefield, Sirus and Louis rolled one of the cannons, undetected, west to the parking lot of the Baptist church. The kids, including Dozer and his two disheveled partners, leaped into the bed of the truck as Virgil fired the engine. While Rob hopped into the passenger seat, Darla pushed Virgil away from the steering wheel, sliding the old man across the worn leather seat. "Sorry, Virgil," she said, "but we're running for our lives here. I don't think going eight miles an hour with our left blinker on the whole way is going to do the trick." She threw the old Ford into drive and slammed the door.

Sirus hitched the cannon to the bumper and helped Louis get Jerry settled in the truck bed with the kids. In the middle of the battlefield, the ghost of Captain Long, his wide-brimmed hat and plume splattered with Rebel blood, pointed with his saber and howled, "They's takin' the cannon! To the ready, lads! Give chase!" The demons turned in unison.

"Oh boy," Virgil mumbled and wiped his hand across his lips.

"They's comin'!" Beans hollered. "Step on it!"

Sirus let loose with his shotgun as the ghouls rolled towards them. "Yeah, I think we should go now," Jerry moaned. "Head for that beam of light!"

Darla hit the gas. The old truck threw dust and gravel into the air, plowed through the ditch, and bounced onto the pavement. With the pedal pressed squarely against the floorboard, she swerved the truck around a Rebel ghost immersed in flames fleeing the location of the Cave Hotel. Seconds later, the truck raced down Bynum, putting distance between them and their deadly attackers and allowing the anxious occupants a brief moment of relief.

Jostled about in the passenger seat, Rob looked in the rearview mirror. "Umm…Darla…honey, I think you might want to get us there as quick as possible. As if we didn't already have about three-hundred problems…we just got a couple more."

"What!" the frantic woman screeched.

Bursting from the woods lining both sides of the road, the mutated Osage Indian creatures attacked with bloodcurdling cries. In search of scalps, the fiends charged forward, firing arrows and launching spears at the vehicle.

"We've got Indians chasin' us!" Rob yelled as he slid lower in his seat for cover. "And what's worse…"

"There's worse?" Darla gasped. "This is a freakin' nightmare! What could be worse than any of this?"

"Well, each of the Indians has two faces for one," he cried, "but we also have a tornado bearing down on us!"

Dropping from the black sky and spiraling towards earth, the twister danced eerily in the distance, devouring everything in its path and leaving destruction in its wake. The kids huddled together in the truck bed, screaming for Darla to drive faster. Sounding like a hailstorm, arrows pelted the rusty metal of the truck. The bear-faced monster leaped from his steed. The horse's mane of slithering serpents struck at the kids as the demon clamped onto the side of the truck with his claws slicing through the metal like a knife through butter. Sirus pressed the barrel of the shotgun against the creature's eye and fired. The beast tumbled to the asphalt and bounced into the path of the charging appaloosas. Ned stabled himself and crawled to his knees. He sent lead flying at the Indians in rapid succession, hammering the deer-antlered ghoul in the chest and throat.

Virgil gazed out the front windshield, his mouth agape. "Oh my god. The beam of light is…is…it's shinin' down on my house!" The perplexed man and his son exchanged troubled looks.

The old Ford fishtailed across the loose gravel on the Millhouse driveway. Barreling over the bumps and potholes, the horrified occupants bounced around violently until they reached the front of the house. Darla slammed the brakes, bringing the truck to an abrupt halt. "Everybody out!" Virgil screamed with the tornado, sounding like on oncoming freight train, only a couple of miles away. "We're headin' for the cellar!"

Sirus and Ned yanked Jerry from the bed of the truck with little concern for his wounded leg, just as a police car with lights blazing and siren blaring pulled up next to them. Captain Pickering heaved his massive frame from the automobile with a distraught Mrs. Morgan and Officer Kunkle following close behind. "What in the daggum hell is goin' on here?" the captain hollered. "I got folks from all over runnin' for their lives, g'tting' chased by corpses! I need me some answers immediately!"

Seconds vital as the deadly ghosts and rumbling tornado bore down on the Millhouse farm, Jerry hopped on one leg with his arms draped around Sirus and Ned's shoulders. "The ghosts'll be here in a couple minutes!" The injured professor said. "You can ask them! I'm sure they'll tell you all about it before they tear you to pieces!"

Filming the scene for posterity and, unquestionably, an award, Louis stomped through the grass, holding his camera as steady as possible. "Look!" he yelled. "The beam of light…it's coming down on that oak tree!"

Virgil and Rob rushed to the cellar on the north side of the house, tugging on the door that had been painted shut several years ago. The group watched in amazement as the beam of light descended gradually from the heavens like a slow-moving elevator, resting on Jared's beloved blackjack oak tree. Witnessing the magical event with great pride and awe, Jerry's mood quickly changed as he glanced over his shoulder to see hundreds of growling zombies cutting through the tall grass north of the Millhouse home. "Uhh, you might want to get the doors unstuck," he informed them. "If you don't, we're all going to die."

Rob pried open the door and bustled everyone down the cracked cement steps into the security of the cellar below the Millhouse home. Bringing up the rear, Sirus and Captain Pickering aimed their weapons, releasing a fearsome volley on their attackers. A shot from the old black man's trusty shotgun slammed into the rotting corpse of a Rebel, taking its right arm off its body, while Pickering, less of a marksman, crippled one of the bluecoats with several shots to its legs from his .38. The two men rumbled down the bumpy stares of the basement as Rob tugged the door shut just before the demons leaped in. Trapped in the door, a skeleton's hand clawed at Rob as he held the door shut. Jared grabbed a rusty hatchet resting against the wall and hacked the beast's arm, crunching through the bone and freeing Rob from its grip. Rob quickly bolted the wooden door closed. The demon arm flopped on the cold cement near his feet.

A frazzled Mrs. Morgan cowered in a corner, her face contorted as she sobbed. "My commemoration! It's ruined!"

Shanks patted the curator on the shoulder. "Aw, that's okay lady. This one here'll be remembered for a long time, I reckon. Besides, festivals is like little league baseball. There's always next year."

Being rather old, the Millhouse home had settled over the years, forming a crack between the frame and foundation that let the light in. Louis stood on his tiptoes atop a rickety stool and pressed his nose against the top of the wall. "I can't see much, but they're still battling each other. We should be safe in here."

Darla rubbed her hands together nervously. "Can you see the tornado?"

"No," the professor replied. "But I can hear it. And it's heading this way." He pulled his face away from the wall and smiled at the frightened kids. "But we'll be fine in here. Not to worry. Farmers in tornado alley have used cellars like these for years to protect them from Mother Nature. Nothing is going to happen to us in here. I promise."

Lying on his side, applying pressure to the hole in his leg, Jerry jerked with fear. Blood soaked his hands and legs. "Oh, no! I think it did hit my artery! I'm bleeding like a stuck pig! I'm going to die!"

Ned peeled his foot from the sticky floor of the basement and studied the sole of his shoe. "You ain't hit in no artery. This place is filling up with blood. It's pumping through the walls."

It was as if the jugular vein of Lone Jack had been sliced open. The horrified group stared at the blood in disbelief. Thick, dark red blood poured into the cellar through every crack and hole, quickly reaching the level of the adults' knees. "This is just great!" Jerry hollered. "We overcome insurmountable odds of survival from marauding ghouls and a flippin' tornado, only to drown to death in the overflowing blood of the dead soldiers, while we're locked in a basement! If I make it outta here alive, I vow never to come to this godforsaken town again!"

Officer Kunkle tromped through the sea of red. "Is there another way out? We have to do somethin'! We're gonna drown in…blood!"

"No," Virgil answered, shaking his head in regret. "I meant to someday build stairs leadin' into the house, but…"

The thick blood reached the height of Jared's chin. Rob snatched his son from the river of red and hoisted him onto his shoulders. "Everybody pick up the kids! Get them as high as you can and…out of this… this…disgusting mess!"

Sitting high atop his dad's sturdy shoulders next to the wall, Jared stared through the crack. His towering oak tree began dancing. "Look! I think the tree is moving!"

As if it had been merely asleep for over a century, the oak magically came to life, stretching its powerful limbs and shaking its branches. The blackjack slammed one of its arms on the solid ground, the force of the blow rippling through the house. It swung at the ghosts with its giant limbs, like a giant squid encountering crazed sailors. The tentacles attacked the ghosts, trapping them in its coils. As the beam of light reached the heights of the massive oak, a powerful force pulled the demons from the branches and hurled them towards the heavens.

Jared spotted Captain Plumb atop his ghastly mount, slashing at the arms of the tree with his saber. Ghosts of the Rebels and bluecoats dangled from every branch. The two-headed Osage Indians and their horses found themselves trapped in the oak as if it were the web of a giant spider. One by one, they were pulled from the massive limbs and catapulted into the sky. Next the light seized the gray-eyed slaves with their heavy chains. Then Captain Plumb and Captain Long, too, were overpowered in the grips of the blackjack. Finally, Mrs. Cave in her black dress sailed through the air. Her face grew to the size of a disturbing, three dimensional billboard. She moaned with a loud, evil hiss, and disappeared into the light.

The moon inched forward across the body of the sun. The winds swirled through the arms of the dancing oak. "The eclipse!" Louis exclaimed. "It's here!" The cellar faded to pitch black.

"Oh my god!" Molly, who was perched on Sirus' shoulders, yelled. "Everybody duck!"

The tornado swept across Bynum Road, ripping up the ground and the trees in its path. It slammed into the oak tree. As if a two-ton bomb had exploded only a short distance away, the house buckled and shook as Jared and Rob ducked for cover. Boards were sheered from the home's skin. Shutters rocketed from its windows, hurling through the air. The mighty blackjack wrestled the twister, fighting with all its magical power.

As the tornado rolled through the cornfield behind the Millhouse home, Jared leaped onto Rob's back to inspect the devastation. His beloved oak had disappeared, roots and all, completely plucked from the ground. Only a deep crater remained to show it had ever existed.

With the possessed heart of Lone Jack gone, the wave of blood in the tiny cellar receded, until it, too, disappeared. Emotionally drained, the group simply stood and stared at one another. Jared looked at his father. Rob smiled at his son. Jared turned to his grandfather. Virgil grinned and shot a wink to his grandson. "Welp," Ned cut through the silence. "That's that. They's gone." A loud cheer of joy and relief filled the damp, cold room.

13

Jared leaped from the old Ford, smacking the pavement with both feet. "Okay, Dad. I'll see ya later."

Rob threw the truck in park. "Wait. I'm coming in with you. I want to check out your room and desk. This is your first day of school, after all, and I am your father."

Jared grinned. "You just want to see her."

Cradling a binder close to her chest, Molly approached, with Jan at her side. "Hey, Jared. You want to walk with us to class?"

"We can show you around school," Jan said, as if the task would be taxing and painful. "Since it's your first day and all, and you're goin' to a new school."

"Hey, Millhouse!" Porker hollered. The rest of the Crossroads gang jumped off their bikes and locked them in the rack. "If the teacher lets us pick our own seats, you can take a desk next to mine."

"That oughtta be a treat for him, Porker," Shanks chirped. "He can watch you fall asleep and pick your nose."

"Bite me, Shanks!" The round boy rammed Shanks with his belly.

"No, you can sit next to me." Sweets placed his arm around Jared's shoulder. "Trust me. You don't want to sit next to any of these guys. They'll get you in trouble."

"Well, well," Darla said, walking towards them with her arms folded. "I guess we have *two* new students today." She put her arm around Rob's waist. "But you look like you might be a little too old, and more trouble than we need around here."

Suds stared at the childish adults with their sick case of puppy love, and then looked at his friends. He smiled, sighed, and then turned to Jared. "Well, welcome to the fifth grade class of Lone Jack, Millhouse. I can't believe summer's already over." The dejected boy shook his head. "Man. Daggum school startin' and all." A bright grin returned to his handsome face. "But, man, we had us one heck of a fun summer, didn't we, Millhouse?"

Jared returned the smile and looked up at his friend. "Yeah we did, Suds," he replied. "Yeah we did."

To contact the author, or for questions or comments, please visit:
www.ghostsoflonejack.com

Proceeds from the sale of this book will be donated to the
Lone Jack Civil War Battlefield, Museum & Soldiers' Cemetery